THE
NAVIDAD
INCIDENT

The Downfall of Matías Guili

Natsuki Ikezawa

THE
NAVIDAD
INCIDENT

The Downfall of Matías Guili

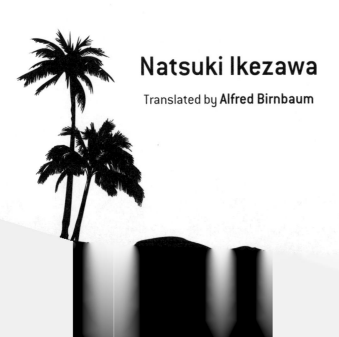

Natsuki Ikezawa

Translated by **Alfred Birnbaum**

THE NAVIDAD INCIDENT: The Downfall of Matías Guili

Original title: **Mashiasu Giri no shikkyaku by Natsuki Ikezawa**
Copyright © Natsuki Ikezawa 1993
Originally published in Japan by Shinchosha, Tokyo.
English translation copyright © Alfred Birnbaum 2012
English rights arranged through Bureau des Copyrights Français
Map illustration copyright © Shinchosha Publishing Co. Ltd.

Cover design by Sam Elzway

This book has been selected by the Japanese Literature Publishing Project (JLPP), an initiative of the Agency for Cultural Affairs of Japan.

HAIKASORU
Published by VIZ Media, LLC
295 Bay Street
San Francisco, CA 94133

www.haikasoru.com

Library of Congress Cataloging-in-Publication Data

Ikezawa, Natsuki, 1945–
  [Mashiasu Giri no shikkyaku. English]
  The navidad incident : the downfall of Matías Guili / by Natsuki Ikezawa ;
  translation by Alfred Birnbaum.
      p. cm.
  ISBN 978-1-4215-4222-5
  I. Birnbaum, Alfred. II. Title.
  PL853.K45M3713 2012
  895.6'35--dc23

                                                      2011047498

The rights of the author of the work in this publication to be so identified have been asserted in accordance with the Copyright, Designs and Patents Act 1988. A CIP catalogue record for this book is available from the British Library.

Printed in the U.S.A.
First printing, March 2012

01

Let us begin in the morning. All good stories start at daybreak.

At five thirty the sky is still dark, but already the birds are twittering. To the east, lacquer black night takes on a hint of blue as the sun hesitates just below the horizon. The birds scatter crumbs of chorus to coax it up, and inevitably—do their voices carry that far?—the first rays tinge the haze over the islands. A new day begins. A common, ordinary sunrise, yet the birds exalt each dawn as if it were a miracle.

Flocking to the treetops, their numbers swell into a ring of voices, louder and louder, until finally the multitude flies off in a dense black squall along the south coast toward the mangrove forests. Suddenly everything goes still. For just these thirty minutes each morning and again for thirty minutes at sunset, the sky is alive with their chatter.

Birds are the spirits of distant ancestors. While dying doesn't turn people into birds overnight, the longer since death, say the island elders, the louder they squawk. But why so many? In times past, when these islands had just risen from the sea, they say there were more people. All of them now are birds; even those birds reborn as humans or whales or bats all died and became birds again. Each must transmigrate through a bird existence to become something else. A bird becomes a bee, breeds thousands of buzzing offspring, then returns to bird form. Those thousands of baby bees in turn become birds. Since before time itself, the birds have steadily multiplied—and at dawn and dusk they are everywhere.

As long as anyone can remember, this place has been called Gagigula, the "noisy islands"; people being born, people passing away, whales and bats and bees breeding and dying, each successive generation sending new spirit flocks gyring overhead in swirling thunderheads of concentric darkness obliterating the very orb of the sun. Seafarers took alarm at these "racketous rocks" overpopulated with birds, and the epithet stuck. Even today, few would affect "international" airs by using the official name, the Republic of Navidad. The inhabitants still speak of Gagigula, the archipelago where sooner or later everyone becomes a bird. Once a bird, hereafter a bird—this human form is a temporary thing. With food aplenty and no predators, these are happy islands thanks to the metaphysics of avian transmigration.

It is now half past six. The sun rises, along with the heat and tangy scent of the sea. Another idle morning is on the way. The islands, just nudging the equator, keep virtually the same sunrise hour the whole year round. Dawn light splits open the clouds the length of the eastern sky, illuminating wavering palm fronds, birds winging south. Out in the gardens, puddles from last night's showers now sparkle in the sun's short ascent. Sunrise does not last very long, nor make as grand an impression as sunset, yet the trees and buildings bathed in that warm citrus glow look lovelier than anything under the glaring noonday sun.

Sadly, not a soul gets up to see it. Beautiful though it may be, nature is boring. People don't make a thing of greeting the sun like birds, much less go to the window to look.

In the long gallery outside the Presidential Villa, ten petitioners stir awake one by one. They've camped out overnight, and it's been uncomfortable. Shaking their drowsy faces and blinking bleary eyes, each looks at the person next to him. Only then do they remember they're not back home on their own little islands but sprawled on a concrete floor in the capital. That's why their grass mats were so hard and cold. Will this be another day of waiting?

Or will they be ushered in to see the President on some executive whim? The ways of officialdom are even less predictable than the weather. There are dozens of proverbs about the heavens, but not one about bureaucrats.

Slowly, each petitioner gets up and shuffles across the lawn, around the main building to a whitewashed plankway beside the three-motorboat dock house, and pees into the smooth waters. Then, flicking off the last drops, each slouches over to the middle of the lawn and washes up at the fountain that sprays silly arcs even in the dead of night. Then it's back to the concrete gallery, squat and wait. Soon some business-minded kids will come to sell them coconuts and bananas and steamed *ma'a* for breakfast.

Six months ago, the President announced he would personally receive petitioners from the outer islands. No one really believed it until one brave soul made his way to the Presidential Villa, knocked on the heavy door, and after just thirty minutes was shown in. The young man reemerged with a shy grin, and three months later workmen actually came to dredge the channel from the outer reef to the village landing as per his modest request. Yes, the Old Man made good on his word—a good deed contracted to a crony.

Even so, getting to see the President is easier said than done. From the outer islands, either you're lucky enough to find space on an unchartered propeller plane, or you hop a once-a-month government cargo ship, or as a last resort you can paddle your own outrigger canoe. Even then, once you reach the capital, the elected leader of this island republic of seventy thousand is a busy man. Sometimes you wait a week or more, and a fortnight's absence makes any islander impossibly homesick. Some can't take it and simply pack up, spouting excuses to their island elders about changes in policy. "The President won't see us anymore." And so, for one reason or another, an ever-changing queue of petitioners idles in the shaded galleries to either side of that pretentious Doric-columned portico.

By eight o'clock, one young petitioner, tired of just waiting, steals over to the great white mansion and tiptoes up to a window to peek inside. High ceilings and thick walls hung with gilt-framed paintings, tall heavy chairs and solid wood tables—as if he hadn't already seen them ten times these past three days. No, what he really wants to see is on the opposite wall, that picture of a woman sitting on a beach in half-profile. Her fine features and full lips tell him she's not from this island, nor from his own. Maybe that big island three hundred kilometers to the southeast could have produced such a face. He's heard tell of beautiful women there. The young man is entranced by her pose, eyes demurely downcast, one hand on the sand. Her wavy hair trained over one shoulder, adorned with a white hibiscus. The sea in the background, that fringe of palms could be anywhere. Only the woman herself is a mystery, locked within the painting. Maybe she lives somewhere in this huge house? It's the first time an image has beguiled him like this, and he's not quite sure what the strange feeling means. How come he keeps returning to the window each day?

Yet as often as he looks, he never sees a soul inside. No one sitting in those heavy chairs, no one standing, no one cleaning. Never seen any doors open. He can scarcely guess what people do in this big building, not that it's any of his concern.

He simply waits. And occasionally, as an afterthought, he imagines how nervous he'll be when they finally invite him in. How small and pathetically out of place his people's request will seem. Though on the other hand, each day his request goes unheard, the more important it becomes not to hurry home, as if sheer endurance itself were progress.

Every once in a while an insider will queue up with a bogus petition, an easy favor to cover for yet another presidential scam. Then everyone is surprised by the friendly and efficient workings of the administration. To the eyes of official visitors arriving by black limousine, all these petitioners are ordinary citizens who love their President, a man they can approach directly. Of course visiting VIPs have no idea how many days these people have been kept waiting; they probably think the President listens to this many people daily. Which is exactly what the President wants them to believe. Clearing a waterway or two is a small price to pay; what matters is appearances, especially with foreign attachés who can influence ODA budgets.

The country is too small to justify setting up embassies or consulates. Navidad merely gets the occasional swing-through diplomatic mission. Journalists almost never come here. Meanwhile, the President consistently ignores foreign media. Seated in his spacious back office, he puts on a show of listening to his citizens, but really it's only to make his own profit-skimming schemes look democratic. Not that he's fooling anyone on the two main islands or that other island three hundred kilometers away to the southeast.

ϟ

This morning, as always, President Matías Guili rises earlier than the birds. Last night it was close to three when he turned in, so he has slept only two hours. These past few years, he's been sleeping steadily less and less, though by inverse ratio his sleep now plumbs new depths. He never dreams. His mind blacks out until seconds before waking. To see him in that state, unmoving, hardly even breathing, you'd think he was dead. Especially since resuming office last year, he sleeps deeper and rises earlier than ever.

The President is honestly beginning to think that people don't need sleep. If he keeps on like this, *he* certainly won't. Those two hours will halve to one hour, then to thirty minutes. His breathing and heartbeat will slow to a complete stop. No wonder he never lets others into his bedroom. Like those sleepless saints of ages past, he knows he's not normal.

His private apartments are done in Japanese style. Every morning, like clockwork, he pops out of his futon, but has no memories of the day before. Everything apparently cuts out in the depths. So the day begins with recouping, and his bath is the place for this. But with his head a total blank, he needs reminding. A note left by his pillow reads, *Take bath. Put away memo.* If not for this, he might well spend the whole day sitting on the *tatami* not knowing what to do, nor even bothering to hide the evidence. Immediately, he files away the note in a waiting letterbox until he takes it out again at bedtime, a nightly routine.

No one else is in on this. If political opponents knew, they could easily assassinate him. All they'd have to do is substitute a different note: *Go to office. Open bottom desk drawer. Take out gun. Put gun to head. Pull trigger.* He is only too aware of the danger, so he never lets on about his sleeping habits, never gets too close to anyone in the late night or early morning hours.

As the note commands, he goes straight to the bathroom and steps into the *hinoki* wood tub, heated from the previous night to just the right temperature. Immersed up to his neck in hot water, he repeats his name a hundred times. This he can do without written prompting: *His Excellency Matías Guili, President of the Republic of Navidad.* He first realized the therapeutic value of a hot bath during his years in Japan. Not long after his return, at a time when no other island headman even had hot water, he built himself a small house and put in a hot tub, complete with boiler ordered from the United States.

Morning baths are good for strategic planning—charting the day's agenda so as not to betray indecisiveness in public—and nine years ago, when first inaugurated, he had a Japanese bath installed in these private apartments. Then a year ago he was ousted. Out of all his many privileges, the thing he missed most was bathtime. Matías hoped against hope that his usurper, Bonhomme Tamang, wouldn't have the place redone American style. Luckily, Tamang's three months in office didn't leave enough time for that. He never took to actually living here. Rather than assert his authority by remodeling the Presidential Villa, he tackled more immediate, pressing tasks. His idea of sincerity, a small man's sincerity. Then, not three months later, Matías came back on the rebound, once again to enjoy the privilege of soaking in his wooden tub any hour of the day or night.

In the amniotic bathwater, he recites his name and honorifics a hundred times, his self-possession returning little by little with each repetition. Thirty minutes later, fully restored, he dons a new *yukata* bathrobe and steps into the adjoining *dojo*, his private shrine. Fifteen minutes here is an equally important part of the morning ritual. The room is twelve tatami mats in size—almost twenty square meters—with a *tokonoma* alcove where hangs a large photograph of the President himself, the very same official portrait tacked up all over the country in full color. Only here it's black and white, mounted as a hanging scroll with a large vermilion seal in the lower left-hand corner. The absence of a national army may have prevented him from posing in full military regalia, but the photographer he flew in from Japan did an admirable job of evoking the Father of the Country gazing down on his people with severity and benevolence, medals stapled across his double-breasted suit. In real life, the President's slight stature might secretly make him a laughingstock in certain quarters, but this bust portrait betrays no such shortcoming.

For fifteen minutes each morning Matías puts his hands together and prays. After the name comes the image; from the photograph he replenishes whatever plenipotency may have leached away overnight—replacing the private person with the official demeanor. He then heads for his study and takes out his executive log to bring himself up to date on all pending business from the previous day.

The older he gets and the more his grip on power increases, the less he discusses with others. Having to pass judgment on each and every issue can be a heavy burden, but it would hardly do to appoint an advisor, let alone ask for advice. Instead, he consults at length with someone he summons in private: himself. During the day at the office, however, he never lets this pensive side show. There he must be seen to dispense decisions without hesitation, though in fact he's worked it all out in this inner sanctum. The only other person allowed in here is Itsuko, the maid. No one else must ever open the sliding door. Itsuko has obviously seen the portrait, but she just sweeps the tokonoma and says nothing.

𝄋

"On the agenda for today…" begins Executive Secretary Jim Jameson—a Navidadian, of course, but so dark-skinned you'd think he was from New Guinea. Young, but competent, a born organizer with a good memory for things, ever ready to pull out the right information at the right time. Which, so long as he lacks the ambition to push things to the next level, is all the President requires of him. The ideal right-hand man.

"In the morning, there's the usual twenty documents for your signature. Then three pending decisions, with respective bureau personnel to make presentations. After that, you're at the Arenas Plantation for lunch, so allowing thirty minutes transfer time, you should probably leave here at twelve sharp. Arenas is experimenting with oranges lately, so if he offers you orange juice, praise his efforts, whatever. It probably also wouldn't hurt to mention those subsidies under consideration. The money does seem a sure thing, after all. Oh, and the lunch menu is steak. After that, ETA for the Japanese veterans delegation is two forty-five, so Your Excellency arrives at the airport at half past. You head up the welcoming ceremony on the airport lawn, after which the delegation goes by bus to the hotel and Your Excellency returns here."

"Who'll be there at the ceremony?" asks the President, reaching for his miso soup.

"The word is five senior staff from the Foreign Office. Also five junior staffers from Home Office, whoever's free. Plus twenty from Island Security. There's supposed to be about fifty of them, so that should make an even match from our side. And we'll be rounding up people and spacing them around the airport, so it won't look too unnatural."

"That's it?"

"No, the Children's Fife and Drum Corps is on call."

"Ah, good. Double-check to see their uniforms are in proper shape. And no slipups when the flags are raised."

The secretary nods.

"And my speech?"

"Very short. You have a dinner with them as well."

"One more thing, those rebel handbills around town, make sure they're all gone."

"That's Island Security's job."

"Well, I suppose. Put in a word with Katsumata for me anyway. What's after the airport?"

"We give them the afternoon off. They'll probably want to walk around town. Later, you have dinner at seven."

"There's a man arriving on the same plane with the delegation, name of Kantaro Suzuki. I have to meet with him, one on one. Today, if possible."

"Your Excellency has an opening between four and five. Or else, let's see, the next slot would be past nine, after the dinner."

"Later's no good. Pencil him in from four to five."

"Anyone else to attend?"

"I think not. We'll be speaking Japanese. State business, but I'll go it alone for now."

Some things are best kept from too many ears, thinks Matías. Not that he doesn't trust his secretary or the boys at the Home Office. But what this spook says at this stage will be off the record and, in all probability, none too realistic. No, give the guy the benefit of a listen, speak sincerely of "mutual ties," then send him on his way. The President looks forward mischievously to letting the man talk, knowing full well it's a no-go from the start.

Having run through the agenda, Jim Jameson withdraws, passing the ever-out-of-sorts Itsuko waiting in a corner of the room with a bowl of rice. The President goes on eating, likewise ignoring her. Following his bath and dojo, breakfast is also Japanese, so his first waking hours are essentially spent back in the "Japan period" of forty years before, though once he leaves these inner apartments, he's all islander. As much as he relishes the Japanese lifestyle, why rub everyone else's nose in it?

Few know that he enjoys Japanese rice with *wakame miso* soup, cucumber pickles, preserved squid *shiokara*, plus a good wake-up-it's-morning helping of tuna *sashimi*. A Japanese breakfast is just the thing, though it's not easy to procure these items here. The rice and wakame seaweed and miso he orders in specially. A hireling at the Tokyo bureau buys small quantities at a nearby supermarket and sends them once a week by diplomatic pouch, ostensibly for entertaining guests from Japan. The President is very fussy about his provisions and will sometimes ask for five different brands of *umeboshi* salted plums so he can select a personal favorite. He's even had local farmers try to grow scallions, but the results have been disappointing. If only they were more like okra, which is practically a weed here!

Matías likes red meat *maguro*, but he just cannot face fatty *toro* tuna belly in the morning. Nor does he much care for *wasabi*. Instead he dips his sashimi in soy sauce mixed with lime juice and a dash of Tabasco, a postwar import from America. The Japanese who camped out down here through the war made do with that horrible powdered wasabi. Nowadays wasabi comes in squeeze tubes, but Matías will stick to his lime juice and Tabasco, thank you very much. He never tires of tuna. It's his power breakfast for the day's activities, so he eats huge portions of it. Fortunately, there is plenty to be caught in these waters, and there's also Itsuko, whose job it is to haggle with the fishermen and keep the freezers full.

Itsuko sees to everything at breakfast. Matías typically lunches with his trusted few in the villa staff canteen, then dines with guests in the formal dining room. Having no family, it's the standing arrangement, though on occasion the President may eat at the hotel or at a restaurant. Either way, Itsuko rarely has to prepare lunch or dinner.

"Is this the regular maguro?"

"Why? Does it taste different?"

The President hates it when people answer his questions with questions of their own. It's not as if Itsuko doesn't know, but she also knows that even if she sasses him, all he'll ever do is grumble. Maybe the old maid has her finger on some dark secret from his past—or so the other servants whisper among themselves.

"No," huffs the President.

"Last night, I was running late, so I didn't have time to thaw it."

"What'd you do? Run it under tap water?"

"No, there's this invention called the microwave oven."

"Hmph," he snorts. So that's why it's so pale outside and still cold in the center. He opens the *Navidad Daily,* a tabloid that exists solely to suck up to the Executive Office. Still, you never know, they might just print something stupid. The headlines read:

VETERANS DELEGATION ARRIVES TODAY FROM JAPAN!
HIS EXCELLENCY PRESIDENT GUILI TO GREET THEM AT
AIRPORT!
ANOTHER STEP FORWARD IN NAVIDAD-JAPAN RELATIONS!

In such big, bold typeface, it looks more like a poster than a newspaper. Is this the best they can do? The President knows better than to expect accomplished journalism, no subtle criticisms that invite a second reading and lend backhanded credence to faulted government policies. One quick glance, a nod of the head, and he puts down the paper.

$\frac{1}{7}$

At nine thirty, Matías Guili is meeting with Finance Bureau Chief Gregory Chan about foreign aid projections for the next year's budget, when the door cracks open and in looks Chief of Island Security Katsumata.

"What is it?" the President demands. The bureau chief turns to look.

"Emergency," pants Katsumata, slipping into the room. "Wanted to report it as soon as possible."

Executive Secretary Jim Jameson peers around him from behind.

"Listen, sorry," Katsumata snarls at Chan, as if a commandant outranked a bureau chief, "but could you, like, scram?" Visibly excited, Katsumata is forever trying to badger others—with little success. Does he honestly imagine this attitude of his gets him anywhere? When Matías first met him, the man was a *yakuza*, a right-wing goon with sufficient promise at bullying young recruits for a certain politician to recommend him. So nine years ago he hired the mobster to beef up the Island Security forces.

Katsumata's forehead glistens with sweat. The President plants both hands on his desktop and braces for the worst. The finance bureau chief has no choice but to leave, accompanied by the executive secretary.

"Take off your glasses!" barks Matías. How many times has he told the man not to wear sunglasses when talking to him? He keeps them on at all times, even during sex they say. Indeed, without sunglasses his face would look ludicrously soft, his droopy eyes more likely to elicit grins than grimaces.

"They did it," says Katsumata.

"*They?*" queries Matías.

"The *torii* gate, they…"

"Who did *what?*" he demands again. Katsumata thinks clipping his sentences makes him sound tough, but he can only keep it up for two or three minutes at most before reverting to his usual blathering self.

"Knocked it down, sir."

"The torii gate at the Shinto shrine?"

"Correct. Word came in and I went to look. It's down, all right. Posts broken in half, no way to repair them."

"Any clue who's behind it?" asks the President, calmer than Katsumata could have predicted.

"They put up those handbills over the rubble, that same slogan, so it's gotta be their faction."

"That's no slogan. Mumbo jumbo, that's all it is. Though it means the louts are serious, pulling off a stunt like this."

"Right. The slogan's gotta be a clue. We did a full-force sweep, but sorry to say…"

"It's *not* a slogan!" sputters Matías. "How the hell did they knock it down? How many men would that take? It's solid stone, shipped in from Japan, joined with cement. Push or pull, that's no one- or two-man job."

"They probably used a car," offers Katsumata.

"Was there a car there at the scene?"

"No, but anyone could figure. Tie one end of a rope to the crossbar, the other end to the bumper, step on the gas, down it comes."

"Right. Anyone see it happen?"

"No, but we'll keep on it."

There's a big difference between no witnesses and no one informing Island Security, thinks Matías.

"Probably done in the middle of the night," continues Katsumata. "No houses, no people around. But put up some reward money, we'll get names all right."

But the torii? More than even the culprits, it's the gate that preoccupies the President. He reassembles a mental picture of it, a landmark he's known since childhood. If the shrine was built the year before he was born, then that torii has stood well on sixty-three years. Feels almost as if he's been knocked down himself. The shrine building was demolished after the war, leaving the torii standing alone for nearly fifty years. And now it's gone.

During the war, Japanese MPs used to patrol near the gate and jump on any islanders who passed by without bowing. Not even kids were spared. The shrine faced south, so bowing at the gate sent a long-distance prayer across the northern seas to the imperial capital. If kids saw an MP staked out there, they'd hide in wait for grown-ups to get beaten up, though they had to be careful not to laugh out loud or the MP would catch them too. Crouching in the bushes, desperately stifling their giggles...Not one of his pals from those days is still around. Or maybe they are? What were their names? Those friends from when he'd just arrived from Melchor Island. He was running errands for the Chinese laundry, so that must make him thirteen or fourteen at the time. The other kids were younger. He can almost see their faces. They must know exactly who he is, but none has approached him since he became president. A population this small and not one of them has come forward. What would his chums think of the old boy now?

Matías snaps back to the present. "Well, then, we can't hold tomorrow morning's ceremony for the delegation there."

"Not necessarily. If we clean up the rubble, they won't know when the torii disappeared."

"Okay, we'll consider it. But even so, something must be done. About those hoodlums."

"Yes, something," mumbles an uncharacteristically evasive Katsumata. "I did issue an alert."

"No, we've got to act now. We don't even need to know who we're dealing with. Here we are, on the verge of improving ties with Japan and getting a major injection of capital. We cannot tolerate such outright anti-Japanese acts. How do we put that across?"

Matías thinks of countermeasures. He's not angry. This is a game of chess, a power play in which a show of anger may have nothing to do with actually getting angry. If he can't hit these unseen enemies where they live, then he has to do something visibly forceful. The point is the punch, not the punching bag. Anything can be the target. Irrational, maybe, but effective. That's how politics works, at least his politics, his way of maneuvering the pieces on the board.

"Katsumata." Matías stares straight at him and lowers his voice. "Burn down a house!"

"A *house?* Whose?"

"Anyone's. No, let's see…a distant relation of Bonhomme Tamang. Somebody ordinary people wouldn't know, but as they catch on they'll come to suspect, yes, he's the ringleader. Find me that somebody and set his house on fire. In the dead of night. I want a real blaze. Pretend we know exactly who our enemy is. That should do the trick."

"Yessir, right on it. And uh, about the slogan?"

"I *told* you, it's not a *slogan!* Gibberish, that's all it is. Just make sure not one of those handbills remains up around town. Meaningless or not, they're an eyesore."

⚡

The Nissan slowly descends the slope toward the airport. The limousine was a "little something," a personal gift to Matías nine years ago, only two months after he took office, during final negotiations with Japan over the war. Japan had no qualms about laying out a sizeable sum, but refused to acknowledge the payment as compensation for wartime occupation and conscription of forced labor. No, it was "goodwill aid." In the end, newly elected President Guili relented; it was his first big job as leader, his first gift from Japan. He regarded it as a personal handout, but when he lost the third term, accountants started making noise and forced him to turn it over to incoming President Bonhomme Tamang. Now back in office, Matías takes renewed pleasure in the limo. It's an emblem of his career, this Nissan President. Could be the name, but he'll never trade it in. Heinrich the chauffeur has been at the wheel the entire nine years, despite the change in passengers.

The car pulls up to the officials and citizens lining the way to the airport— but where's the motorcade? Matías fumes in the back seat. That Jim Jameson isn't on the ball. Or no, this is Katsumata's turf. Didn't he allocate extra budget to Island Security for two motorcycles? Must have a word with Katsumata. No, wait, didn't some freewheeling Island Security rookie wrap one of the bikes around a tree? When Katsumata came to report the accident, Matías himself decided that one bike wouldn't look up to snuff, so they canceled it.

Mind is going to pieces, crumbling away. Is he really getting so old? Maybe he doesn't recover all the particles of memory that sift away while he's asleep. Maybe his morning bath and dojo aren't enough. Like sand through his fingers, his strength is trickling away.

The whitewashed airport building is just up ahead, the very symbol of this island country's existence—built entirely with foreign money. Could we, he often wonders, get by without it? Shut down the borders and make a go of it? Just seventy thousand people, but in today's world no one can cut off all ties and look inward. No self-reliance, physical or spiritual. The earth's not big enough. No sooner would we say, "We're going our own way," than the developed countries would insist, "Oh, but that's so hard." Anything to "protect" us.

Granted, that's how he got to be president. If the job of a politician in a small country is to balance island ideology with pressures from abroad, then clearly he's the best qualified. Okay, so maybe he's leaned too much on Japan, and in ways he'd prefer not to tell his countrymen. Ah, the time it would take them to understand! He had no choice. Still, his self-confidence hasn't flagged, he's managed to keep things on course.

Why in this modern age is value always parceled out in monetary form? The airport terminal was built eight years ago with funds from Japan and the United States—and both have tagged along with Navidad ever since. Predictably, each gave construction jobs to their own contractors, who spirited the donated money back home. They even demanded that his presidential kickbacks be deposited in their own domestic banks, mere paper figures he has yet to withdraw. The airport may be here in Navidad, but it's really just a stepping-stone for America and Japan, a tangible promise of incursions to come.

But just how—with what?—is Navidad to repay those two great greedy powers for these runways scraped out of the jungle with Mitsubishi Caterpillar bulldozers, for the monstrous pseudo-ethnic terminal that dwarfs the surrounding coconut groves, the traditional "praying hands" roof beams clumsily mimicked in reinforced concrete? Lucky the locals don't realize how ugly it is; they probably think all airports in the world look like this.

To either side along the twenty meters to the terminal building stand Island Security corpsmen, chests out at attention. The limousine steers a slow progress between their ranks and stops before the main entrance. Heinrich gets out and walks around to open the back door, when up runs Katsumata. Like a faithful bird dog, he looks pleased with himself. His dark glasses reflect the sky and clouds and plantings of stunted palms.

"What is it?"

"Found twenty-four total, all around town," he beams, holding out a sheaf of handbills.

"Don't hand them to *me*," Matías growls under his breath. The man's gaffes are an embarrassment. He may be good at threatening people but is hopeless at investigating. "Get them out of sight and burn them. Or no, stash them. They're evidence. Are those the last?"

"Yessir, we combed everywhere," crows Katsumata as the President strides up the paved walk to the terminal, the other officials a few paces behind.

And what if they tack up more? Matías almost asks.

"Got men posted at key locations. Won't be a slogan stuck anywhere," adds Katsumata, fielding the unspoken question, but Matías keeps walking. Even if they catch the scoundrels in the act, a whack on the tail won't make the problem go away. The real question is, who's the brains behind it all?

He reaches the terminal in ten steps and heads inside. The interior is air-con chilled. Prior to construction, Matías fought with the Japanese architects. Why the air-conditioning? What's so bad about arrivals feeling the heat? Just open it up to the breeze. Must make a mental note for when it comes time for repairs. If he can remind himself to remember, that is. As he follows Jim Jameson toward the VIP Lounge, he turns and glares at Katsumata.

"Just make sure no vet sets eyes on them. Can't imagine any of them can read Gagigula, but if anyone asks, just say it's a government motto. Meanwhile, find out if it's some old saying or what. Ask around, try some old folks."

"Old folks never listen to us," pleads Katsumata, as if he's been asked to do the impossible. Island Security isn't cut out for intelligence work. Just a bunch of juvenile delinquents from the villages. All muscle, absolutely nowhere in the head department.

"And another thing, about those punitive measures, get on them tonight," says the President, lowering his voice.

"Oh, you mean the arson thing?"

"*Whatever.* Just hop to it!"

Katsumata nods and disappears.

The JAL Boeing 727 carrying the veterans delegation touches down at 14:45, right on schedule. Tourism is booming here. Nearly every flight is filled to capacity three times a week, bringing tourists to these crystal clear waters and coral reefs dazzling with tropical sun and colorful fish. But today's passengers are different. These forty-seven have little to do with the "tourist route"; the only money they spend will be a Japanese government stipend for bus charter and lodging at the Japanese-built Navidad Teikoku Hotel. All the ceremonial whatnot is to be paid out of Navidad's own diplomatic budget, making their visit a rather uneconomic proposition. They probably won't even buy any souvenirs.

Before reaching passport control, a Foreign Office minion swiftly diverts them from that endless queue for the one and only Immigration officer and slips them through a side door to a special waiting room. Seated there on the upholstered benches, they clearly do not resemble any breed of foreigner typically seen on the islands. An all-male group is unusual enough, but every one of them is wearing dark blue or gray wool suits despite the tropical heat. Each, moreover, has a big black leather bag and white hat marked with a single red stripe, an easy mark for the staffer to spot. All are in their sixties or upwards. All except two: one, young and restless, checking back and forth with the Navidad officials, a travel coordinator who packages special group tours; the other, middle-aged and calm, a liaison officer from the Japanese Ministry of Welfare. The old men sit mopping their faces with white handkerchiefs, whispering among themselves. Sharing remembrances from fifty years ago? No, one of them is unfolding a piece of paper and muttering something to himself.

Fifteen minutes later, after the Navidad bureaucrats have duly impressed the foreign guests with the officious propriety of the local system, the forty-seven veterans are shown to a plaza outside and there herded into rows. Facing them are two flagpoles attended by two tanned youths—police cadets?—in green *guayaberas* and black shorts, and a simple podium. To the immediate left and right, yellow-uniformed children of the Fife and Drum Corps stand poised with their instruments. Another twenty green-and-black youths fall into formation on the far left flank, balanced on the far right by a dozen government types. Front and center among these is a man of remarkably short stature, matched only by his girth.

Almost as soon as the forty-seven veterans are in position, out steps one very dark Navidad official. Dressed in light green, he ambles over to the Japanese delegation and, after brief deliberations, persuades Mr. Ministry of Welfare to go stand at a microphone on the lawn. He himself then mounts the podium, squints up at the sky while everyone gets quiet, and launches forth. He's good at this sort of thing.

"Gentlemen, welcome to the Republic of Navidad. We extend our heartfelt greetings to you all. I am Jim Jameson, executive secretary to the President."

He pauses and casts a glance over at Mr. Ministry of Welfare for a translation. The old men all plant their eyes on their compatriot chaperon; obviously no one understands a word of English. The liaison officer renders the executive secretary's self-introduction into Japanese, though his expression reads, *Couldn't they provide their own interpreter?*

"Putting all past misfortunes behind us and seeking to lay new foundations of trust, we are pleased to open every part of our country to your veterans delegation."

Another pause for translation. A total waste of time. Compared to this Navidadian's English, the Ministry envoy's rhetorical skills are far more bureaucratically polished. He could dash off a more proficient speech in Japanese without even listening.

"And now, to proceed with our official welcome: the raising of the flags and our national anthems."

At that the secretary bows out, whereupon a largish boy from the Fife and Drum Corps trots up onto the podium and retrieves a conductor's baton. The green-and-black youth by the right-hand flagpole proceeds to unfold a flag, clip it to the rope, and slowly hoist it as the fife-and-drummers play an odd melody with no discernible chorus. Slowly, slowly, the flag ascends, filling out in the breeze to reveal blue-green and blue stripes with a coconut palm silhouetted in white on the middle green band. Even more slowly, it reaches the top of the pole in unison with the end of the national anthem. All forty-seven veterans take off their hats and stand at attention, respectfully observing the moment.

Another anthem begins, and the other cadet brings out another flag. Plain red on white, instantly recognizable before it's even unfolded. The cadet hauls it up, all eyes ascending with it. Reluctantly, the forty-seven Japanese begin to register that, just maybe, this bouncy tune they're playing could be their own national anthem...the very same *Kimi ga Yo*, "Hymn to the Imperial Reign," they sang each day on these very islands during the occupation, sang each time they saw off comrades-in-arms, and still sing unexpurgated in Japan today, even after losing the war. Reassured by the now-familiar passages, they begin to feel even a measure of admiration for the boys and girls who are mangling the melody so masterfully. If not for the serenely ascending Rising Sun, it might as well have been a Polynesian pop song.

The flag is up. In the haze of silent expectation as everyone gazes up at the sky, the portly man from the government welcoming committee strolls out to the podium in an ever-so-leisurely way on his short legs. Only now do the forty-seven vets begin to feel the strain of the fierce southern sun. Removing their hats was a big mistake.

"Greetings to all of you from Japan. I am the president of this country, Matías Guili."

Matías says this in Japanese. His delivery is smooth, too impossibly fluent to have been learned as a second language. The effect, as calculated, is tremendous. A murmur ripples through the visiting delegation.

"In order to put behind us those days of misfortune, and more, in order to lay new foundations for both our countries in the years to come, all that is past must be put peacefully to rest, and rightfully so. By no means inconsequential are the many strengths both sides bring to this task, a major country in its major capacity, and a smaller country in its smaller capacity. Thus, I feel this visit to be an important first step. I have many more things to say to you all, but rather than go on here in the hot sun, I would like to suggest that we adjourn until dinner, when there will be opportunity to speak at greater length."

Matías concludes his short speech and steps down. The forty-seven veterans are visibly relieved. The sun *is* hot. All the tourists who glared at these old coots as they were waived past Immigration have since been whisked away on buses, no doubt to some place where iced drinks await. Now these old boys are the ones left behind.

"Next, in reciprocal salutation, former Infantry Captain Ueshima," blurts out the Ministry liaison officer, unprompted. Unable to keep silent in this heat, he's jumped the gun.

Out steps a veteran from the far right end of the front row. Admirably disciplined, the old soldier marches stiffly to the podium, bows deeply to one flag and the other, bows to the President now back in his place, then reaches into his jacket pocket and pulls out an alarmingly thick sheaf of folded *washi* paper.

"Ahem, as per that gracious introduction, may I present myself: Kinzo Ueshima, former infantry captain. While hardly the most fit, inasmuch as I am the eldest in our delegation, as well as having held the highest rank, I will hereby offer brief greetings in reply to His Excellency the President."

He unrolls the paper one fold at a time, like a hand scroll. As everyone dreaded, the speech to come is interminable. And even worse, he's had no new thoughts since 1944.

"Starting in 1918, the end of World War I, when these islands, now independent in the eyes of the world, first came into the care of the Empire and in due course were made a protectorate by the League of Nations, a great many imperial officials and Japanese citizens came to reside here, though subsequently when the Empire rose up valiantly in lone resistance to Western pressures upon the lands and seas of East Asia, shedding much blood and tears in the Pacific War, it was the sad fate of our comrades to leave their bones buried in these sands, their bare corpses strewn in the fields, in remembrance of whom we have now journeyed to these tropics to comfort their spirits in the hope of righting those misfortunes..." On and on he goes for half an hour, and there's still a big wad of paper to go.

Now and again he swallows his words, choked with emotion or perhaps straining to make out what's written. The handwriting is so minute he practically nuzzles the page with his geriatric reading glasses, triumphantly raising his voice each time he deciphers a word.

The veterans' reactions divide sharply: some hang on to Captain Ueshima's every word with tears in their eyes; others gaze into space, anxious to get out of the heat. From where Matías stands, the ratio looks about one to four, though he can't quite make out a few at the back.

After a few minutes, someone at the rear does in fact keel over, falling between the rows of red-striped hats clutched at waist level. An accident that was waiting to happen. Matías eyes Jim Jameson, easily more adept at handling situations like this than Katsumata, and the executive secretary sneaks off to the airport terminal to summon two bored Island Security guards. They bring a stretcher and carry the casualty inside, reviving him with slaps and wet towels and ammonia and brandy. But no sooner does this all-purpose remedy have him back on his feet than the next victim has to be hauled in.

Captain Ueshima's speech shows no sign of abating—a long history deserves a long speech—though a sense of crisis is encroaching. Just this side of panic, one old soldier in the captive audience looks up to see—what is that apparition in the sky? Eyes swimming with heat, he tugs at his neighbor's arm and points. His comrade lets out a loud gasp that spreads through their ranks and across to the Navidad officials.

There atop the pole, the Japanese flag is on fire. Ghostly pale against the bright sun, flames lick into the white ground and crimson ball peeking from the folds, a beautifully burning vision. Well, the Rising Sun is supposed to be blazing red, isn't it?

Eventually, Captain Ueshima realizes no one's listening. He looks up and gulps down his speech just as the rope burns through and the last scorched remnants sail slowly, gracefully to the ground. The endless speech suddenly comes to an untimely end.

⚡

An hour later, President Matías Guili is back in his office. The burning flag is still in his thoughts, of course, but he's given Katsumata instructions, so he might as well put it out of mind. He's got the whole night and early morning hours ahead to ponder what it might mean. The executive secretary shows in a guest, another Japanese from the same flight as the veterans, though he reached the hotel well ahead of them. He didn't see the burning flag. Instead, he found a message to come here while the veterans have some free time to stroll around town—although, considering their average age, they might all be in bed recuperating from the heat. They have that luxury; the President has no rest.

The man stands in the doorway and bows to the prescribed angle. He's in his fifties, tall and slim, sharp features, dark for a Japanese. *A burnt tree of a figure*, thinks Matías. Now where did that image come from? Leaves and branches seared away leaving only a charred trunk. Did he see it as a child on his mother's island? Or somewhere in Japan?

Matías stands and greets the man. Then, cueing his secretary to leave, he indicates a chair. The man presents his name card and takes a seat.

"Kanroku Suzuki, wasn't it?" says Matías in Japanese before even looking at the card.

"Yes. Most honored. I've long awaited the opportunity to meet Your Excellency."

"Never mind that. Like I always tell people, I'm not here forever, so let's get to the point."

Hard words to cut a hard image. Not that he believes for a minute his time is so short; he just uses the line to preempt idle chatter. In a developed country he could keep his thumb on the media, but here any two people can talk up no end of rumors. And those rumors spread quickly. A real pain.

"Very well, as you say, let's get down to business." Suzuki opens his attaché case and pulls out a stack of papers. "The project is shaping up nicely. Which is why, rather than write or telephone, I felt I should come and explain things personally."

Polite he is, thinks Matías, *politely pushy. No getting a word in edgewise.*

Suzuki talks fast. "I believe you will have had the opportunity to look over the proposal I sent, along with the cover letter from Jitsuzo Kurokawa. However, allow me to review the main points, just to refresh your memory."

Never did care much for long-winded formal Japanese, Matías reflects. *Too many empty words.* As if the man can't talk straight and respectful at the same time, whatever his ilk. Not a government functionary. Name card makes him out to be director of some globalspeak consulting firm, but that's a red herring. They make up paper companies left and right in Japan. Can't trust corporations. An individual lives only so long, but corporations? They're reborn or gobbled up by other corporations. Can't trust a director's title.

Does this Suzuki have the face of a corporate man? More likely a free agent flitting between politicians and finance and bureaucracy. What drives a man like this? What makes him tick? Money? Personal glory? Craving for power? The thrill of toying with the machinery of nations? Confidence that someone behind the scenes wields more power than the officials out front? Almost makes him wonder what drives a president like himself—but no, he'll push that to the back of his mind. More late-night material.

Obviously Kurokawa's taking his cut on the deal along with everyone else. So will any money swim all the way here? A small country like this, it's hard to balance what benefits the people with what profits oneself. Still, why all the pseudo-officialese?

"…which is to say, the crux of the plan is the petroleum stockpiling facility to be built at Brun Reef by the Japanese government. Construction will of course be funded entirely from the Japanese side, with maritime area leasing to be paid in perpetuity—as long as the facility stays—into your state coffers. Still, the enterprise will require creating a quasi-governmental corporation for negotiations and project implementation…"

What's this man saying? What kind of talk is this? Matías knows only too well: the kind of talk that moves money and people, the most spellbinding language in the world.

"Specifically," Suzuki is voicing almost to himself, "the facility is to be constructed using the simplest and safest methods. Only the smallest portion of the reef will be dredged, just big enough to moor ten refurbished tankers, each with a three-hundred-thousand kiloliter capacity to be filled by other tankers. Alternatively, all ten might arrive already full. I don't have the final word on this. Either way, the tankers will remain at anchor, with no off-loading to other ships."

"What's the good of that?" Matías interjects for the first time.

"Guaranteed security. After the oil shocks of the seventies, the Japanese government understood that as a singularly vulnerable consumer nation we should lay in emergency stores against fluctuations in oil supplies. For decades, we've built stockpiling facilities at various locations throughout Japan, bringing our reserves to a 180-day supply. Half a year's worth of oil. The proposed facility would form one small part of those stores."

"So why build here?" asks Matías.

"Decentralization. Not putting all our eggs in one basket, so to speak. Less to go wrong in any one place. I know what you must be thinking—why so far away? Well, of course, there's the safety quotient of distance. But also, Navidad is situated just off the shipping lanes between the Middle East and Japan."

"Sounds like weapons," mutters the President unintentionally. Nothing you ordinarily need, but handy to have just in case. Just like nuclear weapons.

"To be perfectly frank, Your Excellency is absolutely correct. In peacetime, petroleum is a resource, pure and simple. But should international tensions arise, it suddenly becomes a weapon. Though unlike conventional weapons, it has no offensive attack value. Still, those on the supply side can cripple their enemies just by turning off the tap, making it a 'negative factor' weapon. By planting sufficient caches here and there, we guard against such eventualities."

Suzuki pauses here in anticipation of some comment, but the President says nothing.

"Not only is Navidad in a prime location for Japan, with negligible population to be affected by the construction, but the capital investment would key into this country's economic development, its maintenance and management generating a steady rate of employment."

"Using old ships, isn't there a danger of oil spills?"

"Every precaution will be taken."

"And if they still leak? Everyone's so vocal these days. Five fish belly up, the whole country goes crazy. And not just here, half the world will be up in arms, pointing fingers at us."

"We stand ready with oil fences and other technologies, and in the improbable event of any mishap, financial compensation. It is a Japanese undertaking after all."

"And the remuneration for the maritime leasing?"

"An extremely delicate question." (*At last we get to the heart of the matter,* thinks Matías.) "We may propose various bases of calculation. One way might be in terms of land value, but how exactly to establish equivalents? Whereas compensation for the fishing there, however important to the lives of the local populace, amounts to practically nothing monetarily. Various options deserve consideration before we settle on a plan."

Wouldn't bet on it, thinks Matías. This man hasn't come here without a specific sum in mind. "What if we look at it from the viewpoint of how much this will help Japan?"

"Meaning?"

"Meaning, what if we regard your petroleum as a kind of insurance, then hash out premiums. Say we value the peace of mind from having three hundred thousand kiloliters stockpiled here at one percent of its market value—purely hypothetical numbers. That should be simple enough to figure out."

"At twenty-five dollars per barrel..." Suzuki wriggles his fingers, telling the beads of an imaginary abacus. "That makes 4.7 million dollars a year, or a little over five billion yen. Quite a tidy sum."

"My one percent was purely hypothetical. Insurance premiums are highly arbitrary. In any case, there's plenty of room for negotiation." Matías bides his time, just to impress upon his visitor that he's the one running this discussion. "The main issue is much more basic."

"And what issue might that be?"

"Namely, why should my country let you line up your ugly tankers on our beautiful coral reef and run the risk of an oil spill just to ensure the security of Japan? Did you think I'd jump at the mere mention of money?"

"Nothing could be further from my mind. Which is precisely why, in the order of business, or rather of proper etiquette, I took it upon myself to go over the main points."

"Right."

"As you say, why Navidad? Again, rather than go into all the details, let me just cite the proximity to Japan's oil routes, ideal reef conditions, the small population, the welcome absence of intellectuals to object to a project of this sort, and..."

"...and a president who's easy on the take?"

"Curiously enough, I myself advanced that very same opinion."

To whom? Matías looks the man in the face but shelves the question. Well, consider it an achievement that he's showing a shade more honest slime.

Suzuki smiles back at Matías. "But forget our position. What matters here are your country's long-term priorities. I wouldn't claim to be an expert, but let me offer a few, perhaps untoward observations. My apologies in advance."

What a funny man, thinks Matías. The way he keeps changing colors. Up to a minute ago he was a dyed-in-charcoal-gray bureaucrat, now suddenly he's the visiting lecturer in international relations. Slippery, but also a prime mover. Lubricant that turns to fuel.

"To put it bluntly, your country is too small. Say we posit the optimum size for a country to be a million or more; anything less is a logistical disadvantage—you survive in peacetime, but come war you disappear. A population of seventy thousand is nothing. You get by as islands, but in the middle of a continent your country would never exist to begin with. Likewise, economically, Navidad's national budget derives almost entirely from foreign aid, from US and Japanese ODA," Suzuki argues, hammering home his disagreeable logic.

"Point taken," acknowledges President Guili.

"Up to now that was fine. The underside of Cold War tensions was safe.

Materially sufficient. But in the century to come there will be shortages, north and south will fight over resources, foist toxic wastes onto one another. We're entering a period of global realignment. And when elephants fight, the safest place for a mouse is on an elephant's back."

"So you're saying we should ride with Japan?"

"In a word, yes. Fortunately, Your Excellency's affinities with Japan run deep. Navidad looks to its farsighted President to secure relations between our two countries."

"By means of an oil tanker stockpile?" asks Matías.

"To entrust something of importance is to forge a bond of trust." The bureaucrat resurfaces with his specious phrases. With Japan's strategic materials kept here, any attack would be an attack against Japan. A security pact by default.

"No, what scares me is that the bond will become too strong."

"The bond is not cement. Only a few million dollars a year, surely?"

"There are prewar precedents."

"What is that supposed to mean?"

"I mean, Navidad and the other League of Nations island protectorates in your so-called Domestic South Seas effectively became Japanese colonies or military bases. We saw terrible fighting during the war, then later the Japanese government made no appreciable reparations. I grant that you're our closest major power, and I'm personally acquainted with Japan. That still leaves me plenty of reasons not to trust your country implicitly."

"Most regrettable," Suzuki apologizes. A sentence without a subject. Who regrets? The Japanese people? The government? The man himself? "But those days are gone. Open warfare is a thing of the past."

"Who's to say? The surest way to secure resources is to colonize the resource country. You yourself said as much a minute ago, talking about 'the century to come.'"

"All the more reason to find safety under Japan's wing."

"Suddenly elephants sprout wings. Enough. Let's leave it there for today and meet again tomorrow. We each have things to sort out before then." Not a bad start, thinks Matías, even more inclined to favor the project than before.

⚡

At the dinner reception, the delegation's deputy leader, former Naval Ensign Saigo, makes a speech:

"At this time, on behalf of our entire delegation, I wish to express my heartfelt gratitude to His Excellency the President and to the Republic of Navidad for the magnificent banquet that has been laid before us.

"Thinking back, it was nearly fifty years ago that we sailors of the Imperial Navy came to defend these islands. When I reflect that half a century has passed, my emotions know no bounds. Can fifty years really have gone by so quickly? Can we have aged so much? It makes me realize all the more the impermanence of human life. When we were stationed here, we comrades-in-arms were mere youths in our twenties. Leaving home for the sake of our country, with pride in our chests we sailed to these solitary islands and engaged in mortal combat with the encroaching enemy, losing many before returning to Japan desolate and bereaved. Now fifty years on, treading these sands once again to comfort the souls of the many noble comrades who died, I cannot help but feel their sacrifice was not in vain. In my heart of hearts I know it is because of them that Japan prospers, that the world is at peace, and that their children and grandchildren enjoy the happiness they have today.

"Losing one's comrades is hard," blusters the big bald-headed old officer. "Losing one's subordinates is hard. Men forced to drink muddy slurry for lack of water, to eat grass for lack of food, only to perish with fever for lack of medicine. Harder still is it to see one's friends with arms and legs torn asunder by mercilessly superior American firepower, covered with blood, screaming in agony. It was hard to see them die that way. Yet is it not precisely because of what we endured that we worked so arduously after the war, pushing forward on the battlefield of industry to build up today's Japan? We have come this far thanks to those buddies of ours looking over our shoulders. And so it is only fitting that finally, fifty years after leaving behind their earthly remains to board the sadly departing ships, we return with renewed respect.

"And yet the souls of our comrades-in-arms, the courageous spirits of our bright-eyed shipmates, never thought to linger in this remote and alien place. For though they left their corpses scattered in the jungle gloom, their souls took wing, each and every one, to fly back to their beloved Japan. Some may scoff when I say this," his voice creeping up a note, "but I saw them. I shall never forget the day, April 25, 1944, in the harrowing aftermath of the saturation bombing that obliterated our Command HQ, when I watched as one white bird then another flew up from the bodies of our comrades strewn about the smoldering ashes and, once the American planes had gone, circled the blue sky, then went winging off to the north-northeast. What was that flock if not the courageous souls of the Greater Japanese Imperial Forces who selflessly met their deaths on these lonely South Sea isles?

"I have heard similar reports from other places on the islands. Not a few of you, I'm sure, may also recall such startling scenes. That's right, those fallen heroes turned into pure white birds and flew off to their beloved Yamato. Unable to defend their ancestral homeland in life, they flew northward over the vast ocean to guard the nation in spirit.

"Indeed, I would submit—and in no uncertain terms—that as hard as we have worked these fifty years to give our comrades-in-arms comfort by rebuilding postwar Japan, in a sense it is they who have comforted us. They who have tirelessly watched over us. And so we come now to these antipodes not only to remember those painful times, to grieve together with them as fathers, husbands, brothers, but to dedicate ourselves anew. If by some oversight any of their bones were missed in the repatriation of remains, let us find them.

"Let this be our cause: to consecrate an altar upon which to offer our deepest, purest prayers! Recalling those days of suffering"—his voice sinks low and sinister—"the spiritual strength of our generation must rise again! Those who have betrayed their heritage—our mindless youth—must be opposed! That above all is the true purpose of our noble mission. Is it not time to take action, to lay anew the foundations of the once-and-forever Greater Japan?"

"Right," mutters President Matías Guili in native Gagigula, "just keep telling yourself that."

⚡

The President has visited Angelina's place once or twice a week since 1977 when she first set up on the island. Unlike the Japanese bath in his official residence or the limousine that came with his presidency, this affair with Angelina is strictly private; she's the only true love he's ever known. Most decisions he talks over with Angelina; he needs her to let him see the issues objectively. He's always demanded a lot from his women, but never lots of women. That much hasn't changed from the time of his long stable marriage to María Guili.

Matías makes a brief appearance at drinks after dinner with the veterans, but can't bring himself to join in their mellow mood of nostalgia and ducks out without fanfare. Their positions are now decisively reversed—the politico who was once just an errand boy, the servicemen who are now doting old losers—but they don't know that. They don't recognize the Japanese-speaking local big shot as the little brat they used to boss around: "Get me some palm wine! Get me a woman! Get me some decent fish!" And Matías hasn't the least intention of telling them.

Heinrich drives slowly as he always does these nights, easing the Nissan to a stop behind Angelina's brothel. Matías opens the car door himself and enters the building by an inconspicuous green door. Straight on down a dark hallway, he heads up a small staircase and opens a hardwood door to another dark hall. He pauses to part the heavy curtains along the wall to peer down on the floor below where men in suits or aloha shirts lounge with scantily clad young women, talking in hushed tones or tipping back drinks as they hold hands. The usual peaceful picture, jazz playing softly in the background.

At a table to the far right sit two white men, Ketch and Joel. They never seem to change. Indeed, ever since they started coming here, doing odd custodial chores during the day, they've become a permanent feature. Look in at this hour and they'll be at a table for two with a bottle of twelve-year-old I.W. Harper planted in the middle. Every night it's the same: they down a bottle of bourbon while playing chess or teasing the girls or whispering secret in-jokes. Sometimes they just sit and stare. The two of them polish off the bottle, then retire to their private room where they fall asleep on a queen-sized bed in each other's arms.

There was a time when Matías couldn't stand the sight of them. They reminded him of something, but now they're such cornerstones of his existence that it's become a ritual to check in on them. Seeing the two of them there, he feels relieved. He can dismiss the awkward associations they arouse. He's even grown rather fond of them, and if it suits his mood, he'll go have a drink with them. They're witty, veritable fountains of information, the best kind of drinking partners. Not that it diminishes the problem, though. It's been almost a year since it all happened. Still, what will he do when they finally up and leave?

No chat with them tonight, however. Matías heads on into Angelina's room and pulls a half-hidden cord. The bell makes only the faintest ring, yet Angelina never misses it. At this hour she'll be downstairs directing drinks to different tables, catching up on the talk of the town, fielding gripes from the girls, but as soon as she hears the tinkle she's out of there.

"Evening," says Angelina, a slight Filipina lilt to her English. "What you drinking?"

"Whew, am I tired. Today's been a killer."

"You always say that. But really you got plenty of spring in you."

"It's just pretend bounce. Better give me a hit. Yeah, and a small bottle of champagne."

"Oh? That's fresh," she says, pulling a thin gold chain from her cleavage to retrieve a tiny pendant key. She unlocks an ebony chest and takes out a tiny jar. Then, opening the icebox fitted into the lower compartment of the chest, she extracts a half-bottle of Moët & Chandon.

"What, no glasses? How many times do I got to tell them? Always keep a pair chilled!" She picks up the telephone by the door and calls down to one of the girls. The maid's gone home by now, and Ketch and Joel only work days, their noontime energies evaporated in a cloud of alcohol.

Unexpectedly, a slim young woman Matías has never seen before appears. Not Filipina by the look of her. Dark rosewood complexion, with big eyes. Big lips too, but drawn tight, giving the impression of someone who gets her own way. Where's this face from, thinks Matías, watching her deposit the glasses and leave.

"Who was that?"

"New face. Now don't you get ideas. Hired her as a maid," chides Angelina as she pops open the champagne and pours two glasses. "Remember Magda, used to work here?"

"Not really."

"You had her once. Short girl, big tits. From Melchor?"

That jogs the President's memory. Another Melchor islander, eh? "Ah yes, her."

"Well, this one comes by her introduction. Said she's a friend of a friend. Come looking for cleaning work. But you never know, once she see how much the other girls make, she might change her mind."

Matías is still eyeing the door where she disappeared, champagne flute held between his chubby fingers. He meets a hundred people a day and forgets ninety-nine. Others remember him, of course; that's the privilege of position. Somehow, though, he just knows he'll remember her tomorrow. Hard to forget such an unusual face.

"Something about her," says Angelina. "She sees things. Usually doesn't say a word, just cleans and does laundry. But sometimes she look up and say, 'Storm coming.' And honest to god, storm really does come."

"She can predict the weather?"

"And not just weather. She see a new customer, she say, 'He gonna get drunk and fall asleep.' Thing is, it's true. The john just drink himself to sleep on the sofa."

"Think she can predict the future of the country?"

"Oh c'mon, she's not *that* good."

His face clouds over, he's said something he shouldn't have. He drops the subject and concentrates on the bubbles in his glass.

Meanwhile, Angelina scoops a dab of thick black paste from the jar onto a miniature plate, lights it with a match, and carefully lowers the smoking resin into a coffee cup. Then, covering the cup with a saucer, she passes it to the President. Putting aside his glass, he slides back the saucer lid and inhales.

A warm, familiar, mown-grass smell fills the room. The smoke soon takes effect: pleasure liquefies in the depths of his brain, drowning him happily.

"Makes the champagne taste completely different."

"Even turns water into champagne. Still, you asking for a hit, been a long time."

"Mm. Just so dead tired today. Don't like dealing with the Japanese."

"You, the leader of the pro-Japan faction?"

"That's ideology. Business. Personal feelings are something else. Undress, will you?"

Angelina rises to her feet and peels off what she's wearing, one piece at a time. Not making any special show of stripping for him, nor simply going through the motions, but enjoying the feel of letting each layer lightly graze her skin and fall away.

"No, everything," drones Matías, drowsily pointing to her underwear. "I see you there and the whole world is mine. All the women in the world stand before me while I just watch. You know why?"

Ignoring the query, Angelina reaches around behind her back and unhooks. She bends over, holding her breasts, and lays the bra on the chaise longue. One leg at a time, she steps out of her last article of clothing.

"Give it to me," says Matías, handing her the hash cup. She savors the warmth in the palm of her hands, the smoky sweet fragrance infusing upwards. "I'd be happy just to spend each night like this."

"So why don't you? Just hole up with me someplace."

"Can't. This is what every man in the world wants, and yet it's still not enough. It's the workday that makes the night such magic. Or am I wrong?"

"Do I look like a philosopher?" Angelina stands just out of reach, running her hands leisurely over her skin, midriff to breasts. She takes three steps back and pulls aside a heavy velvet curtain to reveal an alcove bed, where she now reclines. Matías grabs up both champagne flutes together with the hash cup and moves to the bedside chair.

"Really ought to export more of this stuff to Japan. Not for the money. I just want that country to loosen up a bit."

"One diplomatic pouch at a time's not much business," says Angelina.

"And I can't say I much care for dealing with Kurokawa on the receiving end either. Got to branch out. Such a big, rich country, and they're so uptight. They think they're so together, no foreign riffraff. Too damn well behaved for their own good, never making waves. Flood the country with this shit, and we might see some real honest-to-goodness egos."

"Egotists, the whole lot of 'em, but each one alone's such a wimp," slurs Angelina, breathing in a puff of hash. She raises one knee to spread before him the part of her she's most proud of, the part he loves the best. That tuft of pubic hair *is* beautiful: wispy brown against her pale skin, the way it divides into whorls left and right as it covers her little mound, fertile with promise of joys to come. He feels an urge to put his hands together and pray to her, a divinity liberated from the individual person of Angelina. The least bead of dew glistens in the chandelier light. Is this the sanctum, the transcendence that Matías seeks? To worship or not to worship?

"Aw, fuck 'em," he concurs. "They're so simple, so bound to morals. Swallowing every word from the top down, no questions asked. No one thinks for himself. Just give me the proper endorsement, every corner convenience store'd be selling the stuff."

"Worth a try. Team up with some bigwig."

"Not bad. Not bad at all. Get it legalized, supply it single-handed. It'd be fun," he mumbles, fingertips poised not in prayer, but ready to dive in.

⚡

Two hours later, the President heads out without a word to anyone, just like when he arrived. Angelina sees him to the door in her dressing gown, then returns to her room. Stepping back inside, she notices the lingering hash odor. She takes a deep breath and yawns. The salon downstairs is quiet, with probably only Ketch and Joel still around.

She goes to her ebony chest, kneels to open a drawer, and pulls out what looks like a letter. Stripping off her dressing gown, she climbs back onto the messy bed and unfolds the paper. She stares at it for a long time—five minutes, ten minutes—then silently, secretly, begins to cry. Her tears drip onto the page, and soon it's all wet. Big wet words. Words that someone has been posting all over town for more than a week now:

The earth shall accept thee

Angelina doesn't understand what it's supposed to mean. Nobody does. Nobody but the person or persons who stuck them up. All she knows is, it has something to do with the President. Why does she cry when she looks at it? It's been like this for five nights running. Why can't she bring herself to tell Matías, whom this surely concerns—why keep the handbill hidden away? She doesn't even want to think about it. But at night, after the President returns to his villa, she takes it out and contemplates what must bode some grave fate for the President and herself. Just how and when that fate will disclose itself, she has no idea. She feels like praying to this handbill, just as Matías felt the urge to pray to her pubic hair and moistened lips—but she too refrains. She touches the page and goes on weeping.

02

Geographically, the Navidad Archipelago comprises three large islands and a number of lesser outlying islets in the South Pacific. Two of the large islands are surrounded by a common barrier reef; the third lies some three hundred kilometers away within its own reef. All share a common language and an ancient network of trade, a distinct sphere of Navidadian culture generally conducive to a united political destiny. Somehow the islands just belonged together, though nationhood, it goes without saying, was decided elsewhere—so far away, in fact, that to the islanders it might as well have been ordained in heaven.

Significantly, most small countries emerging on the international horizon see their origins tagged with the phrase "it goes without saying." When discussing these countries, it is customary—that is, banal—for writers to trot out truisms about "discovery," the events that introduced them to the world without the locals even knowing they'd been "discovered." No, they are mere accessories to the "historical fact"—and so it was with Navidad.

The archipelago entered the annals of world history in 1645, when the otherwise unremarkable Spanish explorer Baltasár Jarán de Valencia discovered an island surrounded by a coral reef. Warily venturing ashore, the ship's crew found it was in fact two islands separated by a small inner lagoon and inhabited by people who came out to meet them just as warily. Both sides simply stood there eyeing each other from opposite ends of the beach. Narrowly resisting the temptation to open fire, the Spaniards traded glass beads and other European trinkets for island food and water. They refrained from using their muskets, as the ship's log records, because the encounter fell felicitously on the twenty-fifth day of December; hence in the joyous spirit of the season these two vastly different races did not massacre one another. For that same reason, Jarán christened the islands *Las Navidades* after the Nativity, taking the liberty of naming the larger of them Baltasár after himself. What the islanders called the place he didn't ask. Thus, Gagigula appears on no world map.

As Baltasár was also one of the Three Magi, the other main island became Gaspar, and a third distant island, spied but unexplored the previous week, was dubbed Melchor (again ignoring the fact that the inhabitants called it Sa'an). The Spaniards then celebrated by tapping a cask of Maldivian madeira. Did the holy names of *Los Tres Reyes Magos* just happen to mirror this island trinity, or should we read in it some prophetic manifest destiny?

Granted, people had lived here long before this "discovery," and a handful of white men sailing caravels halfway around the globe to plot islands on maps in no way affected their day-to-day happiness. Not for the time being at least. The waters abounded in fish, and should they have wanted for boats to sail beyond the coral reefs—though catches were plentiful in the lagoon alone—the hills were thick with trees. Taro and bananas grew readily, and ma'a, which the Europeans saw fit to call "breadfruit," sprouted everywhere. In short, the islands were generously endowed to support a sizeable population.

Baltasár and Gaspar are shaped like two battling beasts, a variation on the lion rampant. Or rather, to our more peaceable Rorschach-tested eyes, like twins conversing embryonically inside a coral-ringed amniotic sac. The resemblance, however, only became apparent to local inhabitants in the last hundred years. Prior to that, none had ever viewed their homeland from the air, and by the time they had, the islands were swamped in confusing developments even more foreign to the populace.

Baltasár City was not, for instance, laid out on the island of the same name; this capital of twenty thousand strong is actually on Gaspar Island. Were there only a Gaspar Town on Baltasár Island the story would have a happy symmetry, but alas, it was not to be. The main town on Baltasár is simply called Colonia, "the colony." Baltasár City sits on Gaspar exactly where the male member would be on the lion, a built-up quarter of government offices, market halls and port facilities occupying a small cape that thrusts out into the lagoon. Colored urban-red on the map, it all the more resembles a phallus, a correspondence that tickled the cartographers of the Instituto Real de Estúdias Oceanográficas.

But back to the Spaniard Baltasár Jarán de Valencia, the principal agent in "discovering" the islands. About his character, records have little to say. One supposes he was just another sailor of whom Spain, Portugal, and England had a great number at the time. Born in 1605, he came into an early inheritance from his father at the age of twenty, and with that money he bought a small trading concession. Still ship shy, he boarded one and then another of the company's Atlantic charters as a "privileged crewman," and thus gained his sea legs. By the age of thirty-five, having increased his late father's fortunes to a goodly sum, he sailed off for the fabled East Indies. Reversing a route charted by Magellan some hundred and twenty years before, he hoped to veer north to Cathay, but was beset for weeks on end by easterlies that drove him to these Navidads, where he dropped anchor for a few days' respite.

As one who sought adventure only after having first laid up funds for his old age, we can assume he was none too ambitious. After weeks of fighting the winds, he was apparently satisfied with this small claim to posterity; he gave up entirely on Cathay and instead made for Java, where he filled his hold with "divers and sundrie" for the return voyage. Yet even then, this middling mariner was financially favored, for the Javanese cargo tripled his investment. Nothing else comes down to us about this unremarkable avatar of the Christmas spirit. One imagines him back home surrounded by children and grandchildren, recounting his exploits in the Eastern Seas, until eventually he passes on (though of course it's perfectly possible that once back in Spain he was shot dead while making moves on another man's wife).

As a result of Baltasár's reports, the Navidads came to grace the charts of the Empire of Spain. It was something of a miracle that islands this size remained undiscovered in the Pacific, considering the number of fortune-seeking vessels—Spanish, Dutch, and English—that plied those waters. Had it not been Baltasár but instead Garcia Jofre de Loaysa or Miguel López de Legaspi or Sir Francis Drake (knighted despite being an outright pirate) or Thomas Cavendish or Olivier van Noort or Joris Spielbergen or any other less Christian rogue who sighted the islands, their fate might have been quite different.

When the Navidads were claimed as Spanish territory in 1668, it goes without saying (that phrase again), no islanders were consulted. The Navidads were ideally located for guarding the sea route via which Mexican silver was transported to pay for silk and spices and tea from the Philippines. As to legalities, the discoverer was a Spanish subject, reporting directly to the Spanish crown—thus, who could question Spain's sacrosanct right to the territory?

Catholic priests arrived with the galleons. They offered the unbaptized savages a magnanimous choice: either convert to Catholicism—which would save their souls—or else. Of course, the Spaniards had firearms and the islanders had only stone adzes and bows and arrows. Within fifty years, the Vatican received the joyous tidings that all the islanders were now good Catholics, though only a scant ten percent of its original population. The effects of this religious decimation were long-lasting: to this day some sixty percent of Navidadians are Catholics, whose given names are to be found in the Book of Saints.

Much later came the Germans, who were still in the throes of national unification and latecomers to European imperialism. They desperately wanted a colony of their own, but the best places were already taken. Even tiny Belgium had carved out the Congo, leaving only a parched tract of sand called German West Africa.

In the Pacific it was the same story. Tahiti, Fiji, Samoa, Tonga, all the earthly paradises had been snatched up in rapid succession. Fortunately for Germany, Spain had already lost the Philippines and Guam to America in the Spanish–American War. Her other Pacific colonies, the Carolines and

Navidads, were merely jewels encrusting an ornate altarpiece, no longer of any real benefit. They'd converted thousands of islanders and continued to baptize a few hundred children each year, which kept a score of missionaries occupied but was hardly reason for holding on to the territories. Rudely awakened by defeat, Spain understood a full century ahead of her peers that the age of colonialism was over. Sometimes the decline of the state spells better times for everyone; as with certain foods and the opposite sex, countries are most delectable past their prime. Thus at the very end of the nineteenth century, an enlightened Spain sold the islands for 250 million *pesetas* to a gullible Germany that still doggedly believed in the vogue for colonies. And once again, it goes without...whatever, no one bothered to inform the natives.

Together with the Germans arrived, not missionaries, but businessmen. They came to the South Pacific with more immediate goals: to invest a minimum of capital to generate a profit from their colonial enterprise. The question was, what could they ship to Europe from the tropical Pacific? What could these Navidads possibly have to offer to people who wore woolens, ate beef, lived in brick houses, and enjoyed opera? There was only one likely product: copra, the thick, fatty flesh of the coconut, which provides a rich, all-purpose oil for cooking, candles, and soap, and once the oil is extracted, a nutritious press cake for animal fodder. To the captains of industry, it was quite a find.

Not that these Germans saw themselves making millions of marks per annum the moment they saw a coco palm. They had their trials and errors before they finally succeeded in turning the throwaway nodule of this peculiar tree into something they could sell. The move from sun-drying to wasteful but quality-controllable kiln-drying was the inspiration of one T. Weber, Direktor, J.C. Godeffroy Gmbf and simultaneously German Federation Councillor in Samoa. Likewise, it was an agronomist—name unknown, but attached to a German trading firm—who encouraged wrapping the trunks with spiny pandanus leaves to prevent rats and coconut crabs from eating into profits (nowadays they band the trees with tin collars).

If the Spanish enlightened the islanders to the existence of heaven, then it was the Germans who showed them the world at large (life in hell was left for the Japanese and Americans to demonstrate). The copra they produced was shipped far away, and foreign exchange arrived in the form of goods. Did they understand the process? Hardly. The world of commerce, whereby their copra was shipped to cold northern ports, landed, stored in warehouses, sold in the abstract, made into soap and margarine, then shipped off again, was scarcely more imaginable than the economic circuits that looped back. The islanders' world went only as far as the eye can see; what they saw was copra disappearing over the horizon, then returning as cotton print clothes, canned mackerel, matches, steel fishhooks, and nets. To them, the connection outbound-to-inbound was pretty much like the relationship between sex and procreation. Only with copra, the fun part came at the end.

Germany discovered marketable phosphates on other islands, but unlike Nauru or Angaur or Yaluit, the Navidads sadly had none. Nor did fluctuating prices for copra necessarily guarantee quantities of matches and mackerel, hooks and nets on the return voyage. Still, by the beginning of the twentieth century, the islands had a presence in the world economy, proudly standing in one small corner of the same stage with everyone else.

The commodity market for copra also imposed certain rules. When the German trade representative-cum-diplomat said, "Plant coco palms," then everyone planted coco palms. Up until then every island had these trees aplenty, and short of a typhoon knocking down swaths of jungle, who ever heard of making any special effort to plant them? Why harvest more than you could eat? To people living in nature, it was simple common sense. But no, now they had to deal with capitalist nature; they had to plant as many trees as the land allowed, carefully maintain the stock, and harvest it for export. In Ponape, every adult was required to plant ten coco palms a month; in Yap, it was four. In Truk, the numbers were similar, but duties were held individually accountable, subject to forced labor. At one point, each Navidadian was obliged to plant a hundred trees a year. Thus, under the maxim "No responsibilities, no rights," the advent of the modern world tightened the thumbscrews of social management. German policy toward the islanders is masterfully expressed in the words of Minister of Colonial Affairs Dernburgs: "The aboriginals are our most valuable asset in the colonies."

On the other hand, the Germans taught them not to think twice about wasting things. What they were after was copra—nothing else. Of the hundreds of ways to make use of palm trees, the Germans valued only one. No German wove palm leaves into baskets to carry taro and fruit to the village. No German plaited fish toys for the kids, or drank the sweet coconut water, or fashioned coco shells into bowls, or made ropes from the husk fiber, or ate the fresh young shoots, or even took an afternoon nap in the shade of those big swaying fronds (after first making sure not to sit directly under a coconut). To think that they neglected all these blessings and only had eyes for copra! The islanders learned to accept many odd market dictates without really understanding them. Latecomers to the school of international business, they could only memorize their lessons, no questions asked.

After the Spanish and Germans came the Japanese, and in their wake the Americans. Only after extended domination by these four peoples with their various different principles did Navidad finally become independent.

↯

The day after the Japanese veterans delegation's arrival, a dozen islanders are sitting on the palm log benches out in front of the Cooperative Market—"News Central" for the citizens of Baltasár City. Market-goers all love to come here to trade opinions for gossip, then watch the stories multiply. Men and women alike, ages fifteen to eighty-five, whatever their social standing or political views, all become top-notch critics the minute they take their place on the benches—the long-established seat of collective judgment on this island (and the greatest threat to President Matías Guili, though he doesn't know it yet). A bit of advice for anyone—spy or otherwise—who wants to know what's going on in Navidad: instead of reading a week of the *Navidad Daily*, instead of listening to the monotony of Radio Baltasár for a whole day, you'd do better to spend thirty minutes sitting here in the plaza and just listen.

"Last night, a house in Xulong done burned down," says an old man to a muscular fellow in his thirties sitting next to him.

"Yeah, I know. Right after everyone finished supper. House started burning from outside, fire climbed the wall and over the roof. Family was just sayin' how awful hot it was for evenin'," says the younger man loud enough for all to hear, his delivery neat and precise.

"Well ain't *you* the know-it-all," says a fat woman in her fifties sitting on the opposite side, shucking a basketful of beans.

"Well if you must know, I was *there*, visiting relations not five houses away. Right after the fire started, I see this flickerin' light outside, then somebody's callin' for water to douse the house. Didn't do much good, but kept it from spreading. Lucky there wasn't no wind."

"And the family what's house got burned?" asks the big mama.

"Staying with neighbors. They was startled all right, but don't seem too altogether grieved. The kids're havin' a great time. They been wantin' to put up a new house anyhow, had most of their stuff stored with relations. Place was practically empty, so it went up just like that. Burned the leaves off the ma'a tree next to the house too. Might make more fruit come out."

"So why'd it catch fire?" a lanky fellow wonders out loud, swaying on his haunches.

"Somebody had'a set the fire. Right before the flames spread all over, they saw a boy runnin' off. Anyway, a house don't burn from the outside, not by itself it don't."

"The thing 'bout the ma'a tree is true. There's that old saying: 'Once burned black, twice bears back.' Ma'a's a dumb tree, gets scared people gonna use it for firewood if it don't got fruit. That's why in the old days they used to light fires under barren ma'a trees," mutters an old woman listening in. "People nowadays just don't know."

"They ever rile anybody, that family? Do anything to hold against 'em?" the old man asks on behalf of everyone. The marketplace naturally divides between those who ask and those who answer.

"Got me there. All I hear is, they's good people, nice and friendly," reports the village voice.

"S'posed to be fun torchin' houses," sniggers a kid one seat over from the old man.

"Not for normal people it ain't. Wouldn't put it past *you*, though" says the big mama.

"Don't look at me. You'd hafta be brung up twisted. Or from somewhere else."

"There was this fireman in Manila liked to set fires. Kinda makes sense," interjects the lanky fellow, letting everyone know he spent some time in the Philippines.

"Maybe they got the wrong house? Who lives next door?" asks the old man.

"Just regular folk. Mind you, regular folk can sneak their hands where they don' belong. Maybe eye the other guy's woman, put a little hex on the neighbors, but otherwise..."

"No political hokum? Nobody in Tamang's camp?" the old man presses on.

"Come to think of it, three doors down's that family Bonhomme Tamang's niece married into, but who'd set a fire for that? An' even if, they shouldn'a got the wrong house."

"Shouldn't and wouldn't, 'cept that's Island Security for you, heh heh," the old man chortles, which starts everyone laughing.

"Yah, but okay, why now?" blusters the old ma'a woman, stopping everyone short.

"Yeah, and what about that flag burnin' at the airport?" asks the kid.

"Strange, mighty strange, but it don't got the Tamang touch. Most of them Tamangos are modernizers, do things American-style. Wouldn't even know how to use no magic. You even hear they been up to much lately? Sure ain't called to reopen the assembly, so why burn flags?" says the old man.

"C'mon, everybody's anti-Jap. But that don't make us all Tamangos," says the kid.

"Somebody got it in for the President. Bet this is just the beginning," says the skinny fellow ominously.

"How long's it been?" wonders the kid after a moment's silence.

"A year," says the big mama. "One whole year for Guili to shore hisself up nice 'n safe."

"Good thing too. Damn good thing. Politics shake, everything go to pieces. Next thing you know bombs're flying and houses burning, can't be no good," grumbles the old man.

"Least damage anybody could do, that fire in Xulong. Makes you think like maybe Island Security got orders to send a little message to Tamang's camp, probably on account'a that Jap flag."

"Yeah, and that torii gate thing too," the kid chimes in again.

"Just the sort of stunt the President and Chief Katsumata might dream up. But hey, them Island Security boys'd never pull it off. They get their orders, they ain't got the guts. Like they go burn the wrong place. Bet the family even knew what was coming off, so they get out in time. Probably got money out of it too, or an Island Security barrack air-con gets installed by mistake in the new house they build. Who knows?" The man has all the answers.

"You really are Mr. Know-It-All, ain't you. Keep spreading them big ideas around, gonna get you a air-con by mistake too, eh?" sneers the big mama.

"I wish. But from what my cousin in Island Security tell me, them jokers can't keep anything straight. Still haven't heard from him 'bout this one, though. Just a gut feeling."

"Think Guili maybe ordered the fire?" asks the lean fellow, rocking back and forth.

"Probably," says the kid. "That's what his Island Security's for. And that's the President's politics, keeping us down. Hardly matters what we all think about Emperor Matías Guili."

"Not emperor, Guili wants to be dictator," explains the young man, flaunting his powers of analysis. "He's looking for an opening, but nobody couldn't care less how he rules. For him to crack down, people gotta get all hot and bothered, gotta rebel. But government's like winds up in the clouds. Blow this way, blow that way, don't matter to us. Money breeze in from overseas, it just circle around and never even touch the ground. 'Cause he can't rightly pinch our bananas or fish, now can he? A dictator need a secret police, but them boys don't know even know how to keep a secret. Good thing Guili's pro-Japan and Tamang's side's pro-America, otherwise Island Security wouldn't have no work at all. Still, things been awful quiet since Tamang died. Guili's just waiting for us to act up, throw bombs, tack up slogans, something to give him an excuse."

"Interesting, I'll say that. Real interesting, but it ain't got no reality. You make us out like simple folk ain't never seen money, but those days're long gone. Ain't nobody here that principled. We all want our radio cassettes. We want our blue jeans. And specially, we want our rice. The best thing them Japs ever did was teaching us the taste of rice," preaches the big mama. "Worst thing too. 'Cause you can't grow it here, you gotta buy it."

"You said it!" seconds the old man. "I'm from the generation what first tasted rice. Same as Guili. Couldn't believe it, thought I died an' gone to heaven. Make a man go crazy, that taste. Better we shouldn'a known it at all."

"Isn't the President's job to protect us?" argues Mr. Know-It-All. "Keep the big countries outside the reef?"

"But the rice bomb done dropped anyway. President Guili's not gonna stop no tide. Even Tamang did a better job of seawallin' Japan," says the lanky fellow.

"Hamburgers 'stead of rice. Big diff'rence," says the old woman, perking up at the thought of the island's one and only burger joint, though she's never actually tasted a hamburger. If only her grandson would go buy her one.

"Well, maybe not. Isn't easy being a small country," echoes the old man feebly.

"Take away the country, we still got the people," says Mr. Know-It-All.

"But that's just what this global-ation today don't allow," says the lanky fellow, proud of the big words he knows. "Just like we don't like people to leave the village, big countries don't like us little islands floatin' off alone. They got to work us in somehow. Give us aid, sell us junk, send us tourists, build bases, an' we just gotta put up with it. Just the way it goes nowadays. That's why we need somebody like Guili to do the troubleshooting with the outside world."

"That's right," seconds the old man. "Somebody gotta do the dirt work. Even if he is a crook."

"Hang on, don't you think we're all maybe just a little too smart for our own good? Know-nothing island folk talking like regular experts!" says Mr. Know-it-all.

"'Specially since we forget ever'thing soon as we leave this here market an' go right back to being good little villagers, glad to do what our President tell us. Something special 'bout this place," says the lanky fellow, thinking of his time in the Philippines, "even if our soundin' off don't carry far. Could say it's these benches do the talking, not us."

"Yep, the gab goes on, only the speakers change. Our behinds get smarter every day, but we don't never do nothing," the old man sighs with resignation.

"Yah," the old woman tags on, "but what d'ya make of them handbills all over town?"

⚡

Few would disagree that World War I marked the real beginning of the twentieth century (much as the nineteenth really began with Napoleon's defeat in 1814). By 1914, local turmoil was building toward "world" turmoil, albeit limited to European battlefields—a singular moment in time and space for people all over the planet. Only with the twentieth century is everyone implicated in one world, like it or not.

The War to End All Wars may have been confined to Europe, but surrogate skirmishes flared up in colonies all around the globe. In a corner of New Guinea known as Kaiser Wilhelmland, a British Army brigade wiped out a defenseless German reconnaissance unit comprised mostly of natives; while in Tanganyika, German East Africa, Humphrey Bogart and Katharine Hepburn's tiny riverboat did battle with a German gunship. In Micronesia, the Empire of Greater Japan, having severed diplomatic relations with Germany on August 23, landed its First Naval South Seas Expeditionary Force in the Marshall Islands on October 6. This was followed on the twentieth of the month by a Second Expeditionary Force to the Carolines and Maríanas, and a third to the Navidads on the twenty-fifth. The Germans put up almost no resistance. Germany lost territories five and a half times the size of the Fatherland, and Japan gained vast spoils with no actual fighting. It was like picking up a dropped wallet.

And so the inhabitants of these islands were pocketed into the twentieth century. Considering all that followed, that fateful day was either the beginning of a new era or the end of good times. For whereas the Spanish and Germans had endeavored to edify and manage these colonies, never intending to actually live there, the Japanese wanted to emigrate. Japanese settlers came crushing in en masse, as if the islands were uninhabited. They dried *katsuobushi* bonito fillets, they planted sugar cane, they brought rice and soy sauce too. Like the dirt-poor Spaniards who shipped out to the Americas in the seventeenth century, or Irish to New England in the eighteenth, or Chinese to California in the nineteenth, early twentieth-century Japanese headed either to Manchuria or the "Domestic South Seas."

When people move, cultures move with them. So when these "domesticators" came, it goes without saying (yikes, those words again!) the natives found themselves overtaken by Japanese culture. The new landlords built Shinto shrines on the islands, established Japanese schools. Unlike the British who never made the Queen's English mandatory for the whole Indian population—only those ambitious individuals seeking employment with the ruling class—Greater Japan required all the islanders, now second-class imperial subjects, to learn the Japanese language, pray at Japanese shrines, and ultimately—if male—be drafted into the Japanese military.

Among the waves of Japanese who flooded into Navidad at the time was a katsuobushi maker from Kochi, across Osaka Bay on the backwater island of Shikoku. A bonito fisherman in his youth, he'd lost three fingers of his right hand to a tangle of rigging, which dry-docked his career. Up to that point he'd caught fish; now he went over to the processing side and mastered the art of curing them. In 1929, hearing that a new bonito-curing plant was to be set up in the Navidads, he left behind a wife and child and made for *Namidajima*, the "Tearful Islands" as they were then called. Formerly mere ports of call for taking on food and water and bait, these Domestic South Sea islands were now producing great quantities of sugar and katsuobushi, and technical skills like his were in high demand.

Matías Guili believes this Chujiro Miyakura was his father. He's never told anyone, nor is there any official record of his father being Japanese. Still, the idea is not as farfetched as it might sound. Not that he ever met the man or even heard anything about him from his mother. She herself was from Melchor Island, far away from Gaspar and Baltasár. When her parents died one after the other, the orphan made her way to the capital and found employment at a Japanese-run barbershop. Which is where, her son Matías supposes, she met Miyakura. Supposes, because when Matías was only three, she succumbed to a Japanese tuberculosis epidemic.

His mother's younger sister took the child back to Melchor and entrusted him to the care of distant relatives, where he received little attention and, after finishing three years of public school, was thrown out on his own. An unruly boy, he headed back alone to Baltasár. There, an aunt found him living hand-to-mouth and gave him a box—keepsakes from his mother, she told him. Cheap Japanese perfume, a few pencil stubs, a dirty handkerchief printed with a Japanese landscape he would later recognize as the Ama-no-Hashidate shoals, a hairclip made of hibiscus wood and shell…and, tossed in among all this, a single dog-eared calling card:

Chujiro Miyakura
Chief Manager
South Seas Fisheries Company Ltd.
Navidad Katsuobushi Division

That's the size of it. His mother bore him and died unmarried. There were no rumors about this man and his mother; his aunt knew nothing about how her sister came to be with child. Still, Matías found a father in that box. Mere conjecture, embellished on a name card? As far as he was concerned, the card *was* his father. The figure behind it was up to him to invent. No card can make a woman pregnant, but it can beget a father.

Whatever connection existed between this father and his mother he could only imagine. To that ruling-country male who left behind a wife and children to come to the South Seas, was she merely a local mistress, a "shadow wife" in the parlance of the era? Was there mutual affection? Was it a one-night stand, or worse, a roadside rape in broad daylight? Feelings notwithstanding, it might as well have been rape. At a time when the islands themselves were being ravished, how could there be consenting sexual relations between Japanese men and island women? Or so teaches the ideology of anti-colonialism. Matías tried hard to convince himself of the rape scenario; he felt no sympathy for the man. Only— since a boy needs a father—he had to manufacture one. No need to color in a personality; the more abstract the figure, the better. No need, even, to wonder whether a man who raped a woman would then give her his calling card.

Whatever his reasoning, much later, during the several years he spent in Japan as a student, Matías took off one spring vacation and made a special trip to Kochi to find out about this Chujiro Miyakura. With nothing more than the card and snatches of hearsay to go on, he finally managed to locate the address, but unfortunately Miyakura himself was long gone. After just two years in Navidad he'd returned to Japan at the very end of the war, only to be conscripted despite his disability, and shipped off to his death. All Matías eventually heard from a nephew of his, who received him with cool suspicion, was that Miyakura had been a *katsuobushi* maker and a bonito fisherman before that. On the long ride back to Tokyo, changing trains countless times, Matías asked himself what in fact he'd learned. That the man really existed. That he indeed did come to Navidad. That he probably was good at his trade, but returned to Japan two years later because he missed his wife and children. That his family had since split up, whereabouts unknown...but was this what he wanted to know?

The truth was, there was only one question he wanted to ask: "Did you rape my mother?" It probably didn't even matter what the man's answer would have been. *No, it wasn't like that at all,* or *I don't remember the woman,* or

I never had a single woman the whole time I was on the islands, or *Yes, I did take advantage of her, but that doesn't mean I didn't love her*—anything to clear up what Miyakura's name card was doing among his mother's things. He'd just wanted to sit in that tiny house in that tiny fishing village in Shikoku, and put it straight to the wizened shrimp of an old man before him—"Did you rape my mother?"

Maybe he was so insistent because he badly wanted just to distinguish himself from all the other island boys. He was willing to be the bastard product of rape. He wanted living proof that half his blood came from superior Japanese stock. The chances were his father was just a Navidadian with no name card to leave behind. The boy's facial features and skin color could cut either way. Whatever the case, his mother died without telling a soul who the father was. That in itself was not uncommon, but the record was never set straight after her death. Even after the boy grew up and became president, no father ever surfaced. Which gave him the unique freedom to choose one for himself.

It also helps explain what made the boy so bent on success in a place where, given the traditional island lifestyle, he'd never go hungry. Even orphans enjoyed some fat of the land. The local standard of living may not have included rice or soy sauce or soap or cans of Geisha-brand mackerel, but any good Catholic would come into Sunday Mass clothes. He'd still be given a patch of earth and allowed to make his own canoe. Still guaranteed a back row seat at ceremonies. That should have satisfied anyone, but no, Matías made up his mind to renounce the land of plenty.

The good thing about the South Seas is maybe just a little too good: if you don't really have to work for your food, why stake your life on rebelling against foreign domination? Not that colonial administrators ever got around to oppressing the islanders into starvation. But if the drive for change is altogether foreign, where did Matías get his social-climbing ambition? That achiever mentality could only have come from a Japanese: a vision channeled into the mind of a Navidad orphan by an imaginary rapist father. And so it was, urged on by Chujiro Miyakura, the boy began his long ascent to the office of president.

⚡

What, then, of his mother? Where did she figure in the inner life of the boy Matías? We know she was from Melchor Island, the third distant light in the Navidad trinity. Relations between these islands are a story in itself. Ordinarily, two large island twins might be expected to overpower a third smaller one, but here the isolated, less populated, not especially prosperous Melchor has always held spiritual sway over Baltasár and Gaspar. The other two even sent tribute. Not because of any organized religion or political clout, but the clairvoyance of the Melchor Council of Elders. At the end of the nineteenth century, when the Ponape islanders revolted against the Spanish, and Navidad debated whether to take up arms as well, the Melchor Elders advised against using force. Spanish rule, they said, wouldn't last much longer, and their pronouncement proved correct: Spain lost the Spanish-American War and abandoned its colonies in the Pacific (although other foreigners moved in to take their place). Everyone was mystified. How had the Elders known what historical changes were afoot?

Like a homebound sister who develops visionary powers while her able-bodied brothers go out to farm and fish, Melchor left everyday concerns to Gaspar and Baltasár but would reliably divine the right path in times of serious crisis. Thus, anyone coming from Melchor to the capital was treated with a certain respect and often called upon to solve difficult situations, for it was widely believed that everyone born on Melchor had this sixth sense.

Matías made the most of his Melchor origins, although with his tenuous family ties, he never really thought of Melchor as a homeland. Had the twelve-year-old orphan stayed on Melchor, he wouldn't have gone far, wouldn't have been given the chance. So around the time that Imperial Japanese Navy cruisers first dropped anchor off Navidad, Matías left his home of nine years, his mother's keepsakes under one arm, and crossed the waters to a different life.

On Baltasár, his first job was as an errand boy for a Chinese laundry that served the Japanese. Three years later, with a little luck, he found employment as a busboy in the naval officers' mess hall. There he made use of his most salient skill—conversational Japanese. Three years of pointless grammar drills at public school had taught him next to nothing; still, he was different. Buoyed by a faith in his Japanese blood, he made extra efforts to learn passable daily speech. Simply speaking the language of the colonial overlords raised him that much above his peers. Here for the first time the orphan discovered his own worth, and the earnest way he cleared the tables made him the mess hall pet.

One officer in particular had his eye on Matías. Second Lieutenant Kazuma Ryuzoji was paymaster for the troops stationed on the islands. What was it about this scrawny brown kid that piqued his interest? He'd call the boy over and listen to his Japanese for mistakes, even tutor him in *kanji* characters and arithmetic if he had a moment. The other officers razzed him, "Hey, Kazuma, didn't know you were the type!" but to Ryuzoji it was simply a charitable gesture. Teaching gave him some small pleasure—at least that's what he told himself.

Or perhaps the real story was that Ryuzoji caught a glimmer of himself in this youngster, living by his wits, tempering his ambition by force of intellect. Matías wasn't just aware of being different, he was dead set on turning that half-breed distinction to his advantage. What else did he have? Here, Japan's incursion into the South Pacific was instructive: Matías realized early on that cultural enrichment came from rubbing shoulders with everyone, but politics worked the other way around, by excluding outside elements to consolidate power, by putting oneself forward at the expense of others. Ryuzoji saw how the boy picked up on these things almost instinctively.

Ryuzoji himself was born into a poor family in Kyushu, and the navy was the quickest way up—if only as a temporary step. He took up accounting at the Naval Academy with the idea of learning a skill he could fall back on in civilian life, whenever that might be. Accepting an unglamorous posting as a paymaster, his hands-on application was all that kept the books balanced at a time when Japan was seriously out of kilter. The mercenary mentality agreed with him. Bravery and loyalty and determination aside, wars were waged by moving men and materiel with businesslike efficiency.

By early 1943, however, supplies were running desperately short, and many of the vessels that weighed anchor from Navidad never came back. The islands would not fall under direct attack for some time, nor did the Navy men here sense the impending peril. Ryuzoji alone could see it coming. That April, a few days after the shocking news that Admiral Isoroku Yamamoto had been killed in ambush at Bougainville, Ryuzoji formed a bold opinion he dared not share with his fellow officers. Instead he took Matías into his confidence, though he'd only known him for three months. That noon, when Matías brought him the daily special of taro curry and salt-grilled reef fish, Ryuzoji invited him to his quarters after dinner.

"Tell me, boy, do you have any idea why Japan is the greatest country on earth?"

"Because Japan's got great people," replied Matías.

"Wrong. There are great people in Japan, and there are slouches too. Brains and idiots, nice guys and crooks, in just about the same proportions as any country, anywhere. Well, maybe we're a little more hardworking, but even that comes out about the same, give or take. People everywhere work, only some never really get down to business."

Matías just listened. This abstract stuff was tricky.

"The Empire of Greater Japan owes its success to His August Presence, the Emperor."

Whatever you say, thought Matías, half wishing he could go back and change his answer.

"Humans are weak. One person alone can't do much. If just for themselves, people won't till the fields until after dark. There are hungry children at home, old folk, that's why they work. Even school children, they study because they want to take home good marks to their mother." (*Not me*, thought Matías.) "The desire to work is the wellspring of community spirit. There's no greater pleasure than to live up to others' expectations. Just as there's no greater joy than to sacrifice one's life for someone you believe in. That's how it is."

Matías listened silently. This was getting too difficult for him.

"And the one who's watching over all of us Japanese subjects like you and me, that's the Emperor. Because we always feel His eyes on us, we work for Him, we do battle with the enemy, we struggle through every setback. And why do we struggle for the Emperor?"

"Because the Emperor's so great," said Matías, the groomed student providing the expected answer.

"Wrong," said Ryuzoji, the patient teacher. "From here on is my opinion, so don't say anything. Just listen, and don't tell anyone. If talk gets out, I'll be in deep trouble."

"I won't say a word," promised Matías.

"It's not because the Emperor's so great that Japan is a superior country," argued the logical imperialist. "No matter what His nature or countenance, we Japanese subjects revere Him and work ourselves to the bone for Him, grateful to have been born and raised under His Imperial grace. No, it's not because of His character, it's because His August Presence binds us together as a nation. It's this arrangement, it's the system that's so superior. Do you understand?"

"I think so." He didn't understand at all.

"In American-style democracy, there's nobody at the top."

"What about the president?" asked Matías.

"Yes, America has a president. But let me ask you, can people really revere someone elected by a popularity poll? Do you really think he can pull everyone together, heart and mind? Our Emperor didn't rise up through the ranks, He descended from above. The Emperor is the Emperor, that's why He unites a hundred million hearts together as one."

"Even us islanders?"

"It's a question of your own heart. Your spiritual rectitude in standing before the Emperor, your awareness. Islander or native of the Yamato homeland, the only thing that matters is what you've got to offer the Emperor. For those who think only of what they can do for the Emperor, for the nation of Japan, there is no inequality."

Makes sense, thought the fifteen-year-old island boy. *If I do my part, nobody can hold anything against me.* He conjured up a gigantic aircraft carrier, like the one that once anchored inside Navidad reef. Fighter planes zooming off the flight deck in tight formation. The thrusting roar, the hair-trigger response, himself in the cockpit. What a thrill!

But then Second Lieutenant Ryuzoji made a startling comment.

"Just between you and me, this war is going to end. In form only, Japan will lose. By now I'm reconciled to the fact. The true victory, however, is much farther off. Sustained by the Emperor even in defeat, the Japanese people will work together all the more and win a completely different kind of fight. Only then will the true power of the Emperor come to the fore as a unifying force. The authority of the state will bind up all the selfish individual loose ends. I've studied governments around the world, and in this regard the Empire of Greater Japan is undoubtedly the most highly evolved. Yet in order for our country to assume its rightful glory in the world, we must now first taste defeat. Affairs of state do not reflect upon His August Presence, so our losing this war will in no way be His responsibility. The Emperor is unconditionally above blame. Rather, by suffering ignominy this once, the true meaning of the Imperial Order will shine through all the more. After this defeat, Japan will be the nation to watch!"

"And what'll happen to me?" asked Matías, unable to keep up with the officer's leaps of conjecture.

The question was so untheoretical, so real, it threw him. The man was drunk on his own rhetoric, intoxicated with the happy freedom to speak his mind openly where none of his colleagues might hear. He was rehearsing a speech to an assembly of thousands, when all of a sudden his flights of fantasy were pulled down to earth.

"You? Once this war is over, you'll know your true worth," he extemporized after a moment's thought. "If you turn your back on the Emperor, you'll end up as just another islander. But if you give yourself once again to the Japanese race, the glory that awaits us can be yours to share as well. And if you ever are in a position to lead these islands, it may be in your power to bestow the bounty of Greater Japan's prosperity upon your people."

What could possibly have lodged such ideas in the mind of this naval officer? It was still a mystery to Matías years later. What he recalls of that night is Second Lieutenant Ryuzoji's strange elation, his assertion that if and when

Japan lost the war, the demoralization would only be temporary and a strong country would later reemerge. At the time, however, Matías still had no idea of any way he could possibly "give himself to the Japanese race."

That was the only time Ryuzoji spoke like this. In the days that followed, he still tutored the boy, goodwill beaming from his quiet, friendly eyes—but nothing more. When the war turned ugly and all hell broke loose, Matías fled Baltasár back to Melchor. He never saw Ryuzoji again in Navidad.

BUS REPORT 1

On the island of Gaspar, passengers are forbidden from drying their laundry on bus windows. During the Japanese occupation, when bus service was introduced between Baltasár City (then Shokyo, the "Showa Capital") and the village of Diego (Dego), a rumor spread among the womenfolk that laundry hung on bus windows dried more quickly, so buses came to be used more as clothes driers than as transportation. The sight of brightly colored clothing fluttering from every window, however, conflicted with the aims of a modern conveyance, so the gravely concerned bus staff adopted a strict ban on "boarding the bus with wet clothing." The phrasing "with wet clothing" failed, however, to specify whether the people were carrying or wearing the clothes. And in a land of sudden tropical showers, what use are buses that refuse service to someone who happened to get caught in a downpour? Thereafter, the rule was amended to read: "Passengers are forbidden from boarding the bus with wet clothing, except for what they themselves have on." Thus, women from the village of Diego who did their wash in Marna Creek, which flows into the lagoon near where the airport is today, were effectively banned from carrying their laundry home by bus (and drying it on the way). Discussions were held between the women and the transport company; the drivers maintained there was no plausible reason why laundry draped out of bus windows should dry any faster than elsewhere, and the housewives claimed from personal experience that it most certainly did. As a last resort, the bus company called in the Japanese Military Police, who declared the drying of laundry on bus windows in Navidad to be a punishable offense. Eventually the custom was forgotten. After the war, when Navidad became an American protectorate by United Nations mandate, the rule was automatically perpetuated, even though young housewives today are quite unaware of the practice.

Notably, no such problem exists on the island of Baltasár, as there are no buses on Baltasár and never have been. Only now, with petitions demanding a bus link between the city of Colonia and Tabagui village, does the problem threaten this peaceful island. If buses are introduced, as almost certainly they will be, debate will no doubt rage again over this long-forgotten regulation. We await definitive reports based on scientific experiment to settle once and for all the question of whether or not laundry actually does dry faster on bus windows.

That afternoon, the President holds his second round of discussions with Suzuki. No more abstract nation to nation, big country squaring off with little country—he can think over all that at his own pace, in his own time. He's been balancing powers ever since he assumed the presidency, and if need be he'll debate the pros and cons with anyone, local or foreigner. But now's not the time. Detailed information in Suzuki's portfolio, particularly about what resources the Japanese financiers and bureaucracy are prepared to muster, that's what he wants to hear. The scenario may not be as unlikely as he first thought; there's still a good chance of steering things to his advantage. Then, if this does come off, he can leave the rest to paper pushers on both sides. Turn it over to Jim Jameson to rubber-stamp. But let's not get ahead of ourselves, Matías cautions himself. We haven't decided squat yet.

Today he has to coax some figures out of Suzuki. Just how much would this project, should it reach implementation, personally profit President

Matías Guili of the Republic of Navidad? Unless it benefits both himself and the country, however insignificant the population, what sense is there in leasing out sovereign territory on Brun Reef to the Japanese? They'll have worked out where and how to arrange the appropriate slush fund payments, but what about *why*? Matías Guili has his morals. He has no intention of whitewashing a clean facade like Bonhomme Tamang; still, he'd rather not pilfer from his own country. Better to take from foreign concerns. He's got to stand shoulder to shoulder with Navidad.

"What's in this project for me?" he asks straight out at the start of the second session.

"As regards that point, I have a secret plan from the Ministry," whispers Suzuki.

You bet you do, thinks Matías. No need for any Suzuki to come here without that. There's plenty of sharper errand boys out there. Otherwise the deal could be done just as easily by post. The President maintains his easy manner. "And?"

"The monetary indemnity to Your Excellency is to be one percent per annum of the amount paid into the national coffers. Not a huge sum admittedly, but as long as the facility stays, whether or not Your Excellency remains in office, the funds will be sent in perpetuity."

"You think maybe I'm due for retirement?" asks Guili, looking him hard in the eye. He knows his stare packs a punch. Most islanders would look away at this point.

"We're not in the business of hypothesis," answers Suzuki, looking right back at him. The perfect officialese reply. "Naturally, when we first proposed the project, we had to consider whether this was to be a payment to Your Excellency the President or a personal gift to Matías Guili individually. And it was our unanimous decision that it should be the latter. On this one point, there was no tie, no mixed opinions."

"No tie, no collar," jokes the President, repeating an old pun he heard long ago when first studying in Japan. "No, seriously, I understand. Please proceed."

"Of course, we recognize that the amount is hardly in keeping with discussions of this scope. However, we fully intend to express our gratitude to Your Excellency by other means, so please consider this one percent a mere ribbon on the box."

"Other means of thanking me?"

"A plan to ensure increased security far and above Your Excellency's present position. By reason of which, any quibbling over the aforementioned one percent to Your Excellency personally or to the President becomes a moot point."

"I'm not interested in any foreign power guaranteeing my position."

"Nothing like that, I assure you. Our methods are much more indirect. Please, just hear me out, as this involves the project itself. In building such a facility to stockpile petroleum, certain precautions must be taken to safeguard supplies. Terrorism is now a global political force, which we must take into account. Suppose twenty armed men were to occupy the facility and issue outlandish demands to your country or ours. Realistically, they could blow holes in the ships' hulls, causing huge oil spills. Imagine the public outcry."

"I was planning to augment our Island Security."

"Grateful as we are that you've thought of taking such steps, they're not quite sufficient to deal with terrorists. With all due respect, your present Island Security is barely capable of staring down the local citizens or breaking up peaceful demonstrations, is it not?"

"Well, yes, that is more their speed," says Matías sourly. He knows only too well there'll be more and more jobs Katsumata's not cut out for. Can't expect to turn over the entire law-and-order business for the whole country to a washed-up yakuza, thinks Matías, recalling Katsumata's baby face. He's been okay until now, but the problems are escalating.

"Which is why Japan will take on the expense of upgrading the Island Security, plus practical training. Your men would take turns being posted to Japan for training and return home with the appropriate weaponry and communications devices. This would occur in three-month rotations, so in a year's time the entire militia would be in fighting form. Peacekeeping tactics, suspect surveillance and questioning, terrorist group containment and eradication: they'd be brought up-to-date in all the latest SWAT techniques. Whip them into proper shape."

The present Island Security is none too popular. Some two hundred and twenty guardsmen all told, a national unit paid for out of the state budget, but effectively Matías Guili's own private army. It's obvious to everyone. Largely inactive and untested up until now, though should it ever come to fighting, there'd be a major row over its role. If, however, they were guarding these oil reserves, that might just wipe clean the "private army" taint. He has to hand it to them for their insight into where things stand in Navidad.

"In addition, we will establish a *Marine* Island Security with two patrol boats."

"Hand-me-downs from Japan's Marine Self-Defense Forces?" quips Matías.

"If I might proceed further in the direction we started," Suzuki presses on with one self-important breath, ignoring the President's remark. "Your Excellency's current position is far from secure. While on the surface the country may appear quite stable, one wonders if there are really no foreign plots afoot, no clandestine rebel elements among the people. Forgive me for saying so, but it's hard to believe Your Excellency has a full grasp of such developments. To be perfectly honest, looking from a distance, it makes us anxious to think that, were something to happen, we might not be able to come to your aid in time. It is our heartfelt wish, of course, that Your Excellency should maintain the serene dignity of the presidential office for ever and always." (Here Matías waves his hand to cut the honorifics. Today's Suzuki is pure bureaucrat, and when a Japanese government type turns on the florid phraseology he knows he'd better watch out.) "But viewed objectively, Your Excellency does not stand on one hundred percent solid ground. What's to stop an armed band from surrounding the Presidential Villa and staging a coup d'état? We cannot afford to lose Your Excellency at this point."

"Is my presence so very convenient to you all?" Matías enjoys tossing out sharp rebuttals to throw respective arguments into us-and-them relief.

"It's not that simple. Even should other new politicians be waiting in the wings, surpassing even Your Excellency in ability, it is still Japanese diplomatic policy to value continuity. Big changes may have bad consequences. Then there's Your Excellency's fifty years of relations with Japan."

"That's a big figure you've dredged up."

"I make it my personal duty to know all there is to know about Your Excellency, and I repeat, Japan can ill afford to lose such a good partner in the West Pacific. At present, Your Excellency has disbanded the legislature while a soft martial law stays in effect for the sake of domestic stability, but it is our experts' opinion that your Island Security lacks effective muscle."

"What you mean is, you'd set me up as a real dictator."

"Not in so many words. Different countries have different stages of development, and the forms of governance vary accordingly. As Navidad faces up to the stringencies of the twenty-first century, she will need your guidance all the more. Not for just another five or ten years—Your Excellency must lead the way forward for much, much longer. And to guard against instabilities that threaten your benevolent regime, Island Security should be strengthened."

"The more you tell me, the more I feel myself turning into a puppet."

"Not at all. It's for the mutual good of Navidad and Japan. Both countries need you for decades to come."

"Who's to guarantee that what profits both sides will coincide forever? Rather dangerous, dancing so close. More natural for two countries to recognize their respective differences and just check in from time to time. At any rate, I have no intention of becoming another Yuan Shikai selling out a South Seas' Manchuria."

"What a memory for names you have! I'm not so well up on my history, I really had to think there for a second. No, please don't forget that the full command of the Island Security would be in Your Excellency's hands. We would merely offer technical training, nothing more."

"Technical training. And secret indoctrination sessions on the side. Brainwashing our best and brightest with the idea that Navidad's well-being is best served by sucking up to Japan. That's how they'll come home. With maybe a couple of rabble rousers in their midst. Or else you'll send us Japanese technical advisers to keep them drilled. Then one day you'll turn some upstart with ambitions against me, and I'll be out just like that."

"You exaggerate!" Suzuki protests, unconvincingly.

"Historical imperative, if you'd care to study up on it. Not that I'm against it necessarily. If I thought it were for the good of the country, I'd gladly step down. I just don't like being jerked around. And not just me, none of us living on these three islands have ever had much stomach for that. The less that's brought in from outside, the better."

"Moving people and things creates wealth."

"Yes, transport brings wealth to one end, but makes the other end poor. Value flows in one direction."

"Not at all, both sides get rich on exchange."

"That's a basic tenet of trade, I grant you. With my business background, I don't doubt it." Matías is beginning to enjoy arguing with Suzuki. Now that the petroleum facility issue and Island Security training have been nicely eased into the background for the moment, time to extrapolate and digress; it makes the game more fun. Size up the adversary's position, plot out what both sides will say. Intellectual games like these have made Matías who he is today—a shrewd political thinker, confident that no Japanese will ever get the better of him. At least he knows of no race of people worse at debating than the Japanese.

Matías would happily spend the whole afternoon matching wits with Suzuki, when not fifteen minutes later in barges Katsumata. Once again, unannounced.

"I'm in a meeting," hisses Matías. Ordinarily he can overlook the clown's lack of manners, but not while he's receiving important visitors from abroad. And especially not when the subject of discussion is the restructuring of Katsumata's Island Security.

"Sorry," stammers Katsumata in a clumsy stage whisper. "Emergency."

All right, this emergency had better be good, thinks Matías, grabbing him by the arm to walk him back toward the door. "Okay, out with it!"

"The veterans delegation…they're missing," says Katsumata just out of Suzuki's hearing range.

"They're what? Did some of them wander off somewhere?"

"N-no, all of them, they're just gone."

Got to think here. If it's anything like what he seems to be saying, we might just have a sticky situation. "We can't talk here," says Matías, who turns to tell Suzuki there'll be a brief recess, then drags Katsumata into the next room and slams the door. "Start explaining!"

"This morning at nine o'clock we held the bus tour launch at the Shinto shrine, right?"

I know, thinks Matías, *I was there.* The Ministry of Welfare escort duly lectured everyone on keeping pomp to a minimum, so it finished quickly. No burning flags, no fainting old men, and the remains of the toppled torii gate cleared away as per orders. No one who hadn't been there recently would notice anything amiss. Matías waved goodbye to their yellow-and-green-striped bus. Yes, everything went smoothly this morning.

"According to today's schedule, they were supposed to go by bus to Diego and walk into the jungle for the first memorial service."

I know that too, thank you. Matías had reviewed the schedule several times over. Diego had been the site of a Japanese Navy Wireless Corps outpost.

"After that, lunch at Tonoy House, then on to Sonn."

"And another memorial service in Sonn, then back to the hotel," Matías cuts in curtly.

"But," says Katsumata, pausing theatrically, "the bus never arrived in Diego. At two o'clock, Tonoy House calls the Foreign Office asking when they're going to arrive. The Foreign Office calls us, and we send out our motorcycle. The bike phones in from Tonoy House, no sign of any bus anywhere between here and Diego."

"That's ridiculous. Then what?"

"We send out a Jeep with three more guards. The bike goes on ahead to search the road to Sonn and all side roads in between. Nothing. That's when I thought I'd better report in, so I came here."

"What in hell's name is going on?"

"No way anyone could get lost on that road."

"That's for sure. Straight line, ten kilometers at most."

"No, ten miles. That's sixteen kilometers."

"Whatever. Doesn't the motorcycle officer have a mobile phone?"

"It's broken."

"So why didn't you have it fixed?"

"No parts."

"Did you send anyone beyond Sonn? To Naafa, for instance?"

"No, wanted to wait for word from Sonn. They've got to be somewhere between here and Sonn."

"Let's go look." President Matías Guili strikes a decisive pose. "I'm coming along."

Katsumata just nods. This time, apparently, he sees how serious the situation is. Too many people involved here. And not just anyone, important guests of state. If word gets out, he'll never hear the end of it.

"You go by Island Security Jeep. I'll take the Nissan. We'll meet up in front of the Public Works Bureau. And get all your info straight by then. At least I'll be able to use the car radio." Matías practically pushes Katsumata down the hallway, then returns to his office.

"The strangest thing just happened," he tells Suzuki. "The veterans delegation has disappeared."

"All of them?"

"The whole bus."

"With how many people in it?"

"Forty-seven Japanese and one of ours, a staffer from the Foreign Office. Plus the driver."

"Forty-nine people. Do you think it's a hijacking?"

Uh-oh, didn't think of that. Could someone on the island really pull off something like this? Never any kidnappings here. The only crime's when some joker gets drunk and goes berserk, or a village idiot threatens people with a shark harpoon. No one even thinks of nicking a tourist's handbag. So then who was it knocked down the torii gate? Who put up all those handbills around town? A bus can flip over or run into a palm tree or something, but vanish without a trace? "Impossible," he says, dismissing the hijack hypothesis flat out. "But just in case, I'm going out with the search team myself, so with your permission I'd like to continue our discussion tomorrow or the next day."

"Very well then, I'll stand by at the hotel. Let's hope and pray they come back safely."

That sounds ominous, thinks Matías as he sees Suzuki off.

⟡

It's late at night in the President's private apartments. All is quiet. Outside, the night sky swirls with stars, but the only ones who'd care are fishermen eager to read next morning's weather conditions. As ever, the beauty of nature bores the locals.

President Matías Guili sits on the sofa and mulls over the afternoon's events. Earlier in the evening, he visited Angelina's for a small snifter of cognac and commiseration, too preoccupied for much else. It's been one hell of a hard day.

Today's events call for otherworldly insights, the kind a spirit he knows can provide. He must summon him properly but can barely bring himself to say "Lee Bo," the ghost of a name.

He rises from the sofa to fetch a candle, which he lights with the seldom-used coffee table cigarette lighter and places in the equally clunky ashtray beside it. Then he gets up again and turns off the room lights. No drafts enter the room, yet the flame wavers briefly before coming to a stable pinpoint of illumination. As age increases, so does ceremony. He looks at the candle and shakes his head; nothing but protocol lately. Politically, he pretends to tackle each and every situation, but it hardly takes more than a superficial mental swish. Real judgments are rare; he merely moves from ceremony to ceremony. Not once in the last year has he actually had to shift out of autopilot. Probably the last time was that Tamang decision. And he wonders why the days are so monotonous.

The flame stays perfectly still, not a flicker of movement. He stares until all thought settles like ash. Presently the flame appears to flare. He strains his eyes, then looks up to see sitting there before him…Lee Bo, glowering head-on. Matías nods. The apparition nods back.

Lee Bo—the erstwhile Leigh Beau—is formally attired in late

eighteenth-century English frock coat, kinky hair tied behind in a queue, an intense scowl on his black face. His dark complexion could make him a Navidadian beachboy who chases pale-limbed Japanese tourist girls as they deplane; only his clothing and stern expression would seem out of place.

"Been a long time."

"Aye," says Lee Bo in a mannered basso profundo. "How fare the islands in my absence?"

"Lots going on, but nothing new at all. Same as ever here below."

"Words becoming a man half unencumber'd of this mortal sphere." The voice trails off into echoes, this visible form a mere shadow of his real self millions of leagues away. "Or do you feign this distant air?"

"Just as you might be putting on airs for me."

"Nay, a cursed habit, that."

"You speak from experience? Your time in London?"

"My conduct is inconsequent. 'Twas you who summoned, was it not?" Lee Bo steers the conversation back on course.

"So it was. I called you because something's come up. Today, an entire bus disappeared on the way to Diego with forty-seven Japanese and two Navidadians on board."

"Not each conveyance shall reach its destination," muses Lee Bo.

"True. But the problem is this one bus—why didn't it get there? It's not the general principle but the particulars that concern me."

"Ah, but did not you yourself just say that tho much transpires, little signifies? The vagaries of one coach, methinks, are of scant interest."

"I'm a politician, so by day at least, I can't be so casual about things. A bus has gone missing, and I need to know. Was it a natural accident? Was it a plot? And if so, by whom?"

"And the diff'rence? Is not the plotting of the human mind a work of nature?"

"If I wanted to take a philosophical view, I'd turn in the keys to my office. Politics is a hands-on job. I can't just look on from above the clouds."

"The coach is safe. As are those on board."

"Then you do know! Who's behind this?"

"Ah, the undercurrents are deep indeed."

"When will they return?"

"Alas, I can no more divine the morrow than the next man, being privy to but one small part of the present scheme of things, as you must know."

"I suppose so, yes," admits Matías, even as his mind races to consider the ramifications of the delegation's predicament. Yet if Lee Bo can't read the future, who is he to try?

"This Suzuki is an evil knave," says Lee Bo out of nowhere.

"There are no saints in his position."

"Nay, far worse than that. The reek of money is on him, the stink of blood and filth."

"That too comes with the job. Though his proposal does have its appeal." He assumes the spirit already knows of the plan to build up the Island Security forces.

"As well it should. Man was born to desire medals and regalia and his own men-at-arms. Once the thirst for wealth and women has been quenched, that is."

"Damn my honor. Do you trust them, tying me to Japan with that half-assed scheme?"

" 'Tis a difficult strait that lies ahead. Especially when your own ship rode in on a wave of independence."

"Promising a clean sweep of Japanese ties served its purpose. It got me elected."

"Not once, but twice." A momentary silence falls between them. "Tho 'tis deep inside, you have a mind to see the islands return to Japanese thralldom. You'd have Japan stay a short sight out to sea for an aire of freedom, whilst granting you boon and protection all the same. You'd like to see that, wouldn't ye? You've always been more Japanese at heart than any Japanese."

"Think so? I can't really tell, myself."

"It lies frozen and awaits the thaw, perchance in that miracle cooker in your servant Itsuko's larder. Yet from the headings you have taken, I can tell:

you fain would tell them to abandon this pretense of oil stores. You'd have them lay in a full-rigged naval base as grand as anything the Yankees have, the better to check the Chinaman's advances in the South Formosa Sea and the Spratlys. Propose that, and ye'd no longer be some tick on the map no one e'er heard of. You'd be world-class. Have you no such ambitions? That lot who toppled the gate are after the same thing."

"That lot? Who?"

"The waves are moved by many tides."

"Damn it, man! Do you have something against proper names?"

"'Tis no longer my world. I see but the pitting of forces and take no int'rest in affixing names each to each. To be sure, you have a dire conspiracy in your midst, above and beyond whate'er plots you may ascribe to Suzuki and Kurokawa. Either you fail to notice or already think you know…"

"And which would be better, from your perspective?" asks Matías inadvertently.

"I merely observe the theatre of this world," answers the spirit with neither expression nor gesture. "'Tis most enjoyable, but brooks no comment. I favour your conversation, but 'twould not do for any words of mine to alter the course of the drama. All is as natural phenomena: we may predict the weather but ne'er control it, therein lies the fascination. And yet I do espy a seed of turbulence in ye that might well sprout a typhoon. Most promising."

"Then there's still something I can do about it?"

"Can and must," laughs Lee Bo with a dry, ghostly cackle that echoes back two centuries. "Just last night, you met with someone who will o'ershadow your future more even than this Suzuki."

"Who do you mean?"

"Aye, you noticed all right. You were quite taken."

"And we talked?"

"Nay. You did only behold. But that trice suffic'd to cast her spell."

"That new girl at Angelina's?"

"The very same. Think on it. That face bewitch'd you. Made you yearn to see her, to speak to her, somewhere without Angelina."

"Possibly. But haven't I shown interest in new faces there before?"

"'Tis diff'rent this time. Heretofore was common lechery, pursued with Angelina's grace and knowledge. Better she indulge your appetites wi' plain consent than leave ye to nibble in secret. Full confidence has she in your mutual affections."

"I didn't look at the girl that way, not this time. For one thing, she's there as a maid."

"Nay, you didn't view her with a carnal eye. But mark my words, that wench will furrow deep in your life."

"Come on, I just heard she was from Melchor and looked her over. I used to see faces like that as a kid, but that's all."

"Aye, the countenance of a clan given to spiritual insights."

"So whose side is she on?"

"Neither friend nor foe. Naught in this world is fix'd from the very outset. Tho 'twould be wise to pay court to her. Methinks your courses are bound to cross and mark a turning point."

"Now that you mention it, Angelina did say the girl was maybe psychic. But only about little things."

"Clairvoyance has no great or small. 'Tis the doer makes bold or weak. Nor shall the clairvoyant necessarily profess all she knows. Any more than all vessels disclose true position…" And with that, the spirit vanishes.

03

Once again people have gathered on the benches out in front of the Cooperative Market. They've come to town to load up on fish and mangrove crabs, sweet thumb-sized baby bananas, fiery red chilis, green salad papayas, arm-long beans, imported rice and other provisions. Then they cross over to the supermarket for canned goods, wire, fishing lures, and lollipops for the kids. Finally they hunker down to lay in a supply of rumors and add their share to the cumulative intelligence of the island. Compared to cash and produce, the currency of word-of-mouth makes for infinitely more convoluted transactions—faster too.

"'Dja hear about the bus?" a fifteen-year-old asks a sixteen-year-old, both come from the village of Mill to buy a basketball for the gang. They hitched a ride in with some grown-ups and are now waiting for the promised return ride. The boys have been sitting here for four hours, though with their purchase rolly-polly on their knees that doesn't seem such a very long time.

"It went missing, yeah?" says the other, looking not especially interested. He's upset. First of all, he's thirsty. Secondly, they don't have any money left to buy another Pepsi. Third, it irks him that a kid one whole year younger is pestering him. And fourth, they're still a long way from their village, where he knows he can get something to drink. Of course, there is a water tap at the rear of the market, but he doesn't know that. "Sure, I heard. With a shitload of old fogeys from Japan on board, right?"

"Right. Well, Island Security's been looking and it's like nowhere. Zilch. Where d'ya think they'd hide a whole bus?"

"Who?"

"How should I know? That's the mystery."

"But hide a bus?"

"Well, then where is it? It couldn't just disappear."

"What if it got loaded onto a ship by mistake? Or mixed up with some other buses?"

"No, they hid it all right. Somebody did. Dug a hole and buried it."

"C'mon now, a bus? It's not like you're burying a coupla coconuts." He leans forward emphatically, challenging the offbeat line of argument.

"But what if you used a bulldozer? You could dig a big hole..."

"And what you gonna do with the dirt you dig up?"

"Don't be a dumbo. A bus is hollow, right? It's just a shell. You fill it up with dirt easy. First you dig a hole in the road and pile the dirt to one side. Then you put the bus in and fill it up with your extra dirt. Then you tramp it down nice and level, and nobody's gonna suspect nothing. Gotta do it at night, though."

"They buried the bus?"

"Well, maybe they trapped it in a pit. Covered over the hole, so the bus comes along and—*wham!*"

"And what about all the people riding?" It seems he's forgotten his thirst.

"People got legs. They go off somewhere on their own. Probably just eating or sleeping someplace. But anyway, the bus is buried underground. Might even be right here, hey?"

The fifteen-year-old stares at the ground in front of them. He can almost see the buried bus take shape beneath the burned red soil. There are lots of things under the surface. The subterranean world is far more mutable than anything here above.

✨

A few meters down the long bench, two men lower their voices. One is a fisherman come by early morning boat from Tabagui village on the far side of Baltasár Island, the other a young baker he bumped into on the plaza. Distant relations it turns out, from five generations back. Navidadians set great store by family ties, and once a bloodline connects them, secrets can be spoken. First they chat about this and that cousin, but soon the talk turns to the bus.

"Hear the thing about the bus?" the baker asks the fisherman.

"I did, I did. This morning, in the market. But c'mon, who the heck'd wanna steal a bus?"

"What are you, simple? Nobody stole no bus. It was the Japanese inside they was after."

"There was Japanese on board?"

"Don't you know nothing? Forty-seven members of an old soldier tour from Japan gone missing. Them and two Navidadians. Makes three days since they disappeared."

"Maybe they all went out swimming or something. Underwater, with those, whatcha call 'em tanks on their backs. Tourists from Japan like that kinda stuff. Big problem's when they catch too much, though."

"Old folks gone deep sea diving? And sheez, who stays submerged for three days?"

"Guess you got me there. But y'know, this one diver from Japan, he told me old buses make darn good fishery reefs. That's what they do up in Japan. Sink 'em the right depth, and lots of fish come live in the wrecks."

"Well, fish breed in sunken ships after all. Good fun going diving to look at 'em."

"You dive?"

"Just once. I was showing around this oven company rep from Manila. It was pretty nice, I'm telling you. So many fish swimming around in that old Japanese Navy hulk."

"See? So a bus'd be just as good."

"That's not what we're talking about here. Nobody said hoot about sink-ing no bus."

"Okay, then, what's the story?"

"Dunno. But y'know," the baker leans over, close to the ear of his distant relation, "from what I hear, seems Island Security's mixed up in this somehow."

"Island Security stole the bus? They wanna go for a ride somewhere?"

"If you'd just listen, nobody said Island Security stole no bus. What they wanted was the Japanese inside, so what they done is hide the bus, passengers and all."

"What for?"

"That still ain't clear. The whole tour was old folks, maybe VIPs." He probably imagines Japan to be like their traditional island society, where old people are still held in high regard. "With them nabbed, we get some lev'rage on the Japanese government. That's why Island Security's got 'em hid away somewhere."

"You got it all figured out, doncha."

The fisherman nods with deep admiration, thinking how he's going to spread the word when he gets home to his village. His fish didn't fetch as high a price as expected, but the day trip to the capital was worth it for this catch of news alone.

⚡

Still another ten meters further along, two old men stand chatting. Both well over sixty, regulars on the plaza, they meet here practically every day to toss pearls of insight into younger conversations. But today the famil-iar faces have yet to arrive. And those two kids aren't about to lend an ear, nor is that baker party to local hearsay, so that leaves the two of them to talk to each other. Little do they know they're onto the same topic as everyone else.

"Japan's behind this, mark my words."

"You figure? I thought as much."

"Japanese Navy, the way I see it. I detect their hand."

"Hold on there. Japan ain't got a navy anymore. Only a Self-Defense Force."

"Same thing. In any case, Japan's saying their boys died here in the war, so they send over a bunch of their buddies from back then to pray for their spirits. But that's just a cover for their navy to sneak in and whisk 'em away."

"What for?"

"To put the squeeze on us, that's what. They're gonna try to push something on this country of ours. Gonna build a navy base or make us a Japanese territory. Same ol' story all over again. Okay, China's come up this time around, so they can't slice that pie, but Navidad's small fry. They send us a bunch of their old boys, then secretly escort 'em back home to Japan and demand we hand 'em over. Which we can't, so we owe them. That's their game."

"Guess that makes sense. But how'd they steal a bus?"

"Simple enough. Remember, back when the Americans landed here, they used those strange-looking boats? Personnel carrier whatsits. They land one of them thingies up at Pearl Beach or somewhere and load the whole bus on board. Then they just head out past the reef to the mothership waiting out at sea. From there, they make a beeline back to Japan. Probably already in Yokosuka or Sasebo by now."

"But the driver, he's from here. And I hear tell there was a coupla young fellas from the Foreign Office." So far their information is halfway accurate, thanks to their daily sorties to the plaza.

"Them Japs were probably packing pistols, the lot of them. All they had to do was stick a gun to the driver and them Foreign Officers, hijack the bus to Pearl Beach, smuggle 'em on board that personnel thingy, and off they go. Simple as that."

"But why Pearl Beach?"

"No other patch of shoreline you can get a bus out to. Everybody's watching the airport, but there, just hide it in the palm groves till dusk, ain't nobody gonna see you."

"No, that don't quite jibe. I'll grant you Pearl Beach is the perfect place for that kinda thing and the Americans did land from there, but that's east of Baltasár." Meaning Baltasár Island across the lagoon from Gaspar, not Baltasár City the capital.

"So?"

"So how'd they get across? Your putt-putt boat between Sonn and Mill can't carry no bus, and the ferry's still being repaired. On account of which is why my son's car is stranded over in Colonia. Just happened to drive over there when the ferry grounded."

"Well ain't that a shame. And a bus can't cross by itself, now can it?"

"Nope, and even if it could drive across water, well, everybody'd see it. Anyway, the bus went missing on Gaspar. Shouldn't have gone all the way over to Baltasár."

"You think? Well, maybe not." Our naval theoretician acquiesces.

"No need to explain no disappearing bus," the other old man proclaims slowly, looking deeply philosophical. "Buses do go missing from time to time. And then they reappear."

"That's it?"

"Well, think about it. The world's full of these stories. Buses disappear, then pop up again. No rhyme or reason, that's just buses. Any smart modern country's gonna keep a few spare buses on hand. No point goosing ourselves out of shape over this, we just gotta wait is all."

"I'm with you there. You don't see me worrying."

"For a fact, same thing's happened in these islands before. Only it wasn't no bus, it was a troop of infantrymen led by an officer on a horse."

"A horse, you say?" His face brightens. "Was this back in the Japan era? Funny, never heard anything of the kind up to now."

"Nah, before that."

"German era?"

"Bingo, the Ponape Incident. The German administration wanted to plant coco palms, so they divvied up the old land system claims among the commoners and paid the elders compensation. Which tickled their fancy. Only now them Germans pressed the Ponape people into road construction, beat 'em with whips—or so they say. Got 'em fighting mad, killed the governor and technicians. Three months later, German troops arrive from New Guinea, the islanders are put down, fifteen rebels put to the firing squad."

"Mighty well schooled, say that for you."

"I used to be a teacher. Taught history."

"You don't say. So then?"

"So right after executing those fifteen, in order to keep the rebellion from spreading to other islands, German troops came here to this island too. Even brought over a horse. The detail did a once-round the island, realized there wasn't any rebellious folk hereabouts, but still they decided to pitch camp for a while near Diego."

"Brought over a horse, did they?" For some reason that impresses him. "And then?"

"And then, with no sign of rebellion, they pretty much take things easy. But then one day, two weeks after they get here, the whole platoon goes out on recon and don't come back."

"And the horse?"

"The horse too. Only two soldiers stay back at camp, and they raise a real squawk. They comb everywhere, top to bottom, but nothing turns up."

"The horse too, eh? Bet they were in deep trouble."

"Trouble for sure. No way to get reinforcements, wasn't even a ship in port. At least no ship they could commandeer back to New Guinea. Eventually a packet boat did come, but not for another three months. Meanwhile, the two soldiers had the whole island on alert."

"And not a trace? Not even horse shit?"

"Well, uh, no," he says, skirting the other's obsession with horses, "but from time to time there were sightings. They were marching up the road, they were sleeping in the forest, they were out swimming…One report even had the commanding officer leading a charge in the middle of the night. But the two soldiers were sure there'd been foul play and feared for their lives."

"Can't say as I blame them. Right after a revolt and all."

"Exactly. Even us Navidadians had to think something was up. Well, things were getting mighty tense, when just then the missing troops came back."

"The horse too?"

"What's with you and this horse?"

"I just like horses. The Japanese forces brought horses, right? Well, I was a groom. Handsome animals, they are, horses."

"I'm sure. But like I was saying, the whole platoon and horse came back unharmed."

"That's wonderful. The horse with 'em too."

"Er, yes, but, funny thing was, when the two men asked the others where'd they'd been so long, nobody could give a clear answer. Don't rightly know, is all they'd say. They all looked healthy enough, like they had a pleasant time and all. But as to what exactly they did and where, they didn't remember. The commanding officer made no report, ordered his men to keep their mouths shut about the whole business. In actual fact, no one had any complaints. No hardships, didn't go hungry, nothing like that. So it must've been nice, wherever."

"Fancy that, not knowing where they been. Bet that horse knew. Smart animals they are."

"No doubt, but you can't get a horse to talk."

"True, true. Can't get a horse to talk."

"So that was that, the whole incident escaped the German high command. My grandpa told me the story as a boy."

"News to me. Never knew there was horses on the islands before the Japs brought 'em here."

BUS REPORT 2

At 6:00 AM, lowest ebb tide, a bus was sighted crossing the lagoon between Gaspar and Baltasár islands, sending ripples across the surface. The yellow and green vehicle careened this way and that, racing gaily over the crystal blue shallows. The first rays of the morning sun over the low central hills of Baltasár glinted off the windows as the bus took to the water out past the airport bearing northeast, skimmed the tip of Tsutomu Point, then disappeared in the direction of Colonia.

Four o'clock in the afternoon, the Presidential Villa. All morning it's been cabinet meetings, consultations with officials, receiving well-wishers, and other face-to-face business that dragged on into the afternoon. Now at last Matías finds himself alone in his office, mulling over various papers. Negotiations with Suzuki have been on hold these last three days. He's had plenty on his hands trying to answer for the disappearance of the Japanese tour group. As president, he personally took charge of search operations while everything was in an uproar. But eventually, with still no clues, people tired of searching and things settled down. Matías reported nothing to the Japanese Ministry of Health and Welfare; there was no explaining an incident like this. Behind this lapse lurked the wishful thinking that the bus would simply show up sooner or later.

His hand signs this document and that, but his mind is elsewhere. If early morning is his time for abstract thought and formulating strategy, then late afternoons are for tackling specific problems. Right now, however, he doesn't quite know what to make of the subtle waves he senses around him, a premonition that change is in the offing. He doesn't want to believe in anything called fate, but experience tells him there are times when everything proceeds smoothly, and then there are times when everything bristles with resistance like banners brandished in defiance across a vast plain. Generally there are no alliances between the banner bearers, and it only happens once every few years.

This might just be one of those times, he thinks. Time to be on guard, that much is certain. But against whom? First of all, there's Suzuki. He's got the upper hand for now, but Matías can easily turn the tables in their negotiations, take the offensive instead of just hearing him out. He can make demands, push discussions in more favorable directions. He can press for concessions to benefit the country and himself as well. It will be fun to see how far he can go. Suzuki is a manageable adversary. Matías also knows the moves for dealing with all the politicos hovering in the background in Japan. They pose no problem.

No, the problem lies in unseen quarters here at home. Strange things happening all over Navidad of late. Who are these people posting their strange handbills even at village crossroads? Sheets with printed slogans on them—it's not just two or three people doing this. There has to be a whole group bound by some sense of mission. Which doesn't sound like the Navidad he knows. Can there really be an underground cell like that here in this country? Somebody had to stick up those bills and topple the torii at the old shrine. A Japanese flag did go up in flames at the airport. And now a bus carrying Japanese vets is five days missing. Must he admit the existence of a single movement behind all these ominous events? And if so, are they closing in, slowly tightening the noose around him?

Another thing occupies his thoughts, that new girl at Angelina's. Why was he so bewitched by that face of hers? He's never been one to obsess over women, so why did his eyes follow her around? Do her Melchor origins have some special significance for him? Beguiling women from that island are no rarity here, that alone shouldn't mean anything. No, even Angelina must have noticed something odd. Does her clairvoyance bode other foes as well?

Matías has lost none of his self-confidence. The banners are all still a long way off, and the means to combat them are all in his hands. Whatever happens, he's still president. Navidad's ground plan is right here in his head. Despite the domestic situation, when it comes to those all-important dealings with other larger countries, he's the only one around with negotiating savvy. Who knows? Woman or not, the new arrival might even prove a useful ally. He has drawn on the strengths of women any number of times before. Maybe this mystery girl has powers he can use to his advantage. A leader taps the potential of all those under him and shares out the spoils in return. What's the difference between men who advance by their abilities and women who wile their way in on their charms? So treat her like any other woman up to now. Just stand strong and nothing can go wrong.

Having thought that far, he pauses as he sorts through his papers—a letter. The envelope is cut open, like all the others, but why has his secretary flagged this one with a little note?

Another FI letter, Sir. Did not break the inner seal as per enclosed instructions. Do not believe size or weight indicate explosives. If in doubt, will open for you.

Inside is a single sheet of stationery and a very thick envelope with no return address, only the words "A Friend of the Islands" on the back flap. How many of these "inside communiqués" has he received these past few years? This "Friend of the Islands" in who-knows-what government bureau in Japan always surfaces to deliver some important piece of top-secret Navidad-related information, always just in the nick of time. Lately the letters had stopped, so there's something almost nostalgic about receiving one, even if the tidings they bring are not, in most cases, good news. Navidad has pursued a path of goodwill toward Japan, and the better part of that policy, Matías likes to think, is of his own making. Yet all too often Japan chooses unscrupulous methods to undermine Navidad's position. Learning beforehand about Japanese treacheries is potentially helpful; what's difficult is not letting on that he has advance information. Opening these letters is always touch and go.

Underneath the address on the front is a bold red CONFIDENTIAL, but the secretary cut it open anyway following standard protocol. The inner envelope, however, remains intact. Marked TO HIS EXCELLENCY MATÍAS GUILI PRESIDENT OF THE REPUBLIC OF NAVIDAD along with yet another CONFIDENTIAL, it bears an overblown warning:

Proceed no further. To be opened solely by the President himself. Contains no hazardous or noxious materials. A good official knows his place.

Phrased the same as ever, though he has to admit, it does the trick. He picks up a pair of scissors and carefully slits open the inner envelope. Inside are several sheets of official stationery written in masterful Japanese calligraphy. As on other occasions, the paper is stamped in the lower left-hand corner with a small seal—that of the Ministry of Health and Welfare, which doesn't necessarily place the sender in that ministry. Most of the information supplied up to now has come from other government sources: the Ministry of Finance, the Ministry of Foreign Affairs, financial circles. He lays out the pages and reads.

To His Excellency Matías Guili:

Please excuse the lack of communications. While it no doubt speaks auspiciously of relations between our two countries that there has been nothing to report for so long, an incident has arisen and we can no longer afford to be so complacent. Let me convey what information I have obtained.

I am aware that His Excellency has been engaged in discussions with secret emissary Kanroku Suzuki concerning the projected construction of an oil-stockpiling base at Brun Reef. In all likelihood, his presentation consisted of first outlining the plan, then detailing how the project would benefit you personally.

There is a hidden agenda to the plan. No doubt they intend to tell you at some later stage, probably once the ten tankers are lined up in place, along with a Marine Island Security patrol boat and newly built Island Security armory equipped with the latest weapons. To not inform His Excellency of the truth until all this is a fait accompli, however, is tantamount to blackmail. Considering the hidden realities, I believe it would be most inadvisable to base relations on such maneuvers.

Their present plan does not call for all ten tankers to store petroleum. At least one of these will be a Japanese Marine Self-Defense Force warship disguised as commercial transport. From the outside it will appear identical to the other tankers, but inside it will secretly house considerable firepower, repair and maintenance supplies, and dry dock facilities, as well as a complete medical clinic with surgical capabilities. None of which, if the truth be told, has any place in an oil-stockpiling depot. If fuel storage were the real objective, inland on the main islands would be far more realistic. What they want is a military base, a foothold; all this talk of oil is mere subterfuge.

The Japanese government is set on assuming a more active political role in the Asia-Pacific region, fully implementing a Self-Defense Force presence throughout Southeast Asia. To do this, Japan must secure sea lanes by readying at least three tactical bases. Hot spots such as

Cambodia and the Spratlys are seen as threats to the stability of the region. Beyond the immediate countries, Japan now unilaterally counts herself as a concerned party. Naturally Japan cannot come out and assert territorial rights. According to my sources, rather than embark on a policy of direct intervention, Japan intends to co-opt participation by backing lesser nations in the vicinity. Hence, positioning a Self-Defense Force base on an outlying reef close to international waters would carry great significance in the wider strategic scheme. That is the general picture.

Nonetheless, considering domestic public opinion and the reactions of other nations, it would prove difficult to openly pursue such a plan. Before all else, again according to my sources, they must start constructing clandestinely in the Navidads, then watch and wait before gradually expanding the project. Part of the scheme apparently includes staging the rescue of a merchant cargo ship, using a Marine Self-Defense Force cruiser to drive off a pirate vessel in international waters in the South China Sea. The aim is to heighten the image of Japan's Self-Defense Force as a maritime power comparable to the American 7th Fleet.

As His Excellency will have gathered by now, I am an insider to this policy-making process. I am neither pro nor con; my only thoughts on the matter are that, given the times, this is what we can expect. As always, His Excellency is at complete liberty to choose how to use this information. One might affect ignorance, or lay one's cards on the table in order to steer negotiations in a more beneficial direction, or break off negotiations altogether, a slap in the face to Japanese duplicity. Whichever the path taken, your judgment will decide the future of the Republic of Navidad, and I will be glad if this letter has been of help toward that decision.

Unfortunately, now is neither the time nor place to reveal documentary evidence of the Self-Defense Force's camouflaged warship plan. His Excellency will just have to be satisfied that I happen to be in a position to write this letter. I look forward, however, to that happy day when

I know my sincere efforts have in some small way favorably influenced the fortunes of your country.

Respectfully,

A Friend of the Islands

Matías ponders the psychology behind this inside indiscretion: the idea of belonging to an organization, while secretly upholding different principles; obeying a double set of directives, invoking one or the other according to the circumstances; following the organization to the letter on minor points, yet disavowing it on major issues to stand upon higher moral ground.

But is this really an inside informant's letter? Even assuming a secret plan actually exists, a warning could only serve to steer him in a certain direction, a ploy to get things moving at the appropriate moment. Come to think of it, hadn't most of the tip-offs he's received from this Friend of the Islands ultimately played into Japanese hands? All information easily conceals background disinformation. On the one hand, we have Suzuki's smokescreen negotiations; on the other, ostensibly from different channels, these contrary signals. No, let's trust our Friend and his offering of intelligence. Japan *is* trying to pull a fast one. Building a military base in another country without its consent—isn't that outright invasion?

Why do they have to do things in such a half-assed way? It makes him furious. He's the president here, no one else. Why can't they just come to him straight out? Instead of sneaking around, why not ask to build a Marine Self-Defense Force base right up front? All they have to do is come up with sufficient compensation. This Suzuki doesn't have to spell out the difficulties that lie ahead for a tiny country, as if Matías can't read the grim realities himself. In actual fact, Navidad can only prosper by strengthening her ties with Japan. That much he can do himself. And not as a stooge, but as the father of an independent national policy, able to justify his relations with Japan to any and all nations in East Asia. And yet, perversely, they choose to jerk him around? How is he supposed to deal with them? The foundations of his political life are starting to shake. A time of change is drawing near.

BUS REPORT 3

As the afternoon Southwest Airlines charter departed with 113 passengers on board, including ninety-nine returning tourists from the previous week's charter, a bus was sighted taking off directly behind their Boeing 737. The bus moved down the runway at the same speed as the plane, nosed up at exactly the exact angle, and rose skyward in similar style. It was like a child playing airport.

For some reason, no one in the control tower saw this development as dangerous. It wasn't until both the bus and the 737 had disappeared into the clouds that it occurred to anyone that even by sheer determination a bus without wings should not be able to get airborne. The traffic control crew contacted Regional Airspace Authority in Guam, though of course they balked at reporting a flying bus. Instead they reported a near miss between a Boeing jetliner and a small craft. The radar in Guam, however, picked up only the passenger plane, which was flying on course; their reading was that there had been no accident. The Southwest Airlines jet itself likewise called in "no sign of any aircraft in the area." The small craft had submitted no flight plan and by now was probably off in some other quadrant.

One week later, when the next Southwest Airlines Boeing 737 arrived with another 122 tourists, the off-chance hope that the bus might also return failed to materialize.

"I'm thinking of calling that girl over here," says Matías.

"Indeed," thrums Lee Bo, waiting on his flesh-and-blood counterpart.

"I want to have her nearby to see how psychic she really is."

"And have you no int'rest in her as a woman?" taunts the ghost.

"Not in the least. If you mean wanting to see her naked, or sleep with her, then no, I don't particularly need to stake a claim. I just want to ask her things."

"If that be so, 'twould serve as well she stay at Angelina's, and foolhardy to try to possess her. E'en now, she belongs to no one. As quoth Angelina, that one is not for sale."

"I told you, I've got no sexual motives. But I would like to know how she came to work there. And no one's going to convince me she's an ordinary maid. Clairvoyance—as a politician, that's something I'd like to keep on tap."

"Verily," says Lee Bo without a trace of irony. His words hide no duplicity, and Matías likes that. "Tho what would Angelina think?"

"She'll be all right with it. I'll explain. All I want is a few predictions. She's not the sort of woman to get jealous over something like that."

"Nay? In times past, you took your wenches to bed at Angelina's, but always wi' her say-so. 'Tis only her forbearance about a man's philanderings that things ne'er got serious."

"And I'm not serious now. I'm not interested in her as a woman. It's her psychic powers, dammit, which Angelina herself told me about in the first place. I just want a closer look."

"Whate'er, your manner is strange. 'Tis doubtful you'll be able to convince Angelina."

"Well, maybe this once I won't explain."

"These past four nights after she told you of the maid's premonitions, you've hardly look'd Angelina in the face. Ye ha'nt been yerself. Not touch'd any hemp, nor spent the night there. She knows something's amiss. If now you call the maid to the manor, your Angelina will not be pleas'd."

"You don't really believe she could possibly be jealous? She knows me too well. If occasionally I take a fancy to one of her girls, Angelina doesn't say a thing. But that's still nothing to do with my reasons for asking that girl over here."

"Aye, but how strong the grip of lust upon the adult male. When I dwelt on my isles, I did my share of wenching. Alas, 'twas child's play. I ne'er knew adult license ere I cross'd o'er...Nay, not to counsel 'gainst the maid, but the risk may be higher than you think."

"So you hinted the other night. That's why I want to keep the girl here beside me. Lately, there're signs of change all around. Powers shifting.

Everything's buzzing, closing in. I need to go on the offensive, and summoning the girl may just do the trick. If ever there was a time I needed to read the future, it's now."

"Aye, I grant you that. She has the look of a sorceress about her."

"So she *is* a medium? I want to hear what she says about the Japanese delegation disappearing, ask her about Suzuki's plan and that anonymous letter this afternoon."

"Perchance, if medium be the word, she can predict the future, but how she means to use those powers of hers is another question. As I say'd, she may foresee, yet not foretell. I can see things ye can't, but e'en so, I am not privy to the future nor can I read minds. My eyes see only the powers at play a little clearer than ye do."

"Okay. So what you're saying is, whatever benefit I may gain by having a psychic on call, I risk bringing unknown forces into this house."

"Uncharted and unharnessed."

"But as you yourself know very well, there comes a time when one needs to take risks. I have a feeling now's such a time. It's not about my tastes in women."

"As I say'd, lust can bewitch as much as any wine, tho not in the same way. And if the girl hath powers twice o'er, I see trouble ahead."

"Sexual witchery? Yes, I suppose some men do get hooked by it."

"Verily."

"Did I ever tell you about that time with Heinrich, my driver? The weirdest thing—really surprised me. Showed me I didn't know jack about sex."

"How so?"

"Once, just on a whim, I had him fuck someone with me present. Just wanted to see what it felt like to be a voyeur. Sex movies, stage shows, that sort of thing I'd seen in Japan. Probably even have a few videos stashed away here at the mansion, if I felt like digging them out. But all that's phony. Playacting. No, I wanted to see what a normal man would do, given the chance. So we drove to Angelina's, and I told Heinrich to come in with me. He didn't seem to know what I was saying at first, but when he caught on, he balked."

"What did you expect? Startled the poor man, and for what craven purpose?"

"Well, I set him clear on that. Told him I was happy with his work, so I was giving him a bonus. Anyway, I had him go upstairs to the corner room. It's set up so you can peek in from the next room. Then we sent in Magda."

"Magda? Can't say as I know her."

"She's long gone. A lady of leisure somewhere up in Manila now, married with kids. Or so her letters say. Angelina reads them to all the girls as an object lesson: work hard, get yourself a good john, one day you'll be on easy street. One smart cookie, Magda was."

"As is your Angelina. Hardworking too, yet ne'er cold and calculating."

How well did Lee Bo know his Angelina—and *how*? Did the ghost watch the two of them get it on? Could he be seeing her on his own? Matías has no idea how much the phantom gets around. "You'd expect a woman of her profession to be cold?"

"Nay, I'm the bloodless one, remember? On wi' your story. About Heinrich?"

"Well, he was unbelievable! A completely different man. Normally so reserved, so cautious. But once inside that room with Magda, he went insane."

"Oh?"

"Magda tells him, 'Let's take a shower, shall we?' like with any customer, but he doesn't even hear her. He just grabs her with both hands and throws her down—*wham!*—headfirst onto the bed. Magda's used to a little rough stuff, that's her job. All kinds of men in this world, no telling how they'll behave with a prostitute. So they'd better be ready for anything."

"'Behave with a prostitute'? Lo, a scientist!"

"Give me a break. I may not be the most sex-driven male, but still. I'm happy to have Angelina as my special bonus for the long hours I put in as president. I might enjoy the occasional night with one of the girls there too, though I wouldn't miss it if I didn't."

"Wi' some men, physical desire may blossom into a desire for power."

"It never ceases to amaze me how you, who died just barely adult and never even had a grown woman, could know all this."

"I saw a few things in me time."

"And since?"

"Aye, for the most part since. Life alone wasn't time enough. But go on, what of Heinrich? 'Tis an eternal twenty-one-year-old you're talking to, so gi' me the bump and grind."

"Be patient! Like I was saying, Heinrich went wild—"

"Details!"

"First, he started ripping off her clothes. Magda put up no resistance, but that only turned him on even more. He was all over the girl. Swept her arms aside, big hands pawing her breasts, ripping at those, you know, those drawstring knickers to grab her ass, pushing her legs wide. Like he only had fifteen minutes before they took his toy away."

"Some men're like that."

"But we're talking about a man with a wife and five children. Can you imagine him doing that to his own wife?...Do you believe in rape?"

"Believe, you say?"

"Taking a woman against her will, by brute force."

"Seems mere cockmanship to me."

"No, it's a power thing. Like Heinrich had to show Magda who's boss."

"But, go on, what next?"

"You're impossible. Anyway, he gets Magda naked, but she's smart. She just rolls over and waits for the beating she knows is coming any second. Meanwhile Heinrich's eyeing her the whole time while he steps out of his trousers, one leg at a time, like a soldier."

"Took off his belt and thrashed the wench, did 'e?"

"No, there you go again. He took off his pants, but he was still wearing his chauffeur's jacket. That's how he climbed onto Magda."

"Aye, the captain's vice."

"Strange, don't you think? His tool was charged up from the moment he got his pants off. An ordinary size cock, at least from what I could see."

"An *Everyman* piece, was it? And the moral?"

"Only that I don't understand sex. Or no, I don't understand people. You suppose Heinrich's so frustrated? So pent up in his daily life?"

"I daresay, no."

"Well, the moment he shoots his load, he's off her in a flash and crouching down beside the bed. He still doesn't say a word. And I heard afterwards, even when Magda's telling him how good he was, how virile—things to boost a guy's illusions—it was like he didn't even hear her. He never spoke to her, start to finish. Like some little demon was pulling his puppet strings, no better than a spook."

"I beg your pardon! E'en we dead have our pride."

"A slip of the tongue, I assure you. But tell me, Lee Bo, what makes us humans dance?"

"Don' look at me. I died at twenty-one, too cursed short a plank to reel or jig."

"Some excuse. You've had plenty of time since. Two whole damn centuries."

"True. People come in all stripes and ev'ry one thinks hisself normal—except when none are looking on. Prob'ly all wipe their buttocks diff'rently too."

"But we're talking about him—Heinrich. That night, I had Angelina send him off alone—I didn't even want to look at the man—and Angelina drove me home herself. The next morning, when I saw him, it was like nothing ever happened. Maybe he knew I was watching. Maybe he acted that way because he wanted to give me my money's worth. I never asked."

"And what say'd Angelina 'bout it all?"

"Just that men are a mixed lot. And that if you built a place like that for women to have their way with men, women would be a mixed lot too. And here I imagined all men were alike in bed."

"People lie together for all manner of reasons. The only ones who do it always for the same reason are harlots, very likely. So what's your verdict on the new maid?"

"Ah yes, that was the point of all this, wasn't it. My mind's made up. Tomorrow I tell Angelina to send the girl over. Things have changed course. Having her close by might just make things change course again. That's my move."

BUS REPORT 4

A fisherman set out by canoe from the village of Uu and paddled through a southern break in Saguili Reef to the outer coral slopes and the open sea, where there are big fish to be had. Only this day, he had no luck. From morning low tide until afternoon, he didn't see a fish worth the name. Some days are like that. He was about to call it quits and head home, when a large something cut across his field of vision—a very big cabrilla. Stealthily, he dove after it; the fish didn't notice it was being chased. Cabrilla are none too bright, but curious, which makes them easy to catch. The fisherman was closing in from behind when suddenly the fish darted off. He wanted to give it one last try but ran out of breath, so he had to surface and hope he wouldn't lose his quarry by the time he dove again. He found the fish calmly feeding on the coral in the distance. Slowly, he swam toward it, this time coming right up on the fish; he pulled the rubber sling on his harpoon gun and let fly. The point pierced it straight through.

That's when he felt he was being watched. Strange things do happen in the sea, he remembers thinking, as he turned around to look—and there behind him was a bus, and peering out the windows were old men! Their faces looked yellow underwater. The passengers waved at him, pointing at the fish skewered on his harpoon, and even clapped their hands, applauding his achievement. The yellow and green stripes on the bus seemed to dance in the rippling coral sea light, yet inside it was apparently dry. Perhaps the chassis was waterproofed? He smiled through his diving mask and waved back at the old men, then went up for air. But when he ducked his head under to have another look, the bus was nowhere in sight. He deposited his fish in the canoe, and dove in again, but no bus. Only when he went home to his village and told his mates did he learn it was the missing bus.

Matías first met Angelina in 1977, when he was forty-nine. The place was an upscale brothel in Manila where he was taken one evening as part of the VIP treatment on an official visit to the Philippines. He wasn't really in the mood, but he went anyway—and Angelina was one of two hundred girls in the establishment. She was twenty-eight at the time, just about ready to leave that line of work. The favor was clearly a passing gesture to a dignitary whose emerging nation was still a little-known quantity, and Angelina perhaps got to do the honors because she hadn't been in demand lately. But whatever the motives on the Philippine side, Matías was taken with her the moment he saw her. That first night, she received him warmly and graciously, suppressing any here-we-go-again expression in the tradition of the trade. A pretense that should have fooled no one, yet Matías was so fresh off the boat he imagined she might actually care for him. The fact was, up until then he'd never really fallen in love.

It wasn't until much later in life that he realized how many special favors he enjoyed from those around him. Believe as he might that his attainments were his own doing, how very different his fortunes would have been without other people's goodwill. During his Japan days, there was an older woman who generally looked after his needs. As a dark-skinned foreigner, short even by Japanese standards, with no economic pull, that was something in itself. Not that he'd have missed female companionship— he honestly felt no yearnings in that direction—still most of the time there was some woman around. He was also befriended by men, so it wasn't all maternal instinct. Cornelius, the first president of Navidad, for instance, had looked out for him and helped set him up in the world of politics, though the alliance was brief.

He also had his share of women the first few years back in Navidad. The faces changed from one to the next at some unspoken signal. Homebodies good at cooking and housework, beauties made for taking out and about. He'd put in his twelve hours at Micael Guili's shop, eat lunch and dinner on the job, and get back late at night to find the woman waiting and himself irritated at having to make some semblance of conversation or love. He didn't know about other men, but he could get along just fine without a woman.

Six years after he started working at Guili's, Micael the proprietor fell victim to the islands' first traffic accident, leaving Matías to run the store single-handed. Two years on, seeing the amount of cash in circulation, Matías reckoned the islanders' purchasing power merited a healthy boost in imported goods. He refurbished Guili's general store, turning it into the first super-market in Navidad. He swept all sex from his life; there simply was no room for a woman in a routine of sleeping, waking, and eating behind the counter. Everyone was so used to seeing him spend all hours at the grindstone that it came as a shock when in 1963 Matías married Micael Guili's widow María. He was thirty-five at the time, María fifty-six.

Rumor around Baltasár City made it out to be a marriage of convenience designed to give Matías complete control over the burgeoning M. Guili Trading Company. Which was not entirely incorrect, though not the whole picture. Certainly María was amenable to a union with this man who had been toiling away for her; in that sense the nuptials did have a clear economic basis, a merger of their business selves. And Matías, for his part, didn't think twice before annulling his own virtually nonexistent maternal family registry to take on her surname. Micael and María had no children, so Matías became an adopted Guili.

Yet despite what anyone might think, the two of them passed unfailingly enjoyable days together, blissfully unaware of their age difference. Not only was there no pause for pretty young things to insinuate themselves closer to the richest retail proprietor in the country, but even the marriage-of-convenience stories subsided. Getting together with María gave Matías his first real taste of a home, and for all of fourteen years, until María passed on at seventy-one, nothing clouded their selfless partnership. More than enough time to drive the disappointed gold diggers into compromise marriages of their own.

What was behind this miracle? Very simply, Matías was a stranger to romance. The sensation of falling hopelessly in love with someone to the exclusion of all else—*that* he never knew. He had no idea people could agonize day and night over such things. Had accusations reached his ears that his marriage to María was calculated, he might well have asked, "You mean there's anything else? Men and women can relate in other ways?" The marriage suited him; working all day, staying up talking late into the night, it seemed an ideal life. Short on romance, perhaps, but full of affection. María was a woman of superior intelligence, much brighter than her deceased husband had ever been and studiously careful not to overstep her prerogative. Pundits quipped that Matías got his savvy from her, from their nightly kitchen talk. Not surprisingly, when death claimed María just as Matías was entering into politics, he mourned a lost confidante as much as a soul mate.

Now this same Matías suddenly found himself in love with someone he met in a Philippine brothel. Infatuation hit him totally out of the blue and left him reeling. He dragged himself from her bed at four in the morning and spent the whole of the next day contriving to see her again. It was the longest day he'd ever known. The basic equations of his life no longer added up. If a man could feel such electrical storms of emotion, where had he been for fifty years? Scarcely able to wait out the daylight hours, he made his own way to the establishment of the night before and found the same girl, Angelina—her name long since committed to memory.

For four nights straight, he visited Angelina, always staying until dawn, prolonging the hours of lovemaking with installments of his life story. Hers he never asked, fearful that he might babble, "What's a nice girl like you doing in a place like this?"—the oldest line in creation. Why would a professional woman tell him the truth anyway? Meanwhile, his days were a parade of perfunctory meetings with Philippine officials, his evenings spent in dinner engagements. Afterward would come invitations to other brothels, but he'd bow out—only to find himself racing to Angelina, his knees practically giving out by the time he reached her. *This isn't normal*, he thought, *this isn't normal at all.* If Angelina was at all perplexed, she never let it show. She had herself a good customer who'd be heading back to his little island in a few days' time. No matter how far the guy pushed his luck, what harm could he do? She listened to what he had to say and asked questions at appropriate intervals. *This is one smart woman*, thought Matías. *María was smart, but this one's smart and beautiful too.* She had her own views; she didn't just palm off what she thought he wanted to hear.

But if Angelina thought her islander just a one-week special, she was sorely mistaken. On the fourth night, Matías proposed. Angelina just stared back at him and gave the only intelligent response possible—she laughed. She laughed until tears came. It was a good minute before she caught her breath and saw—she could scarcely believe her eyes—that her suitor was dead serious. Matías ardently restated his case: he had standing in his country and real prospects for a more powerful position. This was the year after Navidad gained independence from American protectorateship, and newly elected Representative Matías Guili was in the good graces of President Cornelius. In fact, the President had appointed him as his personal emissary to the Philippines. Matías stopped short of telling Angelina that one of these days she'd make First Lady, but he hinted at something close.

"You give me till tomorrow to answer?" asked Angelina. Coming instead of the outright "no" he expected after such fits of laughter, Matías was elated. The whole of the next day, with no official chores, he roamed the busy pavements of Manila. He may have wondered what the hell he was doing, but he never doubted he'd taken the right course.

At last it got dark, and he went to see her. The old lady at the door recognized him and showed him in without a word. Matías blushed like a high school boy awaiting a reply to his first love letter (though only he could tell, his skin was so dark). Angelina greeted him with a serious expression and sat down silently at a small table beside the big bed. *Hardly a beaming bride-to-be*, thought Matías. He didn't dare breathe until she said something.

"About you proposing, I'm happy you want to marry me, really I am. But me, somebody's wife? Well, that's not me. I been living in this world too long now to stay cooped up. What am I gonna do? Cook meals, do laundry?"

"You wouldn't have to do any of that. You'd have a maid."

"No, that's not the point. I'm a damn good cook, you know, but picture me trying to look like a good little wife. Me, arm-in-arm with you in public?"

"I don't see why not."

"I'd feel wrong. I never even think about it till now, I never get used to it."

"You'd get used to it in time," he pleaded desperately.

"No, it never work. So…" Angelina paused pointedly. "I just have to say no."

"Oh," sighed Matías. His voice hit bottom.

"But...I got an offer of my own."

Matías looked up.

"I'm maybe not wife material, but we can still stay together. I only know you this very short while, but I like you. And I can't keep on like this in Manila forever. It's a young girl's game, you know. So here's my offer: I ask you, please take me with you to your country."

"Without marrying?"

"That's right. I wanna run a place like this in your Navidad. Take no customers myself, I just manage the girls. I run a class house, invite a few girls from here who wanna tag along, hire local Navidad girls too. That way you get to see me every night, we drink and talk and sleep together just like this week. But not like a wife—I have my own work. No bother with home life, we both get something better—a secret partnership."

Thus Navidad's very first brothel was established and met with great success. Backed by Matías, enterprising Angelina signed a twenty-year lease on a public hall—bargained down to a nominal price—from the Navidad government. Originally built by the German admiralty, then used as Japanese officers' housing, then occupied by the postwar American administration, it was a grand affair. She completely redecorated the place to her own taste and brought in a hotel chef and a few girls from Manila. Within a year their numbers doubled.

Angelina had a real knack for business. Overcoming all initial difficulties through good old hard work and acumen, she succeeded in teaching island males the modern market value of sex as a commodity. Granted, she catered to a privileged minority of island society, plus wealthy vacationers and VIPs from abroad, yet it wasn't long before others followed suit with slightly less upscale establishments. But by then, of course, Matías was President of the Republic and Angelina his trusted nightly advisor. How right she'd been to choose the divan of commerce over the housewife's overstuffed couch.

BUS REPORT 5

One hot afternoon, a housewife living near Naafa Village set out for her taro patch. Gathering taro is much easier in the cool morning hours, but first she'd gone to the river to wash some clothes and the sun was already high before she realized the taro basket was empty. Oh no, she thought, now I'll have a thirty minutes' trudge before I wade into the muck in the noonday heat. She was waist deep in the taro patch when something flicked past the corner of her eye. Strange, she thought, shouldn't be anyone about. Maybe a dog? On looking up, however, she swears she saw a bus the size of a full-grown sow racing across the fields along the banked earth paths. It was painted in green and yellow stripes, very pretty.

The woman watched the bus drive off, when it struck her: Buses aren't that small, and they don't go puttering around taro fields. She let out a gasp and strained to get a parting glance, but by the time she reached the embankment—one leg sucking up a thick slurp of muck, then the other—the bus had vanished into the banana trees. Now wait, she told herself, that bus didn't even reach as high as the lowest bunch of bananas. Words that figured in her official testimony and later appeared in Foreign Office documents about the missing bus.

The woman made her way over to the banana trees in question and peered into the undergrowth, but the bus was long gone. If only she could have seen if there were tiny people on board or some other species of passenger. She waited around for an hour or so through the worst of the midday heat, until finally—still no bus—she put her basket of taro on her head and trudged back home.

Matías first met the two of them after losing the third presidential election, when he was at a very low ebb. He hadn't just lost his job and authority, word had it—leaked by accident or possibly on purpose—that this new President Bonhomme Tamang's investigators were closing in on him day by day. Papers detailing his under-the-table dealings in connection with the construction of the Navidad Teikoku Hotel might soon fall into Tamang's hands. Meanwhile, for what it was worth, Matías kept passably busy compiling a list of Tamang's political errors as ammunition for his comeback in the fourth election. Though if the shit hit the fan over his own corruption, there'd be nothing he could do. Fleeing overseas would be suicide. Living in Japan on his bank accounts posed no problem, but what would he do with himself each day? No, exile was out of the question. Think as he might, he was at an impasse.

Predictably, his hours at Angelina's increased considerably during this career slump. Matías would have happily taken up full-time residence, but Angelina wouldn't hear of it. He was the mainspring of the business, and with him out of government, official guests had already dwindled; if he continued to sit there on his ass, she'd lose all her customers. He could still come around at night via the green door, but if he insisted on spending his days there, holding court in the salon, meeting with his not-so-secret informants, then others couldn't help but see. This was her brothel too. And if the great man didn't get up on his own two feet, Angelina scolded, how was she expected to stand behind him?

One night, having crept in the back way to Angelina's bed, Matías picked up on something in her daily recap. A couple of new customers had come in. Europeans, different color hair and eyes, but otherwise they could have been twins. Thirtyish—no telling white people's ages—they just stood there, hesitating, in the doorway "Welcome, step inside," encouraged Angelina, who happened to be close by. Actually, the men told her, they weren't looking for women. They were gay and, frankly, quite content with each other. No, what they wanted was a drink. The hotel and guesthouse bars had the odd bottle, but not the label they were after. Someone had suggested, however, that Angelina's might have the very thing.

"So what's your poison?" asked Angelina.

"Twelve-year-old I.W. Harper," said the fairer and slightly taller of the two. "Got any?"

"Sure do. Come on in. Is that really all you want?"

"That'll do just fine," he said, smiling at his friend. ("A real beautiful light-up-the-sky kind of smile," Angelina told Matías.)

The two of them came in and sat down. Each ordered a shot glass and a big chaser. They stayed on for what must have been six hours, sipping their bourbon nice and slow. Savoring the taste, smiling at each other, exchanging quiet jokes, they practically polished off the whole bottle while remaining, to all appearances, sober. At first the girls eyed this odd couple with curiosity, but when neither man showed the least interest in them sashaying past en déshabillé, they finally gave up, disheartened.

"They probably still down there drinking right now."

Just then the intercom buzzed from the ground floor salon. The two men were saying they wanted a room for the night, was it all right? Angelina thought it over for a second, then said, "Well, if they wanna make this their hotel, why stop them? Only give them the smallest room, number four. Can't really charge them same as for a trick."

The following evening, hearing that they were back, Matías decided to take a look for himself. With Angelina's permission, he made a rare foray downstairs into the salon and found the two sitting happily at a corner table with a bottle planted between them.

"Mind if I join you for a while?" asked Matías.

"Not at all. Please do," said one of the men, the other nodding in unison.

"I'm Matías Guili. Up until a few days ago...I was president here."

"I'm Yin."

"And I'm Yang."

Funny, thought Matías, *they don't look Chinese.*

"Or no, I'm Port."

"And I'm Starboard."

Seamen were they now?

"Er, Laurel?"

"Hardy."

"Castor."

"Pollux."

"We're a mixed-up couple, the two of us. Call us what you like, we're inseparable."

"Each just a part of a pair."

"Care for some bourbon?"

"Uh—no," said Matías, lifting his champagne glass in disconcerted response to the jabbering duo. "I'm okay with this."

"Ah, you got us there."

"An equally fine tipple. The French sometimes do get things right."

"Excuse us. We still hadn't settled the name question. Seriously, my name is Paul Joel."

"And I'm Peter Ketch."

Finally, thought Matías, *some real-sounding names!*

"Totally unrelated, yet people say we look alike."

"Unrelated? Well I like that! We're lovers. I hope you don't mind that sort of thing."

"All the same to me. East and West, everyone's got superstitions about twins and the like, but there's room for all sorts in this world."

Joel was blond and blue-eyed, and Ketch had chestnut hair and dark brown eyes, yet in actual fact the two did look very much like twins.

"We're *so* glad to find this bourbon here."

"Give us this and we're fine anywhere."

"Weren't we just saying, if we had this every day, we'd be happy doing almost anything?"

"Which makes me curious," said Matías, "I hope you don't mind my asking, but what *is* it you two do?"

"Whatever. We do magic tricks, done our share of boxing too."

"First off, we worked as coal miners in Sweden, then we were doctors in Madagascar."

"No no no, you got it backwards. The longest was that stint in the circus. After that we sold gibbons, worked as dance instructors, that sort of thing."

"More recently, we headed up an advertising firm."

"In Manhattan."

"Truth is, we've even killed people."

"Yes, we *have* killed people. Can't go into details, naturally, save to say it was a CIA job."

"What are you talking about? It was Mossad."

"Stasi."

"Okay, anything but KGB. That really would be too much."

"So you see, we're fickle. Can't stick to any one job for more than three years."

"Eventually, we got tired of doing different jobs altogether. Thought we'd take a break, lie low for a while. So we started island-hopping across the Pacific...and here we are."

"Pretty soon, though, the money's going to run out. We'll stay while the drinking's good, but when our last bottle's gone, we'll just have to look for gainful employment, now, won't we?"

"Go work for Mr. Harper."

"Goes down easy. Tickles your throat from the inside."

"Er, you two," Matías finally managed to get in an awkward word, "being homos and all..."

"That's right. That's how we can be happy, just the two of us. Granted, having beautiful women around is nice too, though perhaps we're a tad disappointing for the ladies. Especially considering the line of work here," said Ketch (or was it Joel?), gesturing with a shot glass toward the girls entertaining the other customers.

"With Joel beside me and this to drink, what else could I need?"

"With Ketch beside me and this to drink, what more could I want?"

In the end, Matías never did learn anything reliable about them—except their names. Back at his own house later that night, however, he checked the dictionary just out of curiosity. Sure enough, he found that a *ketch* was a two-masted Bermuda-rigged sailboat, differing slightly in the position of its mizzenmast from a yawl or jolly boat, derived from the German *Jolle*. Not "Joel," but suspiciously close. And wait, Peter and Paul, weren't they the two principal Biblical apostles? Aliases again?

A few days later, when Matías was feeling even lower and more insecure, he struck a deal with the two to retain them as handymen at Angelina's and—if and when the occasion should arise—as his personal bodyguards. In return, they'd be granted room and board and all the I.W. Harper they could drink, for as long as they stayed on the islands.

Every day they did their allotted duties around the premises, and every evening they happily downed a bottle of Mr. Harper's finest, then retired to their tiny room number four and fell asleep in each other's embrace. Not the least bit secretive about their gay proclivities, they were, however, reluctant to have their morning slumbers disturbed by Angelina sending one of the girls to wake them up. This arm wrapped around that shoulder, they'd grumble about the knock on the door, but a contract was a contract.

BUS REPORT 6

The warm coral-reefed seas around Baltasár and Gaspar islands are home to a number of rare species of plankton not to be found in any other waters. Similarly numerous are the foreign scientists who come to the islands with proposals to set up permanent research facilities. Attractive though it might be to see a generation of local boys and girls grow up to be world-renowned plankton experts, the President has no intention of agreeing to this—at least for the moment—and douses all such offers from abroad in a cold shower policy. Nonetheless, among the undeterred visiting researchers, one young scholar from the Wood's Hole Oceanic Institute set up a laboratory in the basement of the third cheapest guesthouse in Baltasár City. During the daytime, he boated about the lagoon casting his plankton nets, then spent the late afternoon classifying the specimens collected, and typed up his findings by night. A reclusive fellow, only rarely did he ever go out on the town.

One afternoon, this David Crosby spied something extraordinary swimming across the eyepiece of his microscope. Could that have been a yellow and green bus? He distinctly saw some little old men cheerfully waving from the windows. For the next hour or so, he toyed with the knobs, frantically adjusting the magnification and focal plane, but the bus never reappeared.

Understandably, the very next day, he packed up his research and headed back to America. When life-changing good fortune comes along, one mustn't let it slip by. We can only hope that when he told his colleagues about his amazing experience, they were equally appreciative of the significance of his rare discovery.

04

One slow evening, Ketch and Joel are ensconced at their usual table in a corner of the near-empty salon, while Angelina stands by the door on the lookout for customers. The younger girls are all chatting in threes and fives, underscored softly by Miles Davis—a 1953 New York recording with Sonny Rollins and Charlie Parker on sax, "Round Midnight" medleying into "Compulsion." Angelina's extensive collection of jazz rarities is lost on the islanders, but it's been known to draw the occasional gasp from foreign visitors. For jazz aficionados Ketch and Joel, this cache of several hundred records is a source of immense enjoyment.

In the far corner sits the young woman from Melchor. The same age or younger than the rest, she most decidedly is not one of the girls. She has never been "kept" by parents nor madame nor patron. She rarely talks to the others; she either does her chores or sits in her corner. She aspires to invisibility: never enters into gossip, never the butt of any jokes, yet everyone notices if she's there or not. Imagine someone leaving a big package in the salon; people might learn to overlook it in time, but they'd still wonder what was inside— that's her. Normal-looking as can be, though since she hardly ever talks to anyone, there's little opportunity to see her face straight on. She always averts her eyes and rarely glances around the room. But tonight it's so quiet, she seems transfixed. Maybe it's Miles Davis who's cast a spell on her. Just now, two Indian traders come in, hurriedly choose partners, and disappear into the back rooms, but the maid from Melchor just sits listening to Miles's trumpet, oblivious to their exit. Even when Joel calls Angelina over, nothing can make the maid look up.

"Slow night," says Joel, as Angelina takes to a plush sofa.

"Uh-huh, that's how it goes. Men all got better things to do. Business or family or sick parents or somebody's wake, it all put this good-time establishment off-limits. And no one in from overseas either, unfortunately. Everybody got off-nights."

"Gives everyone a breather," says Ketch.

"Nice change for one night maybe. But if it go on like this for a month, heaven help us."

"Not much chance of that. You've got a solid reputation. The President's a regular here, VIPs always pass through," Ketch says reassuringly.

"You don't like drunks, do you?" Joel asks her, apropos of nothing, his impossibly blue eyes glinting in the chandelier light.

"No, I happen to like drunk men *and* women. *I* even been known to get drunk myself."

"But skin-to-skin in the sack's better than just drinking, right?"

"Who says you gotta choose one or the other?" she counters logically. "We make our business here offering both. Most johns knock back a few drinks before they take a girl."

"But not us. We just drink and go to our room. On busy nights when you'd kill for an extra room, nonpaying guests like us must put a crimp in your profits."

"Never cross my calculating mind. Paying customers or not, you're guests of this house. I happen to like you two."

"We're so happy to hear you say that," says Ketch.

Joel looks skeptical. "Do you really mean it? Are you really happy to have us here?"

"Sure. And not just me, the girls all enjoy having you here. And there's your contract with the President," she adds in a lowered voice. "We all welcome you."

"Nah, c'mon," says Joel.

"Plus, you two have your uses. Wanna know why?"

The two men nod, clearly drawn in.

"Too many women staying together is a mess. Before your time, we have the girls selling, we have the johns buying, and we have me taking care of business, that's it. Often the girls fight, a little too often, steal customers back and forth, bitch bitch bitch…stupid stuff. Then you come along, and all that stop. The difference is, somebody looking on. Not a customer, not another girl, somebody they can trust, somebody they respect, somebody from a whole different world, but near enough to understand. The girls all feel your eyes on them, so they act nice, on their best behavior. You're not women, so no competition, nothing to get catty about. And you're not men—well, you know what I mean—so no need to flirt. Ideal housemates, no? Or you already know this, and just playing along?"

"We knew it. But then we're always drunk."

"Which is fine. You gay and you boozers, so that make you double distant."

"So it's all right for us to stay drunk? All right for everyone here, I mean, not ourselves."

"Why not? You both fun, you good with words and charming, and most of all," she searches for the proper phrase, "you satisfied with life. Drinking helps. It really does."

"Now *that*, I must say, is something I've given considerable thought to," says Joel.

"Joel here's lectured on 'Drinking as Social Consciousness,'" says Ketch, gazing off.

"That's right, at an Alcoholics Anonymous meeting."

"No! Really?"

"To harden their resolve, they decided to expose themselves to opposing opinions, or some such crazy notion. So I went and talked about the contribution of alcohol toward pacifism."

"Joel's a good speaker, very persuasive," adds Ketch.

"All in good fun, a bit of a lark. But you know I don't remember a thing. I was drunk at the time. Anyway, it was Ketch who wrote the text."

"Just notes, really."

"And what exactly did I make of those notes, Mr. Ketch? You were there."

"Well, Mr. Joel, you talked about the drunkard as the most evolved genus of peaceable creatures," says Ketch. "I remember it all very well. The gist of it was, for starters, that we humans have too many desires. We want to conquer other countries, or we want the most beautiful woman in the world for a bed warmer, or we want that rare one-of-a-kind ancient vase for our mantelpiece, we want it all. But the effort to acquire these things costs so very much, both for oneself and for others. Especially others, too many sacrifices."

"Did I really say that? Are you sure you're not just making this up?"

"Not at all. Based on my simple notes, you extemporized most convincingly, Mr. Joel. To wit, that alcohol serves to cut those outlandish desires down to size and conveniently evaporates any lingering dissatisfactions. Or more to the point, getting drunk makes you feel as if you'd already realized your desires. And alcohol's a lot cheaper. Not this high-class stuff, of course," says Ketch, holding up his glass of I.W. Harper. "But still, compared to a battleship or diamonds to entice a beautiful woman or a rare antique vase, it's a whole lot less expensive. Thanks to alcohol, people can just skip all those over-the-top desires."

"That's right. Alcohol's an imagination amplifier," adds Joel.

"Very well put. It amplifies us drunkards into the most highly evolved peace-loving dreamers in all creation."

"But horses and cows and whales don't drink, and they very peaceful," says Angelina.

"Most certainly. That's because horses and cows and whales are innately good. No such thing as a bad horse. No evil whales. We must ingest alcohol to return to that happy horse and whale state. And compared to drugs and bondage and sexual disorders, alcohol's pure. Don't know about plankton, but it's the nearest thing to grain."

"Talk of sexual disorders, where does that put you two?" asks Angelina, speaking with a knowing confidence that she's not offending.

"We're both one hundred percent normal. We're friendly with our own kind. We never sleep with women, nothing so perverted."

"Tsk tsk, he's just teasing. We're normal, the customers who come here are normal, the girls are normal. It's people who can't get it on without slashing their partner to ribbons who've got a problem. Now *that's* a disorder."

"So there you have it. Taking the argument to its logical conclusion, we showed that a highly evolved drunkard species is just about as peaceable as horses, cows, and whales."

"Within one week, a full third of the AA members quit the organization."

"Really floored us, it did. Made me feel as if I'd done something wrong."

"Oh, come now. It was all in the power of words. And none of them even knew just how 'amplified' you were at the time."

"No, they knew," says Angelina. "Same as I know drunks are basically good. Mind you, there's better or worse at everything. We get some lousy customers in here, make a nuisance of themselves, but given time even they get the hang of it."

"See? They evolve," quips Ketch.

"Well, don't you evolve too much. We all love you as you are. We wish you could stay drunk forever. And if you can, we just want you to see us as lovely ladies."

"Don't we always?"

"Yes, always," echoes Joel, pouring himself another glass of bourbon.

Angelina wonders whether to have one herself, but then looks up and notices the maid from Melchor is gone. No, she'll pass on the drink; it's too much trouble to go get a glass.

"This bottle, though, wish they'd done a little better by the shape," chides Ketch. "What's inside is so good. Why'd they have to make such a god-awful bottle?"

"Square bottles are unnatural, the fake cut-glass work is uncalled for. The cap's too big, it looks cheap. They wanted something to set this twelve-year-old apart from the run-of-the-mill bottle, but they overdid it."

"Round, slender bottles are the thing. Better to fit right in the palm of your hand."

"Don't you two ever disagree on things?" asks Angelina.

"Certainly. All the time."

"Actually, we don't get along at all."

"Funny, I never heard you arguing."

"Only when we're alone. And without screaming or shouting."

"Oh, then you really *do* get along. Shut out the world and you have your own little world to yourselves."

"You think?" says Joel.

"Listening to records every night, laughing, whispering. What on earth you two talk about? Everybody want to know. What you got so much to discuss?"

"Call us creative."

"Alcohol heightens creativity. Some say the best part of human culture is distilled from it."

"Like a toy choo-choo train, running on alcohol. That's humanity."

"That's why, while we do reminisce from time to time, most of the time we make up new things."

"New things? Plans, things to do?"

"No, worlds," says Joel matter-of-factly. "Inhabited by people doing all sorts of things, with unexpected events in the offing so there's an element of change. We make it all up. Natural backdrop and human actors, settings that've been there forever but the scenes keep changing. You know the sort of thing—a world."

"Or two."

"And *that's* what you make up?"

"Well, in words," says Ketch.

"We toss out different ideas, sketch in the details, then put it all together."

"Care to let me listen in sometime? At the creation," teases Angelina, a rare note of coquetry in her voice.

"One day," says Ketch.

"All in good time," adds Joel, noticing something out of the corner of his eye. The maid from Melchor is now standing in the corner of the salon staring this way. Intrigued by their conversation possibly? Or no, thinks Joel, was that a spark of defiant challenge in her eyes? As if to say, we'll see who's better at making up worlds! One brief flash of eye contact, then she retreats to her room.

BUS REPORT 7

Sunday morning, Santa María Cathedral in Baltasár City, the bus attended First Mass at seven o'clock. As parishioners took their seats and the priest approached the altar, the bus was already there, at the end of a pew far to the back. Throughout the service it sat quietly with its engine off, so despite its size, only those sitting in the same row and the priest and acolyte who faced the congregation even noticed it. According to testimony from those seated nearby, during the hymns and litany two voices came from inside, probably the driver and young Foreign Office staffer assigned to accompany the veterans group. A former choirmaster went on record as saying that one sang at a high tenor pitch, the other bass.

When the collection basket was passed around, witnesses saw an arm reach out from the driver's seat and contribute a substantial amount of banknotes. However, when the time came to take Communion the bus did not rise. Most probably it—or they—felt unworthy to partake of the sacrament. Later, this puzzled people: on the one hand, if there were any sinful people on board it had to be the Japanese ex-soldiers, not the two locals duty-bound to drive and assist them, though they too presumably felt guilty consorting with wrongdoers. The subject of these most uncatholic venalities was much debated among the faithful of the capital.

Once Mass was over, as if to avoid any questions, the bus slipped outside as unobtrusively as it came. The backing maneuver was a feat of consummate skill. People ran after it, but all they saw were the taillights rounding a bend in the road. Others ambling about the cathedral lawn infused with righteous grace after Mass saw the bus leave but for some reason didn't think of giving chase by car.

Another rather more secular question people later asked themselves: what exactly were those Japanese doing all through Mass? And the answer was, quite obviously, they must have been sleeping. So the only two good Catholics on board, the driver and the Foreign Office aide, probably had conspired to take the bus to church, even though the sinful forty-seven inside slept right through the angelic hymns of praise.

President Matías Guili, habitual early-riser, is pondering a question in his dojo: whether or not to call that young woman from Angelina's over to the Presidential Villa. By all measure of daytime logic, which is to say in the language of politicking—bureaucratic institutions or persuasive rhetoric or sharing out monies—the act carries no obvious merit at all. He already told Lee Bo, he can't even explain why he wants her nearby, so probably he shouldn't give it another thought. Still, he has the feeling this is an important decision for him. Shifting and shapeless, a nocturnal vision born of the shadows between late night and dawn, the implications are unclear, yet compelling nonetheless. For in some spiritual sphere, far from workaday events, other powers hold sway. Somewhere, he knows, she's connected with him. With so many strategic judgments to make in the weeks ahead, keeping her around will have its advantages. For psychic support, for guidance. She probably won't know herself if something she says is prophetic or not. Even if nothing happens, some of her powers might just rub off on him. All very iffy, he knows, but that's a risk he'll have to take.

Matías isn't discounting how Angelina might react. Didn't he tell Lee Bo he can't afford to lose her? She's everything to him, the incumbent dictator of his desires. Yet sex aside, there must be something Angelina's not providing, or why would this maid from Melchor even bother him? Highly irrational, but so are the extenuating circumstances of the moment. Doesn't her very advent signal strange times ahead? Why else would he brood over a woman he's hardly seen head on, let alone spoken to? Everything's changing directions so quickly, escalating thick and fast, the usual channels can't deliver. With so many unknowns volleying at him from all sides, reflexes alone won't do.

Now's no time to be standing idle. The music's playing, so you better dance it to the end. And if you think before you move your arms and legs, you ain't dancing. You can't lose the moment, that flash of decisive inspiration. He's been here before. Just like when he decided to ask former Imperial Navy mentor Kazuma Ryuzoji to sponsor his studies in Japan. Or the anxious months before he finally brought Angelina here to this country, when he felt like he was fraying on the edge. Or when he first ran for president. Even after losing the presidency, the road to reinstatement was paved with snap decisions, like that contract with Ketch and Joel; the minute he met them, he knew it was no coincidence. Knew it without a second's hesitation. Call it a gut feeling—*Yes, here's a solution!* And now, this maid from Melchor is practically waving another contract right under his nose. But first, better read the fine print!

Matías reaches a decision. Before breakfast, he takes out a sheet of his personal stationery and pens a short note to Angelina:

Need an extra hand at the villa. Lend me that maid from Melchor for a while.

Matías

He's dashed off memos to Angelina before. He hates to telephone and would rather not rely on others to relay urgent messages. Heinrich, however, he can trust to deliver a simple note. Nothing new about that. Only this time, he'll be bringing someone back with him.

What will Angelina make of this snap request? He thinks it over. Any way he looks at it, the maid takes first priority. He'll have plenty of opportunity to explain it all to Angelina later. Or no, she'll catch on soon enough without his having to explain a thing. He needs the maid's powers to overcome the crisis he faces. Angelina picks up on these supernatural vibes more than he does, Matías tells himself. She'll understand better than anyone.

At eight thirty, Heinrich arrives. Immediately the President summons him to the back office and hands him a sealed envelope. "Take this to Madame before midday, wait for her instructions, then come back here."

Heinrich, expressionless as ever, takes the envelope and heads for the garage. The President half-listens to Jim Jameson read off the day's lackluster schedule as he thumbs through a stack of papers to be signed, his eyes barely skimming the words. None of it sinks in. All documents have been prepared according to ministry manuals and precedents on file: minimal bureaucratic meddling, hand delivered by his excellent staff for the executive secretary to scrutinize before reaching him. As a rule, he'd read each one, but this morning he just can't seem to focus and signs them perfunctorily. He gets up and saunters from the office, touching base with Jameson now tackling mountains of paperwork out in the foyer.

"I'm stepping out for a bit. Be back in thirty."

It's so unlike him to simply walk out in the middle of his morning session that Jameson rises in alarm, but the President reassures him.

"Just going out for a little walk. Won't take long."

And with that, he leaves the startled executive secretary behind and walks down the hall. First President Cornelius undertook the construction of this Presidential Villa immediately after assuming office. While hardly luxurious by foreign standards, the sprawling neoclassical structure with its imposing whitewashed walls is the biggest thing ever built on the islands. In the beginning, opinion was not entirely favorable, but eventually the islanders came around to the idea that a president was bigger than all the clan elders put together; he needed a building this size to inspire international confidence. Even simple folk from the tiniest outlying villages know by now that in today's world, image is everything.

Matías likes the building. Admittedly, it was only after he became president he realized how much he liked it, how much he went in for big things in general. Construction proceeded slowly. Then six years after independence, just as the plasterwork was to receive the last finishing touches, President Cornelius fell ill and died; he never knew the comforts of living here. Three months later, Home Office Attaché Matías Guili was sworn in as his successor and quite pleased to take up residence. Soon he was having additions installed, with his own private quarters tucked unobtrusively behind, complete with Japanese bath. What he really likes about the Presidential Villa, however, is its formidable frontage, the broad lawn graced with translucent curtains of flowing water, the long galleries in columns end to end. It takes a lot of man-hours just to keep the tropical undergrowth from encroaching, and the illuminated fountain doesn't come cheap either, but the coffers can spare that much. These things aren't for Matías; it's the nation that needs them.

He's lived here eight years, not counting the three months when he lost out to Bonhomme Tamang. His rival never actually resided here during his short term in office—no, he commuted every morning from his own humble bungalow—or rather, just as he was moving in, the "American" president up and died.

Matías ambles through the building with no real urge to go outside. The villa is big enough for a good walk. The U-shaped two-story Palladian pastiche centers on a faux third-story facade surmounted by three flagpoles. At most times, when there are no visiting dignitaries, only the Republic of Navidad flag waves from the middle pole. Most of the ground floor is given over to various executive staff offices, in name at least; only the right wing is actually occupied. Walking the long hallway toward the left wing, behind which hide his private quarters, he passes the occasional secretary bearing a briefcase or an armload of papers. Each without exception is startled to encounter the President wandering about at this hour and fumbles to come up with a salutation. He ignores them all and keeps walking. *If only he were a ghost, invisible to others!* sighs an inner voice, his stray thought surprising even himself. He's still got plenty to do, too much in fact. By the time he runs into his fourth underling bowing clumsily, he's already regretting this whole exercise.

He makes straight for a stairway, which leads up to the grand hall that occupies the better part of the upper floor, a formal reception room for inaugural ceremonies and fêting guests of state. To either side are passages that run the length of the left and right wings upstairs, leading to various waiting rooms and some ten spacious guest suites. Apparently Cornelius had different ideas for the Presidential Villa; Matías has no intention of putting up guests here, official or otherwise. He occasionally has food catered in and will hire temporary help for special functions, but it's no fun being a hotel. Nor will he make a single budgetary concession to hire extra help. A once-a-week cleaning is the only time anyone comes up here. The beds where no one sleeps in rooms where no one stays are draped with white drop cloths. The President walks the corridor devoid of human presence, reaches the end, turns around, and walks back. He turns a corner, passes through three sets of double doors to the grand hall, turns another corner, reaches the other end, and returns. Back and forth.

He thinks of the man who had this mansion built. His dark face and ash gray hair, that winning smile, his unshakable sangfroid in decision-making. Unlike Matías, he could openly boast about his one-quarter German blood, and at age thirty he anointed himself battle-ready with that *nom de guerre*: Cornelius. An air of megalomania wafted about him and propelled him into the presidency, fulfilling an already tangible promise of greatness. If the man hadn't come along at the right time, the country might never have adopted the presidential system. Certainly no one else would have built such a grandiose Presidential Villa, nor put up such strong opposition to America. Yes, but if as a result Navidad drew closer to Japan, which in turn led to this Brun Reef oil-stockpiling thing, who was to say that trading off America for Japan was really an improvement? Seen against the growing estrangement between those two countries, was choosing a nearby major power over a distant superpower such a smart move?

⚡

Walking the corridor, it all comes back to him: Cornelius's face, his proud-chested stature, his deep rich voice. Whatever else you could say about him, the man had all the makings of a president. Compared to which Matías's own small frame is almost laughable. Not that Matías strikes people as especially short. There's something about him; he has only to ignore his height as if it were a trick of perspective, and those around him are forced to overlook it as well. Seated, no one ever notices how short he is; on his feet, good manners dictate that others pretend he just happens to be standing in a lower spot.

This presents problems when he has to meet guests at the airport and cross the wide tarmac apron, so he makes a point of always waiting inside the terminal. Which constitutes no particular breach of protocol as long as the visitor isn't of equivalent rank—but foreign heads of state never come here anyway.

No, the respective heights of Cornelius and himself are not the issue. More to the point are those unresolved mysteries: *Why was the great man so nice to him? Why should he have invited Matías into the independence movement, then given him the nod to be his successor?* These doubts have niggled at Matías for over a decade, questions he's turned over in his mind hundreds of times. When Cornelius and he first met, Matías was just a supermarket owner with an honorary seat on an administrative hearing committee, which he attended purely as a matter of form since he had no say. Sure, Matías had financial connections, his share of acquaintances overseas, and maybe that made him someone of consequence in others' eyes. But political ambitions? None to speak of. Of course, Cornelius was not yet president, though he personified Navidad's hopes of breaking away from America. As Matías turns a corner in the corridor, he swears he can almost see Cornelius standing there at the far end. The huge double doors to the grand hall are shut, but the goings-on inside are clear as day: there's President Cornelius, and all around him the many formally attired guests, officials, and dignitaries, outer island leaders in their traditional robes, women in their finery attending the first-ever National Day celebration. Well, the great man was right after all. No one else could have fit the job description for president with all his qualifications. Not even Tamang, an Illinois University graduate who spent years in Washington as personal assistant to a certain lobbyist from Hawaii. If Cornelius had been coming in as third-term president, he'd never have gone digging up dirt about his predecessor. What a dumb thing to do! An invitation to chaos, a meaningless gesture to a handful of do-gooders. Nothing any self-respecting politician ought to do.

Tamang was always surrounded by his crowd. He and his pro-America pals, a real ruckus of a democratic party, deciding everything by noisy consensus. Still, he himself stood head and shoulders above the lot of them, and when they lost him, his followers ran out of steam. Despite intimations about a strong leader somewhere in their midst, not one of them took up the reins. Matías knows they hold a grudge against him, but who among them has the stuff to really oppose him in the political arena? Cornelius provided for Matías Guili as his successor; Tamang lined up no next generation. He had just taken office; maybe he hadn't planned that far ahead. At this thought, Matías stops in his tracks. *And what about me? Ever considered who's to come after me?* Times change, generations change, new ideas displace old truths—Cornelius knew a thing or two about social mechanics. He recognized that when the time came to step down, he should step down. He understood politics as it plays out over decades. Different though they were, Cornelius died believing Matías a worthy successor. Is there no one equally worthy to whom Matías can pass this heavy chalice? That someone must be out there, waiting in the ranks of officialdom. Maybe some game young entrepreneur on the way up. Or is he just kidding himself? That executive secretary of his, for instance, Jim Jameson, will he ever be president material? Or what's-his-face, the deputy head of the Home Office? Only time will tell, but that time has not yet come. He'll just have to carry on, the dynamo of the nation. The country's still not ripe for handing over. A crafty old leader for an immature country, a fresh young leader for an old country—that's how it works.

After several trips up and back along the corridors back, he realizes he's deliberately burying his head in the past and future in order to ignore the problems at hand. Nothing good can come of this. He's decided to summon that maid, and that settles that. Not that he intends to put her to menial work. Say he puts her in his private quarters, nominally under Itsuko, what use is he to make of her? What will Angelina's reaction be? What's the girl got hidden inside her? Nothing but unknowns. He'll just have to wait. Better go downstairs and get back to work.

But just as he reaches the stairs, the strangest thought comes sailing at him like an arrow: *What if he's doing exactly what Cornelius once did? What if Cornelius didn't really have a clue what was going on either? What if he was doing the bidding of some external power?* Behind this painted backdrop reality, maybe some stage director and props men and all kinds of mechanical contraptions are moving things about? How does he know there's no puppeteer pulling his strings? Suddenly he gets the distinct impression that every joint in his body is tangled in invisible threads. He sweeps them away and hurries downstairs to the office.

↯

Heinrich does not return by noon. The President leaves instructions with the staffer on duty that Heinrich's passenger is to be shown to a waiting room; he himself is going to the canteen for talks over lunch as scheduled.

The prospective lunchee is a heavyweight legislator from Baltasár Island who's fairly close to the President. He'll be accompanied by several junior legislators from his camp, so Matías has asked Jim Jameson and a middle-echelon official from the Foreign Office, nobody especially prominent, to join them. A year ago, Matías disbanded the legislature as an emergency measure in response to the uproar when former President Tamang died under unusual circumstances. All authority was reeled in to the Executive Office, ostensibly as a three-month or half-year stopgap, though in fact the clamps are still on now over a year later. The only reason one doesn't hear legislators grumbling is that the President has co-opted all avenues for complaint, inventing pretexts for a lunch or dinner invitation especially to hear them out.

Thanks to his previous eight-year double term, he is up to running the country with no legislature *and* virtually no complaints. A legislature has its role in breaking in a new president, but beyond that—just to reflect the will of the people? Who needs it? His dictator-in-mediator's-clothing stratagem has worked remarkably well. At least no disgruntled noises ever reached his ears, no dissident movement has reared its head. Until recently, that is—the torii gate, the handbills, the burning flag...Signs were surfacing.

The topic of discussion at lunch is how to solicit ODA funds from Japan for road improvements between Colonia city and the village of Tabagui. The heavyweight legislator's clan sell imported cars and gasoline in Colonia, as well as do automotive servicing. Gaspar's surfaced roads have long been a source of envy to them, as Baltasár Island has yet to be blessed with any such incentives to motoring, save for a few paved streets in Colonia itself. But run blacktop the length of the island, and who knows?—they might conceivably bring in tour coaches, maybe even rent cars. Or better yet, receive the contract for public buses. That would be a big boost to the local economy, *their* local economy.

The President dishes out comments that could be taken for either yes or no as he spoons up his octopus curry. A Creole dish introduced after the war from across the Indian Ocean, it made quite a hit with the Navidadians, who love octopus, and now serve it not only in hotels and restaurants but also in ordinary homes as everyday fare. As luck would have it, the Japanese had already paved the way for acceptance with their version of "curry rice" during their years here. The trick is to tenderize the raw octopus meat by pounding it before simmering; you don't have to be a chef to know this—every housewife in the islands does as much.

The big man in Colonia fills Matías in about local goings-on, but stops short of broaching the subject that everyone's talking about—the disappearance of the bus—for fear it might upset the President. Matías himself, however, is thinking about the Melchor Island maid he's impulsively invited to the villa with no explanation. No clear answer issues forth on the road improvement plans, not out of political gamesmanship, but simply because he has other things on his mind.

"How about it? Sound possible?" asks the legislator.

"Fifty-fifty I'd say," comes the classic noncommittal politician's response. "It'll be easier to push this ahead as a direct request from your people once the particulars become clear. Let the public know the petition system isn't just for the outer islands; main island folk can do their bit too. Wouldn't be such a bad thing to create a precedent."

Even so, there's no guarantee of paved roads. It's not clear whether the President means to use such petitions as a basis for ODA negotiations with Japan or take other budgetary measures, or if he means anything at all. In the end, the legislator refrains from mentioning the missing bus and leaves the table talks without any solid promises. The President sees the group to the end of the corridor. As they walk across the circular drive to their waiting car, the Foreign Office man confides that "the President's tone sounded fairly reassuring." Little consolation, when what the legislator really wanted was a firm pledge he could promise to his constituency. Looks like he'll have to dig in a little longer; this issue will take more canvassing than he thought.

⚡

After lunch the President returns to his office and immediately calls in the villa steward to ask the whereabouts of Heinrich's passenger.

"Waiting in room 117 is the word from Administration. Shall I have the visitor sent in?"

"One seventeen? Is that a meeting room?"

"Yes, I believe so. Not a room that sees much use. But with so much paperwork to go over today, the staff just spread out to whatever rooms they could find. So that was the only available space."

"I'll go myself."

The steward is surprised; the President never goes to meet a guest, conference room or not. The entry in the agenda he received this morning reads only *Presidential guest, Rm 117, 12:25*—no name. The President leaves the puzzled man behind and walks off down the corridor.

Number 117 turns out to be at the east end of the main building, just around the corner from the wing leading to Matías's private quarters. The President knocks first, then opens the door. The room is dimly lit, the curtains half drawn. The maid is sitting on one of two white-dropclothed sofas, her face an indiscernible silhouette against the scant northern light from the window. She turns, rises, and bows demurely as he enters the room.

"Sorry to keep you waiting," says Matías, taking a seat on the sofa opposite her and gesturing for her to sit. "I believe you know me, we met at Madame's place."

The young woman nods. She is wearing a white blouse, her slightly wavy hair tied back in a ponytail. As his eyes adjust to the half light, Matías can make out the proportioned features he's seen before. Not striking especially, but certainly a Melchor face, one that betrays no emotion. She looks at Matías because he happens to be sitting there before her, but otherwise her eyes show neither curiosity nor dislike, no interest whatsoever. She doesn't even seem concerned that it was the President himself who brought her here. Maybe she could see it coming. Maybe she knows she has a role to play. Or then again, maybe she's just a dimwitted country girl. A voice in his head is telling him he's made a mistake in bringing her here.

"You're from Melchor, aren't you?"

Another nod.

"My mother was from Melchor. Died decades ago," begins Matías, for lack of any other way to launch into what he has to say. Just how long ago was it she died? Fifty years? Sixty? Seems like ages... when out of nowhere he recalls her face. How's it possible? A face he couldn't remember for the life of him, now suddenly clear as day. And the woman before him doesn't even look anything like her. *No, better stick to business.* He collects his thoughts.

"I'm thinking to have you work here for a while," he adds quickly—and his mother's face disappears. "What's your name?"

"You call me what you like." Her voice is low, all undertones, but straightforward and clear, a voice that carries well. He could enjoy listening to this voice, though the gist of her reply catches him by surprise.

"But you must have your own name, from when you were born."

"New job, new name," says the voice.

"At Angelina's—I mean, at Madame's—what did they call you?"

"María. María the maid. There were two other Marías in the house."

"They say all women are Mary," he observes. "So let's not use María."

"No, better something else."

"Well then, how about my mother's name?" Once again, his dead mother's face floats into view. "Her name was Améliana."

"A good name. Please use it," says the young woman.

"About the work here," the President continues, "I want you to look at people. Once a day, for maybe an hour or two, when I meet with someone I think is important, I want you to come along. Then afterwards, you tell me what you make of him. While we're meeting, you don't say a word. You just pick up on what sort of person he is, what he's thinking."

Matías never intended to spell it out like this right from the outset. He thought he'd let her get used to helping out in his private quarters under Itsuko, but after seeing her face, hearing her voice, something tells him to put her in an advisory role, appraising people, even though he's not sure she really has that sixth sense.

"The rest of the time, you can relax back here. There's bound to be chores to do, but don't feel obliged to do any if you don't want to."

She nods slowly. Brought to a new workplace, given only the haziest job description, she accepts. There are scores of women public servants here in the capital and surely a good hundred more schoolteachers counting all the outer islands, but none has been given similar duties. Probably not one woman in all the world has been offered such a non-assignment. *So what am I doing?* thinks Matías, when just then he notices the young woman's face starting to flush with color. A faint glow rises through her tawny complexion, her eyes shine, her lips part slightly. This is a completely different face from only five minutes ago. Her expression—or rather her impassive lack of any—remains unchanged, but that tentative drifting air has given way to some strong sense of grounding, of arrival, a transformation that plants her right here in place. Her very presence can now draw attention and halt one's thoughts. The astounded President takes a moment before he regains sufficient composure to pick up the interdepartmental phone on the coffee table and ring Itsuko's extension. He gives the room number and tells her to come quick. Rarely does he ever summon Itsuko to the main building.

"These next few weeks," he tells his new assistant, "I have a lot of important people to meet and important decisions to make. Of course I can get advice from specialists, but I'd like to ask you for advice of another sort. All you have to do is say what you sense. Whatever you say about someone won't be your responsibility, just tell me when no one else is around. I hear you have powers to see other people's worth, their plans and ambitions. I'd like to test those powers."

"I can only see so far," whispers the newly christened Améliana, reverting to her quiet former self. "There are limits to everything."

"I know, just tell me what you can."

Having said that much, the President realizes there's nothing more for him to say. And this is someone who has no inclination for small talk—she as much as told him so. For the very first time, Matías considers objectively what others must make of him bringing this young woman into his inner circle. Ordinarily it'd be some sex story, and if that's what people want to think, fine, that interpretation serves his purposes well enough. Though actually, looking the woman in the face, he feels no desire to take her to bed.

With any luck, it will take them a good long while to work out who she really is. If the clerks and secretaries want to talk, let them talk. Better than him trying to invent some plausible job title. The President stares out the window and continues to turn things over in his mind before Itsuko shows up; the girl is silent. Matías rises abruptly and opens the curtain. Bright light comes streaming into the room. Outside, the lawn is dotted with petitioners sitting and lying on the grass, waiting for those in charge to summon them inside. A car drives away, most likely the Colonia legislator and company. *They've taken their time,* thinks Matías. *Probably means they've been talking to someone else here after lunch. Now who could that be?* Dictators are always seeing conspiracies everywhere, doubting even the most reliable information. It's an occupational hazard.

A knock comes on the door, and in steps Itsuko.

"Ah yes, there's a little favor I need to ask. I want you to look after Améliana here."

"Yessir," says Itsuko, without enthusiasm. Just dragging herself out of the President's private quarters was already a bother, and now to be asked to oversee some new girl. What's going on here?

"Any light work will be okay. But send her to me when I require her."

"Is she to come in by day?"

He hadn't even thought of it. "Do you have a home here in town?" he asks.

"No," she answers.

"In that case, you can live in, like at Madame's."

Améliana nods.

"Find her a room in back. I leave the rest to you."

"Very well, then, this way," says Itsuko, as she leads Améliana out of the room.

The young woman steps through the door and away, followed immediately by a flutter of lilac butterflies. *Now how did they get in here?* wonders the President, as the room grows colder with their exit, leaving him with the distinct impression that something is missing.

After a moment, Matías walks around the coffee table and heads for the door when he notices the painting on the wall behind him. It's a room no one uses, so he has never seen it before, but today the painting stops him in his tracks. He just stares at it: a picture of a young woman sitting sideways on the beach, a sarong wrapped around her waist, with two small, perfectly shaped breasts on her naked torso. Her slightly wavy hair is trained over one shoulder and adorned with a white hibiscus. And the face, it looks so much like Améliana just now, it could be her.

No, it can't be, he thinks, taking a closer look. It's not a portrait but an archetypal woman's face, chased of all extraneous detail save the essential femininity, with the result that the two faces give the same impression. That's the only explanation. And yet, this Améliana sat looking straight at the likeness the whole time and didn't bat an eye. Matías is mystified. Who painted this picture? Who hung it here?

⚡

Late in 1947, Matías made up his mind to go to Japan and wrote Lieutenant Ryuzoji a letter. Word had blown in that the defeated Empire was in total chaos, but however unrealistic his hopes, he badly wanted to believe that he could make his way in that big country. There was every reason to hesitate. Wasn't life good here in these islands? It never even occurred to the locals to leave. In other islands in the Pacific, he'd heard, it was customary for those who came of age to leave their homeland at least once in their lives, but the Navidadians stayed put where they were born, raised, bore children, grew old, and died. Even at the very tail end of the war, when the Empire of Greater Japan urged all her subjects to rally to the cause, next to no one left of his own free will. It wasn't that they lacked courage or felt disloyalty to that distant imperial reign, they simply couldn't get their head around the idea of leaving the islands. The Japanese could round up any number of voluntary laborers to construct an airfield there, but recruitment campaigns for active service overseas foundered miserably.

Three years after the imperial forces were routed, however, Matías got the bug. Being an orphan at the bottom of the pecking order among his late mother's relations back on Melchor Island and with no other means of support, the prospects were slim. Even his above-average intelligence and popularity with other kids his age counted for little in traditional clan society. No, he'd have to make his way to Japan and build himself a life there. So remembering Lieutenant Ryuzoji's parting promise, he drafted a letter saying he was determined to come. For all its faults and childish wording, it was a moving letter. Ryuzoji's reply arrived seven months later, when Matías had all but forgotten about it. Ryuzoji wrote that his new postwar career was on a stable footing with enough financial leeway for him to guarantee Matías an education. He'd take care of the necessary procedures for him to make the trip. An elated Matías accepted the invitation and didn't look back. He was twenty years old at the time.

In those days, of course, there were no flights between the South Pacific and Japan. There were hardly even any regular ships either, just the occasional lone freighter carrying consumer goods to and from Osaka. Ryuzoji instructed him to sign on as a merchant sailor, enclosing a letter to present to the captain when the next ship anchored at Baltasár City. What's more, tucked inside that thick envelope was all manner of documentation for when they docked in Osaka: detailed directions, a map of the city, even an application form—complete with address and message—for the telegram he was to send from Osaka Station. The funds for the telegram, his train ticket, and meals en route were double-sealed in yet another envelope. Matías could scarcely believe the money reached him unscathed, but he had to admit, Ryuzoji saw to everything. When he thinks back on it many years and numerous benefactors later, Ryuzoji emerges as the first and brightest beacon of goodwill at a major turning point in his life.

Eventually the ship arrived in port, and a timid Matías sought out the captain with letter of introduction in hand. Half unsure just how far he could trust Ryuzoji's word, he found the outcome more than satisfactory. He was quickly shown on board to see the captain, a stalwart soul who'd sailed to Navidad repeatedly during the war, and right then and there he was taken on as a single-passage crew member and given a seaman's passbook already inscribed with his own name, which had been waiting in readiness in the ship's safe. The young man was literally floored. How meticulous could these preparations be? Matías ran to tell the good news to the owner of the flophouse where he was staying, gathered up his things, and hurried back to the docks.

All he remembers of his time on board was that the other crew members generally made a fuss over this short, dark-skinned, hardworking island lad. His job consisted entirely of cleaning. He quickly learned what it meant to run a "tight ship." For a small vessel, there was plenty to do: swab the decks, tidy the officers' cabins, mop the mess, brush down the hull, and as if that weren't enough, don goggles and chip off the clots of rust that encroached on any exposed metal surface. Not bad work, he thought, sitting out on the deck in the hot sun from morning to night, banging away with a hammer. He can still hear the happy rhythms he'd pound out but can't recall a single face among his fellow crewmen on that twenty-day voyage, nor even that of the kindly captain—proof positive that his memory is selective.

The ship sailed within sight of the mountains of Kyushu and Shikoku, then negotiated the Kii-Awaji Strait, finally docking at the Port of Osaka. He was unaware at the time just how much clout Ryuzoji must have had to muster in order to arrange this highly irregular means of getting him to Japan as a one-way seaman. He merely breezed on board, then breezed off, thinking that's just how things went. He even received a little pay to boot. The port where he disembarked didn't tell him much about the size of the country; ports everywhere large and small look pretty much alike. But when he caught a train together with a seaman on home leave named Shimizu, he had a hard time suppressing his backwater astonishment that such a big machine could move at such speeds. His first-ever train ride—a rush of nervous excitement and exhaustion that ultimately deposited him at Shinagawa Station in Tokyo, where he was met by Ryuzoji. His elation at that moment has long since crowded out any recollection of the days that followed. (Selective memory again?)

Ryuzoji was hitting a peak just then. Amid the returning demobilized troops who hustled left and right, he'd been quick to read the pulse of the times. He had the knack for building connections through moving material goods; he was sharp enough to see postwar Japan before the war ended. It would take years for young Matías to even begin to understand the cogs that turned the man's world around them. But of course, that was just one small part of piecing together the big picture of Japan, an engrossing intellectual adventure.

Ryuzoji, as it turned out, was now in the brokering business; scooping up things with the right hand, passing them on with the left, and mostly odd unrelated flotsam at that. Many of the items were black market. Defeat not only broke the forges of production, it disrupted intangible avenues of trade. Many items just never got to where they were supposed to go, and any middle man who found takers for all the merchandise afloat could name his price. In Ryuzoji's case, while he himself gained some pull in the currents of resurgent nationalism, a loyal network of contacts among former soldiers and imperial ideologues provided information on goods. From Matías's perspective, Ryuzoji's sphere of enterprise was an extremely advantageous perch from which to observe what moved the vast mechanisms of Japan. Here he learned the principle that it was not the capitalist out in front, nor the manufacturer nor the consumer, but the man in the middle who decided everything; goods or ideas, the important thing was to position yourself midstream in the flow of things.

Fresh-off-the-boat Matías was given work as a warehouse guard for Ryuzoji's company Shinheiwa Kogyo—the auspiciously named "New Peace Industries." It was a live-in job, thereby solving both his employment and housing problems in one go. Ryuzoji roped in a country cousin's third son, and together during the day shift he and Matías managed incoming stock and handed over ticketed goods to customers who came with large carts or three-wheeled cycles or trucks. In the meantime, they just had to hold the fort and patrol two times a night. To Ryuzoji's credit, he sent this underemployed pair to school, though not both at the same time, of course, as that would have left the warehouse unguarded. The other lad, Ken'ichi, attended regular daytime high school classes, while Matías boned up for night school. With a trumped-up rural middle school diploma that was dubious at best and his entrance exam scores that were as bad as could be expected after only two months' cramming, he still made the grade, thanks again no doubt to Ryuzoji's political clout. In the end, however, he proved himself to be an earnest student capable of very good marks. Warehouse guard duty afforded time for his studies, and Ken'ichi rose to the head of his class, making him the best possible tutor. Ryuzoji, presumably, was pleased at having paired them up.

After four years, Matías graduated with decent marks for a foreigner. During those years Shinheiwa grew by leaps and bounds. The postwar enterprise of shuffling about secret caches of local goods leveled off, and business moved on to aid supplies from America, especially with the start of the Korean conflict. During his last year of school, so many goods poured in they sometimes couldn't finish storing them all during daylight hours and had to continue working late into the night, forcing him to forego classes. Anyway, the future looked bright for the company when the newly graduated Matías became a full employee. He still lived in the dorm room above the warehouse, but meanwhile the warehouse underwent renovations and the wood-frame structure was expanded into a sturdy block-and-mortar building.

One evening in mid-March, Ryuzoji summoned Matías to his home, a large house he'd bought just fifteen minutes' walk away. Before the war, this showpiece of "modern living" had been the residence of a pharmaceutical executive and had luckily somehow survived the firebombing of Tokyo. Here Ryuzoji lived with his wife, whom he'd married three years before; already they had two children. Matías was invited into the parlor, where his host stood sipping imported whiskey, a samurai sword mounted on the wall behind him, looking rather incongruous with the faux-Western decor. What Ryuzoji had to say was this: Matías should study a little longer in Japan, then return to Navidad.

"I believe you know this from all you've seen, but for the time being Japan has to look after itself. Any talk of forming a Great Alliance like before is still a long way off. In other words, until then, this country can't afford to take in people like you as foreign-born Japanese subjects and must treat you as foreigners. Do what you might, there's little prospect of your rising to the top here in Japan. From the very beginning, not even I thought I could make a Japanese of you. That's not why I brought you here. No, it's always been my intention to send you back home once you finished your studies so you could be of service to your own country. Navidad will see changes, but there's no future in letting your know-nothing clan elders decide things on a whim, or allowing a bunch of young upstarts to run the show just like Uncle Sam tells them to. Son, I want you to become a politician. One of these days I'm going to stand for elections myself. It's not my turn yet; they still call my brand of thinking 'backwards,' a 'throwback.' But mark my words, there will come a day when people will realize that they must be true to their Japanese spirit. My ear-to-the-ground says it won't be so very long. So you go back to your country and become a person everyone respects, someone who can run the islands. The place has gone American. It's supposed to be a democracy, right? So there ought to be more room for a young person like you to get into some decision-making position. Scratch the surface of American democracy and you'll find plenty of iffy notions—lies—but up front it offers opportunities for even youngsters to succeed. Equal opportunity is not a bad thing. What's more, you'll be fresh back from Japan. Of course, I know there are those who'll say that since you fought on our side, you lost with our side too, but there should still be some mature people around who understand the Japanese spirit. After all, we turned back the white powers as far as we did; we said what we had to say with blood and steel. That kind of spirit is something your islanders can understand. So pack on home with Japanese spirit in your heart and Japanese connections in hand, and your island folk are sure to respond in kind."

Ryuzoji was happily intoxicated. Matías listened in silent doubt. Did he really have the political animal in him? Someone so awkward, so outcast, so short, so fed up with Navidad society, could he really stand up and speak in front of a crowd? Inspire confidence and decide important matters? Negotiate with foreign countries? Build up a political machine? Matías knew very well where Ryuzoji was heading, though the more he understood, the less it seemed to have anything to do with him. On the other hand, he also appreciated Ryuzoji's generosity in bringing him here to study. And if becoming a politician was what it would take to repay him, well then he'd give it his best shot. Or so he vowed, until he tried to picture the island elders even pretending to listen to him. Matías the politician may have been Ryuzoji's dream, but to Matías himself it was more like a hallucination.

It was another four years before he actually returned to Navidad. He left the room above the warehouse, rented a room elsewhere (board included), and began to commute to work. Shinheiwa Kogyo engaged in a little export business by this stage, and Matías was out in that department. He also went to night school to improve his English, and learned to write standard form letters. Meanwhile, Ryuzoji took him places: to business negotiations, to quasi-political gatherings, to a whole range of functions. Everyone recognized Ryuzoji right away by his young briefcase-toting assistant, the short one with the dark skin, though few would ever have thought this was his protégé. To be honest, Matías understood very little of what went on. Who were these people? What was being discussed here? Ryuzoji generally just dragged him along with no explanation before or after. Whether exchanging tip-offs on where surplus goods were to be had, or brainstorming about raising funds for Representative So-and-so, or exploring ways and means to end a dispute, the sessions remained a mystery to him. What Matías ostensibly gained from sitting in on them was the realization that person-to-person connections made the world go round. Men like Ryuzoji had absolutely nothing to do with creating anything. From the word go, things existed as goods to be bought and sold—sugar, bananas, ships, yams, gasoline—goods in all shapes and sizes moving in one direction, money moving in the opposite direction. Anyone in the middle stood to make a profit, which of course he'd then have to share out properly or it would cause squabbles later on. It also struck young Matías that politics must work the same way: the broker who could arbitrate a peaceable accord between those in the middle of the road and those off to the side could shore up his own power base in the process. Something to remember.

One more thing, during this time Matías learned about women. Up until then, he'd lived quite uninvolved and unconcerned. He never played with girls when he was a boy in Navidad, never had time once he came to Japan and started working. Japanese schools had yet to go coeducational, and even after becoming a Shinheiwa employee he never went out drinking, knew nothing of gambling; he was a mama's boy without a mama. It took his new landlady to make a man out of him.

This frumpy, plain-at-best Tsuneko was a war widow. She looked close to forty, though her real age was just a little over thirty, and while she could expect no suitors, she seemed to enjoy her solitary freedom, supporting herself by partitioning her eight-tatami-mat living room to take in three young lodgers, for whom she provided breakfast only. Matías rented the makeshift two-and-a-half-mat "room" in the middle with flimsy plywood "walls." Hurriedly married just before the end of the war, Tsuneko's husband was sent off to the front in the South Pacific soon afterwards and never returned. That was the end of the story, but she never complained. She hardly talked much anyway, not even to her three boarders. It just so happened that one of Tsuneko's distant relations worked for Shinheiwa, and he sent Matías along to her, guaranteeing him to be "of good character—for a foreigner."

For all of a year, Matías was only a lodger, and Tsuneko would just serve him breakfast without comment. But then, her two Japanese lodgers moved out one after the other, and no new faces came to fill the vacancies. There was a virus going around at the time, and Matías stayed home sick with a fever. Tsuneko nursed him back to health, coming to his bedside with ice packs, even wiping his sweaty body. Matías had heard the other two lodgers call him "jungle boy" behind his back, so while he did sense a certain reserve on her part, he was pleasantly surprised at her kindness. And one evening when he'd almost fully recovered, Tsuneko came to him *in bed*. At first, Matías didn't know what was going on; the storm of sensations caught him totally by surprise. *So this is what everyone's always talking about,* he wondered vaguely through the haze of exhaustion.

"A cute guy like you must be popular with the girls," she told him in the middle of the night, as they both lay there looking up at the ceiling. He was astonished. It had never even occurred to him that he might be considered "cute," although come to think of it, people generally did treat him rather nicely for a "jungle boy." Not that he had a whiff of sex appeal by conventional standards. Yet there was something about this short, foreign-born youth that made everyone only too glad to look after him. The intimacy with Tsuneko became a steady thing. He was both a toy-boy lover to her and a young innocent who needed mothering, a partner with whom to share daily conversations about the weather, snippets of good news, odd topics around town. She decided not to take in any other lodgers, and entitled him to evening meals as well. The sex was fun, but it wasn't everything. This homely woman took such pleasure in watching him eat that soon she was happily scrubbing his back at home instead of sending him out to the public bathhouse. Matías had to admit it was a good life. One reason he became forever fond of Japanese baths was surely that bathing at Tsuneko's house was such a treat.

On the job, Matías gained a working knowledge of trade; from Ryuzoji he learned more abstract lessons in political maneuvering; and Tsuneko's gift to him, the ease of knowing what it was to be loved. None of these things could have conceivably prefigured his later thirst for power, yet Ryuzoji's neo-nationalist thinking may have to some extent colored the future president's views, if not given him an edge on the all-important métier of managing personalities. This same Ryuzoji later went back to his hometown in Kyushu and was elected four times to the local prefectural assembly before serving three terms as a rank-and-file legislator in the Japanese National Diet.

Kazuma Ryuzoji had always been an exceptional individual and his own thinker—especially in his youth. This may not have counted for much in the war zone, where he kept his ideas to himself, but back in Japan he brought them to bear on the economic battlefield through the company he set up. Every friend, every acquaintance was a human resource to be developed. He tirelessly performed favors, smoothed ruffled feathers, and charted avenues of compromise between divergent camps without either side losing face. Matías, too, was a case in point, though the investment in someone so young was exceedingly long-term. Ryuzoji paid older associates their due respect and never resorted to intimidation; rather he dispensed influence, then when he was sure of his backing he moved in to collect—the classic Japanese politician's ploy. If Matías eventually proved a bigger fish than Ryuzoji, it was a credit to his mentor. Matías only wished his *sensei* could have seen him sworn in as second President of the Republic of Navidad.

Ironically, after lingering in Japan to see Ryuzoji's gradual ascent, the event that ultimately sent Matías packing was when Shinheiwa went bankrupt. As should have been obvious to anyone, a temporary pinch caught the company critically short of capital and a temporary pinch sent it under, though barely three months later Ryuzoji was back on his feet and had formed a new company. But whether Matías took it as a sign or an opportunity, he didn't let his good thing with Tsuneko hold him back. Eight years in Japan was just a little too long. Twenty-eight was the right age to be heading home to prepare for the next decade or two. And so it was that in August of 1951—the year Tsuneko and Matías heard over the radio at breakfast that General MacArthur had been relieved of his post as Proconsul of the Occupation Forces in Japan and Elvis Presley topped the charts with "Heartbreak Hotel"—Matías left Japan behind and returned to Navidad, now a protectorate of the United States of America.

༄

At ten o'clock two mornings later, the President is sitting in a special VIP room at Navidad International Airport waiting for his airplane to be readied. Beside him is Executive Secretary Jim Jameson and a young official from the Home Office, together with the maid from Melchor who just two days ago received the name Améliana. Seen through the large window, the clear skies look made for flying.

Half an hour ago, when the President appeared at the entrance of the Presidential Villa with an unknown young woman in tow, the other two were taken aback. Who *was* this girl in the white blouse and long green skirt splashed with a yellow floral print? She didn't look like any public servant they'd ever seen.

"Think of her as my personal advisor," said Matías by way of introduction. He apparently had no intention of further clarification, nor did the others dare to ask. They all climbed into the Nissan President, and fifteen minutes later, no one had spoken a word.

"It's all so sudden, so we can probably expect a brief wait," the executive secretary finally informed him just before Heinrich deposited them at the airport. The President had only brought up the idea to go on a reconnaissance run to Brun Reef that very morning, and the government Islander prop plane was already booked for the day. It took some doing, but the prior reservation was canceled so the plane could be reassigned to the President. Now they're waiting on pre-flight maintenance.

The door from the lobby swings open, and in steps Katsumata. Two corpsmen stand guard by the entrance to the VIP room, but of course they do nothing to stop the chief of Island Security, who strides right up to the President. Only then does Katsumata notice Améliana, and he casts her a suspicious glance.

"What's up?" asks the President, intercepting the man's probing gaze.

"Nothing really, I just went by the Presidential Villa to present my routine report, and they told me you were heading out on a trip. I thought I might still catch you, so I came here."

"Do you actually *have* anything to report?"

"No, nothing special. No bus, no leads. No new information on the flagpole incident either. The fact is, there's been no other incident since. No more handbills, everywhere's quiet."

"And you still haven't solved one damn thing," growls the President.

"We're trying. We just need a little more time," he says, eyeing Améliana again. He wonders whether he should warn the President about letting unidentified persons get too close, but decides against it. Island Security's ID checks are nothing to boast about.

"No protection today?"

"Don't need any."

"Are you sure? In times like these?"

"Idiot. Brun Reef's a hotbed of activity, is it? Move. Out of my sight."

"Okay then, take care," says Katsumata, leaving a stronger impression in reverse than he realizes.

The door to the tarmac now opens, and a gust of hot air blows in a man wearing a white pilot's short-sleeve shirt with epaulets. "All ready, sir. You all can board whenever you like."

Everyone rises and files out onto the apron. The weather is perfect, if a tad windy. The President takes his customary copilot's seat. The two officials leave one row empty and sit in the third row to help balance the aircraft. Améliana sits behind them, alone in a seat on the right-hand side. The pilot immediately revs up the engines, ticks his checklist with a ballpoint pen while reading various meters and gauges, then calls the control tower for flight clearance.

"It's Brun today, wasn't it?" he shouts over the engine noise.

"Correct," answers the President, also shouting.

"Didn't wanna be taking you to the wrong place," jokes the pilot, handing the President a spare headset and gesturing for him to put it on. The instant Matías dons the gear, static-riven cross talk leaps into his ears. The control tower is telling them they have right of way ahead of the Continental flight to Guam. Well naturally, knowing the President's on board.

"Excellent weather conditions, so we should have a smooth ride," the pilot assures him, switching from control tower to intercom. Always busy talking, this man.

"When we get there, could we circle a few times around the reef before we land?" asks the President into his microphone.

"Sure thing. She's your plane today, sir," comes the reply. "Your word is my command."

Clearance for takeoff has apparently been given, and the Islander cuts along the taxiway in front of the Continental Boeing 737 and onto the runway. Then, in the moments before becoming airborne, even the pilot falls silent to concentrate on the operations at hand. They start to climb, reach cruising altitude, and nose off in the direction of Brun Reef, at which point the commentary resumes. Okay, so he talks a lot, Matías still likes the guy. Part of the reason he sits up front in the copilot's seat is to watch him play with all the buttons and switches while chatting over the intercom; no one else in Navidad is as frank and open with the President. Originally a crop duster from America, he somehow drifted across the Pacific and up until two years ago was working for PMA, a small-time carrier that ferries missionaries from island to island. Then he was piloting Cessnas and Pipercubs for a private concern in Guam, when he got himself fired for causing a minor accident (that just happened to affect Matías's fate in a big way). At which point the Navidad government picked him up and gave him this cushy job as an offering to appease Providence on the part of Matías. And ever since, the President has flown once or twice a month in the man's Islander.

For the entire thirty-minute flight, the pilot holds forth on his favorite subject: what a waste it is for the government to keep a plane like this all to itself when it only flies full capacity, what?—three, four times a year? And there's the redundancy of separate government bureaus flying twice in one day to the same island on different errands. Turn this into a national airline and carry civilian passengers, why they could almost operate in the black. Navidad only needs to lay out the venture capital, then leave it to him to run; he guarantees much cheaper, more convenient air service than now. A win-win proposition the way he tells it.

"So you buy another plane this size and hire two more pilots, because you gotta pump it up first. But in the long run, you'd be saving the country money, and I'd be making some myself too. The demand is there...Ah, look, there's Brun."

Sure enough, up ahead under a wisp of cloud is a long, thin land form. The pilot eases the throttle and gradually brings the plane down closer to the reef.

Brun is a ring formation broken in one place, a very misshapen ring, with the widest patch above sea level at the point furthest east from the break. It's here that a few fishing families live. A kilometer away is a simple landing strip; otherwise it's just a handsbreadth of empty land and coco palms. Inside the reef are two or three tiny unoccupied islets, used only for fishing operations. Today there's not a single wave; the waters around the atoll are absolutely calm. A single car can be seen moving along the lone stretch of road that runs up the bare backbone of sand. As instructed, the pilot flies three complete circles above the reef. According to the diagrams included in Suzuki's plan, the oil depot would be built inside the ring, to the immediate right of the break. That's where they say they can moor deep-draft tankers with only minimal dredging.

A pickup truck is waiting beside the landing strip. Two wardens from the government outpost watch the plane land, their expressions immediately changing when they spy the President on board. One of them shouts an apology as he runs up to the Islander while the engines are still roaring. "We only heard someone was arriving from the capital. We didn't know His Excellency was coming. We only have this truck."

"Doesn't bother me. You two ride in back," the President tells the executive secretary and Home Office man. Améliana he seats up front before getting in next to her. The two Brun wardens take a minute to discuss the situation, then one takes the driver's seat and the other climbs in back. The dirt road glares white in the blazing sun. Once the plane's engines die down, everything goes absolutely still, the better for the pilot to take a noonday nap in the shade before the return trip.

The President instructs the driver where to go. They drive for twenty minutes, with the sea to either side, until the road gives out. The President gets out and prompts Améliana to follow. The three men from the back of the truck dust themselves off as they set foot on the white coral ground. By the side of the road is a hut, whose only occupants, children, peer out startled by the sudden visitors. Their clothes are ragged, but they themselves look bright and cheerful. There seems to be no adult around. No boat tethered to any post where nets hang drying near the water, so maybe the father is out fishing. But where's the woman of the family?

The executive secretary and Home Office man stand by idly, looking utterly confused. What made the President want to come here to this godforsaken place? Matías ignores them and walks off down a footpath into a coconut grove. He disappears among the trees, with Améliana close behind. The other four men have no choice but to follow. And twenty paces back, their curiosity piqued, the children tag along cautiously.

Several hundred meters through the coco palms, the President emerges onto a beach. Before his eyes the coral steeps pure blue in the crystalline waters, but across the lagoon he can see a dark gray line. To the right must be the exit to the open sea, not quite visible from this position. This side of the mouth is a small deserted islet, concealing the opening on the other side. There's not a boat anywhere inside the reef. Probably all gone out after big fish at this time of day. Most fish school on the outer shoals, right where the reef drops off into deep water.

The President sits himself down on a toppled coco palm. The trunk is still rooted and arches up into the air, so his short legs dangle. The four men look on from a distance, hesitating to go near. Améliana, however, approaches and leans on the tree trunk. Matías mops his forehead with a handkerchief and gazes at the sea before him. The sea breeze is wonderful.

According to Suzuki's plan, the projected facility is to be built between that deserted islet and this side of the reef. Ten tankers all moored together in a row, and right about here on this beach they'll build an office in an Island Security compound. The road will need to be extended up to here from back at that hut. The crew for the facility will probably sleep on board ship, so other personnel will have to commute back and forth by motorboat. No way for them to build a bridge across. A floating causeway perhaps? The biggest issue is the dredging. A good mooring depth is one thing, but if they have to dredge the channel to bring in the ships, it'll be a huge undertaking. Rip into the reef and fishing will suffer.

The President calls over his two men and asks them to tell the local wardens to go take a hike somewhere. Améliana stands behind the President. The children hide among the coco palms a safe distance away.

"This is where the Japanese want to build an oil base," Matías tells his three companions. "They proposed it the other day, and I'm considering the ramifications." He has to speak up over the breeze that blows Améliana's hair in waves. "See that little island? Between there and this beach here, they want to moor ten thirty-thousand-ton tankers."

"That Japanese visitor the other day?" asks Jameson. He's good.

"The very same. As he explained it, Japan has been readying reserve oil for a long time now, and apparently this amount here would give them some measure of security. We lie nearby the shipping lanes from the Middle East, and politically we're stable. Our ties with Japan go way back. So it's ideal, he says. The annual maritime leasing fees would generate a sizeable income. Though of course, by the same token, we'd also become much more closely tied to them. Still, all in all, not a bad scenario, I'd say."

"The scale of the operation would be tremendous," says the executive secretary.

"Absolutely—it would take five years to complete."

"Who would be assigned to it on our side?" asks the Home Officer staffer. A typical green young bureaucrat's question, straight to the technicalities.

"How about setting up a new coordinating office especially for the project? After all, it would involve the Home Office and Foreign Office and Bureau of Outer Islands."

"Right, there may be difficulties negotiating with the locals here," Jameson comments. "Even with a massive settlement, folks around here aren't going to budge."

"That's where you boys come in. It's up to you to do something about that," says the President. "I don't want any opposition in the capital. The legislators will go along with it. The Tamang faction has been quiet lately. No real grounds for ordinary citizens to get up in arms either."

Yes, but what about those strange handbills pasted up around town? he remembers. *Whoever's been doing that just might try something.* But supposing Island Security gets that backing from Japan a little earlier—that would make it much easier to squelch any opposition movement. Actually, once this project gets under way, it should facilitate things politically.

"And have you already committed to this plan?" asks the Home Office staffer, his tone polite but heavy with innuendo. He has no personal objections to the President's directives and never really expected to be taken into consultation anyway. All he wants to know is where things stand, a practical career concern.

"I wouldn't say so," Matías responds evasively, walking a few steps toward the lapping water's edge. Well, *has* he made up his mind? One thing and one thing alone is clear: the decision will be his. He's only talking up the plan to the two of them now so that when the time comes, they'll be able to move on it as required; he's not asking their opinion. So what will it be? He sees Améliana sitting on a rock not far away. What does she make of this setting? Or won't she say? She just sits there staring at the sea, not a thing written on her face. Matías walks across the sand toward her. A hermit crab scurries out of the way of his feet. He does not see the creature, but Améliana's eyes race after it. She cringes slightly. Matías sits down next to her.

"What do you see here? Won't you tell me?"

"Do you really want to know?"

"Yes, if there's something you see."

"Up to now you've closed your eyes to what you did not want to see. Isn't that so?"

"Meaning what?"

"Exactly what I said. Sometimes not knowing is better."

"No, I want to know. For better or worse, I want to know everything."

"Oh. That's brave of you," says Améliana. There's not a trace of irony in her voice. The matter-of-fact words are whisked away in the wind. She takes up his hand from where it rests on the rock beside her and grasps it firmly. She looks out to sea.

Matías looks out at the same sea, his hand in hers. Inside the reef all is still, nothing moves even on the further shore. And beyond, above a horizon hidden from view rise layers of stratus cloud. But that is far, far away. Overhead there's not one single cloud, only the sun slowly, patiently heating the earth below. Let the palm trees put out all the shade they can, the tree trunks would still be baked through to the core.

Matías wipes the sweat from his forehead with his linen suit sleeve.

His mind dives beneath the lagoon. As far as the eye can see, the inner reef is alive with schools of tiny brightly colored fish. A shadow slants down as a big fish passes above. In a flash, fingerlings light off in all directions, and for one brief instant, the water shimmers with countless invisible scales. When was the last time he saw such a scene with his own eyes? Even as president, Matías still feels the urge to go diving. Not with those overblown scuba tanks, but just mask and fins and snorkel. Here, on a quiet shore far from the Presidential Villa, his hand entrusted to a young woman, gazing on a silent sea. More silent than silence.

Something comes into view above the surface. He watches as a large dark *presence* looms into view between the beach and the far shore. Perhaps several hundred meters out. What can it be? With no discernible shape, it just hovers there, motionless to the naked eye. No, it's not moving. Just a chain of black shadows cast darkly upon the surface of the sea. The sun beats down as harshly as ever, his forehead still beads with sweat, yet everything suddenly goes dark, his body is enveloped in a strange chill. As if he's been shut inside something. The shadows grow darker and increasingly real; their weight almost ripples the calm sea.

Matías strains to see as there before him, slowly, very slowly, the shadows take on substance, becoming a line of long objects. Ships. A cordon of ships squatting low in the still waters. Immobile bulks, never to budge. They've made their last voyage and come here to die. After logging so many thousands of leagues back and forth from the Persian Gulf to the Far East, bellies filled amid desert sand and salt tides, they sailed off past Kharg Island, withstood the fiery wastes of the Indian Ocean, squeezed through the narrow Malacca Strait to prow northward time and again, only to end up here for eternity, their final mooring. It almost makes Matías feel sentimental. He's not himself. What does he know about tanker routes?

The shock of realization brings ten massive tankers into menacing focus. He knows he's sitting on a beach hundreds of meters away, and yet he can see each ship in amazing detail. There's a bridge with railings jutting out from both sides. The round portholes of each officer's cabin. The vestigial smokestacks of the gas turbine engines. The huge pipes that run the length and breadth of those vast hulls, the countless valves and pumps, the catwalk extending over the bow, the rigging all so impossibly clear. Men stripped to the waist, running laps on the deck. Anything to relieve the endless boredom. Well, how much work can there be for the crew of a stationary ship? They hardly speak as they slouch past one another.

On closer observation, Matías can make out reddish spots of rust on the broad sides. The crew have grown sloppy, it's been ages since anyone did any hard work and scraped the hulls. He remembers how much he himself once enjoyed the task, yet here no one lifts a finger...And now they're gone, there's not a soul left on board. The jogging crewmen have all disappeared and left the ships deserted. Little by little the rust encroaches, no longer just on the pumps and pipes and gadgets, but penetrating deeper and deeper into the very structure. Sea spray and oxygen join forces, sending feelers into the cracked paint, corroding the toughest iron. Below the waterline, the decay advances even faster; seawater presses at every nick and dent, drawing ever nearer to the tonnage inside through some magnetism of liquid to liquid, enticing the crude to come out.

Then one day, two ships burst their bottoms. Winds whip the lagoon, and the oil spreads slowly but surely out to sea. It may take a year or three times that long for it all to leak out, but that's nothing compared to the tens of the thousands of years that oil and water are fated to commingle.

Soon the other ships join in, their hulls ravaged by gaping holes, the metal plates emitting a sulfurous stench. The bombs come flying over the reef from distant seas and are followed in turn by satellite-guided missiles. The rumble of explosions is heard in Baltasár City, black smoke rises into the stratosphere, visible for hundreds of kilometers around. Citizens tremble in fear. It was all quite foreseeable: hoarding so much here in one place was practically asking someone to steal or burn or sink it. No need to look very far for a motive either; if the intention was to deal a major blow to the pride and economic might of a hated power, the locals can readily oblige. The notion that the other man's gains come at one's own expense is as old as humanity.

The crude oil slowly sinks to the bottom of the lagoon. The hundred-year-old cells of coral suffocate one by one; the ocean floor is sealed in a sticky euthanasic shroud that steadily kills off the schools of fish that once lived here. Dead coral looks so much like human bones. A mere coincidence of nature? But bones are bones, and there are deeper parallels to be drawn, lessons laid down—for whom? By whom? The dead coral? The people who killed them? God? No, not God. God died before all of them. If everyone here has Catholic names but no one goes to Mass on Sunday, it's because God is dead.

Dead. The beach is littered with the oil-choked bodies of seabirds, just more bones and a few feathers slicked down with tar. A vision of pitch-black depths. Three million kiloliters of crude oil now cover everything inside Brun lagoon, a symbol of things to come for the earth at large. Sadly, not a soul is left to witness this scene, much less mourn. There's no one left at all.

The ships break apart. First one, then another. Devoured by rust and battered by winds, the welds split open in the rocking waves, reducing the hulls to scrap metal, irregular lumps of oxidized iron. Red bones beside white coral bones, both foaming gently at every high tide. No fish to be seen anywhere. The shores deserted, though the sky is still blue. Only the white clouds look down silently on the remains of the ten tankers.

In a daze, Matías wipes his forehead, now slick with sweat, then disengages his hand from her grip and stands up. Just standing on his own two feet should break the spell. At least he can turn his back on all he's seen and look up at the sky. The blue, however, is no different from the sky in the hallucination. It changes nothing. He looks behind him and sees the children still peeking from behind the palm trees a few paces away. This helps bring him back to reality, until he detects a look of alarm in their faces as well, which only makes him more afraid. *Have those kids seen what I just saw?* he wonders. *Even without channeling through Améliana's hand, did they see the same things on their own?*

Matías turns away from their troubled eyes and looks warily toward the sea. The lagoon seems as calm and clear as ever. Glancing to the right, he sees Jameson and the Home Office man drawing something in the sand with sticks. Os and Xs, a game of tic-tac-toe. Those two didn't see a thing. At most they must think their boss was just sitting there surveying the water with that strange girl. The children, however, saw. They witnessed those visions.

"Was that the truth?" he asks Améliana under his breath. He was dead right in thinking this woman has special powers, but their effect is so distressing and unfavorable to him personally that it puts a quiver in his voice.

"'Truth' isn't to be trusted," says Améliana. She chooses her words precisely; her tone is unerring and deliberate. She wants him to understand. "Better not use that word. Grasp at 'truth' and you'll only get your hand cut off."

"So then, that was all your…" He searches for the best way to put it. "That was *you* envisioning things?"

"I don't have such powers. All I can do is pick up on the currents taking shape here and now."

"Which means one day all that might really happen?"

"That I can't say. The future's not that simple. I'm only a switchboard. So many things pass through me and scatter in all directions. What you saw is only one of many futures for the choosing. It's you who are in a position to decide. Unless you choose to make it real, it's only a hallucination. Don't you see?"

"Unbelievable. Totally unbelievable. Let me ask just one more thing: how many years would it take for all that to happen?"

"That I can say least of all. It isn't for us to know. It's all just hints and signs. Five years? Two hundred? I can't tell. But if it's two hundred years, you can safely take that course. The plan should bring us many benefits here, no one is going to fault what you did two hundred years ago. But…" Améliana starts to speak, then drifts into silent thought. The wind rustles the palm fronds overhead. Behind her, several butterflies flit about, the bushes stir. The sweat dries on his forehead. "But if it's only five years, then what would you have me say?"

"I get the picture. Don't say anything. I saw what I needed to see. And I now know the kind of power you have. The rest is for me to think over good and hard on my own. Well, then, let's be going."

05

Five AM. Matías wakes. Breathing only a few times a minute, he hasn't so much as twitched until now, yet when his internal timer switches on, his wake-up circuits surge with juice. Microscopic solenoids in his eye sockets throw tiny levers, springing the hinges of his eyelids. His retinae make out a blur of ceiling. Slowly he raises himself upright on his futon and looks around. His head is a complete blank.

A piece of paper lies beside his pillow—*Take bath. Put away memo.* That's right, he's supposed to do what's written there. No need to think, just follow the instructions (conscious thought he can jumpstart later). Somewhere in the back of his mind he knows the handwriting. He even has a sneaking suspicion that it's a note to himself and that he's done all this before. Minimum brain functions can manage this much activity. No self-destructive impulses this morning

He files away the note and heads for his Japanese bath. He slides open the door, steps in, tosses his yukata night robe into a hamper, opens a second inner door, and carefully crosses the slippery wood-slatted floor. There's a window, but outside it's still dark. One by one, he removes the planked lid from the tub and steps over the lip of the tub, slowly shifting his weight to the foot in the water before stepping in with the other and lowering himself down. He stretches out his arms and legs. His body weight is buoyed by the water, his muscles support only the neck up.

He soaks, relaxed but not letting himself drift back to sleep. He must concentrate on reviving his mental capacities little by little. No, that's backwards, a dog chasing its own tail; his mind has to revive before he can concentrate on anything. He repeats his name and title: *His Excellency, President of the Republic of Navidad Matías Guili*, consciously moving his lips...one...two...*That's you*, he tells himself, *the President. Without you this country has no leader*. It would be sheer chaos, an invitation to ruin. So put some feeling into it! Like a real potentate with his grip on everything.

One hundred repetitions. *Wouldn't it be nice*, the odd thought skims across his not-yet-himself mind, *if we could recite other names for a change?* Somewhere deep in the recesses of his memory he hears a beautiful, rhythmic chorus. A litany of names, an ever-permutating sameness. Generation after generation, a dizzying trail leading all the way from mythic past to pre-modern times. Buddhist monks chanting dawn service in a temple. How many decades ago did he hear them for a month of mornings?

> *Mahaguru Vipashyin Buddha*
> *Mahaguru Shikhin Buddha*
> *Mahaguru Visvabhû Buddha*
> *Mahaguru Khrakucchanda Buddha*
> *Mahaguru Kanakamuni Buddha*
> *Mahaguru Kâsyapa Buddha*
> *Mahaguru Sakyamuni Buddha*

Seven generations. Only then did the historic Buddha Gautama Sakyamuni enter the picture. And still the novices drone an interminable succession of disciples, voices echoing in the dark worship hall, white breaths hanging in the chill air.

First Patriarch Mahâkâsyapa
Second Patriarch Ânanda
Third Patriarch Chanavâsa
Fourth Patriarch Upagupta
Fifth Patriarch Dhritaka
Sixth Patriarch. . .

From Western heavens to Eastern lands, the Lamp of Dharma passed down to their own present-day *roshi*. A hypnotic recitation of enlightened transmissions master-to-disciple, ensuring a collective body of wisdom. If only he could chant such reverend names! But no, this is all he's got. No tradition, no lineage, just a farce of fealty.

First President Cornelius
Second President Matías Guili
Third President Bonhomme Tamang
Fourth President Matías Guili

End of service. Hardly six generations of holy ancestors culminating in the Buddha. Nothing but idiots, himself included. All three of them put together couldn't boast a hundredth of the wisdom of any one of those Zen patriarchs. Nor does Matías believe this short list is in any way legitimate, especially not himself.

Back then when Matías was in his twenties, Ryuzoji training at a Zen temple every morning, he'd rise before dawn and sit in the cold, mouthing incomprehensible sutras, followed by that endless invocation of Buddhas and patriarchs. Then finally he'd receive a scant serving of watery gruel for breakfast. He remembers nothing else. No, there was something, a strange phrase—*If you meet the Buddha, kill him. If you meet a patriarch, kill him.* Ruthless, but vitalizing words—what was *that* all about?

Thoughts waft through his head like vapors rising from the tub. The coarse imperfection of the spoken word. The sound of his own voice as it reaches his ear. The flimsy excuse of a name. Another silent voice tells him, *These things are you.*

His hundred repetitions finished, he glances around the dimly lit bathroom, then looks down at a pathetic drift of pubic hair and a shriveled cock, thighs refracted even shorter in the water, feet vanishing in the murk. Reaching out, he sees his own two arms. Totally naked, totally meaningless. Better he should hand rule over to the best-looking man in the country. Wouldn't citizens look up to a fine, strong physique? Wouldn't somebody who embodied such obvious qualities, anybody, make the people happier? Why didn't they do things like that in America or Japan? Maybe then they'd stay contented on their own turf and not come bothering everyone else? No, nations are bullshit.

He gets up out of the tub, dries off with a bedsheet-sized towel, tramps into the changing room, wraps himself in a fresh yukata, and walks down the hall. Twenty steps, then he opens the door to the dojo. Before him scowls his formally attired official portrait. He kneels down solemnly before it; an image of himself the way others see him. Yes, this is the man the country needs. He must drill it in, take on that role and work another day.

Fifteen minutes later, President Matías Guili returns to his private study, unlocks a desk drawer, and takes out his official log. All of yesterday's events he himself will have written down there the night before. He just has to read through his notes, a motley of memos on salient works-in-progress, questions to be decided today along with assorted commentary. The issues for immediate consideration this morning are public servant salaries; whether to allocate state assistance to the latest Arenas agricultural venture; selecting someone with no conflict of interest to head the vastly expanded M. Guili Trading Co; and then there's that big conundrum—what to do about the Japanese oil depot project. Reference materials from the Finance Bureau on the salary question are in a separate envelope. A three-percent wage hike seems perfectly in order, but the hard part, as ever in all countries, is funding it. If a natural incremental increase in customs duties won't do the trick, then by some other means. Navidad's income taxes are next to nil. How about shifting the entire educational budget, teaching staff and all, onto ODA and asking Japan to foot the bill? Got to take a tough stance toward Japan, find an angle they can't refuse. Support for the Arenas farm is fine by him. Those oranges were good. And if it means he can bring the Arenas folks into his camp, then a share of the assistance package will find its way back as a political contribution to him, completely cutting out the Tamang faction, with no strain on the state coffers. He takes running notes on a handy memo pad. Just business as usual.

After that there are another twenty-odd items to consider. Why the hell does he have to decide all this crap? Which is to say, why have all three presidents—Cornelius, himself, and the three-month wonder Bonhomme Tamang, but especially himself because he's been in office the longest—why have they failed to foster either a responsive bureaucracy or reliable legislators in this country? It's a struggle for the Executive Office to get the various bureaus to crank out any paperwork at all, let alone propose new policies and enact them. He can't delegate anything. Whether financial matters or diplomatic relations or even domestic in-house business, the sad truth is they barely manage to nod their know-nothing heads as prescribed in some imported textbook, when the real task is for them to see the big picture, line up a battery of proposals in response, then submit their write-ups for presidential approval. That's the only way to get on with work. But no, they overbudget willy-nilly so nothing balances. They project annual revenue growth on no basis whatsoever, then inflate budget figures to match. They draft bills that don't do anybody any good. And the legislators are even worse, never thinking beyond what might profit their own constituent villages, using any means possible to squeeze the state for money, anything to maintain a thin veneer of political prowess. Legislative referendums are a circus. He's put up with these shenanigans for eight years now. Oh, he tries to get those idiots to see reason, scattering the necessary incentives their way, applying pressure behind the scenes. He's done his best to run this place like a real country, and not once have that lot come up with a single constructive idea. All right, he's slipped up on occasion. He never intended to lose his elected seat to Tamang. Not because he especially wanted to cling to power, but simply because he knows there's no one else who can keep the brainless bureaucrats and even dumber legislature in line. Predictably, after just one month in office, Tamang ruined everything.

And then the very next month he provoked that ridiculous squabble with Japan. He put on such a big show—Proud Leader of a Self-sufficient Modern Nation!—despite Navidad's singular lack of any industry. Matías should have ignored the fool and just gone back to minding his M. Guili Trading Co. With all the bureaucratic ties he'd cultivated over eight years, he could easily have told them not to come poking around. The country could go fuck itself, he'd keep his enterprise afloat until things eased up enough for a comeback. But no, Tamang had to go stick his silly little fingers where they didn't belong. He initiated a detailed review of certain "pet projects" Matías had okayed as president. He looked into the Navidad Teikoku Hotel and the story behind its construction. Undue scrutiny that served no one, nothing but a self-righteous bid for popularity. A genuinely stupid move.

Then the stupid heroics were cut short by his death. And in the ensuing turmoil when something had to be done and fast, when national opinion was unanimous that former President Matías Guili must resume office, when the enticements and timing dovetailed so perfectly to win him over, Matías came forward. And this time, without hesitation, he disbanded the legislature. Extreme circumstances called for emergency measures, so for the interim the President decided to rein in all powers save for the judicial authority of the court (with one proviso, to overturn that as well if necessary). The United States took exception—"Somewhat less than democratic," regretted the cordial diplomatic letter—but he gave them desultory assurances that it was a temporary recourse until stability was restored and the legislature could fulfill its proper duties. Predictably, Japan made no comment. Matías's deep, dark channels to Japanese politicos guaranteed benign acceptance. And so a year passed. The legislature stayed out to pasture with no plans for reconvening, and meanwhile the Executive Office assumed the functions of all seven ministries to effectively run the country. The President decided everything, aided by a handful of the more able staff directly under him.

Call him dictatorial, call him authoritarian, the nation needed a strong man on top just to stay on course. But now, as the President eyeballs the papers spread out before him—Suzuki's outlined proposal, the letter from the "Friend of the Islands," his own notes on administrative issues—that course is about to change in a big way. A Japanese oil depot at Brun Reef is no mere question of maritime leasing affecting only the outer islands; it will tie his little country to Japan for decades to come. Matías has always focused on strengthening Navidad's Japan connections, but this takes things to a whole new level. Colonization by force would be one thing, but to voluntarily enter into another country's dominion like a good little slave? He can just hear the outcry. If anything goes wrong from this moment forward it will all be blamed on this decision, one made without even the semblance of a vote. He'll be sealing his own fate; he might as well declare himself an out-and-out dictator. Is he ready to take such a big step?

Even more problematic, what if that "Friend of the Islands" is correct in his information? A secret Japanese military base? People will be more than just outraged when they find out after it's already built. Why is Japan acting so covertly? Couldn't they come clean with their old buddy Guili? Isn't there enough fish to go around? Whose idea was it, at what stage, to sweep this under the tatami? How much of this does Kurokawa know? If he doesn't lay claim to it, then other elements must be operating under cover of his political apparatus. So here's the real problem for Matías: should he tell Suzuki he knows about the Marine Self-Defense Force base? If Kurokawa's not in on it, then Suzuki won't know either. Or else Suzuki will know that Kurokawa doesn't know. Or maybe our "Friend of the Islands" is simply playing games to undermine the whole petroleum stockpiling scheme. All sorts of different possibilities suggest themselves.

If the part about the Self-Defense Force *is* true, then taking the long view, it doesn't really change the name of the game, it just raises the stakes. No, let's just consider the oil question for now. Here he is, Matías Guili, a man who's devoted his entire career as president to improving economic relations with Japan. No, even before that, when the islands were an American protectorate and they were gearing up for independence, Cornelius could see America's postwar influence giving way to Japan. Cornelius was so farsighted, thinks Matías. Does he himself have as much foresight? In his position, would Cornelius make the same decision?

And how about Tamang? Tamang was more pro-American than Matías ever was pro-Japanese. Had he remained in office long enough to backtrack on everything Matías ever accomplished, he'd have sucked up to the American government and American money. Okay, they weren't all that different, the two of them; they both relied on bigger guns. Come to think of it, Cornelius was probably the closest thing Navidad ever had to a true independent. Sure, he entrusted relations with Japan to Matías just as he looked to Tamang for dealings with America. Clearly balance-of-power jockeying. Did that make Cornelius less anti-American than he liked to appear? How close were Cornelius and Tamang anyway? Maybe he's fooling himself—maybe Matías wasn't the heir apparent. What if that sly old fox Cornelius was a more devious politician than Matías gave him credit for? What if his scenario was to first elicit Japanese support during Matías's four years in office, then to use the next four years under Tamang to kiss and make up with America? It saddens Matías to think of it. If he really wasn't the only successor, then he's ruined the grand Cornelius Doctrine by eliminating Tamang, hasn't he? But then, Cornelius never set up any political structure capable of counterbalancing him and Tamang. The only thing they could do was cancel each other out, though Matías had the competence to hold onto the presidency much longer (*if you can call a violent end to Tamang's chances a question of competence*, he mutters to himself).

What would Tamang have done in his place? Supposing it were America instead of Japan talking up this petro-military base, what decisive action would President Tamang have taken? Politically, economically, the very idea of an independent country of seventy thousand is patently absurd. New nations have shot up like weeds in the postwar world, but how many ex-colonies really have the stuff to make it on their own? Past some cutoff point—half out of guilt, half out of powerlessness, or else simply to drop dead weight—the colonial masters just acquiesced to all the rumblings for independence. The United Nations heartily supported the move, the earliest independents heartily welcomed the extra company. Mere regions with hastily sketched outlines and no special qualifications were granted nationhood. Navidad being one of them, as if Matías didn't know. The smaller the country, the easier to win a consensus and turnkey an administration. No different climates or economic zones or religions or ethnicities to unify, so no need to drum up external enemies. No political acrobatics, no eternally-in-our-hearts-and-minds imperial family, no presidential elections every four years (though Cornelius judged correctly that the royal road would never work here and opted for an electoral system).

Size does matter, reflects Matías. The main problem for us micro-countries is that we have to align ourselves with others to make us look bigger. The world is thick with friendship accords and economic conventions all vying to compensate for size. And Navidad is one of the smallest fish around in that swamp. But hey, we wanted independence—we couldn't breathe shoved up under America's big fat armpit. People seemed to think independence meant one-hundred-percent freedom handed out just like that. So the primary task in leading this tiny speck of a country is to reconcile popular awareness to the realities of international politics and borderless economies.

Again Matías thinks, *What if Tamang were alive?* Immediately after his unfortunate death, the rumor mill in Baltasár City went wild: Tamang wasn't really dead, the body in the coffin at his funeral had been a dummy, the man himself was being held prisoner in a secret dungeon beneath the Presidential Villa. It was all Matías Guili's doing, he imprisoned our man and grilled him for days on end. . .When the actual truth is that Tamang lies six feet under in the Baltasár Municipal Cemetery, and that Matías never needed his confession or advice on anything. *And yet, what if Tamang could voice some opinion regarding the present circumstances*, the thought keeps nagging him, *what the hell would he say?*

Or instead of another president, what view would a whole other political system have to offer? What if—pesky creatures, these "what ifs"—what if this country had a normal functioning democratic legislature? What stance would it take toward Japan's offer? They'd debate the issue a hundred times over, reject taking any active steps, and wind up in a muddle. Matías pictured each legislator, each face; he did a mental tally of their schoolboyish factions and their cliquish votes; and he came to the same conclusion: that countries, like individuals, should be decisive. Yes, one pilot works best.

The world takes a dim view of dictators. Fine, let them criticize him after he's dead. Let them curse him, dig up his grave, what does he care? Let it be known, there are times when one man has to call the shots for his country. Matías is getting worked up now. He's a regular wizard of a politician, he is, and will be remembered for generations to come (not that he's sired any offspring of his own, one proof that he's on the level. No nepotistic dynasty to follow, thank you, that's not his style. No stashing or bequeathing the wealth. It's just his one generation, and he's not glued to any seat. Everything for the sake of his country! Or is that too shameless? Still, he has to admit, the lack of children was providential. That's why he married María Guili, the perfect barren companion. That's why raising a family never came up when he proposed to Angelina. And anyway, all Angelina ever had to say on the subject was that a pregnant whore was the lowest of the low).

No, he stands alone. No children but his countrymen. Whether they accept it or not, Navidad's seventy thousand are all his babies. Men and women, children and elders alike, good farmers and poor fishermen, incompetent officials, self-seeking legislators and hopeless businessmen, youngsters napping in the banana groves, kids diving for crabs off the reefs, the working girls at Angelina's—everything he can con out of Japan he shares with them all. When you're dealing with a big unaccommodating country like Japan, it's either con or be conned, so you're lucky to have Matías Guili on your side. He'll take them for more than they ever take from Navidad, and do it so they don't even know. That's the make-or-break challenge, thinks Matías. That's his conclusion for the morning.

Just then, he flashes back to what he saw yesterday at Brun Reef. What *was* that? If the base gets built, is that going to happen anytime soon? Think: Japan and Navidad aren't the whole story. So many countries now dispute that lazy stretch of the South China Sea, which until recently only saw the occasional fisherman. Interests on all sides are bristling at the mere scent of oil in the Spratlys. China even sent gunships and planted flags there, fabricating national myths that the islands had always been Chinese territory. To which neighboring Vietnam and the Philippines naturally reacted sharply. Everything hangs in the balance between force and rhetoric. If now the Japanese get in on the act, pursuing their own claims to steady growth, they'll want their own strategic outpost near those "developing" oil fields in the south.

It's just a premonition, but the day may come when even the Navidads become pawns in international ambitions for the Spratlys. Why else would anyone target mere fishing shoals if not to wipe out a base? Would Exocets do the job on the tankers? Or would it be larger, longer-range missiles for a "clean strike"? Kiloton-class fat boys with inertial guidance systems. He can just see them homing in, the entire lagoon evaporating in a blinding flash, leaving Brun Reef uninhabitable for centuries to come. Stockpiling crude oil is fine, but a secret Self-Defense Force base is practically inviting an airstrike. Though of course, an attack like that would really put Navidad on the map, decimation granting instant entrée into international society. That was the vision he saw yesterday.

Or it could all be a setup. Say Améliana isn't clairvoyant and it was just hypnosis. A bogus emissary sent as part of a cheap plot to throw him off. No politician worth his salt would get skittish over cheap scare tactics. Matías perks up as Améliana's face fades away. He must have been seeing things, the terror he felt some kind of mistake. Magic tricks don't last out the early morning hours. Stay real, man. Run the state without running off into imaginings, stay close to the ground and focus on the immediate play-by-play of political forces. Leave the distant future to philosophers with no responsibilities. Three months, half a year, a year, three years, five years from now, the Brun Reef project won't seem so bad at all (the words "ten years from now" don't exist in politics). If need be, yesterday's vision can be interpreted into the next decade. The world may be teetering on the brink of disaster, just let the present order hang on for another shaky ten years. Then let big change come. Time enough to gather strength. Which is why a base in Navidad will come in handy. He'll go through with the plan.

That's his decision for the morning. Enough rumination, thinks Matías, breakfast awaits. Time to move on to the pleasures of white rice with plenty of sashimi, miso soup, seaweed, and pickles.

⚡

Two thirty PM. Suzuki flies in again on the morning flight and finds a message left for him at the Navidad Teikoku Hotel requesting a meeting ASAP. He beats a path to the Presidential Villa and is ushered into the largest conference room, where he's met by the President, Executive Secretary Jim Jameson, a junior official from the Home Office he's met once before, a middle-aged man introduced as a section chief in the Bureau of Outer Islands in charge of Brun Reef, and a young woman whose presence no one bothers to explain. Probably a stenographer or whatnot for writing up the talks, Suzuki imagines, balking at the number of people he's up against. Here he thought he'd be one-on-one with the President like before.

The President shows him to his seat, then speaks. "Regarding your country's proposal to build a petroleum stockpiling facility at Brun Reef, the Republic of Navidad is prepared to make an official response." Matías pauses briefly and gazes up at the ceiling.

Can they really be prepared to take things to such a decisive level? wonders Suzuki, as he waits for what's to follow.

The President now fixes his gaze squarely on Suzuki. "Brun Reef is a sacred and inseparable part of the Republic of Navidad. We cannot, as a matter of principle, accede to its use merely to accommodate another country. Nevertheless, Navidad and Japan enjoy a long history of friendly relations. The peace and prosperity of the nations and peoples of the West Pacific depend in many ways on our continued mutual cooperation. Thus, at this time, in the spirit of friendship and in keeping with the basic directives of our nation's administration, we wish to accept Japan's proposal and promise to offer our full cooperation toward the joint realization of this project."

"Thank you very much indeed."

"May I suggest we now set up a steering committee comprised of representatives from both sides to handle the various aspects of planning until actual implementation. Then in, say, six months' time, when preparations are in place as per the committee's guidelines, the project can be announced to the general public."

Suzuki listens without comment, distracted by the young woman who keeps staring. It's as if she can see right through him.

"Let's wait to put anything in writing. Today, we'll do this all verbally. We need to elicit ideas from both sides." That much on the table, the President quickly turns off his official face. "How about this? You take our reply back to Japan and assemble your team, then draw up papers and courier them here so we can convene a plenary conference. I imagine you'll be dealing mainly with these three men. I'll just check in from time to time. That'll work, won't it? Of course, you shouldn't expect us just to kowtow to Japan's demands."

"Of course not."

"These must appear to be real negotiations. So be prepared, we might even scrap the whole plan."

"I understand."

"And one more thing, about our little talk the other day on what stance Navidad should take internationally regarding the project, we'll think of something. We're an independent nation, we can come up with our own directives. At least for the time being, we have no intention of opening that up for discussion."

"I apologize if what I said was presumptuous. Please strike it from the record, if you will."

"Fair enough. It was fine as opinions go, but no longer needed. I'll think for myself."

Suzuki falls silent and lowers his eyes. The young stenographer doesn't seem to be taking any notes; she just looks at him ominously.

"That's it for now. From here on, you contact Jim Jameson." The President leaves it at that and stands up, takes a couple of steps, then turns around. "And as for that generous offer the other day, the bit about training our Island Security, let's just say it never happened. We'll defend ourselves, thank you, if you'd kindly inform whoever dreamed that up."

Suzuki shakes his head. *Why the heavy sarcasm?* He watches them exit one after another, but just as the young woman is almost out the door, she turns and looks him straight in the eye, then silently turns away and disappears.

Alone in the big conference room, Suzuki is left standing directly under a cooling vent, yet suddenly the air feels unbearably hot.

BUS REPORT 8

Naafa Village in the mid-afternoon. The villagers were stretched out on their sleeping mats at home or lazing in the shade of palm trees or secretly sharing someone else's bed. Right at the peak of the afternoon heat, a bus strolled into the local general store. The shop-keeper was dozing in the back room when he heard someone calling, and hobbled out to find a bus waiting at the counter.

"Sure is hot," said the bus.

"Yeah, mighty hot," said the shopkeeper. "I's jus' napping."

"Sorry to wake you. Some folks asked me to buy some things."

"Like what, f'rinstance?"

"Well," said the bus, glancing at a shopping list, "twenty bottles of Coke, ten bottles of Fanta Orange and three of Fanta Grape, plus five Dr. Peppers and eleven Sprites."

"Tall order," said the shopkeeper. He hurried to round up the required items, but came up short: only seven Cokes and four Sprites were chilled. So he did what any self-respecting shopkeeper does. He headed off to the stockroom for the missing number of bottles and mixed them in with the rest, warm or not. The bus didn't seem to notice. The shopkeeper took ages ringing up the bill, but the bus just waited patiently, handed over the money, loaded all the bottles, and drove off in a cloud of blue exhaust. The shopkeeper then returned to his nap.

The next day around the same time, the bus reappeared.

"More soda pop?" asked the shopkeeper.

"No, come to return the empties," said the bus, lining up the bottles on the counter.

Again the shopkeeper took ages calculating the deposit before paying out a grand total of $2.45, whereupon the bus collected its refund and left.

When Matías returned from Japan to Navidad at the age of twenty-eight, he spent the first half-year just looking around. A little cash went a long way in the islands, and with his modest savings he rented a hut cobbled together between three ma'a trees on the outskirts of Baltasár City. There was no hurry to find work, and anyway no employers in Navidad advertised openings in those days. Public administration attracted boring Guam University types, while the best jobs went to the brightest returnee graduates of the University of Hawaii or West Coast colleges. The few US-interest companies likewise hired returning American alumni. Local capital was scarce; island businesses were small and got by with a workforce of extended family relations. Never mind, he told himself, he'd take it easy and wait. If he returned to Melchor Island, all he could do was fish or tend banana groves or help out with simple carpentry. But he had his pride and enough money set by to wait for something better. He just had to find the right opportunity.

Guili's was one of many mom-and-pop general stores that sold everything from groceries to clothes. The only particular advantage this one store had was its location in the heart of Baltasár City, and Matías heard they were looking for help. Old man Guili was getting on in years and was disinclined to carry heavy goods from the stockroom or do strenuous deliveries. As luck would have it, this Micael Guili also had Melchor origins. It was a start.

The wages were rock bottom. Matías expected as much; his visiting great-uncle from Melchor used to curse "that skinflint Guili." Matías, however, was thinking ahead. All he needed was a base of operations for his Japanese-style start-up venture.

Matías wrought great changes at the store. He got in Mr. and Mrs. Guili's good books through a show of honest hard work, then began to restock the shelves his own way. He started rumors about "the newfangled goods at Guili's," relying on hearsay to entice consumers to try new things. Just modern marketing. When the calculating Mr. Guili and keen-eyed Mrs. Guili saw their sales soar, they too overcame their conservative instincts and learned to trust their worldly young employee implicitly.

In January 1959 Matías took a month off to go to Japan. His sole aim was to find something major to market in Navidad. Ryuzoji, now an up-and-coming right-wing politician, paid for his passage in return for regular detailed reports on Navidad (Matías learned not to question Ryuzoji's motives for wanting this intelligence). By now Matías himself was no mere overambitious employee; he saw Guili's as his own enterprise, and his breakthrough came in the form of instant ramen noodles.

American aid dollars gave the islanders as much buying power as they'd had during the Japanese era. But what new product would strike people's spending fancy? Matías just knew it had to be some kind of food. The islanders already bought California rice, Campbell's pork and beans, and luncheon meat from America, soy sauce and Geisha-brand canned mackerel from Japan. None of it daily fare. Compared to the island staples—taro, ma'a, bananas, and reef fish—these were purchases for special occasions. The idea of opening a can of mackerel, topping it with soy sauce, and serving it over steamed rice came as a revelation, but it wasn't for every day.

While in Japan, Matías bunked at the Shinheiwa employees' dorm and bought packaged foods at a neighborhood shop to try out. Out of all the items he tested, instant ramen was clearly the most saleable. He could just see the islanders sitting down to packaged noodles once a week at village feasts. An instant offering to impress the kinfolk. Just put the noodles in a dish, add hot water, cover, and wait. Those magic three minutes of anticipation gave the illusion of participating in the cooking process, a tantalizing emotional hook that Matías recognized as a key sales point.

The very next day, Matías located a wholesaler and borrowed enough from Ryuzoji to buy seven gross of ramen—a thousand single-serving packages—plus a hundred plastic bowls and fifty kettles. He himself did the export paperwork, then hired a small truck from Shinheiwa to transport the goods to a shipping agent's warehouse. Matías knew he was onto a sure thing, and Ryuzoji took his young protégé at his word. Didn't success stories always start like this? A jubilant Matías flew back to Navidad via Guam, while the noodles and paraphernalia followed behind like poor cousins.

One link that he carried over from this time into later life was Itsuko, now his housekeeper; at the time, however, she was working at Shinheiwa. Three years earlier, a few months before his return to Navidad, Matías overheard Tsuneko complaining that her younger sister was out of work. She was also out of luck with men, but that was nothing new. Apparently, this Itsuko was forever chasing after lovers who subsequently ran off with her savings. The upshot was that Matías, taking Tsuneko's word for it that the girl had a high school education and office skills, asked Ryuzoji to take her on at Shinheiwa.

However slight the expectations of her unexpected employment, Itsuko turned over a new leaf and became a dedicated worker, not even eyeing her young male colleagues—or so Tsuneko reported in her letters to Matías. Of course, the real story wasn't so cut and dried; Itsuko still had her share of men troubles until finally, unmarriageable and unmanageable, she put love behind her. When Matías met her again on a visit to Japan in 1985—Tsuneko had died several years earlier—Itsuko was no longer broke but simply "bored to tears," so she accepted a job at the Navidad Presidential Villa, where she showed a surprising talent for housekeeping and cooking.

But back to the instant noodles (they should be ready by now). Once the thousand packages had safely arrived, Matías took the unprecedented step of actively promoting his product. First, he invited a few steady customers to a show-and-tell ramen tasting. The next day these regulars came back to buy some for their families, and the word slowly spread. Stock began to dwindle, sales picked up pace. Soon they'd half sold out. Matías hurriedly wired Itsuko instructing her to ship five thousand more packages. The ramen rush had begun, and Guili's held a monopoly. No one else knew where to source the product, but in those days before competitive merchandising, no laid-back island merchant would go out of his way to hunt down what sold well elsewhere. Whereas Matías went even further and introduced the first proof-of-purchase campaign: bring ten empty wrappers and get one package free! No one on the islands had ever seen anything like it.

The ramen sensation stirred up every household in the nation. To the islanders' uncomplicated way of thinking, ramen for Sunday luau became their idea of bliss. Navidad had entered the age of cash commercialism, and Matías was right at the center of it all. Just what Micael Guili thought of all this, he never said, though it's not hard to imagine. Seeing the business take off so dramatically under Matías, he must have been of two minds: pleased as the proprietor, but probably also feeling left behind, a vestige of an aging social order. Dynamic changes were overtaking society, that much he could embrace. But given his mere supporting role, all the new hubbub generated by his business surely made him feel awkward. By the time Micael died at the age of fifty-seven in 1962, he was feeling lost and betrayed; the orphan he'd taken in had walked away with everything.

Since ancient times, spoils to the victor have always included beautiful women. In the case of Matías, the beauty was María Guili—alas, at fifty-five, an older gem. The following year, after a regulation mourning period of seven months, the widow and Matías were wed. Romance wasn't a deciding factor. For Matías at thirty-five, upper-class María was an ideal partner for his ambitions.

The next task for Matías the entrepreneur was to transform Guili's General Store into Guili's Supermarket, the first ever in Navidad. The couple had come across this new model of retail outlet on their honeymoon in Japan, and Matías was excited; he saw the future and convinced María that here was a real investment opportunity for all the ramen earnings. He envisioned a gleaming new premises stocked ceiling high with Japanese products, maybe eventually even branching out into automobile sales. Ryuzoji's marketing and sales empire provided a ready example he could apply to his own country—all the more brilliantly for lack of any competitors. Yes, they would be riding the wave of commercialism that was sweeping the rest of the world.

In a tiny island nation, change always comes from outside. After Japan pulled out, and people still had no idea what the American era would bring, there was another man who was willing to wager on overseas connections. Born the noble son of a Gaspar Island clan elder, Gmataram Hogihoki Saranalak Yala Tombe Hati'ik Krami—the honorific titles go on and on, though better known as Cornelius—was heading up a not-so-covert independence movement and stoking expectations for the nation to come. Naturally he was eager to meet the man behind Navidad's new commercial mood swing. By then, Matías Guili the tycoon had expanded his supermarket into a chain, with four stores on Gaspar, three on Baltasár, and even one on Melchor.

American rule lasted twenty years, until 1965. It was high time for independence, both Navidad and America agreed. Situated between Subic Bay Naval Base in the Philippines and a major US Air Force presence on Guam, Navidad didn't need a military installation; indeed the absence of a base here made granting independence an easy choice. Why keep pouring money into a handful of useless rocks in the middle of the Pacific, when they could give the locals control and only minimal assistance? And while Navidad drew its share of criticism for not entering into a federation with Yap and Truk and Ponape, the population of seventy thousand decided to go their own way.

As leader of the independence movement, Cornelius sought strategic leverage away from America. He needed some country big enough to lend support, with ties to the region, though of course not part of the communist bloc. That could only have meant Japan (neither Spain nor Germany were realistic options at this late date), just as Japanese connections could only mean the Supermarketeer. Independence was practically contingent on enlisting Matías to the cause. Soon Matías found himself flying to Japan to drum up support among Ryuzoji's political and financial contacts.

Ryuzoji was then sitting in for an incumbent from his hometown in northern Kyushu whose sudden death left a seat open in the Japanese National Diet. He may have been only a conservative junior MP from a minor breakaway faction, but a parliamentarian's badge still carried clout. Ryuzoji introduced Matías to Japanese power brokers for secret talks. *This is the life*, Matías had to think, *when things go right*. Thanks to Matías, the Cornelius Doctrine succeeded in playing off America and Japan.

So when Cornelius fell ill in the middle of his second term, who was voted in as the next president? Matías Guili, architect of the pro-Japan national policy! Matías Guili, symbol of Japanese aid! Of course, there was also a matter of secret campaign funds from various well-connected sources in Japan.

Ryuzoji himself died the year before, after losing a fourth term in the Upper House, but by then Matías had already found a new fundraiser in one Jitsuzo Kurokawa. A Ryuzoji introduction even closer to the underbelly of Japan and, as crooked politicians went, much more skilled at making money, Kurokawa urged Matías to marshal a private guard in order to keep a lid on dissenting voices who might question his rewriting of the Cornelius Doctrine. Kurokawa had just the man for the job. Thus Island Security was born, with detective-turned-yakuza Katsumata heading up a hundred island boys. Decked out in green guayaberas, shorts, and army caps, they prowled the islands on surveil-lance and crime prevention duty, leaving the existing police to direct the next-to-nonexistent traffic.

The first achievement of the new president was to get Japan and America to review their foreign aid packages to Navidad. Let America think the Japanese no longer entertained territorial ambitions in the South Pacific, while Japan picked up a greater share of the ninety-percent US-supported island budget. He padded negotiations with all sorts of extra conditions: Japanese trading concerns should please increase their investments in island industries. And while they were at it, there were many natural scenic spots around the lagoon that might do nicely to develop into tourist venues for divers. Navidad may have lost out to Taiwan on intensive shrimp farming, but scallop exports still held promise, should anyone care to bid. A banana plantation on Baltasár Island was already bringing in a sizeable income for a Japanese produce cartel, and one of these days there'd be Arenas Orchard oranges to sell.

Most recently Matías had his Japanese think tank weighing the rela-tive risks and merits of realigning the dollar-pegged Navidadian currency to Japanese yen. With so many Japanese business dealings, why bother with exchange fluctuations all the time? This was just one more concrete step in his pro-Japan policy. Of course, certain pointy-headed intellectuals would grumble about Navidad forfeiting its economic independence, warning that encroaching Japanese corporations would pollute with impunity, calling it a step backwards toward colonialism. But hey, he's the President, what harm could there be in overlooking a few alarmist critics?

ϟ

Late at night in the Western-style living room of his private quarters, Matías sits talking to Améliana over tea. There's something he wants to ask her. The aroma of Earl Grey fills the room.

"That Japanese guy I met with this afternoon, Suzuki—what do you make of him?" asks the President.

Dressed in the same white blouse and mousy gray skirt from the daytime, she says nothing at first as she watches the rising wisps of fragrant steam. "That person knows very little," she confides to the teacups. "He says ten when he means three. A bad man, but only a messenger. Hides a lot behind his story but has nothing of his own to say."

"So he's just an errand boy. He hardly said a word today, but usually he's the type who likes to talk big."

Améliana says nothing, then concurs. "I can see that."

"And what about me?"

"I can't say." A firm answer. "If you speak to him directly, he changes. I can see only half—it's all misty, like the light between night and dawn."

"And what you showed me yesterday at Brun Reef?"

"What I showed you when?"

"I tell you, I saw it myself."

"Yes, but the future isn't clear. As I told you at the time."

"Since when have you been able to see these things?"

"Since I was a child, every now and then." She pauses, then speaks again. "When I was three, my mother had a jar of jam. It was from America, very precious. Once a month she bought bread for us to eat with the jam. We ate tiny dabs of it, so it lasted and lasted. The jar was up on a shelf. I saw how dangerous it was, and I said it would fall. But my mother said not to worry, the jar was far back on the shelf. The next day the jar falls and breaks. From the back of the shelf, suddenly it just falls. What could we do? We ate the jam off the floor, careful not to cut ourselves on the glass. We all thought it was funny, but my mother was heartbroken. These things happened many, many times."

"Where were you born?"

"In Ku'uda, on Melchor."

"Never been there, but I know what they say. That there are many people with special powers like yours from there."

"Yes. One time, I see a storm coming, so we all head for the hills. The storm comes, destroys all our houses, but no one was hurt."

"Were your parents pleased?"

"No, they scolded me."

"Why's that?" Matías asks, leaning forward.

"They said things happen because you say they will. You make the jar fall, you make the storm come!"

"Parents would think that, wouldn't they. Then what?"

"I tried to stop, but sometimes I just had to speak. And each time, they scolded me. When I said a friend would get hurt and it really happened, they said I mustn't play with my friends anymore, or the other parents would blame them. They called me a bad luck child."

"You never saw any good things?"

"Never. Only bad things."

"Sorry to hear that," mumbles the President, trying to imagine a life of constant calamities.

"…but nothing about myself, so I was never afraid. Sometimes I hurt myself, but I never knew until it happened. Because if I changed what was coming, made everything come out happy, I'd become a different person."

"How would that change you?"

"I'd lose my foresight. I'd become an ordinary girl."

"That quickly? Overnight?"

"I don't know, but soon enough."

"So you were told not to play with the other kids and you played all alone."

"I have three brothers and four boy cousins. I have girl cousins too, but I never played with them."

"Only with the boys?"

"Yes. We went up in the hills. Or sometimes we went walking on the sea."

"You did what?"

"Only when no one was watching. Sometimes we flew too, but that's dangerous. Because if someone sees you from below, you fall. Once a boy on a cliff saw us out on the sea and we sank. We all swam back laughing. But the boy never told on us. We made him doubt his own eyes and think we were swimming all along."

"Can't swim if you fall from the air, though."

"No, but we played other forbidden games."

"Oh?"

"We all went hiding in the woods, to feel around inside each other's clothes."

"With your brothers?"

"And cousins. We touched between our legs. All of us together."

"You were the only girl?"

"No other girls allowed. No girls ever came near me."

"And then?"

"Then later I began to have bleeding, I grew breasts, but still we played. We had fun, my brothers and cousins and me."

"And your parents didn't yell at you?"

"They never knew. They scolded me for going out with the boys, but it was better than me seeing other children get hurt."

"Your brothers never got hurt?"

"Sometimes, but I never saw it coming. Like with myself, I couldn't see with them. Then, my belly got big."

"You did *that* with them too?"

"Yes. All of us together. Even my youngest brother. He was only twelve, but he got his little thing up. It was cute."

"Naughty kids."

"Were we wrong?" Améliana asks Matías to his face. "Was it bad?"

"Well, badly handled," he hedges. He looks up at the ceiling and something catches the corner of his eye. Butterflies? He turns, but sees nothing there. Butterflies don't fly at night, not ordinarily.

"Perhaps. My belly was big, so my parents found out. They wanted to know the father, but I had no idea. It was the child of all seven boys."

"Didn't you see where your fooling around would lead?"

"No, what happens to me I don't see. I can't see it at all."

"And so?"

"I had a child. A beautiful little boy. But my mother took him away and told me to leave Melchor. I came to Baltasár City and finally found work with Madame Angelina."

"And the child?"

"The boy is three years old, being raised on Melchor. I go to see him as often as I can. He thinks I'm a much older sister."

"And your brothers?"

"No more fun and games for them. They come to see me when I visit, and we talk the whole day. My brothers and cousins all listen to what I have to say."

Strange woman, Matías thinks to himself. *Is hers a commonplace story, or is she totally mad?* Whatever the case, her powers of prediction might just be the real thing. Only, how to use them? They're wasted on her, and anyone who believes meets with misfortune. And what about her three brothers and four cousins? His political instincts are intrigued. Can they all be worked into some scheme of his?

The Legend of Lee Bo

On the ninth of August, 1783, the East India Company merchantman *Antelope* grounded upon the coral-reef'd isle of Coorooraa in the South Pacific. Having weighed anchor in Macau a fortnight prior, she met with a squall on her southward passage via a new route east of the Philippines but continued apace through high waves until First Watch, when just after Captain Henry Wilson ordered First Officer Benger to the helm, the wide open sea suddenly conspired to heave the vessel upon a sunken barrier that skirted a hundred-mile archipelago later known to the world as Pelew or the Palos Islands, though as yet unknown to the English Captain & crew of the *Antelope*. Whilst under full sail, with nary a warning, her keel struck coral just below the waterline, and she listed to a halt.

The tropic moon through the clouds that night shewed the acute nature of the *Antelope*'s predicament. Much to the consternation of all aboard, she had voyaged alone, hence without a sailing partner to pull her right. With no hope in sight, the luckless Captain called all hands on deck to cut down her three masts lest they tempt a toppling wind, then lowered two rowing boats laden with water, provisions, weapons & compass over the side away from the reef, and thus made ready to abandon ship, explaining that whilst none were dead or injured, the chances of survival in those uncharted waters were slim.

Came dawn, they sighted land some three leagues to the south. And as the sky grew light, other formations appeared to the north and east, although so indistinct in the distance as to be unapproachable. The Captain sent out the two rowing boats to reconnoiter the closest outcropping to the south, with instructions that should they meet any native inhabitants they were to comport themselves agreeably. For well did the enlightened European of the age know that not all primitives were man-eating hostiles, and their own precarious position left them little choice. Savages whose paths they crossed might indeed oblige them with fresh water, sustenance & knowledge as to sailings for more civilised realms.

In the intervening hours until First Dog, the crew lashed together the cut masts to fashion a raft as a precaution lest the *Antelope* go asunder. Presently the boats hove into sight with tidings good & bad. They had in fact landed, and discovered a cave of habitable aspect, as well as potable spring water, but the isle appeared to be singularly deserted and without food. Whereupon they hastened to load the raft with supplies and make for the cave ere nightfall. As the raft afforded no grace for personal belongings, each man donned as much clothing & withal as he could muster, which measure proved hazardous under the circumstances. The Helmsman Godfrey Minks did doubly clothed fall into the drink and, thus twice encumber'd, sink and drown ere his mates could lend a hand. Unfortunate man!

Much disheartened, the others remaining, together with two dogs, five geese, and a multitude of guinea fowl, were towed cautiously across the chop drawn by the rowing boats.

Reaching the isle past Second Dog, the sky dark and night well nigh, they moored the raft and waded ashore whilst the two boats returned to the ship. What joy it was to be safe on dry land! Lighting a fire, they supped on rations of hardtack & cheese & water, and so began their life in isolation. The following morning, one of the rowing boats delivered unhappy news. The *Antelope* was irreparably damaged; accordingly their sole recourse would be to salvage as many timbers as could be prized from their trusty vessel, ferry the planks to the isle, and there to wright a lesser craft.

Apparently their beachhead was but a small island in the chain, abundant in water, yet far from sufficing in provender to feed fifty hungry men. Thus marooned, they dared not hope for a passing ship, principally because no Europeans yet knew of this sea route, let alone an entire archipelago. Nay, salvation would not be forthcoming by sea. What then of the larger isles in the offing? Surely there might one find human settlement, whose inhabitants should have noticed a great ship run aground, boats oaring to & fro, bonfires by night. Though would such natives be friendly or belligerent? A most unsettling question.

Two days later, on the morning of the twelfth of August, two canoes were seen approaching. On the beach stood waiting the Captain & Bengal sailor Tom Rose whose command of several tongues had commended his hire in Macao as Interpreter. The other crewmen fell back into the trees, having been warned not to provoke their visitors unduly. Tom Rose hailed the canoes with a shouted greeting and was at first met with silence. Then presently came a response in Malay, which as Providence would have it, was one of the languages Rose possessed. He offered as they were from the wrecked English vessel, traders, not men of war. The two canoes landed a rank of savages naked save for their tattoos, who

spake Malay through one man, whereupon the conversation proceeded amicably. The other crewmen came out of hiding, and as
the hour of the noontide meal was come, they shared their rations
with the visitors. It was learnt that this was Oroolong in the Isles
of Pelew under the sovereign rule of King Abba Thule, who sent
his two younger brothers & their canoes to bid warm welcome to
the strangers. How fortunate for one & all!

Though in truth what were their fortunes? Their ship had foundered but not sunk, the deck boats had not been lost but were within
rowing distance of a tiny isle, both Englishmen & Pelewans had
Malay speakers amongst them (the native Interpreter, a Malayan
called Soogul, had likewise been cast away here some ten months
prior, and thence learnt the local argot), and the two canoes had
arrived in time to enjoy a repast, thereby tempering all quite peace-
ably. Most fortunate of all, the Pelewans were not given to clubbing
strangers and eating them, but rather accommodated them with
gracious civility. Or as Captain Wilson was later to remark, 'The
barbarous people shewed us no little kindness'.

Properly, all things in perspective, they need not have feared
cannibals. Throughout the countless atolls and archipelagoes of the
Pacific no race of man-eating primitives ever lived, save in Western
phantasies. Indeed, the very notion to simply feast upon unknown
travellers would scarcely occur to persons anywhere. Cannibals,
such as did exist in remotest New Guinea & Fiji, rather preyed as
warriors upon malefactors from rival clans, presuming to consume
the spirit resident in the hearts & organs of their valiant foes. Even if
fabled Cathay accounts of Chinese gourmands eating anything four-
legged save tables & chairs or two-legged save their parents (siblings
beware!) may not have been entirely exaggerated, in no regard had
they any parallel in the peoples & cultures of Micronesia. Had our
English wayfarers but known!

That said, first encounters are a most delicate moment in social
intercourse, the initial reactions of either party affecting greatly the

poise & demeanour of both. Moreover, having been wreck'd and
left atremble at Nature's wrath through wind & wave & reef, and
with the imprint of terror yet upon them, had our Englishmen mis-
construed the least hostility in the queer mien of their visitors, they
might easily have over-reacted in kind. How fraught with tragic
misunderstandings the meeting of disparate peoples has often been!
Yet glad to tell, the people of Pelew rather 'shewed no little kindness' to the shipwreck'd strangers, greeting them with such warmth
as to reaffirm our belief in the innate goodness of humanity. What
luck it was, the crew thought to a man, not to have met with hungry lions or tygers or wolves (though again we should note, these
creatures of the wild tend to shun humans unless provoked). Not
only did the Pelewans soon regale them with food & drink, but
even exchanged gifts & emissaries. King Abba Thule bade one of
his brothers assist them and learn their ways. In grateful response,
Captain Wilson offered tools & clothing & sundry tokens of civilisation, all personally delivered in his stead by his own flesh & blood
brother, the ship's Navigator, Mathias. When the Englishmen gave
a demonstration of blunderbuss shooting, a duly impressed Abba
Thule prevailed upon them to put down a rival clan, thereby proving that alliance with the White Men could be a most commodious
stratagem.

In due course, a bricollaged schooner was completed by Wilson
& his crew and christened the *Oroolong* after our waylaid travellers'
tiny dry-dock home away from home. By November, fair summer
weather in that Hemisphere, the Captain was making plans to set
sail, when one of his men named Blanchard, a common sailor afore
the mast, confessed his wish to remain behind. This was beyond the
good Captain's comprehension. Why should an Englishman born
and bred, apprenticed in the honourable profession of sailing, har-
bour such unfathomable whims as to make him forsake his duties
and dally in these God-forsaken hinterlands? The swab, however,
was adamant, wanting only his sailing papers revoked and thus to

be unencumber'd of further obligation. Yea, an early convert to the lure of the South Seas!

After much deliberation, Captain Wilson assented to Blanchard's request. More than a purely occupational calculation, the Captain had thought in some form to repay his hosts the Pelewans & their King Abba Thule, and decided to offer several muskets for the King to maintain the upper hand over contrary islanders. There was no time, however, in which to impart to his warriors the divers skills of musketry, hence it seemed apposite to leave behind a person practised in the art. These being the circumstances and the Captain a civilised English gentleman of seasoned career & ethic, he welcomed it when Blanchard volunteer'd for this role. Verily it seemed a godsend.

Yet even now Henry Wilson met with a further complication. Abba Thule asked that his second son might travel to England with them. If Blanchard's madness to linger in those Southern climes foreshadowed the Romantic Era, with its love of the Noble Savage, we may also discern in the young Prince's curiosity to see Europe some enlightened current of the times, an instinctive passion for knowledge. During the Englishmen's brief three-month sojourn on the isles, the Pelewans had watched them at close quarters and learnt to mimick the rudiments of their wiles. Reckoning that these strangers definitely possess'd a powerful magick, albeit presently held at bay owing to their shipwreck'd straits, they knew the isles could not remain isolated forever. Nay, the next visitors from afar would doubtless not lend their services to help Abba Thule vanquish his enemies, but rather fire upon the King himself. Thus, whilst Blanchard's folly was his alone, the young Prince's motives were in spirit stamped indelibly with the hopes & fears of his isle, of the entire archipelago.

Whether privy to the Pelewans' plight or not, Captain Wilson consented to this exchange of envoys, albeit this time the balance tilted heavily askew. King Abba Thule, for his part, granted

Blanchard leave to remain, and emptied his coffers to bestow upon his son a generous allowance. Yea, like an early stipendiary scholar!

The Pelewan Prince was named Lee Bo, later Anglicised to Leigh Beau, a youth of some twenty years of age, handsome of coun-tenance and favoured with intelligence, most visibly embodying the difference between commoner & crown. At their first interview, the Captain overcame his reservations to enquire through the ship's Interpreter how it was that a native nobleman who can scarcely have imagined the months ahead at sea had reached so bold a deci-sion. To which Lee Bo answered, although most eager to visit the many lands across the long water, he would meanwhile exert himself to eat what the English ate, learn to speak their tongue, and other-wise prepare himself to endure several years abroad by observing the greatness of English Civilisation, as was his mission. This sufficiently reassured the good Captain that the Prince would not start mewling the second day at sea, and he promised Abba Thule he would cher-ish his son as if he were the King himself.

So it was that, on the twelfth day of November, 1783, the *Oroolong* set sail from the Pelews. Upon their departure, King Abba Thule addressed Captain Wilson thus. 'You go home, you happy. I see you happy, I happy…ut you go, I no happy.' How the good Captain replied to these emotion-steep'd words is lost to posterity. Very likely he failed for an equally memorable aphorism in response.

The Prince's possessions were meager: a crude mat for sleeping, woven of cocoa-palm fibres, and a length of rope for tying knots so as to record things he found worth remembering; nothing more. We may easily picture the young Prince, gallantly parading the decks in his sailor's kit, fashioning innumerable different knots, the ship with its cargo of dreams sent off by a fleet of royal canoes!

The *Oroolong* now turned her stern to the isles and bore north-west, a mere one-sixth the draught of the lost *Antelope* and far too small to reach Portsmouth. For this reason, Captain Wilson made for Macao, hoping there to transfer to a sister East India Company vessel bound for Britain. Fortunately, they met with no inclement weather in the Luzon Strait twixt the Philippines and Formosa, negotiating the Batanes Channel to make Macao some three hundred leagues distant by the thirtieth of the month. At long last, the marooned sailors had returned to civilised lands, and for Lee Bo his first foreign country.

"How did you feel then?" Matías asks his ghostly confidant.

"In some senses, 'twas as I expected," Lee Bo replies. "From how the English comported themselves, from such effects as even those castaways possess'd, I knew to expect great things. Not to boast nor dramatise, but I must say my surprise was over and done with when first I saw an English musket."

"Yes, but China must have been overwhelming."

"True enough, tho I merely stood in the doorway. Macao was an open port, free for the rambling, but ne'er did I set foot in Canton. Not even the Company factors were allowed overland into Canton. All business dealings were settled on board ship by appointed spokesmen. Nay, the only China I did see was the port and the rabble living on sampans. Once when a yellow boatman asked me for victuals, I pitied him with an orange or such, thinking, a great people, these Chinamen, but not a rich people withal. Ne'er once on our island kingdom did any man beg of me like that."

"But the city? The buildings?"

"All very grand, I warrant. But one gets accustomed to it after the thrall of first sighting. Anything piled up block upon block so high is bound to impress, if only for a day. Thereafter, things are simply there, part o' the firmament so to speak, unless they change their aspect. Tho were I to try to build in stone beside my father's lodge, no doubt I would meet all manner of quandaries, and so take the true measure of the mason's art."

"I guess it was like that for me too, the first time I went to Japan. Things must have awed me, but you can't keep gawking at each novelty. You just have to accept things for what they are and only later stop to admire it all in private."

"Aye, admiring what others have wrought can only rile and vex," says Lee Bo. "All the more so when on foreign shores, shouldering your whole native culture."

Thus, the two kindred latecomers to world civilization reaffirm their common bond, an affinity that draws the Palauan phantom to these neighboring isles of Navidad and makes him seek out the President.

"Mark you, I was made most welcome, being this rarity of an indigene. Macao stood me in good stead for faring on to England. The Portuguese *senhoras* all fussed over me, touching my tattoos. Hong Kong, you ask? Nay, it did not e'en exist then. 'Twas but a fishing village. The Portuguese founded Macao first. Macao, that was the bourne for Europeans. Hong Kong came only much later, after the English commandeered the Territories in the Opium War. Up till then, English ships all called at Macao before bearing upwind to Canton for trading. Macao was a veritable warren of diff'rent races. I felt so favourably disposed as to reckon England would not pose much hardship."

"Smart thinking. Born smart, lucky for you. They set you down far from your homeland, but you knew how to read the territory," says the President.

"The compliment is not unwelcome," allows Lee Bo. "Tho I have felt shocks that buckled my legs. The greatest astonishment was the mirror."

"A looking glass? A vanity?"

"Aye. My whole body shewn in just proportion, as others might see me— oh, the wonder of it! Being but twenty and a primitive with such a weakness for glass baubles as might have bartered a kingdom for a handful of beads, I spent hours before the contrivance."

"A mirror, eh. Like meeting oneself out in the world."

"Indeed, a moment most philosophical. The captain saw me pass the glass so often to and fro, he gave me a hand mirror."

"Not a bad gift for any twenty-year-old."

"Animals were also consternating. At that time, when Palau still had no dogs, e'en the two bitches that Captain Wilson rescued from his ship had our islanders in a dither. And in Macao, there were goats and sheep and cows and horses! Wonders all, even if I could somehow fathom that men had a hand in their breeding. From the moment I spied the wreckage of the *Antelope*, I was in awe of men's capacity to manufacture. Tho a horse, born from a mare—how could they make that? 'Twas most uncanny."

Matías notices how childlike his ghostly friend becomes when talking about these things, as if the centuries-old apparition had returned to his twentieth year. It's such a novelty to hear him chat so freely, Matías just quietly lets him reminisce.

"And what of my prowess with the spear?" Lee Bo goes on. "A gang of shoremen were boasting of their skill, taking turns throwing at a painted wooden bird. One says, 'Ar been to far Madagascar an' learnt me to spear.' All bluster, he was, ne'er hit a thing. Well, they see me watching and taunt me, 'Have a try, Jimbo.' So I take up the spear, let fly, and pierce the bird right through the head! I was so pleas'd I could beat the Europeans at something!"

"I had a similar experience," Matías wants to say, but the ghost doesn't hear. He's deep into his reverie, two hundred years in the past.

As Providence would have it, several large English ships were in port when they arrived in Macao. Captain Wilson then enter'd into negotiations with the Company to secure his men return passage to England. Having lost a vessel did not help his bargaining position, though as the Isles of Pelew did not yet figure on any charts, the blame for the shipwreck was not entirely his. On the other hand, he found advantage in his misfortune by drawing up an accurate map of the islands, which was naturally well received, as reliable charts represented the cumulative product of many such brave misadventures.

Presently the crew split up, each to his allotted ship by seniority. Lee Bo travelled together with the Captain aboard the Company's Indiaman, the *Morse*, a huge ship three times the size of the *Antelope* carrying 285 chests of Chinese tea. Crossing the Indian Ocean, the *Morse* rounded the Cape of Good Hope and headed north up the Atlantic, with Lee Bo hard at reading and writing throughout the voyage. When they called at St. Helena, that tiny Rock of Empire in the mid-Atlantic where unbeknownst to our returning travellers the defeated Napoleon would be exiled thirty years hence, Lee Bo met up with his friends from the *Antelope* who had arrived by another ship, and they were amazed at his progress.

Finally, on the fourteenth of July, 1784, the *Morse* docked at Portsmouth. The Industrial Revolution was upon England in that hour, even as Gibbon penned his *Rise and Fall*, and Boswell & Dr Johnson conversed on matters philological. Eight years since the American Colonies declared independence and five prior to the French Revolution, this was the age of Mozart, Diderot and d'Alembert, just before some say Europe's star began to wane, or at least a sweet hiatus whilst the hypocrisies of the nineteenth century remained at bay and human happiness was still the measure of worth. In this age, our Lee Bo breathed the air of England, and rode in 'a little house which was run away with by horses' all the way from Portsmouth to London. Yea, this was the age of six-mile-an-hour carriages. A mere trot, yet to our Prince accustomed to strolling the hibiscus & bougainvillaea & ylang-ylang-flowered paths of Pelew shaded by cocoa & pandamus palms & betelnut trees, it was like rocketing through the heavens. Needless to say, the Portsmouth Road presented vistas dismal, cold and gray, the English summer a blighted winter to his eyes. Nor did anyone see fit to inform the Prince that highwaymen still plundered the carriageways, or that murderers were often strung up in plain view.

Inside the carriage, the other passengers bounced and chafed like groundnuts roasting in a hot skillet, but Lee Bo slept, noting only later that 'whilst we went one way, the fields, houses and trees all went another'. The carriage stopped at Petersfield and Mousehill, changed horses at Godalming, then continued on to Guildford, Esher and Kingston-upon-Thames before arriving in London proper. From there they barged downstream under London Bridge and Tower Bridge, docking on the south bank in the seamen's quarter of Rotherhithe. Here lived many a sailor's family amongst chandlers that supplied sundry tackle to the trade; here boats heading upstream to land cargo often tied up overnight and sometimes tarried in dry dock to repair damages from tide & current; here rumors of the Seven Seas were the talk of the town. Stopping in first at St Mary's Church to attend a service, they continued a short walk further to Captain Wilson's home in Paradise Row where Lee Bo was to live as a full member of the family.

"What was it like, the house?" asks Matías.

"Grand and finely appointed. In Palau, three strong men could throw up a house in as many days, whereas the London builder must have needed thirty hands for well on a hundred. And the furnishings! I was given a room of my own with a bed of my own, complete with canopy and curtains. That bed was a room in itself! But even this I soon grew accustomed to."

"Highly adaptable, for an islander."

"Foreign cultures were ne'er a distress to me. Or perhaps I simply enjoyed the good fortune to live like a prince in the captain's house. A move up in the world, if you will."

"Really?" says Matías.

"Aye, materially greater. The sheer scale of wealth to invest such labors in a private home, and more, to send ships halfway round the globe to some tiny isles in the Pacific."

"So living in that big house, what did you do every day?"

"I attended the Peter Hills School in Southwark, to learn to read and write and do arithmetic—your 'three Rs'—but fun, to be sure. Nor were the pupils so very biased."

"Children of the empire could afford to be magnanimous."

"Perhaps, but it being a seafaring village, the sailors' sons welcomed strangers from afar bringing their strange customs and foods and handicrafts. I was introduced as such, an exotic import, if older than my classmates. Schooling serv'd me well; they taught me to pen my own name—Leigh Beau."

"Did you do anything else besides go to school?"

"Certainly, I was fêted by the leading lights of London who, it must be said, regarded me as a kind of pet, a domesticated wildchild."

Matías doesn't know what to make of the ghost's remark. Is he being sarcastic or simply reporting the facts? Or else priding himself for reasons Matías can't hope to understand?

"One dandy of a poet, a George Keates, oft invited me to his house. There I met with many diff'rent persons for tea and biscuits and talk. Politely put, I was made to feel most popular; less nicely said, I was a curiosity on display."

"Did it make you uncomfortable?"

"Nay, quite honestly, I gave little thought to inequalities 'twixt Great Britain and lowly Palau. Only later, in death, was I raised up off the ground, as it were, to a bird's-eye prospect of the world. At the time, I had scarcely the height to see. I was like a skittle fending off five players at once, the balls coming hard and fast. In some senses, perspicacious death becomes me more than life."

"Then it wasn't so bad, your being a showpiece?"

"To be alone in a foreign land is to be one against many. Of course the English who sailed to our islands and back were in the same boat, made the objects of Londoners' curiosity, so I cannot say as it was unfair. After all, I boarded the ship of my own free will. Thinking back on it now, the days pass'd in blissful fascination."

"What did you aim to get out of staying in England? What possible profit?"

"Aim? Profit? Hard words born of the evils of modernity. Eighteenth-century Europe was ne'er so horridly calculating as that."

"But surely it wasn't just to see what you could see?" the President asks.

"Perhaps I thought to turn me into a proper Englishman. Is not that the truth? The intrepid soul who ventures out to foreign lands and learns their foreign ways enjoys no higher compliment than to be told, 'Ye're as good as English.'"

"Well, I guess. Going to Japan, I learned to use chopsticks and take a Japanese bath, to appreciate the seasons. What's different between us, though, I didn't have any gentleman of means to watch over me, no polite salon culture, so I never got in as deep as you. No one even pretended I could be 'as good as Japanese.'"

"These two centuries I have thought on it a score of times, that had I dwelt full fifty years in London, what would my lot have been?"

"Like they say, he who sits between two chairs falls flat on his ass."

"Indeed. At first I did entertain a modest plan: I would stay in England two or three years, learn all there was to know, then return to my homeland embolden'd with my newfound mastery to fortify ourselves against foreigners. A scheme of modernization, if you will. The conceit was to void my vessel so as better to arm me with their cannonry. Yet study as I might, my one lifetime could not span two worlds."

"It's next to impossible to embrace two cultures in one person."

"I despaired. Half a year dash'd my hopes. How I yearn'd for my beloved Palau, yet knew I must stay on till capable of explaining the English and their ways to my father."

"State scholarships carry big responsibilities."

"Unlike your free and easy travel papers."

"Let's not start. I had my share of hardships."

"Each to his own. Young as I was, I quash'd my homesickness and immersed myself in daily study. Literacy, however, was of less consequence than observing civilisation at large. I did even see the Great Wind Bladder, which delighted one and all."

To be specific, the Italian Vincenzo Lunardi demonstrated his invention, the hot air balloon, on the fifteenth of September, 1784, the first aeronautical experiment of its kind ever seen in England. A consummate showman and self-publicist, Lunardi had taken out prior advertisements in various gazetteers, and an unprecedented multitude turned out to witness the launch from the City Artillery Park in Moorfields, paying one guinea a head on the gate. Good Captain Wilson, however, did not see the merit of Lee Bo mingling with great crowds at such a spectacle, nor especially the value of spending a guinea for the same, so the Prince did not attend the festivities, but rather went to preview the bladder placed on free public display some several days in advance. Likewise, on the date of the ascent, he stood a safe distance outside the park to watch it 'float like a blowfish' toward the northern skies of London.

Contrary to the acclaim High Society heaped upon Lunardi, Lee Bo thought little of 'the foolish man imitate bird'. Apparently not a few learned Londoners, the eminent natural historian Sir Joseph Banks and writer Horace Walpole among them, also scoffed at the aerial enterprise, hence our Prince was not alone in his quite rational evaluation of this 'inhuman presumption'.

Indeed, Lee Bo's own voyage, uprooted from his isle to this distant northern clime, surely represents a far more fantastic transit than the brief sojourn of that dashingly charming Secretary of the Neapolitan Embassy or his short hop of a mere twenty-five miles to the sleepy village of Standon-Ware in Hertfordshire. But whilst the famous Lunardi enjoyed the 'heaven-sent' assistance of one brave sixteen-year-old farmgirl named Elisabeth Brett in landing his craft, the Prince was never again to alight on his native soil. For, alas, he died in England.

By December of that year, having lived in the company of Europeans for thirteen months (five months since docking in Portsmouth), he had attained a considerable degree of fluency in English. No one could impugn the sincerity of his educational ambitions nor his progress in the same, for as George Keates remarked, 'His application was equal to his great desire of learning; and he conducted himself in school with such propriety, and in a manner so engaging, that he gained not only the esteem of the gentleman under whose tuition he was placed, but also the affection of his young companions.'

And yet on the sixteenth of December, he complained of discomfort and was confined to his bed. A rash of blisters broke out over his body, indicative of smallpox. Captain Wilson and his family had presumably been aware of the danger of contagion. Already by 1796, Dr Jenner had experimented with inoculating humans with pus from cowpox blisters, based on prior empirical recognition that someone once superficially infected did not risk further infection. So, too, must he have known that a visitor from afar would be helpless against diseases that prevailed amongst Europeans. Surely part of Captain Wilson's enjoining Lee Bo to shun the crowds at Moorfields was the fear that he might pick up 'bad airs' there. Yet despite all precautions, the Prince took ill and lost weight. The Captain called in the prominent physician Dr James Carmichael Smyth to examine him, but the prognosis for recovery was nil. The Captain and those of his kin not yet inured to smallpox were to stay away, leaving but few friends to inform the patient why.

Lee Bo met his last with great equanimity. On the twenty-seventh of December, a cold season in a cold country, before even seeing in the New Year, our Son of the South Seas passed away at the age of twenty-one. Bearing in mind how many indigenes the world o'er were later to perish of this disease borne by men of civilised countries, it is most ironic that he should have been a pioneer in this regard as well.

"So what's it like to die?" Matías asks the big question.

"'Tis not half bad. You should feel no menace when your time comes, I assure you. As soon as I learnt that dying means merely moving across to this side, I realised that one's place and time of death are no reason to fret. Indeed, to take leave of the physical body is justly liberating. One can study things as one pleases. Back then I was so ignorant."

"But at the time, you must have been one of the most knowledgeable Palauans around," says Matías.

"To the Western view, perhaps. Though I do believe my father was better versed in the lore of the world than e'en Captain Wilson. Seven years on, when a young Captain McClure sailed his ship the *Panther* to Palau and told him of my death, my father did not even react. To us island folk, death is literally of no consequence—nothing follows."

"So what you're saying is, I have nothing to fear from death?"

"Not in the slightest. That, I had to think, was the greatest diff'rence 'twixt Europeans and Pacific islanders. Thus, even the intelligence that I had perished in London was of little concern to them, whilst the English seem'd to fault themselves, however slightly. As my last request, in my stead, I had the *Panther* take four cows and two bulls, one Bengal ram and ewe, seven she-goats and four males, four breeding sows and one stud pig, a pair of geese, and two pairs of ducks. Not a bad trade—I daresay, it pleased my father."

BUS REPORT 9

Early one morning, a bus on a rural route on Baltasár Island was slowing at a crossing when another bus zoomed in from the left. Both vehicles jammed on their brakes, just barely avoiding a collision. Luckily, the fringe of trees at the intersection was clear of undergrowth, so they could see each other coming for twenty meters. The driver of the first bus leaned out of his window (cars drive on the right in Navidad, drivers sit on the left) and yelled at the other unfamiliar bus, "Hey, watch where you're going!"

"*You* watch where *you're* going!" came a voice, but not from any driver he could see.

"You're on a side road, you're the one who's supposed to stop," corrected the first driver.

"Didn't think anyone was coming," said the voice.

The driver strained to make out the speaker, but the morning sun rising behind him reflected off the windows of the other bus, making it impossible for him to see inside.

"I drive this road every morning. This is my route."

"But you ain't got no passengers, do you?" sniped the voice.

"Passengers or not, this bus runs on schedule," said the driver.

"Pity for you."

"And what about *you?*" the driver challenged.

"*I've* got forty-nine people riding," boasted the voice.

"Forty-nine passengers!"

"Forty-eight, plus the driver."

"But that's you, right?" the first man countered.

"Well, uh…" the voice hesitated.

Strange, thought the driver, taking another good look at the other bus, there didn't seem to be anyone in the driver's seat. "You mean there's no driver?" he surprised himself by asking.

"Why, of course there is. He's asleep in a back seat."

"But then, how do you stay on the road?" he fired back sharply.

Silence.

"Okay, so who's doing the driving?"

Again, no reply. Then suddenly came a growl, "Outta my way!" and the phantom bus shot across the intersection.

"Hey, I got the right of way!" shouted the first driver, fighting an urge to ram the upstart off the road. But no, instead, he just waited for it to go by. He wished he could give chase, but that again was not the way of a scheduled route bus driver. Banishing such thoughts, he pulled out across the intersection and looked to the right, but the phantom bus had vanished in a cloud of dust. There was nothing but mangrove swamps to the right, so where—the driver wondered as he headed off—could it have been going in such a confounded hurry?

06

The next few days pass without incident. The mysterious handbills have leveled off, and there's no other torii gate left to topple. The bus and veterans group are still missing, but no bodies or debris have been found. *Not too bad,* Matías has to think, *for a state of emergency.* The capital, Baltasár, is calm. No scoundrels have come out of the woodwork with long-range laser beams to burn the Navidad flag in front of the Presidential Villa. Suzuki has returned to Japan with the go-ahead for the Brun Reef oil depot, while the legislators sans legislature remain nice and quiet. Bonhomme Tamang's grave is never without flowers, but then Cornelius's always has three times as many, long after his death.

Navidadians customarily show their reverence with flowers and think nothing of grabbing blossoms from their garden or hedge, woods or roadside to pay their respects (who would ever think of *buying* flowers?). Matías has Tamang's and Cornelius's graves kept under secret surveillance, and every other week Island Security delivers a list of flower-givers. Of course the "secret" part is just wishful thinking; the people all know they're being watched, and in fact there hasn't been a new name reported in three months. No, the Matías Guili regime is on track. All's right with the world.

The President's daily routine sees no real changes: pre-dawn meditation, tuna sashimi breakfast, morning paperwork, afternoon meetings and functions, evening parties and get-togethers, followed by intimate nightcaps at Angelina's. The only new variants are the young woman who sits in the corner unannounced whenever Matías meets with anyone and his distracted air on visits to Angelina, which have dropped off overall. Yet his nights away merely find him alone in his private quarters, writing copious notes in his ledger, or nursing a long drink and thinking of days gone by. He's not playing games, even Angelina has to admit that. Should she ask what's up, he'll offer some reasonable response; he avoids neither her eyes nor her hash-perfumed pleasures. And to be perfectly honest, there's no arguing about him "getting old" whenever things don't go quite right during these tête-à-têtes (until now Angelina had never realized how liberating the excuse of aging might be for a man). Still, something's not right. He might not even realize it himself, but he's not all here. So where *is* he then?

"How she doing?" Angelina asks him.

"Who?"

"María. The Melchor maid from here."

"María…oh, you mean Améliana. She's proving useful."

"Was *that* her name? News to me."

"It's a better name, she says. Strange girl."

"So what she doing, this strange girl?" asks Angelina, stroking his shriveled cock. Both a caress and a threat, it occurs to Matías.

"I have her look at people with those all-seeing eyes of hers. She's pretty much on the money," he answers, again without dissimulating. His edginess prior to summoning the girl to the villa, hesitations about what it might mean to Angelina, fractious questions he deliberated to distraction and even referred to Lee Bo—all that is completely forgotten.

↯

One morning, Matías is in his office plowing through a pile of pending decisions, when Améliana sidles into the room. Usually at this hour she would be helping Itsuko with the housework or out walking around town.

Odd, thinks Matías, though of course she has his permission to come in whenever the "feeling" strikes.

"Am I interrupting?"

"Not at all," says Matías, setting down his papers and reading glasses.
"What's up?"

"I'd like some time off."

He has to think. He summoned her here from Angelina's with no employment contract to speak of. How many days has it been? They never even
discussed salary. Her position is nonexistent at the Presidential Villa, though
presumably he can put in a word with the executive secretary to get her the
going rate. She even seems to spend her Sundays here with no days off. All
right, she's no ordinary employee, and he never really saw her as villa staff;
he just wanted to have her on hand. Maybe he ought to pay her privately
himself. But for now, time off seems to be the issue.

"How long?" he asks.

"Five days."

Why not a week? He has no important visitors scheduled for the present.
A calm and uneventful hiatus—dull even. Might as well not even be here
himself this coming week.

"Okay," he says, then pauses to think—*why these five days?* "Maybe it's
none of my business, but what's the hurry?"

"On Melchor, it's *Yuuka Yuumai* time."

That much he knows. It's printed on every calendar in the country. The
festival, held once every eight years, is even on the presidential agenda. He's
supposed to fly over to catch the final day. Symbolic participation as head
of state in a popular traditional celebration. But what's that got to do with
Améliana? Sure, she's from Melchor, but why go back for it?

"And you just want to visit?" he asks, assuming she merely fancies taking
in the festivities. But wait, wasn't she driven out of her village because of her
"disruptive" powers of prediction?

"I have to. I'm the seventh Yuuka."

It takes a moment for what she's saying to sink in. The Yuuka Yuumai ceremonies are performed by eight high priestesses called *Yuuka*, who wield such

absolute control over the spiritual life of Melchor that no secular power can override them. Their authority comes straight from beyond, and this young woman before him is seventh in line.

"Yes, you go, certainly, if that's what you've got to do," he hears himself saying.

Melchor's spiritual dominion is a constant that holds Navidad society together, the exalted status of its Elders prevailing not on any formalized legal basis but simply as an article of faith. And yet, even higher in status are the eight Yuuka who meet only once every eight years to propitiate the spirits at eight sacred locations around the island.

"The boat is overnight. I get there and the ceremonies last for three days. Then another night on the return. So that gets me back here on the fifth day," she sums up matter-of-factly, as if unaware of the weighty role that is hers to play.

"Are you really the seventh Yuuka?" he dares to ask.

"So I've been told. It's my first time. The last Yuuka Yuumai, I was still a virgin. The *Yoi'i Yuuka* decides everything."

"So I've heard. Or no, the part about being a virgin eight years ago, I didn't know." In his confusion, that's all he can say. Melchor society is essentially matrilineal, with the Great Mother Yoi'i Yuuka from the previous ceremonial cycle on top. For eight years, she searches all the households on the island for new links in the chain of honor. Long ago, Matías vaguely remembers when, as a problem child entrusted to relations, he saw an old woman once come to the door and everyone in the family fall to their knees, bowing and mumbling invocations before leading her to a back room where she was promptly seated on the only chair in the house and offered a cup of precious imported English tea heaped with spoonfuls of sugar. A startling display of piety, even if he hadn't a clue what it was all about. According to Melchor custom, girls who show spiritual powers while still virgins may be given a chance to help out at the ceremonies, but only when the Yoi'i Yuuka judges her worthy is one of them formally accepted as a Yuuka. Judging from Améliana's age, she must have proven herself in only one ceremonial cycle—wasn't that highly irregular?

"When are you going, then?"

"I catch the boat tomorrow. As soon as I arrive, there are purification rituals."

"Okay, I can see it's very important you be there. Just promise me you'll come back here afterwards."

"I promise."

"And be sure to give my regards to the Yoi'i Yuuka."

"I will."

At that, Améliana leaves the President's office. Matías takes a long, deep breath. He tries to picture her in white ceremonial robes, then recalls the intensity of the festivities, the solemnity and frenzy. He's only really experienced a Yuuka Yuumai decades ago in childhood; never once during his years running the M. Guili Trading Co., and later only in an official capacity. It's the single most important event in Navidad cosmology, yet the President has no real role to play in it. *As if there were another separate system of rule here,* thinks Matías, before returning to his paperwork.

⚡

The following morning, Améliana stops in again at the President's office, this time wearing a white cotton dress with red buttons.

"My ship leaves at noon."

"Will that put you there in time?"

"It gets into Melchor at five tomorrow morning. That's plenty of time."

"And the ceremonies?"

"The *Udagan* purification is in the morning. The rites begin at two in the afternoon."

"Well, have a safe trip."

She acknowledges this with a slight bow of the head, then moves to leave.

"Shall I have Heinrich give you a ride to the port?" he asks.

"No, I'll walk."

Améliana disappears, trailing a cloud of phantom butterflies, leaving him alone with his papers.

⚡

At noon, Matías lunches at the Navidad Teikoku Hotel with a visiting rep from a Japanese company hoping to set up a local franchise, but the whole time his mind is on the ship that's soon to sail. A scrap heap of a freighter, probably built in Sasebo or Nagasaki just after the war to run cargo between Kyushu and the northern Ryukyus for the next thirty years before being decommissioned and sold down to Navidad some fifteen years ago. No amount of touch-ups can stop thick scabs of rust from welling up through the white paint. A good, swift kick would put a hole in the hull—or so passengers joke. He can picture them boarding with armloads of belongings, spreading mats out on the deck, unpacking bags of home-cooked food. He knows they'll cast fishing lines off the stern, though for fifteen hours at twenty knots maximum the brightly colored lures will never catch anything. And now Améliana is walking up the gangplank. Today's weather is calm, so it won't be rocking much. He pretends to listen to the Japanese rep's business projections, but all he sees is the ship.

Visions of Melchor and the eighth-year festival haunt him for the rest of the day. The rituals at eight different holy sites, the presiding Yuuka and the attendant crowds, the unremitting recitations in the hot sun by day and the bonfires all through the night, the physical elation of the pilgrims who give themselves over for three days and two nights without sleep, the progress of the sacred barge from one site to the next by sea, followed overland by the priestesses and multitudes. Matías saw the Yuuka Yuumai as a child the year before the Japanese pulled out in defeat. Forty years later—during the previous cycle—he went as a functionary to observe the ecstatic peak of the celebrations for exactly thirty minutes. He offered formulaic respects from afar, then was whisked back to Baltasár City by plane.

The truth is, that's no place for a president; the politician who presents too visible a profile there will be accused of canvassing and see his populist ploy backfire. Sacred powers and secular authority should keep a respectful distance from one another.

That last time—he tries to remember—had Améliana been among the girl celebrants at the tail end of the procession, her face hidden by one of those kava leaf crowns? Had they, in fact, already met? Suddenly all the sights and sounds come back to him. He hasn't thought of the Yuuka Yuumai in years and now he's almost feeling nostalgic for the festivities. He has a sudden urge to go and see the whole thing.

As president, he'll have a front-row seat for the last climactic ritual, but that hardly seems enough. He won't experience a thing, won't know what it feels like to participate as one of the faithful. He wants to shed the name Matías Guili and lose himself, just one more face in the crowd. *But no, it's impossible*, he tells himself, *you're the president*.

Or is it so impossible? He takes a look at his weekly agenda. Aside from the visit to Melchor, there don't seem to be any engagements of consequence these next few days. Discussions with a couple of visitors, two minor meetings, a ground-breaking ceremony for a new middle school. Nothing that can't take care of itself—but that's not the real issue here, is it? The first duty of a politician is to be where he's supposed to be, to show himself to be on the ball, to inspire people's confidence. Actual policy making and judgments are secondary. It's like being a fireman: if you're not there in the right place at the right time, you blow it, the whole shebang goes up in smoke. That's the very first thing Ryuzoji taught him when he entered the political arena in Navidad. No matter how feeble or out of sorts, even if he has to put on makeup, the politician shows his face in front of his people. There's no such thing as down time; he always has to be ready and on the scene. He participates in events, he gets up in plain view and waves. Not to reassure himself of his popularity among the citizens gathered below, but to generate that popularity.

Then, of course, many a politician has stepped out for a moment and found himself ousted in a coup. That's not to say they can't grab power anyway while you're around, but if you're not, what can you do about it? The smart man doesn't go leaving his trusted second-in-command to hold the fort; often enough that deputy will slit his throat on his return. Depart with airport fanfare and you may not deplane to a state welcome. A politician never leaves his seat vacant, not even for a moment. That's an ironclad rule.

ϟ

The following morning at nine o'clock he sends for Jim Jameson.

"I'm going to be away from the office."

"S-sir...?" stammers the executive secretary.

"Just a three-day break. Look after things while I'm away, will you?"

"But your scheduled commitments..."

"Like I said, look after things."

"And the ceremonies on Melchor?"

"I won't be taking part. No particular problems in that department, are there? I'm not needed there in a big way, after all. And there shouldn't be any other urgent business, correct? A little three-day absence, you'll do fine. Only, don't say it's for 'reasons of health.' And no words like 'urgent' or 'emergency' either. Just leave it at 'personal business'; that ought to go down well enough."

"'Personal business,' sir?" repeats Jameson, still incredulous. The President has never talked like this before.

"That's right, something came up I personally have to take care of myself. I'm placing full confidence in you. Just make sure that idiot Katsumata doesn't try anything smart," he says with a laugh.

Jameson gives a strained smile. "How widely do you want this known?"

"Hmm, there *is* the option of not even announcing that I'm away. Have you field everything for the next four days, a week at the outside, and just say I'm inconvenienced at any given time."

"And Katsumata?"

"Guess we really can't *not* tell him. Can't have him think you had me assassinated."

"That's not very funny, sir," he says, looking as deferential as he can.

"Okay, okay. I'll tell him myself. And anyone else in our immediate staff who absolutely needs to know, fine. Only tell them it mustn't get out. In-house rumors won't do any harm. When I'm back in a few days, it'll all be forgotten."

"Very good, sir. What about urgent messages?"

"Out of the question."

"You'll be impossible to reach?"

"Right. I'm going to disappear with no point of contact. During which time, I'm vesting all authority in you. Even if the Philippines declares war and attacks, I want you to handle it as best you can. I won't hold you responsible for any decisions you make in my absence. And it won't be such a bad thing for you to get the view from the top for once."

What is the man talking about? Jameson looks at the President with sheer incomprehension. "I understand, sir. I'll do my best for three days, but please return on the fourth day. Without fail, sir."

"You can count on me. Could you call in to get the airplane ready? I'll be leaving within the hour."

"Where to, sir?"

"To Melchor. To the festival."

⚡

Katsumata is not at Island Security Headquarters, nor to be found anywhere else until Matías is already en route to the airport. Finally, he gets through on his mobile phone and tells him to come to the VIP room at the terminal, there are matters to discuss. Why must he always meet this buffoon at the airport, Matías wonders as he stares at the road over Heinrich's shoulder.

"You going somewhere?" asks Katsumata as soon as he sets foot in the room.

"Just for a short while. So you keep in contact with Jim while I'm away."

"Are you leaving right now? There's no time for me to arrange for bodyguards."

"And none are needed."

That shuts Katsumata up. This has never happened before. Where's the executive secretary? Should he let the President wander off on his own like this? It's unthinkable.

"The domestic front is quiet for the moment." *Except for the handbills and torii gate and missing bus*, thinks Matías to himself. "Thanks to your efforts."

"Nah, really, I…" mumbles Katsumata, also overlooking the obvious security issues—he's such an easy man to manipulate.

"With you around, I know nothing will happen that anyone's going to regret. So what's the latest on the bus?"

Bask in the least glimmer of favor and out of nowhere comes a sting. Katsumata looks up at the ceiling and fiddles with his sunglasses.

"Only hearsay. Nothing solid at all."

"Is that so? Hearsay's a slippery thing to contain."

"Yeah, and difficult to follow up. There's a funny rumor going around about the torii…"

"And?"

"And the word is, some guy says that he met someone who says he saw seven youngsters topple the gate."

"What the hell is *that* supposed to mean?"

"Don't ask me. We tried to track down more details but came up empty-handed. The only real lead is the seven kids. No faces, no ID on any ringleader, no color or make of car, not even the name of the witness who was actually there. No one gives us any answers. It's all just hearsay, like chasing after clouds."

"Seven kids? It could be a red herring."

"Yeah, something that's got nothing to do with the facts." To hear this man use the word *facts* is enough to make anyone queasy.

"Or no, I don't know, it could be the truth. Keep looking."

"Will do, sir, but…"

"But *what?*"

"But nothing makes sense in this place. How are we supposed to conduct serious investigations here?"

"I never expected that from the beginning. If that's what I wanted, I'd have hired someone else, not you. Instead of fussing over finding the culprits, you should be deterring further incidents with those tough looks of yours."

"Gotcha," says Katsumata coyly.

"Well, I'm off," says the President, nodding to the Islander pilot at the door. He grabs up a black plastic bag beside him.

"So where is it you're going?"

"Jim Jameson has the details," is all he says as he heads for the door.

Katsumata is used to seeing the President carrying a spotless leather briefcase. The sight of him toting a garbage bag makes everything seem even stranger. The President makes for the exit, then as if something just occurred to him, he pivots abruptly and walks straight back to Katsumata.

"Lend me those, will you?"

In one swift move, like a skillful thief, he reaches out, takes Katsumata's sunglasses, and slips them into the breast pocket of his suit. Then before the man can complain, Matías has about-faced and walked out the door into the brilliant sunlight. Katsumata is lost without his sunglasses, the storm trooper reduced to a pathetic droop-eyed clown.

Matías doesn't take his usual copilot's perch, but a seat three rows back from the starboard door. The pilot obviously thinks it odd, but makes no comment, aware that his passenger doesn't want to be bothered with questions today. There's a taut urgency to his expression. What can it mean, his wanting to fly to Melchor all alone in such a hurry? It's not like him to show up unshaven either, and with only one carry-on—a garbage bag? The pilot just hopes he's not planning to open the door in mid-flight and dump whatever's inside over the ocean. *Some things you don't want to know*, thinks the usually ebullient American, trying to concentrate on his flying.

Where Améliana's ship took fifteen hours to sail three hundred kilometers, they do it in just under ninety minutes. Mid-flight, the pilot feels the plane jiggle. The President must be moving around in his seat back there. The sky is bright and calm, one-hundred-percent visibility clear to the horizon, not another aircraft in sight. It would be perfectly safe to turn around and look, but he refrains. Big-shot passengers value their privacy.

After almost ninety minutes without a word, they begin their descent. A sudden command issues from the back seat: "Pull up beside the hangar when you land."

The Islander touches down, taxies all the way over to a lone tin-roofed shed at the far end of the tarmac from the one-room terminal, and slows to a stop. The pilot turns off the ignition and wonders, as the engine roar dies away, if he should get out to open the passenger door for the President. Highest office in the land or not, today's passenger somehow doesn't seem to be in the mood for the VIP treatment. Just as he's thinking this, he hears Matías open the door and climb down, then a voice right outside the cockpit.

"Good job. I believe you've been told the pick-up date and time."

"Yessir," says the pilot, looking down to see not the President who boarded at Navidad International Airport in a double-breasted suit, but a beach bum in a faded blue aloha shirt, khaki shorts, yellow flip-flop sandals, an old Taiyo Whales baseball cap and dark glasses. The salt-and-pepper stubble on his chin seems to have grown during the flight, along with years of gray hair.

"My other clothes are in the bag in back. Make sure you bring them when you come to pick me up," says the old beachcomber.

"Sure thi—" The pilot doesn't even have time to finish two words before the squat figure shuffles off behind the hangar. Is no one meeting him? The pilot rubs his eyes in disbelief.

⚡

Rounding the corner of the hangar, Matías walks across the unfenced airfield and straight out onto the road. No one sees him; the dusty streets are deserted. No local officials have been alerted about his visit, nor has any car been sent. He sets off on foot in the direction of the first ceremonial site at Giba, a few hours away, though not ten minutes later a pickup truck pulls up and a stocky-armed matron leans out the window.

"Goin' to Giba?" asks the woman in that old familiar Melchor accent.

"The festival, you betcha," answers Matías, reviving his childhood drawl.

"Get on in," says someone else.

There are already half a dozen people or more riding in back. Matías thrusts one rubber-sandaled foot onto a tire, and a strong hand reaches out to help pull him up. It's been ages since he's hitched a ride in the back of a truck like this and even longer since he's known the goodwill of strangers. To his surprise, he feels elated to be returning to his anonymous roots. Men and women of various ages all nod greetings and the truck lurches into motion. In one corner, a boy of maybe seven is dozing on a mat, his head pillowed on a bright orange lifesaver. It's a wonder anyone can sleep on the iron bed of a truck chugging along an unpaved road, thinks Matías, grabbing the side panel to secure a hold. The boy bounces wildly each time they hit a pothole, but keeps sleeping through it all. Matías watches enviously out of the corner of his eye, wishing he had the knack for such oblivious rough-and-ready rest himself.

Cultural anthropologists have offered various interpretations of the Yuuka Yuumai celebrations. As early as the 1920s, when the eight-year events first came to the attention of the outside world, scholars arrived with their notebooks and pet theories. Here was a cargo cult in somewhat altered form, ran the principal explanation at the time, as the rites centered on a single ceremonial canoe that traveled around to multiple ceremonial sites carrying a hallowed messenger and a sacred object. As soon as the rites finished at one location, the presiding shaman-priestesses headed by land to meet the canoe "delivered" by a team of youthful rowers to the next site, where the ceremony started anew with a ritual greeting on its arrival.

The cargo cult proper was a messianic faith found exclusively in New Guinea from the mid-nineteenth century on, when natives saw white men receiving crates of strange industrial products that could not have been made by human hands and prayed for such heavenly bounty to find the tribe instead. Whereas in times past the gods would have delivered the goods directly, the Europeans were seen as somehow intervening with the gods to make off with items rightfully destined for themselves. So now the tribe entreated the gods to please send things to the correct recipients, typically by prostrating themselves before boat- or later airplane-shaped ritual objects made of wood and vines.

This line of explanation, however, went only so far when applied to what was actually observed on Melchor. The next wave of scholars on the scene saw the Yuuka Yuumai as a ritual recreation of the ancestors' first canoe voyage to the islands, intended to give thanks to past generations for this hard-won birthright and to beseech the spirits for their continued blessings. This theory made more sense, for indeed the verses sung at the ceremonies, however difficult to parse the ancient Melchorian, do seem to tell of the joy of reaching verdant shores and thus, by analogy, of inheriting an earthly paradise. Even so, exactly when people first came to inhabit the island is subject to debate. The local mythology has little to say about any such arrival, suggesting either all recall was lost long ago or some traumatic episode caused them to suppress it. But then, such rites surely bypass verbal transmission of racial memories anyway.

Yet another strong candidate for comparative anthropological relevance is found in the religious practices encountered in the southern Ryukyus and various parts of Polynesia that mime "rare visitant" ancestors and divinities. Once a year, or occasionally at greater intervals, spirits are thought to appear bearing good fortune from afar, whereupon people greet them with rituals and festive performances, before sending them back in due course across the seas. The joyous arrival theme heard in the sacred verses of Melchor thus probably better accords with a repeated visitation than the reenactment of a one-time protohistoric landing. Once every eight years, the islanders rejoice in welcoming "rare visitants" to their rich green homeland, in return for which those spirits—gods or ancestors, it remains unclear—bless the islands with continued abundance. The actual festivities affirm this two-fold character: the symbolic receiving of spiritual gifts is answered by giving offerings in thanks. Hence many scholars today subscribe to this "value exchange" scheme as the most viable interpretation.

The festival runs for two days and nights nonstop. Starting from Giba, the celebrants move seven times to other locations where similar acts of ritual dancing and singing are performed, culminating in the largest ceremony at Sarisaran. All proceedings are directed by the chief priestess or Yoi'i Yuuka, followed by seven lesser Yuuka and their virgin attendants. Laypersons gather around—solemn and boisterous by turns—chanting in chorus and generally making merry for forty straight hours until sheer exhaustion induces a trance-like state; they go "out of their minds," losing all sense of self and even gender before the otherworldly presences they claim to see with their own eyes. This is how Melchor Island gives itself to the spirits once every eight years.

↯

After driving for fifteen minutes, the pickup nudges its way through a scattered flank of people advancing at a brisk pace, until ten minutes later the numbers have packed in so thick around them that wheels are of no use. They abandon the truck in the middle of the road, and everyone climbs down to join the pilgrims all pressing ahead in the same direction. Even the driver gets out and starts walking. Other cars dot the area, but the people just flow around them as if they were rocks in a stream. Matías is walking as quickly as his short legs will carry him, when he remembers the sleeping boy. He turns around to look but sees no sign of the truck, let alone any of the others who were riding with him. Did someone wake the boy? Is he riding on his father's shoulders? He tries to recall his own boyhood Yuuka Yuumai experience. All he can remember from that time is the crush of people and how dark and scary it was at night.

Yes, but night is a long way off. It's barely past noon now, and the sun beats down mercilessly from high overhead. The ground is burning hot. He's sweating. No Nissan to chauffeur him about here; he's walking on his own two legs. Not a soul here knows he's the President, no one even cares that this country *has* a president. It feels wonderful to lose himself in their midst wearing only an aloha shirt, shorts, and baseball cap. But he's no youngster anymore, so how long can he hold out? If his physical strength fails, well, then let it. When the time comes, let him collapse by the roadside and sleep.

That's how the forty-hour festival goes. Whoever gets tired whenever sleeps wherever—and that sleep becomes part of the celebrations, no different than for those who stay awake to sing and dance. Hungry or fed, old or young, man or woman, rich or poor, it makes no difference. You're always free to sleep, if you're a lay pilgrim, that is. The Yuuka, the virgins, and the twenty-odd musicians have no such liberty. All of them must marshal their strength until the very end. The thought gives the anonymous Matías some measure of comfort. Yes, it's hard to be up on high, the focus of attention from below, and such a relief to cast it all aside.

Presently the crowd slows, foot traffic jams back to back. The people in front are now close enough for him to smell their excitement. Short-legged Matías can't see over the heads, not that anyone can see very far; all he can do is absorb the carnival atmosphere passed along the jostling bodies. Pilgrims have come to this island of a mere ten thousand all the way from Baltasár and Gaspar, and from even more distant outer islands. Foreign scholars, travel writers, and tourists push into the fray, all trying to get closer to the Yuuka and the sacred barge, to follow them around the island to the different sacred precincts. Very few will actually see the rituals with their own eyes; their limbs must become feelers to sense the shifting edges of the melee that moves them along like particles in a wave.

Matías tries to creep forward, but the crowd is at a standstill. All forward passage is blocked, so he leans to one side, finds an opening between two stout islanders, and with a decisive grunt, wedges himself under them toward the sound of flutes and drums. For the next hour, he crawls his way through the masses. Most festival-goers are resigned to staying put and react vehemently against the burrowing mole, elbowing him as hard they can. Still, little by little, he works his bulk forward each time anyone budges, until finally he finds himself almost at the outer perimeter of the sanctum. With eight pilgrimage sites, everyone stands a good chance of coming within viewing distance at least once. Experienced pilgrims have their own favorite vantage points, though few would try to take in all eight locations. Crowded though it is here, Giba is apparently a less popular site.

People are swaying to the rhythm of the drums up ahead, stepping back and forth as far as the next person will allow. Some, if they can raise their hands without striking their neighbors, mimic the motions of the oarsmen or the Yuuka who surround the sacred barge, blessing and being blessed. None are yet in a trance, but currents of nervous anticipation spread through the crowd. There is still much, much further to go.

Matías has threaded in as far as he is likely to here at Giba. He can only listen to the music and sense the ritual proceedings, storing up the prevading aura. Buoyed on the energy here among countless strangers, that distant, familiar, gently rippling music transports him—one phrase, then another alternating between breezes—into a state of harmony with the spirit of the occasion. No longer the President of the Republic nor Angelina's lover nor proprietor of the M. Guili Trading Company, he is simply one more Melchor islander again. He has been on his feet for hours, with nothing to eat or drink since breakfast, yet mysteriously his body does not protest; he doesn't even feel tired.

Then, long before the Giba ceremony is over, he decides to stake out somewhere closer at the next site in Zaran. Like a nail drawn to a powerful magnet, he extracts himself from the captivated crowds and, stopping only to drink from a spring, takes a path through a deserted settlement to walk the three kilometers to Zaran. There he finds several hundred people already milling about the village square. Poised in expectation, their faces are expressionless, purged of personality—conversely, a mark of faith.

Matías notices a pickup truck stopped along the road into the square, now half hidden in a sea of people. Some have jumped up onto the flatbed for a better view. Not a bad idea, he thinks, climbing up in back as nonchalantly as he can, and there he waits.

Long, quiet hours pass. Meanwhile, more and more pilgrims engulf the truck. Then, out of nowhere, a frisson of excitement sweeps through the crowd. Matías cranes his neck higher and can barely make out a thin white line—the Yuuka, virgins, and musical troupe—meandering slowly closer. As they approach, people hurriedly shuffle out of the way. Matías strains to see the seventh white figure, but from this distance he can't tell if it's Améliana. He doesn't know if the procession even reflects the order of the Yuuka.

The priestesses advance with resolute steps; they show no sign of having just conducted a three-hour ritual, then walked here without pausing to rest. They enter the square and kneel around a low dais of earth mounded in the center to await the arrival of the sacred barge. There they remain, silent and motionless, virtually asleep, though perhaps in some deeper state of consciousness. Whatever governs their bodies for forty hours straight is well out of the realm of normal metabolisms. Ordinary fatigue and pain and hunger no longer have any meaning.

After what seems like hours, though it might have been only a matter of minutes—Matías has lost all track of time—the sacred barge arrives by sea. Ten half-naked youths stow their oars, step out onto the beach, lift the hull up onto their shoulders and carry it into the square to place it on the dais, then vanish into the crowd. The actual ceremony has still not begun, yet their everyday labors have a natural dignity to them.

Once the oarsmen are gone, the crowd moves in one step closer. By now the back of the pickup truck is so overloaded with people that Matías can't see a thing. But then someone kindly gives him just enough room to squeeze his face through (at least he's too short to block anyone else's view), which effectively pushes someone else off the truck, but the person doesn't complain. Now there's an opening for Matías to crawl through on his hands and knees. After a while he's at the very front of the flatbed. From there, he gets a foothold on the truck door, reaches for an adjacent lamppost, then tries to swing himself up onto the roof of the driver's compartment only to find the space already occupied by three teenagers and a couple of kids. Okay, if he plants one foot on the roof and braces his weight against the lamppost, he has a sightline to the square straight across that sea of people. He can just see the boat and the priestesses kneeling around it.

The invocations are just beginning. The Yoi'i Yuuka mimes the act of sailing the barge across the high seas with the other Yuuka in their white robes and huge leaf crowns striding alongside, front to back, dancing like waves, while the virgins form a ring around them, spreading their arms and swaying to suggest a great ocean. The musicians accompany them with rhythms that, not surprisingly, emulate gently rolling waves. On board the barge he can just make out a sacred plaited palm-leaf box placed before the divine visitant, who sits covered head-to-toe in palm fronds. That role belongs, if Matías remembers correctly, to the third highest Melchor Elder. A lone man among women, his face is entirely hidden; only his arms and legs are visible. He neither moves nor utters a word. Not even when they move on to the next ceremonial site will he lift an oar. Transported together with the palm-leaf box, he is a ritual object whose immobility demands great self-control.

The boat ritual proceeds at a calm, even tempo. The vast sea has been invoked. Without the power of the sea, without the forces of current and wind and wave, the boat and its revered passenger—god or ancestor—go nowhere. These forces must deliver the barge safely to land where the Yuuka welcome it as human inhabitants—or no, perhaps as divinities now themselves?

The sacred barge arrives, the spirits alight and dispense blessings to the virgins, who then dance their joy at length and are answered in kind by the Yuuka, who also dance. The musicians stand, playing. The priestesses recite incantations blessing the ground of the square and, by extension, all of the earth. Then they chant a verse, praying that the boat and its holy of holies fare safely to the next ceremonial site, followed by a long, plaintive song of farewell and vows to meet again—if only two hours hence.

Matías watches all this from his precarious perch. How many hours has he been propped up against the lamppost? He has no idea. It's as if a transparent curtain had descended from heaven to earth, draping everyone and everything in a wholly different time. It hardly matters anymore which of the eight Yuuka is Améliana—or whether she's really here at all—Matías sees *her*, performing with chaste devotion.

The sad, slow song of departure drones on, finally fading into aftertones as the Yuuka and virgins all kneel in place. The more anxious pilgrims quickly break position and start off for the next rendezvous. After a prescribed interval, the Yuuka, virgins, and musicians all rise and also head toward the next ceremonial site via another, more secret path that does not cross any secular road. Their route may take them under bridges or through caves; some claim they must even traverse the treetops—no one knows for sure, though village kids are probably hiding and watching where they go. (Other kids, Matías recalls, never let him, the orphan boy who didn't know his own father, stand lookout.)

He climbs down from the pickup truck and wades into the crowd. Only now does he notice how tired he is—tired and hungry. The sky is now dark, and torches have been lashed to palm trees here and there. Looking up, he sees a brilliant, nearly full moon overhead. There's not a hint of cloud. He doesn't know where he's going, he just walks along with everyone else. Come to think of it, he missed lunch and dinner, but festival pilgrims are free to help themselves to the food set out on boards at each house. Some villagers even divine their fortunes good or bad for the next eight years from the popularity of their offerings: the faster the tidbits disappear, the better the family's prospects. The boards at the first few houses, however, are bare; earlier pilgrims must have eaten everything. *Got to keep going*, thinks Matías, *we're bound to find something eventually.*

"Hey you, where you from?" comes a voice, apparently intended as a greeting.

"You talking to me?" he asks back. It's been ages since anyone addressed him so casually.

"Yeah, you."

The speaker turns out to be an older man—or no, could they be about the same age? At one time he must have been taller, but now the man's back is so bent that he's forced to talk up even to Matías.

"I'm from here, from Zaran originally, but now I live in Baltasár City."

"And you come back for the festival?"

"Uh-huh," says Matías, adding, "Sure am hungry, though."

"Well, there's plenty around to eat," says the old man. "Try the super up ahead."

"The super's handing out food?"

"Yep. During Yuuka Yuumai, most stores got tables out front giving out free eats. Don't you know nothing?"

"I wasn't around last time. It's my first festival in years."

"Started the time before last, musta been. Nice custom."

The two of them walk along toward a halo of bright lights. It's a big storefront thronged with people. Others are standing just out of the light, all eagerly snacking on something.

"See, what'd I tell you? Guili Supermarket's doing a giveaway," says the old man as he picks up his pace. He must be hungry too. Matías follows after him to join a spontaneous queue. It feels strange to be lining up at his own supermarket. He had no idea the Melchor store provided free food to festival-goers. Presumably it was all written up somewhere in the accounts sent to him as owner-operator; no doubt he also could have requested a full report on the scheme, but his presidential duties don't spare him that kind of time. The food chain's been flipped on its head. From highest in the hierarchy, he's down at the bottom begging for handouts. Festivals are funny, he thinks, trying to restrain his hunger.

The festival freebies turn out to be an evolved version of instant ramen—cup noodles. Lined up in front of the supermarket are several large tables piled with boxes of the stuff. Young clerks in uniform blue T-shirts stand by with utility knives to cut open the foil seals on the styrofoam cups, pour in hot water from a succession of large kettles that others relay from inside, and finally hand one hot product and a plastic fork to each taker.

"Step right up! Takes three minutes," spiels a young assistant manager. "Just count to two hundred, nice and slow, while you wait. Or if you can't do the numbers, just watch how your neighbor does it. Gotta give it time, though, or it won't taste so good. Finish one, you can come get another. Eat as many as you like of these lip-smacking cup noodles, the Yuuka's snack food of choice. It's just Guili Super's little gift to all you hungry folks."

Standing on a step stool, the man is a born huckster, ready and able to use any opportunity for publicity. Why sure, the festive atmosphere adds pleasant associations to the taste, tonight's free samples and free spirits helping to trap tomorrow's cash customers. One after another famished pilgrim passes up the traditional boiled taro and bananas set out by ordinary houses, or fried fingerlings lovingly prepared by poorer families, and reaches instead for the Japanese treat directly imported courtesy of M. Guili's capital advantage. Maybe it's a sign of the times? But now, for the first time, the man who rode his instant ramen breakthrough to the top of a new economic model is seeing that whole construct from the bottom up.

The old man gets his cup and fork and moves off, after which a plump girl in regulation blue quickly presses the identical items on Matías. Immediately, the queue ratchets up behind him, so he too moves to the side of the road. He slowly counts to two hundred, then carefully peels back the seal and savors the soy-scented steam before forking up some noodles. While they cool slightly, Matías watches the assistant manager working the crowd. He looks familiar; they must have been introduced at some company function. Good thing he didn't see his boss—the President of the Republic himself—standing right in front of him.

Matías, mouth full of ramen, meditates on his present anonymity: to be nobody in a crowd out in front of Guili's Supermarket is quite different from being an anonymous participant in the festival. To enjoy the blessings that the sacred barge and Yuuka share out is a privilege, but to get hooked on cup noodles merely makes a consumer keep coming back to spend his last handful of change. Even so, this little man in his aloha shirt, shorts, and sunglasses standing by the road eating noodles picks up enough pocket money from those consumers to run his political machine.

Can't a country operate any other way in this day and age? Are the capital interests that would exploit the Yuuka Yuumai so insatiable? Matías had imagined he was here for the age-old appeal of the festival (Améliana's spiritual pull adding an extra tug), but no, he sighs, the scheme of things inevitably involves his own secular connections.

Or no again, the real reason he sighed and hesitated to dig in was that the cup noodles were still too hot to swallow all at once. And honestly, to make things worse, the first slurp was so good—the pasta perfectly firm, each bite-sized ingredient releasing a new burst of flavor in a broth rich with pork fat and vegetable extracts and MSG to tease the taste buds—he can hardly wait for the temperature to come down a few notches so he doesn't burn his tongue. Hell, he may be president and supermarket tycoon and pilgrim all rolled into one, but there's nothing like a good ramen. Pure oral pleasures are the best.

Matías empties his cup down to the last drop of broth and decides to go queue up again, when he spies the same old man, flimsy styrofoam cup in hand, glancing over at him and grinning. For one brief second, Matías flinches—has he been found out?

At the third ceremonial site, Matías doesn't go all the way forward but stays deep in the crowd, letting the energy of the rituals carry to him through the waves of humanity. As the charged atmosphere buzzes late into the night, he can feel himself replenished—by the moonlight beaming down from high in the sky, by the strains of festival music floating nearer and farther, by the unseen motions of the Yuuka, by the mystic powers radiating from the boat at the center of it all. Everyone here feels much the same thing.

By the time the moon sinks in the sea to the west, just as the first intimations of dawn filter in, though the hills block direct view of the eastern sky growing light, the ceremony comes to a close. Not once this time did he see the Yuuka. The crowd starts to break up, carrying Matías along with it. Luckily the fourth location is not far away. As Matías stumbles along, he remembers he hasn't slept in over twenty-four hours. Of course he's been getting by on extremely little sleep of late, but he *is* over sixty-four after all. All eight ceremonies would be pushing his luck, but he feels confident that he can manage one more.

Yet somehow he can't get into the spirit of things at the fourth site, as if the festival magic had lost its effect. He's able to go fairly far forward and claim a place on the beach close enough to see the barge and Yuuka in the distance over the shoulders of other seated pilgrims. People are standing not far behind, but around him everyone stays low and sways on their haunches, all rapt expressions and ecstatic cries. Why can't he get into the mood? No longer one of the faithful flotsam, he's back to being the president just as surely as when he's at the Presidential Villa; a politician soberly observing this superstitious premodern spectacle, this waste of energy that brings everyday affairs to a halt.

Or maybe the festival spirit has given up on him. It's as if someone or something has now denied him entry here. Why this jaded, apathetic feeling? In a celebration of selfless belonging, why is he himself again? After all the secrecy involved in shedding his official identity, why has he suddenly reverted to keeping a watchful eye on civil disruption?

Clouds of suspicion boil up inside him, choking his mind with appre-
hension. It's as if the Yuuka had ritually laid the entire blame for people's
misfortunes at his feet. He's an outsider, he doesn't belong here. Worse than
that, what if people notice he doesn't belong? In their aroused state, they
might turn on him and tear him to pieces. The fear becomes palpable. He's a
crow among doves, he can't stay here.

At the high point of the ceremony, while the virgins are doing a dance of
praise before the Yuuka, Matías turns away and wades out through the crowd
without anyone stopping him. It must be around seven thirty in the morning.
The outskirts of the village are deserted save for gangs of early-rising kids who
clamor to get a view, unlikely though it is that they'll be able see past all the
adults who fill the festival precincts.

He walks along, heading nowhere in particular. What's wrong with him?
Is it just exhaustion catching up unannounced? Better take a breather, go lie
down somewhere and take a nap, but he's not really sleepy. He keeps walking, then remembers that one of his own houses is somewhere in the vicinity.
Not an old family home—he's lost track of his mother's relations for the most
part—it's a property he bought before he became president, as an inciden-
tal investment when M. Guili Trading was beginning to show a profit. He's
stayed there, what, three times all told, a decade ago. Always wanted to rent
it out, but there's no market on Melchor, so he just kept it for when and if,
employing an old pensioner from the Guili Supermarket in Zaran to look after
the place from time to time. Now if he can only jog his memory, where does
the man hide the key? Oh, he'll probably find it once he gets there. He'll be
able to rest up, maybe catch a little shut-eye.

He finds the house and the key in no time. Inside, the air is still. Everything
looks neat and tidy; the old caretaker has been doing his job. There's a bedroom in back, shuttered and secluded, but the sofa in the main room will do
just fine. He's dead tired; he doesn't need nightmares, no shadowy anxieties
coming back to seize him. No panic, no dread, just let him recuperate enough
to go see the next ceremony. People will let him rejoin the festival, won't
they? Thoughts spiral, but his body demands its due until his head gives in.
But more than that, it's the otherness of this island, the aura of Améliana and

the Yuuka that grant him sleep. He stretches out on the sofa and, very much like his nightly blackouts at the Presidential Villa, promptly slides down a steep incline into unconsciousness.

⚡

He wakes in the dark, then slowly recognizes his whereabouts: he's on the sofa in his house on Melchor. What time did he come here and fall asleep? It must have been morning. He can't have slept that long, but that's the full moon right outside the window. Last night the moon had almost completely waxed, and the Yuuka Yuumai begins on the eve of the full moon. Has he slept through one whole day on this wobbly sofa? How many years has it been since he slept so much? How is it possible?

The fifth ceremony will of course be over by now, probably also the sixth. Even if he hurries, he'll be so far back he won't see a thing at the seventh. No, it would make more sense to go on ahead to Sarisaran and just wait. Those earlier fears seem to have mysteriously vanished. Purified by sleep, he somehow knows he'll be accepted among the festival-going faithful. The fifth through seventh ceremonial sites are all the way over on the other side of the island, but the sacred barge circles back for the last observance at Sarisaran, an easy hike from here.

Matías starts walking and almost immediately feels hungry. He can make a short detour over to the supermarket for another cup noodle handout, but he'd rather eat something more substantial. The house up ahead has set out a washbasin full of deep-fried taro dumplings dusted with sugar—the absolute best treat around when he was a kid. There's also a large pitcher of water and cups. No one is about and no one seems to be home either, so he helps himself to a skewer of dumplings and a nice big cup of water. Can't beat simple fare—this is the real thing. So what the hell did he eat not twenty-four hours ago at his own store? What *was* that mass-produced crap he imported by the crate-load from factories half a world away to make his fortune? What does that make him? His wealth, even his presidential career are built on a bubble that a single stick of dumplings can burst.

He tries not to think about it and hurries off toward Sarisaran, passing several pilgrims dozing by the roadside on the way. Fifteen minutes later, he reaches the sanctum and finds a good hundred people there ahead of him, already positioned in silence on the sand waiting for the arrival of the Yuuka and the boat. Matías wanders in among them and locates a free patch of ground. Nothing is happening yet, but mysteriously—at least to him—he blends right in unnoticed.

Suddenly he's completely hemmed in by people. He must have dozed off again—altogether extraordinary after these past few years without normal sleep—but now a stir ripples through the crowd. Every eye is on the young oarsmen carrying the barge up to the final earthen dais, around which sit the eight priestesses and festival band.

The music begins. The Yuuka rise and slowly start their boat-landing dance, with special hand and foot movements, the orientation of the barge and dancers' bearing all subtly distinguishing Sarisaran as the holiest site in the cycle. Even the time spent on each movement here differs from the other seven places. Matías strains to follow every nuance and gesture, not feeling estranged in the least, but as if Sarisaran held him in a welcoming embrace. The feeling intensifies: a rapport he shares with every person here—newly initiated youth and toothless crone, man and woman, rich and poor, sick and well—each imagining himself the sole focus of the ritual. All the Yuuka seem to be Améliana, performing body and soul just for him. Through them the gods have been joyously welcomed from far across the waves, offered song and dance, entreated for eight more years of happiness, praised for things large and small, anger of mountain and wrath of sea assuaged, motions of the sun and all other heavenly bodies assured, in order that the reef teem with fish and fields with taro, that foreigners dripping with money be sucked toward the islands, that healthy children continue to be born and grow up to share in all this bounty. Each and every pilgrim believes it to be so—and for the moment, Matías counts himself among them.

By this final ceremony, how utterly exhausted they all must be. How can the Yuuka and attendants, musicians and rowers have stayed so focused in body and mind for so long with no food or sleep, when he dropped out midway? How can he presume to even ask? And yet there's something very odd about the way he dropped out—or seemed to be driven away by unseen forces that conspired to tell him, "You don't deserve to take part in more than half the ceremonies. You are denied the full eight-fold purification."

Even so, Matías feels elated. To be here on this spot with the festival air filling one's body is to reconfirm the joy of being alive. To be born into this world and feel, looking up at the sky, smelling the sweet breeze, that for once one is truly in touch with the world, *that* is happiness. Even if it lasts no longer than three days, those days are bliss. Whether born a bird or a sea urchin or a ylang-ylang flower or a human being, all births seem equally precious; every bite of food, every footstep and blink of the eye, every ray of sunlight and molecule of oxygen is an increment of that happiness.

By the last dance to send off the barge, Matías realizes he is crying. His tears make the moon swim, the entire torchlit scene shimmer. His eyes blur with saltwater delivered from otherworldly seas to wash away the silt of day-to-day authority. His coming here was a homecoming. Blessed are the nameless for they alone shall know this state of grace.

No one here is a spectator. All are celebrants. They alone guarantee the rituals will be passed on and performed next time. Those who witnessed all eight ceremonies, those who skipped the middle part and those who caught only the finale expecting a few spiritual perks, all now stagger home under a weight of god-given gifts—or perhaps simply stiff from standing or sitting for hours—to get a good rest before returning to their lives.

Matías sits quietly watching the crowd disperse. He's tired, but there are things he still has to do. The rowers carry the sacred barge off to a boat shed five minutes from Sarisaran. There it will stay, save for an annual paddle around the lagoon to check for leaks, until the next Yuuka Yuumai cycle. The Yuuka and their attendants change out of their robes on the beach, two dozen of them forming a ring and, several at a time beginning with the youngest, slipping inside to put on street clothes. Matías sees the circle gradually transformed from pure white and vermilion to denim blue and floral-print pastels and brash T-shirt primaries—the casually chaotic colors of a marketplace. Nothing quite spells the end of the festivities as this does.

Ten minutes later, the women have shed all holy mystery and returned to their secular selves: housewives and schoolgirls who, taxed far beyond ordinary exhaustion, now go their separate ways without any parting words. Out of the corner of his eye, Matías sees them leave, but he's looking for Améliana. At no point in the ceremonies could he single her out with any certainty, but now back in regular clothes with no kava leaf crown to hide her face she's easy to spot. She's wearing the white cotton dress with large red buttons down the front she wore the day she left Baltasár City. He gets up and approaches, cutting in front of her as she starts to move off in a daze.

"A real effort you put in there. You must be exhausted," he says in a voice recognizable as her employer's, back at the Presidential Villa.

She looks at him blankly, as though lacking the strength to even show surprise at finding him here in beachcomber clothes. "So you came."

"Yes, I just got the urge. Dropped my work and came." He hopes his expression shows sufficient admiration for her forty-hour spiritual ordeal.

"From when?"

"From the beginning. I rested out the middle, though. I've got a place here, if you need to sleep." At that, he forges ahead like a guide, not even knowing whether she'll follow. She might have a place of her own, after all. Then, after a few steps, he turns to see her hobbling mechanically close behind like a wind-up doll, no spare energy to consider where she's going or why she's following this man. All her powers have been spent on the festival, for the sake of the island, for the inhabitants of Navidad, for everyone on earth. All to wrest some assurance of eight years of calm and quiet for others, however wrong their ways.

People are heading back to home and hotel as Matías leads Améliana to the house where he blacked out just hours before. She steps inside and, doing as Matías tells her, goes to the bedroom and collapses onto the bed in her clothes.

Matías takes a seat on the sofa in the front room. As he gazes at the morning light pouring in through the window, the tides of festival elation steadily ebb, leaving him grounded in his normal sober self. It feels strange to be out of the Presidential Villa for so long, though equally unsettling—probably because he's been doing something so unusual—to be on his own here. He doesn't really believe Katsumata or anyone else will attempt a coup in his absence, but the driving obsessions, thoughts that the country needs him, are reemerging. Still, he has a few hours before his pilot is supposed to pick him up. He can relax and bask in the sun a while, with a sleeping woman nearby.

Again he dozes off and reawakens with his head in a fog, some afterglow of the festival in his system. He vaguely recalls his official duties, but more than any immediate policy decision or dealings with legislators, the deployment of subordinates or negotiations with Japan, he feels an urge to just go on sitting here and consider his own options. Something's pushing him in a new direction. Something's about to give. Call it a premonition, but some major change is coming; it's *that* time. Time to think not about the days and weeks and months ahead, but much further off, though he can't picture himself as old and wizened like the Melchor Elders, he can't imagine Angelina with a head of white hair like María Guili.

But no, wait, he finds he can look down on himself from high above, from Lee Bo's perspective. There's the bustling village square. The friendly everyday Navidadians. What's going on here? Has he died? How can he be seeing these things? Well, sure, he has to die sometime. No telling when, but this body will perish, another spirit lodged in another body will walk the earth, think and love and work for others, laugh and cry and bear children. A happy soul. With his dead self watching over it.

Will anyone remember him? Once upon a time there was a man named Matías Guili who went as far as to become president and shape the workings of this country, pulled people up to the living standards they enjoy today, skillfully created a network of promises with other more powerful nations and, in exchange for all that, skimmed a lot off the top. He saw the presidential system firmly established here, made various arrangements for the next generation of politicians to carry on, then withdrew—will people remember that? Will they put as many flowers on his grave—or more—than on the grave of Cornelius?

It's not the number of flowers, though. It's not whether people remember him or not. Dying ends all that. All posthumous glory is pointless. An instant after death none of it will matter; all acquisitions and debts will be set back to zero so the mind can rest in peace. Rest in nothingness. So much the better. He can just relax and have nice long talks with Lee Bo or the ghost of Cornelius or Ryuzoji or Micael and María Guili. Eventually Angelina will show up too. And it wouldn't be such a bad thing to see Bonhomme Tamang and apologize. He'll probably never forgive and forget, but in the afterlife how bad can that be?

What *is* he thinking? He must be burned out from the festival, that's what's putting these crazy ideas in his head. He's in this alone and he's going to the next world alone. And anything that happens between now and then, no matter how grand and glorious it looks from the wings, is really just liquidating holdings. No matter how many more terms he serves as president, it's straight on from here for Matías Guili, and that's fine with him.

But what if people *do* forget all about him after he's gone? Who's to guarantee they won't? His name will become a footnote in the history books, his memorial stone obscured by moss, while Angelina goes on to find another lover and the next president (who's it to be?) sets the country on a totally different course. Fair enough, though he'd have liked to leave some lasting mark. Not a soft spot in people's hearts, nothing so iffy as warm feelings or respect—something more indelible.

Ah, if only he had an heir. Why wasn't he so lucky? Tsuneko wouldn't keep quiet on the subject. The desire to give love a tangible shape in the form of a child, it's not like he didn't understand it. Young, ignorant, and bursting with sex drive as he was, he did it twice a day, morning and night with an older and, frankly, ugly woman, and never tired. Took her at her word that she didn't want children—but really she did. She took no precautions. All right, Matías was foreign-born, but he was her last chance to father her child, clearly that's what she believed. Almost fooled him too—squeezed every last drop of semen out of him. And yet, for all the incessant fucking, not once did she get pregnant. Not a hint. And then in the end, as he was boarding ship, she said it—"You have dead seed."

Never considered that. All that time he'd thought the trouble was on

Tsuneko's side. It must have been simply ego that prevented Matías from thinking it through further. Maybe that's what made him not go after younger women and shack up so cozily with María. Fidelity to her meant he never needed to find out whether the infertility was on his side or not. With any other young and willing and fecund partner, of whom there must have been many when M. Guili Trading Company was just hitting its stride, he couldn't have *not* known. Not having risen to the occasion, he sees now, was enough to raze any erection. He blew it twice and for all eternity.

Wait, maybe all is not lost after all. Maybe he just hasn't given it a decent try. What about the girl asleep in the next room? She's young, body brimming with all the blessings of the Yuuka Yuumai, and she's completely conked out. She bore her brothers and cousins a son, didn't she? Maybe she can be persuaded to give him one last chance.

As if germinating in the morning sunlight, strange thoughts arise in his mind, expanding with a life of their own. What if Tsuneko was wrong? There's one way to find out. He gets up, drawn to this available sleeping partner not by some vague, uncontrollable urge, but a specific desire to procreate, an aim so far-off it will almost justify anything.

He walks quietly into the next room and goes over to the bed. He looks down at Améliana lying innocently in her white cotton dress on the floral print sheets, sleeping face-up, eyes firmly shut, arms stretched out to either side. She's barefoot, her kicked-off rubber sandals lying beside the bed. Deep asleep, her breathing is scarcely discernible. He must look like this when he sleeps. She's completely unconscious, in no state to refuse anything, enjoying a special respite granted by the gods. Would the gods punish him for disturbing her? No, the gods have baited this seductive trap and will laugh at whoever is lured in.

He wants to feel her bare skin. Her upper arm shows below her short balloon sleeves. He reaches out and touches the soft warmth, a resilience underpinned by the hardness of bone. But for now he doesn't press; he merely runs his fingers lightly over her. Améliana doesn't move. He places his entire palm on her and waits for her body heat to come across. There are truly all sorts of sensations in this world—hard and soft, rough and sharp, cool and warm, wet and dry—but none as familiar and thrilling as touching the skin of another human being.

He kneels down on the wooden floor and moves closer on his hands. He's near enough to smell the odor of sweat and wind and dust and torch smoke on her. For forty hours, all eyes have been on her as she performed one complicated ritual procedure after another, feet in step, arms waving in supplication to the gods. Eight ceremonies, the dark paths in between, the fierce sun and full moon, the spiritual communion with the seven other priestesses, all the dense, long hours have left layers of scent on her skin.

Améliana does not move. Her sleeping figure doesn't beckon by any stretch of the imagination, but defenseless it is. Will the gods not protect her? Or will lightning strike if he takes another step? This is the body that invited her seven brothers and cousins to have their fun. A body that bore a baby boy. He reaches out and unfastens the first of the large red buttons that run down the center of her torso. He's as nervous as if he'd broken into a house in the owner's absence. Another button. The skin of her neckline is beautiful, dark and gleaming smooth. Another button. She's young. Beauty is no excuse; beauty is always seductive, and whoever falls for it is lost. Which is maybe not such a bad thing.

To his credit, the notion that he is entitled to do anything he wants because he's president does not spring to mind. Given his position, he easily could have told Island Security to abduct her and bring her to his bed at the Presidential Villa, and he knows the world is full of leaders capable of doing so (and not a few young women who would consider it an honor). But Matías was never the womanizer, he was satisfied in the past with just María and now with just Angelina; the few occasions he slept with new girls at her brothel, it was less out of lust than curiosity, a shadow partner's dutiful curiosity. In most cases, one time was enough (the few second times served only to reexamine qualities he may have missed), after which he always reported his findings to Angelina as accurately as possible. No, lust is not his principal vice.

He undoes two more buttons to finally expose her breasts. Just the right size and shape. Small nipples and large areolas nicely set off from the surrounding skin. Springy to the touch of a finger. Améliana doesn't even twitch.

Ever so slightly, her breasts rise and fall with her breathing, two sacred vessels gently resting on her chest. Her expression never changes. One by one he continues unbuttoning. She's not wearing underwear. During the ceremonies, she wouldn't have worn anything so Western under her robes.

The tender swell of her belly comes into view, and beneath that a tuft of pubic hair sprouting like reeds in rich soil. The last two buttons. Below her mons, her body divides into two firm thighs, ending in shapely shins and ankles. Fallen limply to either side, her dress no longer protects her. Can the white folds really abandon their duty so easily?

Her pubic hair is a tiny flame, burning with an intensity concentrated in that secret inner chamber, signaling that inside resides an energy just waiting to be coaxed into form.

He puts his hands between her knees and gently forces her legs apart, then reaches under her calves to spread them wider with only the least passive reflexes of the dormant body—not will or habit, but simply bone and muscle tissue reacting to external pressure.

She doesn't wake. The gods are not with her. She can put up no resistance.

Parted genitals: a complexity that at once forbids and invites. Who can really tell what's open or not? Yet whatever makes it through that doorway counts as intercourse. And in the warm dark interior of the womb, the child will grow for nine months until it's born. At which point, there's no question of with or without consent. His own mother obviously thought so. As did the father. The end result is everything.

She sleeps on. Her pubic hair is beautiful. Her thighs are spread, her genitals glisten. He takes off his clothes, then climbs onto the bed and settles in between her thighs. With his skin touching her legs, her breasts, her midriff—already he's getting a hard-on. Is it him or the gods wanting the deed done? Whichever, the cock is his and it's erect enough by now. His pudgy belly gets in the way of seeing any more than the very tip of his cock, but he knows what to do. He spreads her wide open, presses up close and shoves in.

It's no use. No lack of lubrication, but something isn't right. Can he do this completely without her cooperation? She's still fast asleep, no change in her crotch at all. He's the only one getting off here. Like Heinrich, he gets frenzied, driven to penetrate despite the discomfort. He rocks back and forth, but the tip slips out. No, this won't work. He's got to spread her thighs more... He rides up on top of her, struggling to thrust in on his own solitary power. He pushes her thighs wide, he can feel his tension mounting, he grabs at her ass to press harder and harder, and in the confusion, just when he thinks he's *there* all the way inside—an illusion...—he ejaculates.

Suddenly the room swarms with tiny butterflies, swirling about the two of them on the bed, diving at their sweat, choking all the air in the room. Matías looks up in alarm, unable to make out the walls; all he sees is a fluttering lilac storm. The girl and her butterflies, it's a wonder he didn't see any during the ceremonies. No matter, he's done, he's finished.

He pulls out. Suddenly all the butterflies have vanished. Did he actually see them? Now he's starting to doubt he even got his sperm all the way in, though the close, contained heat he felt was all too real. No, he remembers the spurt of release. Simultaneously, sitting on the edge of the bed in a haze, it comes back to him that his own mother was violated like this. His own act has now come full circle to something that has dogged him since puberty, the notion that he himself is the result of rape. How could he go and do the same thing?

His cock slowly shriveling, he gets up off the creaky bed. Améliana still doesn't move, her legs still splayed apart. *Look at your handiwork*, thinks Matías, reaching over to close them, the very least he can do to cover up his crime. How can she possibly sleep through all this? Should he button up her dress the way it was? That's when he sees it: the stain. A bright red spot on the white cotton fabric just under her behind. No, it can't be. Was it her period? She's bleeding all right. He wipes himself off—semen and fresh blood.

Didn't she say she had a son by her brothers and cousins? How the hell can she still have been a virgin? This is crazy. He gets a towel from the bathroom and wipes Améliana's thighs and genitals. But what to do about her stained dress? She can't help but notice when she eventually wakes up. She'll know.

Matías is starting to get scared, doubt creeping toward paranoia, the fear that he's being pushed about by forces he can't begin to comprehend. Was

Améliana really a virgin? Then why would she have lied about bearing a child? No, maybe she wasn't lying. Those were words put in her mouth on that occasion, lines she recited. She's just a pawn in a much larger game. The mistake was seeing her until just now as innocent. She's not young and attractive; she's part of a huge plot, and this was her assigned role.

Now he's getting angry. Never in all his life has he been so manipulated. If he's up against an unseen enemy, then there's not a single move he can make without questioning. In any case, he can't stay here any longer. This is a crime scene.

He folds the girl's dress over her without bothering to do up the buttons, then runs. At least she's alive. She's just sleeping. He'll have to pretend he played no part in that ugly crime. He can't invite her to ride back with him in the presidential plane as he planned; he's got no time to lose waiting around for her to wake up. She'll need a hell of a lot more sleep anyway. Shielded by this logic, he bolts from the house. If he hurries, he'll get to the airfield just about in time for the plane. Will she catch her ship? What if she doesn't come back at all? Will she never show herself again at the Presidential Villa? If not, that's just how it goes. He can only wait and see—although he would like to clarify what happened within the next nine months.

BUS REPORT 10

A commercial film crew came all the way from Japan to shoot a swimsuit advertisement on location in Navidad. In addition to the cameraman and his two assistants, there was a big-name director and his glorified "go-fer" assistant director, a thirty-something makeup artist, a young stylist, and four models, along with two reps from the sponsor. They booked eight twin rooms and one large suite at the Navidad Teikoku Hotel for two weeks solid, and a local agent from Guili Tours and Travel chartered a motorboat and two four-wheel-drive SUVs for them to go shoot at various places around the islands. The women—models and stylist—arrived three days before the others to get a head start on their tans and, of course, continued their daily sunbathing throughout the shooting schedule. Every day the stylist selected different colored swimsuits to go with the deepening shades of tan so as to create an entire "elegant" to "sporty" fashion portfolio, and every evening the crew watched the day's rushes on the TV monitor in the hotel suite. It was an occasion for smiles all around: the director was very pleased with the images; the reps were satisfied with the progress made.

Naturally, there were other reasons why the three men were so pleased and satisfied. By the second or third night, each had suc-ceeded in singling out a favorite model and chatting her up; the fourth model was the cameraman's girlfriend. Thus, the two twin rooms reserved for the girls went unoccupied every night, but nobody seemed to care. The assistant director and makeup man were a steady gay couple of five years' standing. The remaining two assistant cameramen both tried to proposition the stylist, who was actually cuter and more photogenic than any of the models, but she wouldn't let either of these underlings near her. Duly spurned, the two young men withdrew and spent the rest of the two weeks shar-ing the same room, one snoring, one grinding his teeth, each cursing the other—though secretly they didn't feel quite so bad because they'd both been rejected equally. Meanwhile, the stylist enjoyed a good sound sleep alone every night, so that by the end of the trip, she looked even more beautiful than any of her model charges.

The first three days of shooting, they went by boat around the southern tip of Baltasár Island to Pearl Beach, where they shot at sunset for a dramatic backdrop of brilliant colors shimmering off the surf. A picturesque pair of palm trees further down the beach added just the right accent when floodlit. After that, they did some test shots in the mangroves on Gaspar Island and on the uninhabited islets between the two islands. One day, they went to Uu village, a short drive south of Baltasár City, and enlisted all the local children as extras for a "fun" interlude. Another day, they went to the old Japanese military airfield just north of Colonia Village and shot on the abandoned runway with no sea in sight. Which admittedly was something of a risk in a swimsuit commercial, but the images of bikini babes loitering on an airstrip-to-nowhere turned out so curiously evocative that the director gave the footage his thumbs-up. They could even use these to lay down the main theme and intercut it with different sea shots for balance. Once that was settled, they spent the rest of the time taking pick-up shots at an odd little rock formation inside Saguili Reef to the west of Gaspar. Known as Bird Island, this site afforded a veritable catalog of different land features in miniature—white sand beach, mangrove swamp, tropical jungle, boulder-strewn shingle—all in one convenient spot.

All in all a perfect job, everyone agreed on the evening of the wrap at the Navidad Teikoku Hotel restaurant. They toasted their good fortune over some nondescript "multicontinental cuisine" prepared from a potpourri of ingredients: two-thirds flown in from America and Japan and a scant third, as an afterthought, from local produce. Given that photo shoots are generally plagued by one mishap or another, this had to be some kind of miracle. Toasts rang out all around: to the stylist for scouting these islands (she'd vacationed here two months before, all by herself), to the models for their perfect suntans, to the swimsuits and the manufacturer for its taste, to the cameraman for his sure-shot technique, to the stylist again for her consistent on-the-job focus, and of course to the director for his vision and skill in overseeing the project. No one bothered to praise the two camera assistants, principally because there was no occasion to; they'd done their bit, so while the others were patting each other on the back, they'd already taken the first flight home.

So far so good, but when they got back to Japan and started reviewing the videotapes on professional monitors at the editing studio, they noticed a strange apparition in every cut: a green and yellow striped bus that no one had any recollection of shooting but which was always in frame. In the most perfect takes, just as the models ran up the sand toward the camera kicking up a fantastic spray, a big bright bus meandered across the background. Which was impossible; that was deep water. But each time they replayed the tape, there it was: a bus crossing the waves from right to left. In the crucial airfield footage, a good half of the marvelous background was ruined by that same bus. And in the Bird Island shots, where the models lined up in a row on the beach looking straight at the camera, there alongside them was the bus politely facing this way too. Despite the fact that the cameraman had framed the shot edge-to-edge on the four models, with no room on-screen for anything else, the playback was now four girls plus one bus wide— and the bus was practically fender-to-shoulder with the last model, leaving no margin to crop it out.

When the director arrived and took a look, he couldn't believe his eyes. It was crazy. He hit the REPLAY button mechanically over and over again, but no matter how many times he watched, the bus was there as plain as day. He called in the entire crew; they were struck speechless. The director began to cry. Then, after an awkward silence, everyone gasped in unison, "The whole time on the islands, we never once saw any green and yellow bus." A video camera is made to record only what shows in the viewfinder, so maybe someone had composited in the bus image as a prank? Yet there was no sign of any digital hanky-panky. The two camera assistants who had failed to score and came home early were immediately suspected, but whatever their hard feelings, such precision image synthesis was technically beyond them.

They tried to erase the bus electronically frame by frame, but it was too big. The gaping holes it left were too unnatural to fill by copy and pasting pixels. Moreover, the bus wasn't just in one or two shots; the thing was there consistently throughout the whole two weeks of footage, so everyone had to admit this couldn't be any slipup or freak accident; there simply was no rational explanation. A budget of thirty million yen had vanished into thin air. The advertising agency, sponsor, and director himself ended up splitting the loss three ways, each side still blaming the others—much too late in the game, of course, because they hadn't taken out insurance on the job (though even if they had insured, what underwriter would have covered their outrageous claims?).

The real problem now wasn't money, but time. There wasn't a moment to lose arguing. They had to go find some island where absolutely no phantom bus would spoil the show. Neither budget nor season would stretch indefinitely to permit another remote location, so they opted for one of the outer Ogasawara Islands due south of Tokyo. The crew members canceled all other work, flew in by chartered helicopter, and thanks to good weather, finished shooting in three days. Each take was shot simultaneously by two separate cameras, and each of those two tapes was immediately dubbed to yield four tapes. These were then couriered via different routes—airmail, seamail, helicopter—to the studio, where day after day the editing staff thoroughly screened each new arrival; but of course no bus was to be seen on any of them.

That summer, the sponsor's swimsuits sold well in spite of the rushed remake. Having headed off the worst-case scenario, at least no one could pin flagging sales on insufficient advertising. Boasts about the might-have-been-masterpiece commercial notwithstanding, tall tales of the phantom bus and three-way financial loss were bandied about the industry for years to come.

07

From early morning until just after midday, the plaza buzzes with shoppers and pedestrian traffic, then sees a long lull: a hot, muggy blank until the cool of the evening when people come out again. Still, there are always a few souls who sit out the afternoon heat on the benches and shoot the breeze. The plaza is only ever completely deserted for a few hours in the dead of night.

"Hear anything 'bout the bus?" asks the schoolteacher.

"Seems to be having a good ol' time running around all over the place. Heard it goes to church sometimes and drinks soda pop," says the barber.

"We never hear nothing like that at the station," puts in a Radio Navidad staffer.

"That's cos the real important news doesn't ever reach you. The one person in this town who knows everything is the barber. Always has been," says a housewife, the radio man's older sister.

"That's right. People come in and loosen up and talk. Done heard about all kinds of bus sightings. I say let it have a good time while it can."

"Yeah, but when's it gonna come out of hiding? Or does it plan on staying gone for good? And why'd it go on the lam in the first place?"

"Rumor is, it was miffed with the President," the schoolteacher informs them.

"The bus was?"

"Well, maybe somebody else made it disappear. Somebody who wanted to have a little fun with the folks on board. Somebody bigger than the Melchor Elders, somebody we can't see or hear, who's there and not there like the wind or stars or ants."

"A bigger-than-human something."

"I'm just telling you what I heard."

"So what you're saying is, the President's gotta bow his head and apologize before the bus come out again?" asks the housewife.

"The President prob'ly don't even know his doings have offended them higher up. Which means the bus is gonna stay fugitive and beep around the bush forever."

"Well, the President *is* mighty high-handed. He has Island Security set fire to people's houses," says the radio station man in a lower voice. As an employee of Radio Navidad he really shouldn't say anything bad about Guili and his henchmen, not that he really cares. Nothing said here is likely to be held against him.

"Can't be that simple. It's gotta go way deeper than we know about," says the schoolteacher.

"Plenty of that. Most of what the President does, people don't know hoot about. That's how he works things. The Presidential Villa's another world," says the barber.

"How long's it been like this?"

"Since forever. That's just how he is," pronounces the radio station man, assuming an air of authority.

"Nah, that ain't true. When he took over after Cornelius, he was fair and square. He listened to the legislature and didn't fall over hisself trying to please Japan. He was still on our side," says the barber.

"Right, that's why he got reelected," adds the schoolteacher.

"He was reelected?"

"Why sure, for four years—no, make that eight. I've had to teach our kids that President Matías Guili is the highest man in the land for eight years running."

"It's these last two years, that's when he turned for the worse," reflects the housewife.

"It's the hotel what did it. He really forced that construction through, and for no good reason. That's when people got their first good look at how high-and-mighty he was."

"The Navidad Teikoku Hotel, sure was a big stink. My husband's parents had their land confiscated to build that thing."

"Scandalous."

"You said it. It was Japanese money, all right, but not a bit of it legit. No traceable names, it's all funny money. Nothing to do with the real Teikoku Hotel," says the barber, who obviously wants it known he's done his homework.

"You mean they got a Teikoku Hotel in Japan?" asks the radio station man.

"Yessirree, the Imperial Hotel. Real fine hotel," says the barber, as if he'd actually stayed there, though he's never even been to Baltasár Island, let alone abroad. Come to think of it, none of these four has ever been out of the country.

"A real scandal, that. Island Security throwing rocks through folks' windows, harassing kids, planting stink bombs around their homes. Why I even heard them thugs hauled some poor souls off in the middle of the night for 'questioning' and they come back all beaten up. You bet people were up in arms."

"I know this one family, their house got assigned as the Island Security latrine. Guardsmen'd file in one after the other and piss in the middle of the living room. Some even crapped right there on the spot. Try to give the bastard a whack on the behind with a broom handle, and the thug'd just grab the broom away and whack 'em back. The whole house got to smelling so foul they just gave up and moved."

"But the people who sold out, they got some money out of it, didn't they?" asks the schoolteacher hesitantly.

"Don't you believe it. They didn't get no money, all they got was another piece of land what already had other folks livin' on it. So then *they* had to move even further away, right on down the line. By the time the musical chairs stopped, the hotel got the best property in the center of town and everyone else wound up living somewhere worse than when they started. It's already four years now, and my father-in-law's still grumblin' about it."

"But why would anybody be so gung-ho 'bout building a hotel?"

"It's big money, that's why," asserts a construction supply company employee who's been listening in.

"A hotel like that makes money? Enough to share out profits?"

"No, from kickbacks. Say the President arranges for the hotel construction to go through, the contractor pays him a percentage of the budget under the table. That's how things work in other countries. Guili's smart, he learned all about it in Tokyo and applied those lessons here."

"Okay, but it's not just the money," says the barber.

"Oh no?" questions the supply company clerk.

"No, it's not just money. It's his whole politics. He wants to make this place over into a Little Japan…or a Little America for that matter. The hotel was just the first step."

"You defending Guili?" asks the schoolteacher.

"Nah, hear me out, will ya. That hotel's like a faucet. People pour in, cash pours in with 'em. A tiny skim off that loot floating round and round Japan comes here. Then, with any luck, money'll start coming in from America and Australia too. Just gotta prime the pump."

"So?"

"The whole purpose of the Teikoku project was to hook up this country with the pipelines from the rest of the world."

"But people and cash never came."

"Exactly. That's where Matías Guili's smart. The Japanese sharks who built the hotel with funny money were smart, but your typical Japanese are even smarter; they know there's not that much fun stuff to do here in Navidad. I mean, did they really think people'd flock to some backwater where a disappearing bus is big news? No, for sightseeing, they got Hawai'i. For skin diving in coral reefs, it's Palau. For quick trips, there's Guam. There's just no room for Navidad."

"Don't they got disappearing buses on other islands?"

"Doubt it," huffs the barber.

"So what with the hotel all empty, don't that even bother the President?"

"*He* didn't sink any money in it. Okay, maybe he's disappointed he's not gettin' a little extra income, but he sure ain't out anything. He's too smart to sign some risky contract like that."

"But then he lost the third election," says the schoolteacher.

"That's *why* he lost the third election."

"Because of the hotel?"

"Right. Island Security overstepped the mark. Don't know if Guili himself was aware or not, but folks was furious at the IS. Family ties still run strong here, so if people heard their cousin ten-times-removed was mistreated by the IS, then sure as hell they weren't voting for Guili. That power base was much bigger than he reckoned."

"Yeah, and the bottom line was, the money never got delivered," the radio station man throws in, upping the ante.

"Money?"

"Yeah, campaign funds. Now this I know a little something about. It just so happens I got both sides of the story—from them on the giving end and the take. Couldn't broadcast nothing about it, 'course," he says, casting a meaningful look toward his sister, who gives the expected nod. "This was when the hotel business was still hanging over everything. Guili knew he'd come up short on votes, so he went looking for support from Japan."

"Well I guess, sounds possible," admits the upstaged barber grudgingly.

"So money was sent. Fifty million yen. Cash. Carried on board a light aircraft from Guam. The plan being to pay off important legislators and their constituencies."

"Buying influence, eh?"

"Well, something like that," hedges the radio station man, not wanting to stray into hazy areas. "But the thing of it was, the plane couldn't very well land at Navidad International Airport, so it tried to touch down at the old Japanese military airfield."

"You mean *that* crash?" says the barber.

"Now you're talking," says the radio station man, twinkling triumphantly at him. He's talked this far just to get in that one taunt, which the barber naturally doesn't acknowledge. "*That* very accident. But then folks around the north end of Baltasár Island there say the airstrip's always had its problems. According to the pilot who attempted the landing, on the final approach the runway looks ten meters higher than it actually is. The geography must be strange around there or something."

"Don't you bet on it. Them dead Japs put a curse on the place," says the housewife.

"That was where the last of them fought to the death."

"That's why there's been so many accidents."

"Well, in any case, the pilot thought they were safely on the ground and cut off the engines, but they were still ten meters up. So the plane belly flopped and went up in a blaze, fifty million yen and all. The pilot managed to get out. He's the guy now flies the government Islander."

"I saw the time before that," says the building supply company clerk.

"That plane crash?"

"No, like I said, the time before. Ten years ago, I was passing nearby the airfield when this Piper Cub came flying in lower and lower. Just when there was only a little ways to go, it leveled off and nosed up a bit, then the engine went quiet and it just fell—*wham!* Broke the wheel struts, but it still had enough speed to skid along on its belly, out past the end of the runway and into the trees. Didn't catch fire that time, but the plane was totaled. Pilot broke both his legs, nothing fatal."

"See? It must've look ten meters higher, that runway."

"Sure sounds like it."

"Better that than it looking ten meters lower," says the schoolteacher, a self-styled airplane buff, even though he's never been on one in his life.

"You think?"

"Well, if it looks lower, the plane'll still be nosing down, smack into the runway."

"Okay, so it was an accident," says the barber, trying to wrap up this airplane discussion.

"And Guili's money went up in flames."

"It's still them dead Japs, if you ask me. They see incoming planes as enemy fighters, but don't got no guns, so they mess with the ground level to knock 'em out of the sky."

"Anyhow, after three crashes in a row, they shut down that airfield. The time I saw was the third crash. The fourth time was Guili's fifty-million-yen bonfire."

"And I'll bet the pilot was being extra careful too. He musta heard all the stories."

"I dunno 'bout that. They probably didn't tell that damn fool pilot nothing."

"So anyway, about the election…" says the radio station man, returning to the original discussion. "Without that fifty million, Guili lost. Though the bettin' beforehand had him just barely wingin' a third term."

"Yessirree, he done crashed. And out of the wreckage, we got President Bonhomme Tamang," says the barber.

"Now there was a loser," says the supply company clerk.

"You said it. And his first order of business was to go dig up the dirt on his predecessor. Can't say it was too constructive."

"And then he died."

"Died three months later."

"A little too conveniently."

"And right after that, Guili's bounced back in again. As runner-up in the election, he got the consolation prize. But then, there was something mighty fishy about him disbanding the legislature right after he took office and Island Security chasing the MPs home with submachine guns."

"Yeah, where'd those guns come from?" asks the schoolteacher.

"Who knows? But there must've been at least a hundred of them. And with no special budget to buy weapons either. That was the one and only time anyone ever saw Island Security waving those infernal things around. There's always a chance IS might haul them out again if and when, but it's never come to that so far. Probably got 'em all locked up in some secret arsenal. Or maybe stashed at the Presidential Villa in case of a coup."

"Well, there was that thing at the welcoming ceremony for the Jap vets and the torii gate toppled that morning. Wouldn'a surprised me if Island Security went around fully armed after that, but no, they're still empty-handed same as ever."

"Them goons ain't seen arms before or since. Got handed guns that one time, ordered never to shoot, then disarmed at the end of the day. A greenhorn trooper told me so."

"It's a wonder them kids managed to piss in folks' houses," says the housewife, backtracking.

"Or crap."

"Right...or even crap."

"They all bunk together, so they just do what they're told from the top down. It's a group-motivation thing," says the schoolteacher, speaking from educational experience.

"Yeah, that group-motoration ain't no good."

"Hell no. They get all pumped up with pep talk how they's so different from the lazy chickenshits outside, how the fate of the country rests on their shoulders. It's a boot camp for training them how to pick fights, so where'd they get off thinking they's so special? All brawn and no brain, they get nothing but drills day after day. It's all a trick to draw an us-and-them dividing line. If they'd let the boys go out and play, they wouldn't turn so nasty."

"No, it's Katsumata. He's the nasty one."

"Well, sure, he's the one brought the nasty-ing techniques from Japan. Hit first, ask questions later. Whack 'em up and down. Just waiting to get in their licks."

"But maybe they did need submachine guns to get the legislators to behave," says the radio station man, changing the subject.

"Legally, it *was* a declared state of emergency, wasn't it," says the barber, changing the subject even further.

"Well, I heard the legislators got paid off to keep quiet."

"By Guili?"

"Who else? Though prob'ly Guili was bankrolled by Japan."

"Why? Because Tamang died?"

"Because Tamang had started prying, poking around in Guili's past, especially what went on with the hotel. That wasn't good for his health," whispers the barber.

"So it was Guili's doing?"

"Like I said, Tamang's death just then was mighty convenient for Guili."

"Since then he really become a dictator."

"But not so bad as dictators go," suggests the supply company clerk.

"You think?"

"Other countries got lots worse corruption and violence. You don't see Guili buying a thousand pairs of shoes, do you? Or dragging off all the pretty girls in the country to his own personal harem in the Presidential Villa."

"No, he's got Angelina's for that. Fine little place it is too," admits the schoolteacher.

"You go there?"

"Just once."

"Hmph."

"Nah, more than that, it's the scheming and book-fiddling I don't like. I mean, just how much funny money is Guili laundering for his pals in Japan? I just hope he's not planning to come up with some other big new stinker, loads worse than the hotel."

"Yeah, it do seem like something's brewing," says the housewife, "and it ain't fish sauce."

"I'll say. There's big change in the air. The torii gate was a sign. That and them handbills."

"Nice and nasty, those. Don't know who's posting them, though," says the radio station man, nervously probing to see if there's anything more to be known.

"The handbills stick themselves," says the schoolteacher enigmatically.

"That's right, them as wants to stick will," echoes the building supply company clerk.

"So then they're yours?" blurts out the radio station man.

"Now don't go busting your coconut. Half wish they were ours, but no, when I say the handbills stick themselves, that's the honest truth. Same as the torii gate fell and the flag burned all by themselves. That's how it's always been in these islands."

⚡

The following day, the President rises as usual, takes his customary breakfast, and is in the office by eight o'clock. His spur-of-the-moment absence has left him a backlog of work to deal with; it will be a busy day. Apparently there was no major problem in the interim, no Katsumata coup d'état (as if he could carry out a coup with only truncheons).

After a catch-up briefing with Jim Jameson, who looks relieved to see him back, Matías tackles his papers. Sitting high with his short legs crossed on the seat of his chair, he starts going through various bureaucratic reports when something flits across his field of vision. He looks up, but sees nothing, no stray mosquito or fly. He returns to his papers, skims over the lines of text assimilating the content, writes short queries on his notepad, and signs those items that pose no problem. There it is again, a butterfly. He looks up cautiously, but there's nothing there. Ignore it and just concentrate on business. But the butterfly returns to tease him, dancing at the very corner of his eye, disappearing when he tries to focus on it. He fidgets and can't seem to get back to work.

All right, then, he'll sit up straight, face head-on, and wait and see. Quietly the door opens. Améliana slips in and walks up to the desk.

"I'm back," she announces in a low voice.

He doesn't respond, he can't find the words. He raped this woman. Wronged her. It was, in both senses, a violation. She'd been a virgin. Her white dress was stained with blood. Red on white: the colors of the flag he saluted as a child. The very same that blazed against the blue sky at the airport.

But this was a different red and white, shocking in the secret sunlight through the blinds. The bleeding of a girl who said she'd already born a bastard by incest. Excitement and confusion and pleasure and fear—a riot of emotions swept over him. Guilt, regret, the wish to forget it all.

And now here she is, standing eye-to-eye in front of him. He's speechless; all he can do is stare at her. She looks the same as ever. She's come to announce she's resuming her duties, that's what he hears her saying.

"How was the festival?" he asks nervously, not even daring to say he was there.

"All over and done with." Her tone suggests she has no recollection, either of what went on while she slept in that house, or that they'd met up on Melchor at all.

He lets out a long, slow breath. If that's where things stand, then they can talk. He can easily act as if it were all an illusion. His taking advantage of her defenseless state may have been wrong, but her lying about the child had overcome his hesitations—that's the truth of it. Had he known she was a virgin, he would never have done it—at least that's what he wants to think, but a voice tells him this too is a lie. Either way, saying nothing lets it all remain an unaccountable "incident." Matías perks up immediately.

"That was a big responsibility you had, being a Yuuka."

"Yes, but during the ceremonies, I really wasn't myself."

And what about during what came later? thinks Matías. *Wasn't that you lying on the sheets?*

"You must be exhausted. For the time being there's no visiting VIP I want you to see, so why don't you just take it easy around the place for a while? I'll send for you if I need you."

"Okay. Thank you for the time off."

"The festival was much more important than your work here. Though I must say I was surprised when I heard you were to be the seventh Yuuka." Even as he speaks, he notes the smarm in his own voice, though the mention of her title does acknowledge a higher order than any superficial ranking in this room. The game is on: can the President outwit his spiritual advisor, or is the priestess bluffing a mere layman?

A layman. Did he even believe that much in the Yuuka Yuumai? The excitement, the visitant spirits and the blessings they bring, the priestesses and vestal virgins and sacred barge that serve to guide them in, the holy object and holy man, the festival musicians. And even more, the crowds, the collective spirit. Did he really believe in it all?

"I have no say in it. The Yoi'i Yuuka decides everything."

"Of course, quite right. But anyway, well done."

As Améliana bows slightly and withdraws, he wonders—are those butterflies haloing her hair? He blinks, and they're gone. Just then, a question pops into his head, a secular matter that seems natural to ask her about.

"Oh, just one thing, maybe you can tell me."

Améliana turns and takes two steps back toward the desk.

"What's that?" she asks quietly.

She seems completely at ease, no sign of anticipating any compromising query. Matías can surely forget all about what happened.

"The veterans delegation bus, it's been gone a long time now. I was expecting those old soldiers' angry relatives and reporters and cameramen and TV crews to come crashing in here, a big media to-do. But there's been no coverage at all in Japan. Can you say why that is?"

"The same powers that are hiding the bus are preventing a big commotion over there," says Améliana quite simply.

Is that all there is to it? Case open and closed. The disappearance of the bus was a mystery to begin with; what's one more mystery? He's left as much in the dark as before.

"The bus is keeping out of sight of Japan," she continues. "Their families and friends probably just imagine the men are enjoying being back in the South Seas. Their government isn't worried; it thinks the official they sent is busy doing his job. Or maybe they've all just forgotten about the delegation. No one says anything about it, no one is suspicious. The bus seems to have a will of its own."

Two parallel yet opposite feelings assail him: acceptance and utter disbelief. How can this girl know all this? Maybe if he pinned down these vague clues of hers, he could force the bus out of hiding?

"And when will the bus reappear?"

"Whenever it wants to."

It's no good. There's no catching her off guard, no breaking a Yuuka's resolve. Some other power is backing her up. Inside, she's just a woman—an ordinary woman he's had in bed. A Yuuka merely dances a role at a festival. Any stupid girl who can give the least bit serious response to inquiries about her background can be considered "spiritual" enough to become a Yuuka. Isn't that right? She drew on the mood of the crowd, the power of the place, the palpable presence of divine blessings in the form of the sacred barge. She took on the authority of the festival. Even his raping her, who can say outright that wasn't a trap?

"Very well, we shall wait," says Matías with as much presidential aplomb as he can muster. "You take it easy in the back quarters here. You can probably use a nice, long rest after the festival."

Améliana bows and says nothing, then exits, trailing her lilac butterflies.

No, it wasn't a trap, Matías has to think. It was just a case of her sleeping there, the place, the timing. No question about it. The girl hadn't even seemed enticing, nor was he particularly horny. He hadn't wanted to see her naked, or notch up another conquest, no ordinary sexual impulse. No, he didn't rape her; he simply gave in to some inner longing and delivered what was needed to where it was needed. His cock prodded firmly into that secret place and delivered an important message to a warm, well-guarded address. That wasn't sexual assault; that was discharging his duty to the future.

Oh, come off it. He must be dreaming—and a dumb dream too. Important message? He never had the father-stuff to begin with. His gun is empty, a fancy toy. A dummy, a prop. The booby prize at a kids' raffle. At the races, a losing ticket. The losing horse. A horse they can't even put to stud, the kind they just take out and shoot.

All right, so what? What matters is here and now. To do his duty as president and put this country on the right road, to foster an affluent society and, someday soon, train an able, hardworking successor. "Affluent society"—what a sad cliché that is! A dud of a political promise if ever there was one. Just like this pretentious folly of a Presidential Villa. And what a flimsy excuse for diplomacy! Mere begging masquerading as negotiating, presuming to hobnob with the big powers while the country can barely prop itself up on ODA. Kissing up to the lip-service notion that all countries might enjoy the same boons of civilization, even as the big boys use that posture to make the little guys knuckle under with treaties that guarantee nothing. Have they ever considered how humiliating it is to always be on the receiving end? Lee Bo had it better in his day. Or even a generation earlier, before everything started to go downhill.

Just maybe, somewhere in the back of his mind, he's glad the bus disappeared and those deluded old duffers haven't come back. Doesn't this make the first time ever Navidad has beaten its invader, Japan? Isn't he secretly applauding the bus? Though of course that means he's contradicting his own leanings toward Japan. Biting the yen that feeds him. What a mess! Probably he's just too tired to sort it all out. Yes, he's dead tired. Not physically, not even mentally—somewhere deeper. The most essential part that carries on as a bird when you die, that keeps Lee Bo talking: it's his "soul" or whatever that's so worn down. And him only sixty-four years old, not even really over the hill.

What has he done with his life? And what is he trying to do? Clinging to this chair as it drifts along, where the hell is he going?

⚡

The revolving restaurant atop the Navidad Teikoku Hotel, which broke down and stopped revolving within one year after the building was completed, is a laughingstock for the islanders. *Now diners'll have to carry their own plates around while eating,* they joke, or *Now they'll have to put up sails to turn the thing around,* or *Let's all just hold the restaurant steady while they rotate the islands.* Navidadians have always had a talent for humor, though maybe not quite in the same league as East Europeans or Egyptians, people whose harsher colonial histories have honed their sense of satire razor sharp.

Most of the non-revolving restaurant gags do find their way to the President, generally via Angelina. No doubt the local comedians would be delighted to know their punch lines reached the chief executive's ears, but Matías just shrugs off the sarcasm. It's not his hotel, after all. He may have had a major hand in its construction, but that was it. The place is Japanese owned and operated, so whatever its losses, that's their business. He still receives a fixed sum that he doesn't have to share out with anyone. At most, he'll return the favor by holding the occasional large dinner there, just enough to send a token show of gratitude and support back to Japan. The non-revolving restaurant isn't his concern. Not that he's unaware that a good part of the jokes are directed at himself. Misguided or not, taking the odd potshot comes with the job of president.

That evening, after a non-revolving soirée with a number of influential legislators, an unusually subdued Matías doesn't really feel like returning to the Presidential Villa. He has no particular outside business at this hour, when normally he'd be back in his private quarters writing up memos, but he just isn't in the mood to review any paperwork.

"Take me to Angelina's," he tells Heinrich.

This makes two nights in a row. Last night he talked a little about the Yuuka Yuumai, leaving out his own participation and what went on afterwards. Somehow, perhaps because of keeping mum about Améliana, he wasn't up to sleeping with Angelina. How will it be tonight?

The gently purring Nissan President pulls up behind the building as usual. Matías opens the passenger door himself, heads for the unobtrusive green entrance, and goes in. He walks up the dark corridor to his room and sits pensively on the sofa. A tug on a special cord in one corner of the room will ring a tiny bell in the salon one floor below, which Angelina should hear and respond to immediately. What expression, then, should he wear? With Améliana now acting as though the whole incident never happened, it's tempting to just play along and forget about it too. But that almost seems to make the two of them partners in crime. Funny, one-on-one it never occurred to him; only now, faced with a third person, Angelina, does conspiratorial guilt make problems.

On the other hand, had Améliana come back and made a fuss, it might have actually strengthened his ties with Angelina. A president is allowed his selfish little indiscretions, especially if the circumstances encouraged that sort of thing, so if the girl screamed bloody murder, there'd be ways to deal with it. Pretty high-handed reasoning, but the world is full of high-handed individuals who'll tell you the best kind of self-help is taking a big helping for yourself. Still, Améliana didn't say a word.

No, his motives were different. That's why his sense of guilt with Angelina is so strong. If it had merely been a sex thing, his having gone too far and raped a sleeping girl, he could make a case—spurious or not—claiming that any man in his situation would have done the same. Angelina, by occupation, is used to men's excuses; it's practically the first rule of her profession. But his intentions at the time hadn't been anything so simple or selfish as plain lust. It was something else, unrelated to any desire he usually felt for Angelina's body. It was as if—how to put it?—the womb of time had used his cock for its own ends. How can he tell Angelina that?

Between what Améliana won't let him say and what he can't bring himself to say to Angelina, they're going to drive Matías crazy, these two women. Two strong females towering over a homunculus cringing beneath their gaze. He has to regain his position as president, as de facto owner of this brothel, as Angelina's one-and-only man. She'll forgive him anything. She'll hear him out. No, he can't put things that way—makes Angelina a mother to his naughty boy.

Matías reaches a decision. He tugs on the cord to the inaudible bell downstairs, then settles back into the sofa, loosely cross-legged, and waits. A knock comes on the thick oak door.

"Make me so happy to see you two nights in a row," chirps Angelina as she enters.

"How's it going tonight?" he asks, maybe because the Navidad Teikoku Hotel's finances were a topic of discussion earlier in the evening. That deficit is their problem, but he can't afford to be disinterested in the business prospects of this establishment.

"Lots of young people," answers Angelina. "Livens the place up, the girls like it too."

"Locals?"

"Mostly. Drinking a lot too. Three separate groups came in, then they all got together, it's like a party down there."

"Any other customers?"

"Two American old-timers. And three Filipinos, they're already gone to the back rooms. Not a bad turnover."

"Good. That's what I like to hear," says Matías. "So you're not needed downstairs?"

"No problem. If anything comes up, they'll call. The girls can handle things. No rough customers tonight."

"So how about catering to this lonely old customer?"

"Lonely, are we?"

"No, I just wanted to see your face. I just might come here every night from now on."

"Now that's what I want to hear."

"I could sleep here every night, nice and sound until morning, then go to work at the villa."

"You can't do that," says Angelina. "You be grumbling right away how you can't get any work done. In nine years, you try that three times already, and all three times you end up going back in the middle of the night. You never ever stay here till dawn. And after you go, I have to go back to sleep all alone."

"I know, I know."

"Yesterday, you seem tired. How about tonight?"

He knows what's on her mind, but what does she really expect of him? It's not like he's obliged to come here and sleep with her, after all. He takes his pleasure when he damn well pleases. He makes the demands and she responds. Okay, he was tired and he didn't feel up to doing anything, what's wrong with that? Of course, Angelina would say she understands. Though when has she ever come forward and said "Sleep with me" or "Don't sleep with me"? On the other hand, has he ever asked her how she spends her daytime hours? She could be having some wild times with those two damn homos Ketch and Joel for all he knows. Skilled technicians, those two, did what he needed done. Foreigners or not, he owes them. No, Angelina probably just quietly gets on with things. She's not the type to screw around. He knows her too well.

"Let's have some hash. And yeah, some champagne."

A good start, but the night doesn't function. The hash gives almost no buzz, the champagne tastes like carbonated *blanc de blanc*. Angelina's sensuous physique is showing her age, as if he's seeing her with different eyes. The usual sense of security he feels coming here after a hard day doesn't gel. He waits for lust to rear its head, but nothing comes. Meanwhile, the odd realization overtakes him: what a long time he's spent with this woman. Somehow the idea of Angelina aging cuts closer than his own befuddled decline. Either way, old age will come for both of them. For now, she's still beautiful. Better enjoy her while he can, take pride in the fact that she's his.

But even so, tonight things just don't click. Pretty much as expected. His trusted tool doesn't show its worth. However long he caresses her skin, nothing goes any further, until finally a sobering chill sets in. Not the hash or champagne, nor her still buoyant breasts or soft whorls of pubic hair or taut brown thighs or glistening coral-toned inner parts, can prevent him from cooling off.

"Getting old," mutters Matías.

"You're just tired," says Angelina. It's her regular line, calculated to explain away the lack of vigor in this nocturnal refuge as the toll of a secular daytime routine.

No sooner have his ears intercepted the words, however, than out of nowhere a great wave of sleepiness descends on him. He throws an arm around Angelina's shoulder and nuzzles in toward her breasts, and the last thing he remembers is a fleeting premonition that he'll probably stay asleep until morning. This isn't like his sudden plummeting blackouts; it's too easy, too natural, too much like his sleep on Melchor. Hell, he might even dream tonight. Hopefully a nice dream—and then he's out cold.

⚡

The housekeeping staff have all gone home, and Améliana and Itsuko are sharing a simple supper. Normally they eat Japanese food—salt-grilled or soy-simmered fish, sometimes sashimi—dishes Améliana knows the President has for breakfast. She's not averse to the taste of rice and fish with soy sauce, but occasionally she'll go into the kitchen and boil some taro, which Itsuko eats without objection. Their two schools of home cooking are apparently not mutually exclusive, nor maybe even all that different, though the Navidad fare is generally blander and closer to the natural flavors of the local produce. Even so, until she was given a room here, Améliana—like most Navidadians—had no idea the President lived in a "Little Japan." Previously, only Itsuko and the President himself were in on the secret; the rest of the villa that the house-keeping staff sees is done in a faux-Western style with Navidad trimmings that might pass for "Filipino modern."

Only once did Améliana ever see the President dine here in his private apartments. It was a Sunday, and only two other housekeepers were left on duty. Itsuko cooked not the usual Japanese fish, but a big, thick American steak. Améliana prepared taro and ma'a as side dishes. As with his breakfast, the President took his dinner alone at a precise hour, after which he retired to his study for the remainder of the evening. Afterwards, the women ate at their leisure; there was even a small cut of steak for everyone. Itsuko told them that once the President retired to his study, he never called for her; he didn't touch coffee at night, always mixed his own drinks. Very easy to work for, she added.

Tonight, however, the President is not dining in. It's just Améliana and Itsuko having a simple supper. Itsuko, in typical fashion, never talks about herself to Améliana; nothing about how she came to work here or what she used to do in Japan or where she first met the President. It's as if she has no past. So Améliana never reciprocates with stories of her own, never mentions the Yuuka Yuumai (Itsuko merely thinks she took time off to visit her family). Quiet meals finish quickly. Améliana cleans up and washes the pots and dishes as has become her habit. Meanwhile, Itsuko takes a bath, and when the kitchen is all in order, she makes a few preparations for tomorrow's breakfast. That's the last the two of them will see of each other before they turn in.

Two hours later, Améliana sneaks out of her room, just three doors down from where Itsuko is sleeping. Améliana has never once heard a sound from the old maid's room, but still she's extra cautious opening the door. She slowly steps out, returns the handle to a close without it clicking, then quietly pads up the wood-floored corridor toward the President's study.

There is another heavy wooden door between here and there. It shouldn't be locked. She gives it a slight push and it opens. She carefully closes the door behind her and makes sure that the President is not about. Tonight is a good chance to snoop around. She's not planning to stay in this big, creepy house forever. The sooner she can find what she's looking for, the faster things can move ahead. It'll be better for everyone.

To the left is the private chamber where each night the President stays up writing memos, updating his journal, and planning his agenda for the following day. Améliana knows there is an extraordinary amount of paperwork in this room. She has come this far once before, the night before she left for the Yuuka Yuumai. The President wasn't in that night either. Probably he was at Madame Angelina's, as happens several times a week—as everyone in Baltasár City knows. The unofficial first couple's imagined antics are the stuff of Navidadian fantasies; for some years now, bored husbands and wives have spiced up their lackluster sex lives by playing Guili-and-Angelina games. If the President isn't back here in his apartments by this hour, then he's got to be at Madame's. She also knows how he spends his time there. Which is why she scoured this study last night. What she's looking for wasn't in any of his desk drawers or the filing cabinet or the bookshelves lining the walls; it wasn't hidden behind the framed portrait of His Excellency Matías Guili, President of the Republic of Navidad. No, it had to be in another room.

Actually, her search began even before coming to the Presidential Villa. She went through Angelina's premises from top to bottom. That's why she got herself placed there to begin with. She assumed that since Angelina was surely involved in drawing up the document in question, it either had to be in her safekeeping or under Guili's own lock and key. She has no idea whether the other pair engaged in the contract might have a copy or not. The big man might have even sent it out of the country. That paper underwrites the security of both sides. He'd have been very careful about where he kept it.

A door across the room leads to a short passage and a thin papered sliding door, easily mistaken for a wall. With a light touch on the finger hold, she gently slides the door open, then feels for the light switch, hoping there's no alarm. She warily presses the button and the lights come on. What a strange room! The floor is fitted wall-to-wall with twelve glossy yellow grass mats. These have to be from Japan. Who knows what they're called? There is a recess in the far wall, an alcove of sorts, where another portrait of His Excellency Matías Guili, President of the Republic of Navidad, is hanging. Only this one isn't framed or in color; it's black and white and pasted in the middle of an oversize length of paper. Is this how they put up pictures in Japan?

This is Itsuko's territory. No one else is allowed in here. No one else could even begin to know how to clean a room so completely Japanese. What she's looking for has to be in this room, she can just feel it. If it's not here, it's nowhere. Which would mean there was no contract, only a verbal agreement. Before she goes digging around in here, she takes a good look at these strange quarters.

There are two more sliding doors: one paper, the other wood. She opens the paper door and finds another room laid with yet another dozen or so of the same grass floor mats and several layers of what look like thick blankets spread out in the middle. This must be his bedroom. On the far wall is a large window covered with vertical wooden slats and a framed glass pane slid partially open. For ventilation perhaps? This place is much more vulnerable than she'd imagined. She knows there's no surveillance system out in the garden. No Island Security patrolling here at night. The President doesn't seem to have given any thought to the possibility of an attack during the night.

She closes the paper door and now tries the wooden one. Beyond is what appears to be a bathroom. The lower half of the walls is skirted in a queer-smelling wood, and there's a large square box over in the corner, covered with the same resinous boards. Even the floor is laid with this wood, the slats spaced to let the water drain through, she assumes, because those two gleaming faucets over there—one with a red knob, one blue—are positioned to pour directly onto the floor.

No, he wouldn't keep an important document in a wet area. Blank walls, no cabinets of any kind, no place to conceal papers. But then, back in the first grass-matted room, there's no furniture to speak of either. The only place to hide papers would be behind the portrait, tacked onto the back of that long hanging mount. Easy enough to check—but nothing there. In the center of the room is a large square cushion, twice shoulder width in size. She thought there'd be a zipper, but the purple silk cover is sewn tight on all four sides and appliquéd with heavy yellow tassels in the corners and center.

She tries feeling the cushion, but it's too densely stuffed to tell if any paper is hidden inside. Maybe it's folded up? Was that something she felt just now? Only one way to find out: get a knife and cut it open. But then how will she ever sew it up again? One look and he'll know the document is missing. In any case, she'd planned to run away as soon as she found it. That was her whole reason for coming here. She'll cut the cushion.

There must be a letter opener in the President's study, something he keeps handy to slit envelopes. She hurriedly backtracks to the desk and soon finds a package knife in the top drawer. Perfect, one straight cut with this and then run. She just hopes Guili doesn't show up and catch her red-handed. She'll slash the underside, take out the papers, turn the cushion back over, and no one will be the wiser. Or does she want him to find out? Isn't that part of her purpose here?

She grabs the knife, returns to the twelve-mat room, and is about to slice open the cushion when a voice comes from behind—

"Just what do you think you're doing?"

She turns to see Itsuko standing there. The woman may be small, but there's a stern authority about her. Instinctively, Améliana's fingers clench the knife in her hand.

BUS REPORT 11

That July, Navidadians were startled by the appearance of a new cluster of stars in the night sky to the south. Roughly rectangular in shape, this grouping of one second-magnitude star with five third-magnitude stars was noticed because of its situation in a darker part of the sky where elderly islanders could not recall having seen any light before. The stars were much discussed among the populace at large, and the Navidad Science Council received letters inquiring what these stars might be. Were they new American satellites, for example? The Science Council, comprised entirely of high school science teachers and Ministry of Education officials, was stumped and embarrassed. Astronomy as they knew it had no ready explanation for the sudden appearance of new stars. One council member suggested they might be supernovas, but the odds of multiple supernovas occurring in close proximity seemed extremely slim.

The Science Council thought to forgo pronouncements pending further communications from abroad, but such a refusal to deal with local issues and inquiries ran counter to its very raison d'être. Thus, rather than offer a scientific explanation, it was decided they would try to preserve some semblance of authority by naming the constellation ad hoc. However, before they could convene their two-thirds quorum, the very day after the stars were first sighted in fact, locals coined a nickname, which rapidly gained nationwide acceptance. This meant, in most people's view, that the name seemed to fit. Officials had little choice but to adopt the popular name, but then proceeded to act as if they'd invented it themselves. They held an "unveiling" of the new appellation—their first and last press conference ever—and the headline in the following morning's *Navidad Daily* read:

NAVIDAD SCIENCE COUNCIL OFFICIALLY PROCLAIMS
NEW CONSTELLATION "AUTOBUS MAJOR"

Whatever nomenclature might later gain currency among the international scientific community, the Science Council opted to let the "bus" name ride in Navidad for the time being. Not that there was any law against something so controversial going unnamed. Yet despite their conviction that this was big news, not one report on the new constellation filtered in from overseas.

The Central Bureau for Astronomical Telegrams (CBAT) of the International Astronomical Union (IAU) was silent on the subject; the major news agencies and wire services issued no press releases. The few operative parabolic antennae in Navidad positioned to pick up electromagnetic spillover from Filipino, Taiwanese, and Japanese satellite broadcasts gleaned nothing about any new constellation.

Four days after the appearance of the new stars, the Science Council started to have doubts. If what should have been the biggest topic in astronomical history since the Star of Bethlehem guided the Three Magi to the infant Christ attracted no attention whatsoever, then, just possibly, these stars were only visible from Navidad (the council member who made this suggestion was also, of course, alluding to the three "island kings" Gaspar, Baltasár, and Melchor that comprise the Republic of Navidad). Were they even stars? The council debated the question back and forth, and finally resolved to take a closer look at the phenomenon. They would conduct observations using the twenty-inch reflective telescope donated by a Japanese corporation to Baltasár High School. A prudent decision, if a little late.

The fifth night clouded over, much to everyone's chagrin, but on the sixth, a clear sky brought even greater disappointment: for where the five stars had shone two nights before was now only darkness—Autobus Major had vanished! Just gone, after all that commotion—and such lovely stars they'd been too! Was it just some freak light display, people wondered, put on for Navidad's viewing alone? A prank pulled by that other wayward bus, showing off, swerving across the night sky with its high beams on?

The Science Council was in a spot. The stars had not been visible from any other country. What they'd taken for astral lumina from thousands of light years away had in fact only been a few kilometers in altitude. It was too bad they hadn't been quicker with the high school telescope or hadn't had a spectroscope to analyze whether those were true stars or man-made light sources or some other heretofore-unknown heavenly bodies.

Just then, word came from Melchor Island three hundred kilometers away that the same phenomenon had been sighted in exactly the same position at precisely the same time as in the capital. Effectively, there was no parallax. Would the mystery ever be resolved? A more immediate problem, however, was that they had gone and officially announced the finding of a new constellation. What to do? Someone suggested they simply pretend the whole affair had never happened. But no, they couldn't do that in good conscience. Thus, several days later, a single-line retraction appeared in the back pages of the *Navidad Daily*:

As of today, the Science Council officially denies the existence of the constellation Autobus Major.

"Looking for something?" Itsuko asks incriminatingly.

She's been caught in the act.

"It's not in that cushion. Better not cut it open or you'll get stuffing all over everything. Nothing inside but kapok anyway."

Améliana accepts the advice without protest and slides the blade back into its sheath, but can't think what to do next. Will this woman squeal on her to President Guili? And how will Guili deal with her?

"Stay right where you are," says Itsuko, then leaves the room. She's probably gone to call someone. Will she alert Island Security? Tell them she found her snooping around late at night in the inner chambers where she doesn't belong, with a knife in her hand? There's no possible defense.

But then Itsuko quickly returns from the next room, looking resourceful. She's fetched something shiny, sharp, and menacing. It's an awl, the one the President uses to punch papers for binding with string instead of stapling—an old Japanese filing system that Guili's partial to. Just what does Itsuko think she's going to do with that thing? Duel against her package knife?

"Don't cut the cushion, okay?" repeats Itsuko, then walks toward the

President's portrait and kneels down beside a thick grass mat in front of the scroll. She thrusts the awl diagonally into the dark fabric edging of the mat; it goes in easily, all the way up to the handle. Now she heaves and the mat lifts. So it wasn't attached to the floor, only set in place like a piece of a jigsaw puzzle.

"Don't just stand there looking. Lend me a hand," says Itsuko.

Améliana helps grab the raised edge of the mat, then slips her fingers underneath. She can see rough floorboards below. Itsuko now tosses the awl aside and joins Améliana in levering up the mat to face level, and there on the subflooring is a plain brown envelope the size of a magazine. The grass mat is bulky, but not too heavy; Améliana can manage it single-handedly while Itsuko reaches for the envelope.

"I believe this is what you're looking for," says Itsuko, handing it over, then grabs the mat. Quickly, Améliana accepts the envelope and Itsuko lowers the mat, tamping it back in place with her foot. Not a trace remains of their exploits except for the envelope in hand.

"You take it," says Itsuko. "It was time for somebody to come along, so when you showed up, I knew it had to be you. I told myself, this is the girl who'll change everything. That's why I helped you."

Améliana just listens. She had no idea this dour old woman could see so much.

"It's time for a change. I could see it coming," repeats Itsuko in a low voice. "The man's been sitting on top for too long. But he slipped up, lost his nerve when he shouldn't have. He'd come so far without any big mistakes, then he went wrong. What he did after the last election was unforgivable. Doesn't matter how incompetent his successor might've been, he should have let him have his turn. But no, he couldn't do that. Oh, it's been quite a show while it lasted, I'll grant you that, but now it's over."

Améliana eyes the envelope. Should she open it here and now?

"Go on, take a look. Wouldn't want you thinking I'd give you a forgery. Better you make sure and be on your way."

There's no telling when the President might return, but Itsuko seems unconcerned; it's almost as if she's certain he'll be at Angelina's until morning, even though he's never once done that before. What makes tonight so different?

Améliana kneels down on the firm grass mat and opens the envelope. Inside is a single sheet of paper written in English, though she already knows what it's all about:

AGREEMENT

Matías Guili (hereinafter referred to as "Party A"), and Paul Ketch in partnership with Peter Joel (hereinafter referred to as "Parties B"), do by their respective signatures on this document enter into a solemn and binding Agreement as set forth in the following terms and conditions:

1. Party A hereby engages the services of Parties B to dispose of the current President of the Republic of Navidad, Bonhomme Tamang.

2. Party A leaves the choice of ways and means of dispatch entirely to the discretion of Parties B, and promises to have no further word to say on the actual execution thereof, with the provision that Parties B shall make every effort to make the said demise appear to have occurred owing to natural causes so as not to arouse suspicion among the public at large.

3. Only once the above conditions are met, i.e. when Bonhomme Tamang has been safely disposed of without arousing any suspicions of foul play, shall Parties B be deemed to have fulfilled their duties as per this Agreement.

4. In return for the successful completion of those duties, Party A guarantees the following compensation:

   a. Parties B shall be allowed to stay at the premises run by Angelina Lasan Carmena and there provided with room and board (not to include sexual services) for as long as they so desire.

b. During their stay, Angelina Lasan Carmena shall provide Parties B with as much beer and twelve-year-old I.W. Harper bourbon whiskey (not to exceed an average 32 ounces between both persons per day) for as long as they so desire.

5. For the duration that the above conditions are in effect, Parties B shall not take leave or otherwise vacate Angelina Lasan Carmena's premises without the prior knowledge and permission of Party A.

6. Similarly, for the duration that the above conditions are in effect, neither the contracted Parties A and B nor Angelina Lasan Carmena shall intentionally reveal the general or specific contents of this Agreement to any outside interests.

We, the undersigned, do hereby undertake this Agreement in good faith.

Along with the date are three signatures: one easily recognized as that of the President of the Republic of Navidad, Matías Guili, followed by two scrawls decipherable only to someone who knows the names Paul Ketch and Peter Joel. There is no indication of Ketch and Joel's nationality or any other particulars. Can an amateurish document like this be legally binding? Can Angelina, implicated by name but not her own hand, be held in any way responsible? No matter, that's not an issue at present. The main thing is that Améliana has what she was looking for; now she can take action.

"Thank you," says Améliana.

"It's not my doing and it's not yours. Just things taking their course. I've lived a long time. First in my country, then in this one, I've had decades to observe the man from far away and close up. It's taken me years, but I think I finally get how things are with him. I may be standing on the bank of the river, but you're sailing down the middle. I hand this over, you take it and sail on. Natural enough, isn't it?"

"Yes," is all Améliana can say. She'd have liked to ask Matías his views on the subject, but there's no time now. There will be another place for that, another time.

"You go now," prompts Itsuko.

Améliana gets up, bows hurriedly, then leaves. Watching her swift exit, Itsuko mutters gleefully to herself, "Princess flees castle with secret missive in hand. House ransacked and plot uncovered. Ever-vigilant lady-in-waiting sees off princess...If only it were snowing outside, this could be a real kabuki play."

BUS REPORT 12

That year, the village of Placia, a thirty-minute walk from Colonia, was plagued by a curious disease. Those afflicted would wander through the village, each via some fixed arbitrary path; some, known as "express" cases, moved at a faster clip than the others and went straight from one end of the village to the other without stopping; still others went back and forth to Colonia once a day. Obviously contagious, though no pathogen was ever isolated, the disease gave those afflicted a somehow "squared-off," "boxlike" appearance with bright, gleaming eyes; hence the malady came to be known (reasonably enough) as "busitis." Aside from running around and not working, however, there seemed to be no other noticeable symptoms or harmful side effects. And since most families typically had one or two slackers who never worked anyway, people may have talked, but no one took it very seriously. Moreover, the epidemic was very brief; according to the regional health authorities, the worst of it died down after only three weeks, and ten days later the last remaining case had completely recovered with no visible aftereffects.

Nonetheless, other reports claimed that even years later, certain of those afflicted still developed bright "headlight" eyes after dark. Likewise, rumor had it that several mothers who became pregnant during the epidemic gave birth to babies with ever-so-slightly "angular," "blockish" features. Husbands in Placia are not normally known to be jealous, so the children were accepted and raised with love, though inevitably some of the womenfolk continued to whisper about that "sexy bus."

Eleven AM. Angelina wakes for the second time. Ordinarily she drags herself to bed around four and sleeps until after eleven, but last night wasn't an ordinary night. Nice though it was to share her bed with Matías for two nights running, after plying him with champagne and hashish he fell fast asleep. It's not unusual for him to forego sex, but to simply conk out? Certainly, he's never slept through the whole night here before.

She felt a little uneasy leaving Matías alone like that, but once he dozed off she went downstairs to the salon. What a strange night it was. The young islanders who had arrived in twos and threes suddenly all found themselves partying together. Soon the girls were joining in the fun. The Americans and Filipinos had already withdrawn to private rooms with their chosen companions, but the remaining seven locals showed no sign of leaving. Even Ketch and Joel, who never mingled with the clientele, were drinking and chatting with everyone. At one point, Joel got up and started dancing. Others took partners and joined in. The place was hopping. Angelina sat watching from the sidelines until, satisfied that everything was happily under control, she returned upstairs to find Matías still asleep. He looked positively serene—a face she'd never seen on him before. She lay down beside him, not to sleep, but just to curl up for the rest of the evening.

Then, in the early morning hours, she hears Matías groaning in his sleep. He's sweating and batting at his head with one hand; he must be having a nightmare, seems to be in pain. Angelina tries to rouse him, but he just keeps struggling. She shakes him harder. It's like hauling up a drowned man from the bottom of the sea. Finally he wakes, looks around, disoriented, then sees her and is visibly relieved.

"What a weird dream," he says. Though blurry-eyed, his voice is returning to normal.

"What kind of dream?" she asks.

"I was in a boat on a stormy sea, rocking this way and that, waves rolling over me…The ocean was so big, the winds so strong, the boat…"

"It's okay, you're fine. No ocean here."

"…like that boat, the sacred barge from the Yuuka Yuumai."

"From the festival?"

"Hey, what time is it now?" he asks, suddenly wide awake.

"Five thirty. Want to sleep some more?"

"Did I sleep that long? Incredible. What's going on?"

"It's a first, all right," agrees Angelina, noting the hint of anxiety in his voice.

"I'm going. Got things to do in the morning," he says, and bolts out of bed.

Angelina also rises and helps him get dressed, then sees him to his limo parked in the deserted back lane. The cool night air is refreshing. Heinrich is asleep in the driver's seat. Matías gets in without a word and wakes his startled chauffeur, who promptly drives him home.

On the way back to the bedroom, Angelina pauses halfway along the corridor and peeks through the curtain into the salon. The young customers have all fallen asleep in their chairs, each with his arm around a girl sleeping by his side. None of them took private rooms, but still she finds this frieze—fully clothed fawns with nymphs en déshabillé—rather touching, really. It's as if the whole lot of them had been sprinkled with fairy dust. Ketch and Joel are nowhere in sight; they must have gone to bed.

Angelina closes the curtain and returns to the boudoir she shares with Matías. She could use a little more sleep herself. Just a few minutes, she thinks, and has barely lain down when whatever fairy strafed the salon sprinkles her with the last of the magic dust, and she's out like a light.

The next time she wakes up, it's almost eleven. She's been sleeping in the "Matías boudoir," not her own bedroom? Lying there, she remembers the previous evening and all the odd things that happened. Matías conking out like that, so many local customers all at once—not that she can distinguish the various island facial types and mannerisms. The girls forgot all about business they were having such a good time. Must be more fun when the johns are their own age. And so much booze too. Did those island boys make it home? She just hopes somebody stayed sober enough to collect on the bills. Come to think of it, isn't it odd that she went to sleep so early herself? Usually she stays up to the very end.

A few minutes later, still half in a daze, Angelina toddles downstairs to learn from the girls that all the guests left a couple of hours ago, and of course, the tabs were squared away. Yes, paid in cash, no mistake. They sure were fun customers, good talkers too. Whereupon the conversation frays into individual recollections, each girl arguing with the others about the boy she liked best, wishing he'd come again. And not one of them even turned a trick. All fine and dandy, scolds Angelina, but this is a brothel, not a bar. Though secretly she has to admit that a few lively customers every now and again might be a nice change. So they're young and can't afford more than drinks, what's so bad about that?

By the afternoon, she begins checking the food and liquor stocks. The cold storage and pantry seem to be holding their own, so she talks to the cook about fresh market purchases for the following day and writes out a quick list of items to order from Guili's Super. Next, the liquor department: almost everything seems to be in good supply for the moment. She tries not to stock too much beer, just enough to tide them over until the next ship comes into port (in a pinch she can always buy San Miguel and Budweiser at Guili's). Plenty of scotch, cognac, gin, vodka, rum, and tequila for the moment; the cellar's full of wine and champagne. And the next ship's in three days, isn't it? Nothing to worry about. Just need to go over the receipts and figure out which drinks are selling, then draw up an order accordingly in the next couple of days.

Angelina prides herself on having the most comprehensive liquor selection in the country. No male bartender, but Joel has been training one of the girls intensively for a year and now she can mix cocktails with the best of them. No, a night of serious drinkers is not a bad thing. Anyway, liquor brings in the crowd. Puts men in the mood, ups the room rentals, makes the girls' work easier. She doesn't want to lose her reputation for keeping a well-stocked cabinet, doesn't want to hear that a customer ordered something she doesn't carry. That's why she takes pains with her stock. Last night's bunch must have put a good dent in those supplies, the way they were drinking. Didn't rent any rooms, okay, but they probably dropped a bundle. It's a wonder they could walk out of here at all. They must have terrible hangovers by now.

As Angelina continues checking the shelves against her inventory list, she discovers a glaring shortage. Impossible. How can it be? She searches the shelves again and again, but no, it's true. The case of twelve-year-old I.W. Harper is empty. She goes to look for more, but there's only that one case. Could Ketch and Joel have finished off the very last bottle? Last week when she looked there must have been at least a dozen. What's going on here? She was sure there was plenty until the next shipment; could last night's crowd have homed in on the Harper's? Would Ketch and Joel have sat by calmly and let others polish off their private reserve? Of course, they'd have thought there were many more bottles on hold for them in back. Maybe they even enjoyed introducing the island boys to their personal favorite. Be that as it may, who's responsible for letting the bourbon run out? Who brought out the last bottle to the salon?

What to do? It was the house agreement: she promised to provide Ketch and Joel with a constant supply of I.W. Harper. She can't just tell them there isn't any. "We're out" is not an acceptable answer. Should she call Manila and have them airfreight a batch? It's Friday, no flight today. No way to get it here by tonight. If she only had one bottle, she could somehow stretch it out. Is there really not one bottle in the salon bar? Angelina has a rare panic attack and runs to check. Bourbon she has: Jack Daniel's, Wild Turkey, and Old Crow, even five cases of regular five-year-old I.W. Harper—but not the square fake-crystal bottle with the clumsy stopper. Aside from a chilled mug of beer during the daytime heat, Ketch and Joel drink nothing else.

Would any place in town have it? Extremely doubtful. Navidadians aren't much for hard liquor; beer is all they ever drink. Hardly even any alcoholics here. No drunks causing trouble; the police never have to break up barroom brawls. Which is precisely why senior officials and businessmen who picked up drinking habits overseas all come here. The same goes for foreigners. There *is* no place else. Certainly no liquor store on the islands, only a token few random bottles in the supermarket "liquor corner." Horrible rotgut for the most part: Sang Thip rice spirit from Thailand, Australian brandy (no reflection on Aussie wine, which is getting quite good, but she still can't trust something called "Kangaroo Kognac"), Vietnamese rum with a picture of a girl in an *aodai* tunic on the label, clear bottles stamped "gin" made in Bangladesh. The clerks don't even try to push the stuff, they know no customer in his right mind will want it.

No, there's not a chance of finding twelve-year-old I.W. Harper for sale anywhere in Baltasár City. So then, plan B. The only other likely place after here would be the bar at the Navidad Teikoku Hotel, though Ketch and Joel have told her they didn't have any there. Still, much as she dislikes the idea of supporting the competition, it's worth a try; maybe they got some in since then. She can't go herself; she'll have to send someone. How long can she go on pretending that nothing's amiss?

Angelina's in a real fix. She knows the breach carries no specific penalties, but seriously, what other recourse does she have than to explain the situation and let them decide what to do? A new shipment is due in three days' time, a mere two-night lapse. Would they possibly make do with some other bourbon? Forget it. She fully understands their insistence on the real thing; she's not about to swindle them by pouring five-year-old into square bottles. No-have is no-have. Anyway, it'll be interesting to see how they deal with this calamity. That's the spirit—grace under pressure.

Angelina finds the two of them outside, cleaning the terrace. Ketch is hosing down the flagstones while Joel scrubs with a bristle broom. The two mugs of beer on the nearby white metal table, however, are for no ordinary workmen.

"I got something to tell you. Come on in when you finish," she calls out to them.

"Sure thing. What is it? We getting a raise?" jokes Joel.

"No, we're getting the axe," counters Ketch.

"Fair enough. We're just hired hands," says Joel, with a good stiff shove of the broom.

"So cut us right off at the wrist," says Ketch, his thumb over the nozzle to concentrate a harder spray. A tiny rainbow arches through the sparkling droplets.

"Don't talk nonsense, come as soon as you're done," she says, leaving them to it.

Ten minutes later, the pair present themselves before her, hanging their heads in playful shame, a glint of mischief showing in their eyes.

"Forgive us."

"It won't happen again."

"Please have mercy on us."

"We're sorry."

"Sit down, this is serious," says Angelina, putting a lid on their jokes. "We have a problem."

Their expressions shade toward curiosity.

"We're out of your liquor. Not a drop of twelve-year-old I.W. Harper in the house."

They're dumbstruck. Ketch slowly shakes his head in disbelief.

"I don't know how it happen. I always lay in a good stock, right? I's sure we had a half dozen bottles. Last night's crowd musta drunk it all."

"They saw us drinking and ordered the same thing."

"And they out-drank us too."

"They didn't buy any sex, they just sat around talking till morning."

"We didn't know they finished everything off."

"My mistake. It completely slip my mind, but it's too late to be sorry. Next shipment arrive in three days, so there's nothing for tonight or tomorrow. I rack my brains, but what's gone is gone. What do we do?"

She throws the question open. Let them decide. No need to involve Matías, not yet.

"We didn't see this coming," says Joel.

"This *is* serious," mutters Ketch, as if faced with a natural disaster.

At least they don't seem to blame her. For them, the situation is simply inconceivable.

"How about some other liquor…?"

"No can do." They both shake their heads.

"We're addicted."

The three of them fall silent. Angelina's said all that she has to say; Ketch and Joel have nothing to add. The silence is painful. Their machinery turns on a continuous fueling of twelve-year-old I.W. Harper. When that runs out, the gears stop. Angelina stares at the flowers on the table between them and waits. There's nothing else to do.

Suddenly something changes, the air stirs slightly. She looks up to see the pair of them, not sullen anymore, but peering behind her. They actually seem to be smiling. She turns around. Standing there is the maid from Melchor, the one who used to be María, but since going to the Presidential Villa has now become Améliana. Where did she come from?

"These two won't be drinking here anymore," says the Melchor girl. Not "they mustn't drink here," not "they can't drink here," she's merely stating a fact. As if her words were final. Angelina has no idea what makes her think she can say this, but for a second it strikes her that, yes, maybe it is the best solution.

"You two are coming with me, to the Melchor Council of Elders," says the girl in the same decisive tone. "The Elders are waiting. There's something they want to ask you. About what you did a year ago. About the contract."

Angelina catches her breath. She can't speak. Nobody should know about the contract but the four people named in it. *How can this girl...?* But before she can open her mouth, Ketch and Joel have stood up. Looking somehow expectant, their faces say they know the time has come, they'll go along gladly, they'll leave this place. She has to stop them somehow—but the greatest hold, the strongest tether to tie them here, the most potent attraction is gone: there's no more Harper's magic elixir.

María—Améliana, the seventh Yuuka—moves to leave. Ketch and Joel follow. Angelina rises on shaky legs and takes a few faltering steps after them. Nothing she can say will make them stay. The Council of Elders has found them out. Matías is done for. If she could somehow will them to drop dead on the spot, he just might stand a chance. But they don't die; they just keep walking.

María pauses at the threshold as the heavy, carved oak doors fan open from the outside, then moves on into the bright sunlight with Ketch and Joel behind her. Not for all the girls' love and friendship and admiration will they be back. No more fixing things or cutting the grass or polishing the balcony railings. Ketch, the encyclopedic jazz aficionado. Joel, the bartending maven who shuns cocktails. Their secret society of two, teased out in unverifiable histories. Their corner table and nightly bottle of I.W. Harper. Their gay half-flirting with the girls, their winning offhand manner. What will the place be without them?

Angelina follows as far as the entrance to the salon and leans on the door handle, squinting into the glare. Outside are seven youths; they've come to meet these three. She's seen them somewhere before. Ah yes, last night: the seven lads who stayed so late, seven innocents who seduced the girls without bedding a single one, seven spies who siphoned off the last drop of Ketch and Joel's precious bourbon.

Clinging to the doorway, Angelina watches the seven guardians encircle the young Yuuka and the two hired guns, then escort them away, until finally they are out of sight. They've gone to the port, where a boat will take them off toward Melchor and the downfall of the President of the Republic of Navidad, His Excellency Matías Guili.

08

The Melchor Island Council of Elders does not meet at regular intervals. Only when some issue arises and several of the Elders call for a meeting do they all assemble in that sacred lodge or "long house" known as the *abai*. The Council is comprised entirely of respected males over seventy years of age; there are no women members, though in special situations the Council may consult the Yoi'i Yuuka. The Elders have the authority to arbitrate in the affairs of the community, but when spiritual issues that supersede their secular wisdom occur, they bow to the chief priestess. Some questions are discussed for days, but never is any formal vote taken. With no particular mechanism for reaching conclusions, all the Elders remain inside the abai for the duration—except to relieve themselves—while their families keep them supplied with food.

When Ketch and Joel arrive under the guard of the seven youths, the Council is already assembled and waiting in the abai. The lodge is framed in heavy timbers and roofed with pandanus thatch—a building style traditional in the South Seas, though much bigger and longer than the average house. From a distance, it resembles an overturned canoe. Inside there is only one large room, dimly lit by small openings along the base of the walls, with banana leaf seating mats on the earthen floor.

Ketch and Joel duck through the low doorway and are brought before the dozen or so men sitting in a circle. The youths see that the two Americans are seated, then leave.

"Thank you for coming long way," says one old man to Ketch's right, speaking in rusty but understandable English. The other Elders look on silently. Their expressions are difficult to read in the dark interior, especially against the backlight from the low openings, but there is no perceptible air of hostility.

"Other day, we receive paper," says the old man. The others probably can't understand much English, but he doesn't bother to translate into the Melchor dialect or even standard Gagigula. What's being said seems to have already been discussed. "Because this paper, we talking about one man who hold our islands, our life in his hands. Your two names also on paper, so we thinking we hear what you say, so we call you here."

His tone is calm but firm. Apparently, the intention is not to accuse Ketch or Joel; the person being tried here is President Matías Guili. The two remain silent, waiting to see what happens next.

"We want you tell us your own words. Is this paper real contract? Was agreement carried out? We thinking maybe yes, but want to make sure before we pass judgment."

The English-speaking Elder pauses for some indication that the two foreigners fully comprehend the situation. Joel raises a finger to ask the old man to wait a moment, then speaks with Ketch at tongue-twisting speed. As ever, these two do all their thinking together. While they confer, neither the interpreter nor the other Elders show the least impatience or start pressing them to reach a decision.

Joel now turns to the Elder. "We understand perfectly. We will try to answer your questions the best we can. But first, there's one thing we need to know." Joel enunciates clearly for the benefit of their interlocutor. The old man nods his understanding of each phrase, before raising his hand to signal for a break in which to translate it all into Melchorian. The other Elders listen quietly, an expression of wise acknowledgment on their faces, then turn back expectantly toward Joel.

"Generally speaking, it's difficult to assess a crime from a written agreement. How do you deal with promises to perform illegal acts that don't happen? They can't be treated like those actually performed, can they? Just from the document you have, there's no clear proof that we did anything criminal, so we would urge you to rule it out as evidence."

Joel chooses his words carefully. A twelve-year-old I.W. Harper fog has lifted for the first time in a year, and he knows it's up to him now to see them safely across this legal lagoon. Ketch pays close attention, ready to correct any mistake.

"For the moment, we are free of any guilt. But answering your questions about what we did or did not do, with no lawyer present, will put us at great risk. Legally speaking, testimony is not the same thing as a piece of paper. Yet it seems our actions are not the issue here, correct? So, providing you guarantee us immunity, we swear to tell the truth, the whole truth and nothing but."

The English-speaking Elder conveys the gist of these remarks to his companions, which provokes various responses, all spoken in even tones. No one raises his voice or becomes emotional. Finally, the Elder seated furthest back, a bald-headed man with an air of obvious authority, makes a pronouncement. All the Elders listen attentively and nod their heads, then turn to face Ketch and Joel again.

The translation comes back: "We understand what you say. This is not court of law. To be honest, we not know how our country's laws apply to foreigners. Rest assured, we do nothing to you, this Council not punish you for your crime. Once we finish talking, you free to leave this building or leave this country as you wish. Maybe Council suggest you leave country, but we cannot force you. Please to say what there is to say."

Ketch and Joel proceed to discuss what they've just heard. Ketch takes a small notepad out of his breast pocket, jots down a few key points and tears off the page for his partner. Joel strains to read it in the dim light and nods. He queries Ketch on a few details, until after a minute the two of them have settled on a basic position.

"We'll tell you anything you want to know," announces Joel. As soon as this is translated for them, the Elders murmur with satisfaction.

"Thank you. Let us begin. Paper we have looks to be agreement between you and our President Matías Guili. It say you kill former President Bonhomme Tamang, and in return you get to stay at place called Angelina's, where they give you supply of I.W. Harper liquor."

The two men listen without comment.

"And did you carry out your part of agreement?"

"We did," says Joel.

Again the Elders buzz among themselves.

"Please tell us more detail."

"We came to this country a little over a year ago, while sailing across the Pacific on an international goodwill organization's schooner. To be specific, we arrived at Baltasár City. It seemed like a nice place, so we decided to stay on for a while."

Ketch hands him another note, which Joel quickly skims before going on.

"In the beginning, we stayed at the Navidad Teikoku Hotel. Very fancy with all the trimmings, but not to our taste. Oh, the place was grand—too grand. All style and no creature comforts, the food wasn't up to snuff either. Mind you, there's such a thing as plain and simple first-class cooking, but the food at the Teikoku was nowhere in that league. The fatal blow, however, came when the hotel bar didn't have our aforementioned favorite twelve-year-old I.W. Harper. We had a couple of bottles to tide us over when we disembarked, but only enough to last a few days. At the hotel, no more was to be had for love or money. How were we to know that Mr. Harper was a stranger to these islands?"

The Elders hear out Joel's rambling account, then listen to the translation but are none the wiser. How can these foreigners be so attached to this one drink?

"So we looked all over town, but there wasn't a drop anywhere. Navidad's an undeveloped country when it comes to liquor, though we could see how its other charms more than made up for it," says Joel out of courtesy to his listeners. "Sadly for us, however, we need that dram of happiness. We were dismayed. To think that such a lovely place with such attractive people and such wonderful food—outside hotel fare, that is—was missing out on such a good thing. We asked and asked until someone finally told us that one establishment might have this rare beverage—and that was Angelina's."

The Elders hear the name and all nod at once, as if they understand without translation.

"That evening, we went in search of the fabled house of dubious repute, and sure enough, the very item was right there behind the bar. The young ladies there who lend their services to men were of less interest to us. We were happy just to sit and sip, and gaze into each other's eyes."

The Elders hear out the translation and again nod their heads. By now they seem to accept the two strangers' strange idea of happiness.

"When we learned we could stay there, we moved all our belongings out of the hotel. Madame Angelina reassured us that hers was probably the only house in this corner of the Pacific to keep twelve-year-old I.W. Harper in steady supply. And there was another happy discovery—a vast collection of jazz records. That very evening, for the first time, we met the recently unelected former President Matías Guili."

As soon as Joel mentions the name, the Elders lean closer.

"That's right, the big man. On the spot, he came up with a proposal and promised us as much twelve-year-old I.W. Harper as we could drink every night. He had our number."

On hearing this translated, the bald Head of the Elders speaks up via the interpreter. "If that all you want, why you come here? You can go somewhere else, some other country to drink. For what reason you not do so? Why you accept Guili's offer?"

Ketch hands Joel a note, as has become their usual modus operandi. Ketch sketches the general outlines, Joel fills in the figures of speech.

"Well, if you want the whole truth, there were extenuating circumstances. That is, we were in a corner. We needed to lie low for a year. That's also why we came by schooner instead of a normally scheduled airline flight, and why we didn't fly off to Japan or Hong Kong or Singapore when we learned there was none of our favorite liquor here. No, an inconspicuous easygoing place where, above all, we could have our favorite tipple, that's all we wanted. So in that sense, Angelina's was ideal. That and, well, we weren't exactly rolling in cash. The job we'd performed—the job that sent us into hiding—involved a rather complicated system of payment. Meanwhile the authorities in several countries had ganged up on us and frozen our bank accounts, so we needed somewhere to tide us over a difficult patch. Guili's offer was almost made-to-order, so we accepted."

At this point, one of the group interrupts, and the English-speaking Elder interprets.

"Was reason you go into hiding because you work as hired killers?"

Ketch tosses off another hurried note.

"Yes, but please let's not go into the nitty-gritty details. Or at least, accept that it has nothing to do with you here. People drop out of sight for many different reasons."

An evasive reply, but it seems to satisfy the inquirer.

"Well, then, as you no doubt already know, Guili's terms were quite simple: get rid of Bonhomme Tamang by some means that wouldn't look too suspicious. Which we accepted because, well, to answer the previous question, we are indeed 'hit men'—specialists in the ways and means of killing."

Immediately they're bombarded with questions, all asking the same thing: that first night at Angelina's, did the two of them meet Guili by chance?

"Pure coincidence. In our line of work, we don't advertise that we kill people, nor did we know he was looking for trained assassins. We're sworn to secrecy outside our organization, and Guili, for his part, gave only the most roundabout hints. We found ourselves playing a guessing game, aided and abetted by alcohol. It was only a matter of time before something like the truth spilled over."

One Elder wants to know, did Angelina take part in these proceedings?

"No, I don't believe she suspected anything beforehand. Maybe she had some inkling, but nothing definite, not until everything was over and done with. Her only stake in the deal was to follow Guili's orders and keep us in I.W. Harper."

"And actual murder method?" asks the eldest Elder.

"Now we're talking business." Joel purses his lips, then turns to exchange a few words with Ketch as the Elders look on with curiosity.

"Much as we'd like just to leave things at 'secret methods using special tools,' I don't suppose that will satisfy you, will it? So if we may beg your indulgence, we'd like you to promise us that not a word of what we're going to say will leak out. We wouldn't want our professional commitments to be compromised by giving too much away. As we see it, you only need to establish that: one, Bonhomme Tamang was murdered; and two, it was our consummate skill behind the attribution to 'natural causes.' So, here's how we did it, on the condition that none of it leaves this building..."

The Elders talk it over and accept the terms.

"At 11:25 that morning, Bonhomme Tamang's right-hand man found the President slumped over his desk at the Presidential Villa, face down on his papers. Unfortunately, this executive secretary wasn't quite so on the ball as Jim Jameson. He called the National Hospital, but by the time the medics arrived, the President was dead—a heart attack was the call. The executive secretary attested that from eight that morning the President met with several people, then at 9:35 he went alone into his office to concentrate on his paperwork. Several others were waiting in the antechamber, but according to their independent testimonies, no one got to see the President for even a second. And of course, the office windows were locked; the room was sealed tight. It could only have been a heart attack."

The Elders listen with interest. Ketch scribbles another note outlining the points for Joel to put into his own words—their methodical division of labor.

"So much for appearances. The inside story is quite different. Our task was to make sudden death look like organ failure, an assassination without assassins. Of course, it would've been much easier to take him out by sniper fire, but that would have cast suspicion on Guili, the man who stood to profit most from Tamang's death. And anyway, we weren't packing a rifle and sniper scope when we came ashore."

As Joel's tale builds, so does the Elders' interest. Evidently the translation must be good. The Elders keep leaning forward; Ketch keeps writing more notes.

"But let's back up a bit. What were we doing the night before? We were busy incriminating former President Matías Guili. Or more precisely, we were typing up a formal indictment listing all the bribes and 'irregularities' surrounding the Navidad Teikoku Hotel construction—the same touchy subject Tamang had been investigating since taking office. And for a fabrication, I must say, it did sound pretty convincing. A perfect piecrust of fact and fiction, truth and lies. A half-dozen or so pages of pseudo-documentation. Just enough to grab our reader and hold his attention for five minutes. Guili himself gave us the outline, so it wasn't very hard to throw together."

The Elders listen in silence. None of them move. Those who understand a little English are quicker to react, the others hang on the interpreter's every word.

"We printed a single copy. Anyone who didn't know better would have thought we were simply writing a business report. The trick, however, was in the paper we used."

Some of those listening may not be able to follow the technical implications, but everyone at least understands that paper came first, then words were laid on top.

"The paper was impregnated with a special poison, invented by the research and development department of a First World intelligence organization. We won't say which—that would be telling—there must be dozens of these 'strategic agencies' around the world. Let's just say we were formerly in the employ of one of them. Anyway, in the course of our spying—did I just say that?—ahem, in the course of our *activities*, we'd been supplied with a pack of this poison paper, of which we still had a few leftover sheets. The poison is very potent: superficial skin contact with only a tiny amount will cause lethal symptoms identical to thrombotic cardiac arrest—a heart attack—in ninety-five percent of those exposed in less than seven minutes. Apparently it's an alkaloid, a lysergic acid derivative of some kind, but that's all we know."

The Elders react strongly to the poison diagnosis. The use of substances to alter the behavior of humans and animals is older than history itself.

"Okay, then, typically the executive secretary prepares the President's paperwork for review the night before. Occasionally there may be urgent items he rushes directly to the President, otherwise he lays things out on his own desk the previous evening, then transfers them all to the President's desk in the morning. All we had to do was sneak into the Presidential Villa late at night and slip our indictment in among the executive secretary's reports. Nothing simpler. With our training, locks and keys are child's play."

Joel beams with juvenile glee. Males, whether straight or gay, always retain some boyish sense of pride in their career accomplishments.

"The following morning, as usual, the President conferred with his executive secretary about the day's schedule before withdrawing to review and sign his waiting papers, preferring to do that on his own. In this respect, Tamang and Guili had identical work habits—maybe Tamang even picked up the practice from him. In any case, among the papers that morning was a particularly riveting document: a detailed denunciation of his notorious predecessor. Tamang read each line with such interest he didn't notice that the style was somehow a little 'off' compared to standard bureaucratic reports."

Joel pauses to survey his audience. His manner suggests a lawyer leading a witness more than someone on the stand himself, but the Elders don't let it distract them.

"Amazing stuff, that paper: ordinary typing bond by the look of it, yet hard to handle—the sheets tend to stick together—which made him want to wet his fingertips to turn the pages, as Guili knew he often did from observing him leafing through handouts at the meetings they both attended. If any of you have this habit, I would strongly recommend you wean yourself off it. It could prove harmful to your health."

This warning meets with puzzled silence. It would seem that few of the Elders have occasion to deal with documents and papers.

"When papers are stapled together in the upper left-hand corner, people turn the page with the index finger from the lower right-hand corner. The area the finger touches is quite specific. As Tamang finished reading the first page, he raised his finger to his lips before turning to the next. This innocent action brought his fingertip in contact with chemical A from page one, which was promptly ingested into his system when he again wet his finger to flip over page two. Chemical A thus began to circulate, until he was ready to turn to the next page, and he touched the same lower right-hand corner of page three, coated with chemical B, which he again brought to his lips and into his system at page four. By the time he reached page six, the otherwise innocuous chemicals A and B had combined in his system to synthesize the lethal poison X."

Everyone gasps.

"Each chemical must be ingested about twenty seconds apart and in the proper order."

The interpreter Elder now asks a question himself.

"Why not poison second page and be done with it?"

"Poison X is highly unstable, effective only for a few minutes immediately after synthesis. That's why the ingredient chemicals must be taken orally, to ensure that they mix in the body of the victim and not rub together harmlessly on facing pages. As soon as we learned about Tamang's finger-licking habit, the method immediately suggested itself. You could almost say that our bringing a few sheets of this special paper to the islands is really what killed Tamang. And what were the chances of that? It's almost as if Guili's murderous intentions are what drew us here."

The question and Joel's reply are translated for the benefit of the other Elders.

"To continue, then. Once chemicals A and B compounded in Tamang's system, there was no turning back. No antidote. He'd have felt something strange in his chest before he got to the middle of the next page, but probably kept on reading to the end. The strange feeling now a sharp pain, he wouldn't have had the strength to call out or reach the intercom button before collapsing face-down on his desk. The executive secretary discovered him in this state forty-five minutes later, the newly elected president dead in the earnest exercise of his morning duties, his desk scattered with papers."

The Elders are silent. One last note from Ketch remains in Joel's hand.

"Bonhomme Tamang died on the job after only three months in office. At which point, as you all know, a nationwide crisis compelled former President Guili to stand up and reclaim the empty seat, which gave him full authority to declare a state of emergency and mobilize Island Security to contain the situation. The entire Tamang incident was sidelined; the autopsy revealed no trace of poison. No accusations—aside from rumors—were ever levied against Guili. Our job was done."

The interpreter is anxious to ask something again, but Joel forges ahead.

"Naturally you're skeptical. What became of the murder weapon, you ask, the accusations that so fascinated Tamang? The document must have been there among all the other papers when Tamang was found. Indeed it was, but the executive secretary was too flustered to even notice. The disarray of papers seemed perfectly normal to him, and anyway he was in a hurry to call the medics. And then when they came, everyone in the entire villa was tripping over each other trying to get Tamang to the ambulance and accompany him to the hospital. A golden opportunity for someone to sneak away with the papers—and I shouldn't have to tell you who. So much for the events of that fateful day."

Joel rests his case. Ketch writes no more notes. All are moved. Brother Bonhomme Tamang has grown in stature, martyred in such a skillful and singular manner.

"We understand," says the interpreter, speaking for everyone. "We believe you simply carry out Guili's revenge against Tamang. Still, one thing, can you say why Guili want so much you to kill Tamang?"

Ketch fields the question in shorthand and Joel extemporizes the longer response.

"As should be obvious from the fact that the murder weapon was itself an indictment of Guili's crooked finances, the problem was his abuse of public office for personal gain. Tamang had been hot on Guili's paper trail and was already preparing an indictment himself. Guili knew he was in a corner; he had to stop the investigation and quick."

The Elders let out a knowing sigh.

"Just a conjecture, it's not like Guili ever told us any particulars. If you really want to know, you'll have to ask the man himself."

"No need for that. Your testimony and agreement paper enough for us. Thank you."

Ketch and Joel bow, then take their leave. The meeting goes on for hours afterwards. The situation is straightforward enough, with little room for dispute. Still, in keeping with tradition, all viewpoints are aired, including odd bits of lore that no First World court of law would ever consider. Once all have been heard, a unanimous decision is pronounced.

The Melchor Council of Elders has a time-honored way of announcing their decisions. A messenger is sent out on foot or, if to another island, by canoe. For this ruling, Améliana is chosen to deliver the word to Matías Guili in Baltasár City on Gaspar Island, borne by the same seven young oarsmen. The canoe is ready and waiting on the beach.

The seven youths guide their dugout through a break in the reef, then brave the open sea beyond, guided only by their knowledge of the movement of the stars night by night, season by season, their experienced sense of when to sail and when to row.

All goes well the first day of the voyage: the weather holds up, as if in support of the Elders' decision. But the next day brings a gale. Huge waves wash over the canoe; the stars go into hiding and the sun is nowhere to be seen. Vagrant winds and stray currents throw them off course. All they can do is bear up passively to what comes at them, and pray that their canoe remains intact and no one is lost overboard.

The following morning, exhausted from their night of terror, they wake one by one to find the waves now largely subsided, wind and cloud in retreat, and the sun burning bright in the east. Their real trial begins from here on. The seven have only their wits and knowledge of the sea to tell them where they are or which way they should proceed. Améliana may have second sight into things, but she merely listens to their conjectures, saying nothing herself. When they set out, the course from Melchor to the reef around Gaspar and Baltasár should have taken them almost due northwest. The problem now is to figure out just how far in which direction they went that first whole day of northerly wind, then where they were blown in the storm that followed. Neither the face of the sea a handsbreadth below the prow of their canoe, nor the layers of cloud far above them point the way toward Gaspar. Sighting only from the disc of the sun, the young sailors bear tentatively to the northwest.

Maybe the heavens are on their side after all, for they reach their destination by the afternoon of the fourth day. The canoe enters the greater lagoon via a southeastern break in the barrier reef, then heads west along the southern coast of Baltasár Island and beaches unobtrusively at the tip of Gaspar near Uu, where the villagers quietly welcome the eight Melchorians. From there, they walk to Baltasár City and on up to the Presidential Villa, their steps showing little sign of fatigue from their long sea voyage.

FINAL BUS REPORT

Foreign visitors to the islands are often surprised to learn that more than a mere means of transportation, buses are so highly regarded here they almost seem to be objects of worship. The bus network links the capital to most other towns and villages, even extending to settlements with only a few houses. As a result, citizens enjoy an admirable degree of mobility for such a small country, a fact which forms the basis of certain customs.

When an infant is born, after its first bath and suckling at its mother's breast, its very next experience is a bus ride. The child's maternal grandparents (and the mother as well if her postpartum recovery is quick) typically board at the nearest bus stop with the swaddled babe in arms. The mother's husband and brothers and sisters see them all off, and they ride to the end of the line and back. The routes are not especially long, so the trip takes thirty minutes to an hour at most, just long enough to answer their prayers for many safe returns. With this "first bus," the child becomes a "full-fare" member of the family who, it is hoped, will grow up strong as a bus.

It is also not unusual for people with ailments to ride buses for their salutary effect. All buses in the country are equipped with a special sick berth for this purpose. Something like a stretcher suspended in hammock fashion, the bed cushions hard shocks on the roughest roads, while the pulsing of the engine is widely believed by the island folk to have curative powers. Navidadians hold that bus vibrations can work wonders. Most sick people who ride around for one or two days will show signs of improvement; some who had to be carried on board will even get off on their own two feet.

Unknowing foreigners may take alarm at the sight of moribund passengers on buses here. This is not because persons in the throes of death choose to ride buses as a last-ditch panacea, but rather that bus travel is regarded as the first leg of a peaceful journey to the next world and even beyond to rebirth—a custom that is known as the "last bus rite."

Today, thanks to tales told by tourists and cultural anthropologists' research, the relationship between health and bus-riding discovered in Navidad has come to the attention of other countries, so we may expect to see similar bus beliefs spreading overseas. We hear that "first bus" practices have already taken hold in certain regions of the Philippines, while recent reports tell of similar trends just now beginning in the southern islands of the Japanese archipelago. Healthy bus, healthy body.

For some reason this morning, the plaza crowd is mostly women. Passing through on the way to the market or work, they scan the benches for familiar faces, and if they happen to see someone they know, they'll sit down for a good long chat. It just takes a couple of grains of salt to form a crystal, and just a few approachable souls to get the gossip going. The first two on the benches today were young women, followed immediately by more and more girls their age. Before long, the shoppers have forgotten what they came to buy, the office workers and hired help have deserted their posts. The whole gaggle of young females is enough to put off any men and other women past child-rearing age.

"Okay, girl, what's with the I-know-something-you-don't-know face?" asks a waitress from the Navidad Teikoku Hotel restaurant.

"Wait'll you hear—a Yuuka done marched into the Presidential Villa!" discloses a young postal clerk.

"No! What's *that* about?"

"It's the Melchor Elders, they passed some ruling on President Guili and the Yuuka came to lay down the law."

"The Yoi'i Yuuka?" asks a girl who was engaged to a boy from one of the outer islands and returned much happier after the wedding was called off.

"Oh c'mon now, silly. Not even the Elders can make the Yoi'i Yuuka do things. They'd do her bidding, maybe. But no, they picked the seventh Yuuka as their messenger. The young one, with the powers. Gotta admire her."

"How'd you hear about all this?" asks a fisherwoman known to match any man catch-for-catch.

"My cousin, he works at the villa. And he recognized her."

"You got something going with your cousin?"

"What's that to you?"

"Okay, okay. Touchy, are we?"

"Well, *anyway*," continues the postal clerk, ignoring the insinuation, "the seventh Yuuka, who used to work at the villa herself, showed up with seven guys. They just waited at the entrance, but she stormed right in."

The other girls are all ears, excited as if they were witness to the scene.

"And then y'know what?" the postal clerk continues, "she walked right in on Guili and laid it on him."

"What'd she say?" they all lean forward to ask.

"Can't quote her, but whatever, she told him off, called him an evil man."

"*I* could'a told you *that*," one uppity girl puts in. "Don't know what he's done now, but from what he's been up to so far I can pretty well guess what the Yuuka'd say."

"Like what?" challenges the postal clerk, echoed by the others.

"Like the Elders withdraw all respect for him."

"That's it?"

"Pretty much."

"Wouldn't they come down stronger, like with a death sentence or something?"

"Or banish him from the presidency?"

"At least strip him of his authority?"

"No, no, all wrong. My grandpa was an Elder. He used to tell me things."

"Wow, you got some family connections. Cool."

"Well, maybe. I'm a runaway myself, though."

"That's cool too."

"I guess. Kinda shy 'bout it. Something dirty happened to me, so I came home."

"Something dirty?"

"Just pawed me and felt me up a bit."

"Hey, are we talking 'bout the Council of Elders or what? Leave the smut for next time, okay? So why don't they just plain oust President Guili?"

"Well, it's like this," the runaway explains, playing it up for effect. "The Council of Elders isn't a court and it's not a police force. They got no way to put their decisions into effect. All they can do is tell him 'We don't respect you no more.' Can't do any more than that. That's what I was told."

"But even that'd be a shock," says the waitress.

"Shoulda done the trick all right."

"Sure did," says the postal clerk. "Came as a total shock. Why, I hear that the minute he got the word, he went white as a sheet. Then he went to his quarters and hasn't come out since."

"Your cousin tell you this too?"

"Yeah, but I doubt he actually saw him go white. I mean, only Guili himself and the Yuuka were there, and she wouldn't tell my cousin anything like that. But the part about Guili hiding out ever since does seem to be true."

"But what about the President's job? Y'know, meeting people, deciding stuff?"

"That other dude's doin' most of it. You know, with the dark skin, the Executive Fall Guy."

"Yeah, right," says the postal clerk, "that Jim Jimson guy."

"You mean Jameson."

"Yeah, like I said, Executive Secretary Jim Jimson. Dark, kinda good-looking."

"Yeah, him. He can do just fine without Guili around."

"So there gonna be another election?" the fisherwoman wonders out loud.

"Guess so," mumbles the waitress. "Wish they'd just let the dark dude do his stuff, though."

⚡

Two hours later, the plaza is now old woman territory. A brood of biddies is sitting cackling away when a couple more crones drop by to share in the morning hearsay and the cackle becomes even more animated.

"Finally done it," says one old girl, trotting over to her friend on the bench.

"Done what?" asks her seated friend, rising to a slight crouch so as not to miss a single word by sitting out of earshot.

"We whupped him!"

"Whupped him and whacked him!" says another old maid just arriving. "Felt good too."

"Whupped *who*?"

"That mean ol', you know..." stammers the second old maid.

"S'no good. Better you start all over from the beginning."

"Oh, suppose so. Well, you heard about the Elders decidin' not to respect Guili, didn'ya?"

"And them choosing the seventh Yuuka as their messenger, canoed over here to tell the man? Sure, I heard. The President was come-upped. He shut hisself in the back of the villa."

"Aw, who cares about Guili anyway? It's Island Security I got a bone to pick with. 'Course Guili's the one gave 'em their orders, but they's the ones who come bargin' in and pissed in my house!"

"Same here. Them IS boys come and throwed buckets of water all over my sittin' room. Got everything sopping wet."

"Me too. My sister's husband's nephew got beat up in a back alley by the IS."

"And just to grab up the land to build that lousy hotel."

"It's all Guili's fault."

The old girl who rose from her seat wants to slump back down again, but her friend obviously isn't in the mood for a quiet talk. She keeps waving her hands and stamping her feet, mussing her hair and grimacing, the better to make her point.

"It was Guili brought in that goon from Japan when he became president. Tamang was gonna disband 'em, but he didn't have time before Guili was back in."

"That's why we all went down to IS Headquarters. To have us a look around."

"That we did, this very morning. Had us a good long look-see."

"And whadya know? Them snotty bastards come tiptoein' out one by one."

"Out of uniform, in regular old aloha shirts and T-shirts."

"So you whupped 'em?" asks an old woman who's been sitting there all along.

"Sure wanted to, but when they saw us glaring at them, they got all sorry-eyed and ran off. Didn't have the heart to chase after 'em, they's just a bunch of kids."

"We just stared 'em down. Then we went in and had us a little talk."

"With who?"

"The Jap with the dark glasses. The one Guili brought in to head up the IS."

"You mean Katsumata?"

"Right, him. Katsumata."

"He was just comin' out, wearing a suit and carrying a briefcase."

"Looked like such a loser with no glasses and those frightened puppy eyes."

"We surrounded him."

"We told him off. 'You're the guy who put Island Security up to all those terrible things, aren't ya? Dressed our boys in uniforms and had them piss in my house!'"

"Was he ever scared! He pretended he didn't understand Gagigula. Tried to make excuses in broken English like we had the wrong person and he had nothing to do with it."

"That's when I spoke in Japanese. 'I know you. You're that no-good Katsumata. You're the biggest bully of them all.'"

"What a laugh! Shocked him out of his socks. He didn't have any idea we could speak Japanese from the war. He broke down and started shaking."

"Told him, 'Your people made us learn the language when we were kids. Glad it finally came in handy!'"

"And then all of us gave him a whack on the head."

"A little something we owed him for taking all the best property."

"And it felt good?" asks one of the plaza biddies.

"Sure did. We whacked 'im till our arms were sore."

"Didn't kick him. We could've, though, with him cowering there like that."

"Thad've been unfair. And besides, rubber sandals ain't much for kicking. Better our hands and fists for pummeling."

"So we whacked him and whupped him until enough was enough, then we pushed him out of the HQ holdin' his achin' head and came here. Had to tell people, if anybody wants to give him a whack or two, there's still time. He's still there."

"Sounds like fun. Let's go."

With that, several old women get up and head for Island Security Headquarters, leaving the others on the benches to return to less pressing gossip. As the excitement ebbs, the conversation turns to speculation about Guili's undoing.

⚡

Parked a short distance from these ever-so-satisfied matrons are two taxis. Hired wheels are few in this country, and only tourists ever use them, which makes it difficult to catch a cab except between the airport and the Navidad Teikoku Hotel. Or to put it another way, any cab driver who wants to take it easy has only to steer clear of those two locations. No tourist ever walks to the plaza expecting to find a taxi; this, then, is the drivers' customary rest area.

"Just had me a strange customer," says one cabbie.

"Strange, like other than foreign?" asks the other driver.

"No, that was the flight from Guam he come on, so he musta been a Jap."

"Not a tourist?"

"No, businessman type, but real dark for a Jap. Had a big trunk and a black briefcase. Standing on his lonesome like a burnt tree in the middle of nowhere."

"Okay, sounds pretty spooky the way you tell it. What else?"

"'Go straight to the Presidential Villa,' he tells me."

"At a time like this?"

"Yeah, says, 'Gotta say hello to the Prez. Just wait in front of the villa, then we'll go to the Teikoku.'"

"So?"

"So I drive and don't say nothing. That's my job, okay?"

"Yeah, but what's a foreigner have to see Guili about? Sounds shady to me."

"Maybe, ain't none of my business. So anyway, I make straight for the villa, let him off at the entrance."

"And he went in?"

"Just like he owned the place. Weren't no guards at the door. But no sooner's he inside than he comes right out again. He's looking kinda sick, sweating like crazy."

"Someone must've told him off inside."

"Reckon so. Looked like he stepped in pig shit. He gets in back and lets out this big sigh. So I gotta ask the guy, 'Hey, what's wrong?'"

"Must've heard about what happened to Guili, no?"

"No, seems he was used to the VIP treatment, but this time they sent him packing."

"So what'd you say to him then?"

"What d'you think? I tell him how the Melchor Elders decided not to respect Guili, and how that meant nobody was going to take no more orders from him. How this really was the end of the road for the big man."

"And?"

"And when I start off for the Teikoku like he wanted, he asks, 'What time's the afternoon flight to Guam?' Okay, what now, I'm thinking. 'Go straight to the airport,' he tells me. So we turn around and I drop him off and collect my fare and that's that. Three hours in the country, and the guy doesn't talk to more than two people—me and somebody in the villa—before he's outta here. I'm telling you, *strange*."

"Musta been buddy-buddy with Guili. Bet we gonna see a lot more of his type."

⚡

Late in the afternoon, people gather in the plaza. Nobody knows who put out the word, but it soon spreads around the capital. All who hear put down whatever they're doing and head straight for the plaza, until their numbers swell to overflowing. Yet even as they all crowd in, they spontaneously leave an appropriate space in the center. There, some enterprising souls have cobbled together a bunch of crates borrowed from behind Guili's Supermarket to build a makeshift stage. Standing at attention to the left and right, the yellow-uniformed boys and girls of the Children's Fife and Drum Corps hold their instruments, ready to play at a moment's notice. Unlike at the airport, however, there are no flagpoles in the plaza. Flags or not, everyone is waiting for a ceremony of some kind.

At four thirty, the people gathered on the side toward the road that leads to the airport and Diego begin to stir. The commotion soon spreads across the entire gathering, then dies down as people gasp and stare. The crowd parts and slowly, portentously, a green and yellow striped bus drives into the plaza, and through the large blue-tinted windows they can see members of the Japanese Veterans' Delegation waving. The driver nudges the bus forward like a boat slowly parting the tides of humanity. Right next to him in the tour guide's seat is the junior official from the Navidadian Foreign Office. The people in the plaza, all smiles, cheer and applaud the bus's return. It isn't like the heroes' welcome accorded victorious troops or a record-breaking mountaineering team or even successful negotiators returning from a decisive international summit; no, if anything it's more like teasing a naughty boy come home at long last from a wild escapade—only the prodigal son here is the bus, rather than anyone on board.

The bus stops in the middle of the plaza. The door opens and out steps the Foreign Office staffer, followed by the Japanese Ministry of Welfare liaison, then the Japanese veterans one by one. The applause stops, though the many watchful eyes continue to bathe the old boys in goodwill. They're still wearing the same dark woolen suits, so totally wrong for the local climate, identical black leather shoulder bags, and even more out-of-place white hats marked with a single red stripe; but what impresses everyone most is how healthy they all look. Their cheeks have color, their posture is good, there's a spring in their step. Why, they're even a little tanned. Those in the crowd who were at the airport for the delegation's arrival will later remark how surprisingly rejuvenated the old codgers now seem.

Another thing the Baltasár citizens can't fail to notice are the somehow knowing expressions on the old soldiers' faces as they file off the bus. Not without reason: the bus may have chosen its own wayward course, but they were only too glad to go along for the extended joyride. There's a conspiratorial gleam in their eyes.

The veterans line up before the makeshift stage. Compared to when they'd just arrived and stood at attention at the airport, their present formation is slightly more relaxed and casual, less imperial military and more Third World, as if the tropics have seeped under their skin. Mr. Ministry of Welfare is also visibly invigorated. The young Home Office staffer, looking relaxed like someone just getting off work, breaks away from the group and ambles around behind the Fife and Drum Corps to greet a colleague in the crowd, then rejoins the others onstage. Now, as if to start his shift, out of the ranks steps Executive Secretary Jim Jameson, who promptly mounts the stage. Everyone goes quiet.

"President Guili is occupied and couldn't be here today, so I've come in his place," he begins in English, which the Ministry of Welfare man translates into Japanese for the benefit of the veterans. "I'm not much good at speeches, but I'd like to welcome back the delegation and say how glad we Navidadians are to see everybody looking so well and happy."

The old soldiers are moved to hear this. Some stare up at the sky transfixed; others pull handkerchiefs out of their suit pockets and unabashedly mop their faces. They give the impression of having just returned from some grand adventure.

"When I heard that the bus had disappeared, I was quite honestly worried. But as there's not a soul in this country who could mean you any harm, we felt sure you were still alive and well somewhere. Every day, we heard different reports from people who'd sighted you, so we knew you'd be back in due course."

Although unpracticed at public speaking, his words do seem to touch these sentimental old men.

"You've had a rather special experience on these islands, which I hope will encourage you to help cement relations between our two countries."

With that, Jim Jameson steps down. Unlike the time at the airport, however, the usually adroit Mr. Ministry of Welfare shows none of his career polish and actually seems to be at a loss for a follow-up. The short notice and the President's absence have also left the local bureaucrats in the lurch. Who's running this impromptu homecoming ceremony anyway? The Japanese vets go into a huddle, then one of them finally steps onto the stage to speak. Everyone is relieved it's not the long-winded infantry captain who caused so many heatstrokes last time.

"Hello," says the speaker. "Putting aside the purpose that originally brought us here, we'd just like to thank the people of Navidad for giving us such a warm welcome and showing us such a good time during our extended visit. I imagine we'll have a chance sometime to tell you all about what we saw and did these many days, but for now I'd simply like to say that, looking back on it all, these have truly been the happiest, most enjoyable days of my life."

Behind him the veterans all nod in agreement. His words speak for the entire delegation.

"The truth is, we've all had second thoughts about what we did on these islands so long ago and about coming back here decades after the war. All our old convictions have been shaken, and after lots of time for reflection on this trip, we've had a profound change of heart. It's a long story, and we've plenty to tell the folks back home. But for the moment, let me just say how nice it feels to be in tip-top shape again. On behalf of our entire delegation, I'd like to finish with a simple word of thanks to the people of Navidad and to His Excellency President Matías Guili, who is absent today but was kind enough to meet us on our arrival, for giving us this chance to change our thinking."

The whole plaza resounds with applause. The crowd's reaction to the mention of Matías Guili is measured, but the veterans don't seem to notice. Again, Jim Jameson mounts the makeshift stage.

"Well, then, this concludes our little ceremony to mark your safe return. Please have a good night's rest in a comfortable hotel after spending so long on the road. Your flight to Japan is scheduled for noon tomorrow, though we hope you'll come back and visit this country again before too long."

Another round of loud clapping.

"And will you, uh, be taking the bus back to the hotel?"

The veterans all shake their heads; they've had more than enough bus riding for now, thank you. Or maybe they're afraid of going missing again.

Slowly, the Ministry of Welfare man leads them off on foot toward the Navidad Teikoku Hotel, as finally, on baton cue from the stocky boy conductor, the patient Fife and Drum Corps raise their instruments and strike up, not the Navidadian national anthem nor an unrecognizable *Kimi ga Yo*, but that old standard *When the Saints Go Marching In*, an island favorite. The rejuvenated veterans pick up their step to the bouncy two-beat melody and wend their way through the crowd.

⚡

Matías does not emerge from his private quarters. He sees no one and does nothing. Official duties he's relinquished to Jim Jameson. The executive secretary can surely handle all the outward trappings of the office, and whatever else behind the scenes he doesn't know won't hurt him. Enough is enough, the game is over anyway. Whether everything simply evaporates or somebody somewhere takes a beating because of it, what does he care? Should anyone come raging up to the villa demanding to see him, Jim Jameson can turn them away. The man's a rock.

He hardly eats. He leaves most of his morning sashimi on his plate, skips lunch, and only has instant noodles for dinner. He must look a fright, but doesn't look in the mirror, so who knows? At night, he sleeps. Not his abnormally deep dreamless sleep, but the ordinary human variety. He dreams more than seems decently possible, sometimes seeing long-lost faces from his past. Waking is hard, although if he knows he's dreaming he can't be sleeping very soundly. Compared to his former narcoleptic states, he's only floating on the surface, his body scarcely half submerged in the waters of unconsciousness. He doesn't blank out anymore; he knows exactly who he is when he wakes and doesn't need notes or portraits to revive his sense of self. He's become a normal human being.

Itsuko looks after him like before. He's told her to go easy on the meal servings, and after seeing how little he actually eats now, by the third morning after his appetite died on him, she's reduced the portions drastically. She doesn't mother him with unwanted urgings to eat to keep up his strength. If he tells her all he wants in the evening is a Cup Noodle, that's all she brings. On her side, Itsuko merely observes this shut-in Matías who seldom even bothers to look out the window.

He knows that witnesses must have come forward with hard evidence for the Melchor Council of Elders to reach such a harsh decision. He's even guessed it was Ketch and Joel and the written contract that incriminated him. With Améliana the agent on a mission—she and her seven slippery siblings, if they even existed. Yes, but how the hell did she lure Ketch and Joel away from Angelina's? How did she get hold of that agreement? Did Itsuko lend her a hand? No islander would ever think to look under a tatami mat, that's for sure. Then there's the question of why Angelina would let those two leave. And why Améliana was so intent on bringing him down. Who *is* she? Who's behind her? None of Tamang's feckless lot could have put her up to this.

Do these questions cloaked in doubt and vague supposition even mean anything? Whether Itsuko was involved or not doesn't alter the reality of his situation. Maybe she's got a grudge he doesn't know about, but she still prepares his meals, punctual as ever, lays out clean underwear for him every morning, tidies the futon. Shut in or not, he can still lead a normal existence thanks to her. Can't ask for more than that. Even if she did help Améliana, he doesn't see her hightailing it back to Japan. Or even leaving the villa, for that matter.

How's Angelina doing through all this, he can't help wondering. Now and again, for minutes at a time, he misses the sound of her voice, the way she talks, her voluptuous body, her amazing woman's intuition and wisdom within certain bounds, the sum total of her attractions. Yes, but he still doesn't want to go see her or even leave the villa. What could he possibly say to her? And what would knowing the reason why Ketch and Joel left her premises do for him? What was there left to talk about? The days ahead are steeped in silence.

What was Améliana up to now? That day when she suddenly appeared and announced the Elders' verdict, she didn't say another word; she just walked right out of the office. So where was Améliana now? Did she and her gang of seven go back to Melchor? She didn't even mention quitting her job, iffy as it was. She might not have had a contract, but technically she was still employed.

More and more, he feels like he's hanging in thin air.

⚡

Late at night in his private quarters, Matías tires of staring at the same old walls and lights a candle, then stares at the flame and waits for Lee Bo to come. Unless he performs this little ritual, the Palauan prince who died two centuries before in England will not appear. Like all ghosts, Lee Bo knows the dead should not interfere much in the affairs of the living. Their role is simply to look on, to enjoy the petty ripples that engulf the living, a pleasure not unlike watching a movie or reading a novel. Occasionally one of them might reveal himself to a favored character and talk about this and that, but he mustn't spoil the drama or discuss those parts of the pageant that the living cannot see. Never commenting on tomorrow's share prices nor on winning horses (not that Navidad has either a stock market or a race track), what counsel they might give is always from a step or two back. No, they come only when called, often not showing their faces even then. Whether the ghost is elsewhere or simply otherwise occupied, there's just no telling.

Matías hasn't seen Lee Bo since the fateful day Améliana strode into his office and delivered the Elders' pronouncement. He's had to work up to it; he didn't want to risk even more confusion. Matías is never quite sure what to make of the ghost and his passing comments; a trusted confidant, but such a reluctant augur of things. No spiritual adviser, he's more like a much older friend—Lee Bo was born in the 1760s, Matías in 1928—one who has made his fortune and long since retired.

Still, with all the pain and uncertainty that has befallen him, Matías has regrets and anxieties he needs to get off his chest. Some moments he's on the verge of erupting in anger, at others he yearns for a strong shoulder to lean on. Never given a proper opportunity to exonerate himself—that's what's so unfair. Though the more he considers it, what possible defense could he have offered? The Council of Elders didn't even deem his testimony worth hearing. Maybe rightly so. Who is he to doubt the wisdom of the Elders?

He's had too much to think about, thought all he can and then some. Now he's calmed down enough to want to hear what the ghost has to say. The time has come.

A youthful face wavers within the candle flame, and by the time Matías looks up Lee Bo is sitting across from him the same as ever: poised, contented and all-knowing, though in no hurry to speak. Still, the fact that the spirit chooses to appear at all must mean he still feels favorably toward Matías. Or is it just mutual curiosity, a performer-and-viewer thing? Whatever the case, Matías is always grateful for Lee Bo's visits, regarding his mere presence as a stroke of good fortune.

"Rough seas you've been sailing," observes Lee Bo.

"You can say that again. Unfortunately I'm the one who made a mess of things, but still it all came down so suddenly."

"Améliana cut your rigging, did she?"

"If that's what you want to call it. Suddenly she was just here and the whole room was full of those damn butterflies. She was even holding a bunch of *bua* flowers."

"Aye, frangipani."

"Nice to look at in a garden. Lovely smell. But in the hand of a caller, the flower of rejection," says Matías almost under his breath, as if searching for the words from a distance. "I tell you, the instant I saw them, something in me died. Seeing her come with those flowers that morning was the worst thing I could've imagined. She wasn't just plain mad at me for what I did after the Yuuka Yuumai. No, that pose, that expression on her face, I knew she was acting on behalf of something bigger, either the Yoi'i Yuuka or the Council of Elders."

"Twin straits," intones Lee Bo.

"Well, it wasn't the Yoi'i Yuuka. Wasn't any spiritual transgression, but a secular crime. Améliana merely held out that bunch of flowers and repeated, 'We withdraw all respect for you.' My heart just stopped, the blood drained out of me. For some time I'd had a feeling something was up, but I had no idea it could be this bad. I sank in my chair, couldn't even move. I thought I was going to pass out. How could the Elders do that to me?"

"Ah, the living can scarce see e'en one pace ahead," sighs the apparition.

"And you dead can?" snaps Matías, almost by reflex, then realizes the absurdity of his outburst. "No, we living can't see a thing."

The two of them fall silent, as if waiting for something to say. There are moments no words can bridge.

"It all started with that torii gate," mutters Matías.

"And the bulletins posted about. Followed in due course by the motor carriage vanishing. Then your meeting a young woman at Angelina's."

"Were they all part of one scheme?"

"One scheme? The world is not so discrete as you might believe. Shew me an individual! The living, the dead, the thoughts and desires and longings of so many, layer upon layer, o'er time they all act as one."

"I don't get it."

"Oh no? If 'twere not so, how should the Yuuka Yuumai draw in so many people? You yourself made full use of the principle—how else could you have fared so far as a politician in this land? And fared quite well, did you not?"

"You think so? The people were just *them*, the people, to me. I alone was an individual with free will—or so I thought.. Though maybe I was nothing more than the forces I tied together. I can't hold it against Améliana for what she did. She was bound up with other forces themselves."

"One cannot hide things from gods and ancestors."

"So there's no place for me to run?"

"In the ultimate sense, no. There is, tho, the path of not running."

"But not still as president."

It's the first time Matías has spoken out loud in days. He's needed Lee Bo here to bring himself to speak. He's the sole friend Matías can really trust.

"No way can I lose the Elders' respect and people's support and still act as president. Everybody would just laugh at the sight of me. Island Security's gone and disbanded, old ladies have beaten up Katsumata. Suzuki's gone straight back to Japan with his Brun Reef Oil Depot plan. No government clerk will give me the time of day. They've even torn down all my official portraits all over the country and burned them. Why, there's not a single petitioner out in front of the villa."

"All this you know?" asks Lee Bo.

"Well, partly educated guesswork. I haven't lost my powers of deduction."

Another silence. Both of them stare at the candle on the table.

"Where did I go wrong? At what point did I fail? With which decision?"

"All questions arising from your own personal perspective. Seen from Navidad as a whole, you were merely the helmsman of the hour, whether it was you needed Navidad or Navidad you. Precious little does it matter now, such stuff is politics."

"I shouldn't have had Tamang offed, is that it? No man should dispose of his political enemies? Was I supposed to just sit by quietly and watch that idiot play havoc with everything I made? Just let him confiscate all the funds I raised? It wasn't just the money, dammit. After all that effort to squeeze investors in Japan and who-knows-where, to just go and shit on so many possibilities, it was criminal!"

"You call him—"

"That's right, a criminal. Tamang was on a rampage. I even went and met with him before it was too late. Oh, I tried to explain—why I was taking a percentage off the top of every ODA package, how I'd put those funds to use over the next twenty years—but did he listen? The fool had no notion of politics today, not a clue about economics. A country this size, government's just a fancy decoration. He couldn't get something so obvious through that thick skull of his: money calls the shots in industrialized countries, bureaucrats in socialist countries, and the army in developing countries. Good thing Navidad's so small we can only choose one of these. It's all we can do just to have our day in the shade of someone else's big umbrella and not find ourselves underfoot. Getting by while getting out of the way, pandering to pretexts of world peace, creating channels for their money to flow this way—it all takes capital. But try to tell him, the idiot wouldn't hear a word of it. He probably thought I was stashing away millions to retire in luxury. Hey, if I wanted a harem of a hundred young Filipinas, I could have that right now. I tell you, the man had zero political imagination. Couldn't see what was going on around him, in this country, in this part of the Pacific, how the world was going to look in the next few years. No idea. Never should have become president. No, dying was the only choice for him."

"I see," says Lee Bo, too softly to tell whether he's agreeing with Matías or merely prompting further discourse.

"If that plane hadn't crashed before the election, if I'd had Kurokawa's five million in hand, Tamang would've lost and not needed to die. Some opposition party! Legislator misfits and fellow American alumni, nothing but a bunch of whiners."

"'If,' you say. One cannot change history on a whim. Had I not died in England, who's to say that Palau might not today be a cultural colossus the rival of London or Paris? 'Tis naught but idle speculation."

"Okay, so the plane crashed. Some old wartime jinx maybe, but that stupid pilot downed it with all its precious cargo right there."

"Dull-witted, perhaps, tho not unskilled. 'Twas no fault of the pilot, that pyre. Indeed, had you founded your own flying folly, he would have made an able captain. His talk of two great birds, painted in green and yellow stripes like that soldiers' carriage...such grand dreams he regaled you with."

"So you knew?"

"Indeed, I knew of your tribulations in amassing funds, the airship enterprise being just one of your ambitions. I may well have known ere you yourself."

"Sure, I always wanted to start up Air Navidad. Decades-old Boeing planes would do just fine. Secondhand hulks from Aloha Air or Garuda. Hell, I'd have even taken old Air Nauru planes. Just three of them, that's all I needed. At eight million dollars each, that's twenty-four million. Throw in all the other equipment, say thirty million. If I invested fifty-one percent, I'd have a fine company, which I could just as easily hand over to the country. My money or the state's, what's the difference? The state coffers don't earn interest, that's the only reason I saved up under my name. In a Swiss bank, one of those famous secret accounts, but that still doesn't make it my own private savings. I'd hand it all over to Jim Jameson tomorrow. Never planned to spend the money myself anyway."

"Tho why an aerial enterprise?"

"You of all people, my bonny Prince from Palau, should know that. For the last few centuries, these islands, this region has seen plenty of foreigners pass through, but no locals leaving. You were the single exception. Unfortunately, you died for it."

"Aye, perished I did."

"Our history's nothing but stories of others bringing things here that sealed our fate. People here never got to choose—only you and me. Don't tell me you don't see us in the same boat. We're allies. Isn't that why you chose me to haunt?"

"Aye, a kindred spirit."

"A fellow islander who made it abroad. Lucky I didn't die away from home, so I could bring back my bounty alive. I imported instant noodles and became president. And all the while I kept thinking, we islanders have got to cross the ocean on our own. We have to take control of our own destiny. We should be the ones to decide who goes where to study what, who we invite here to the islands, how many tourists we let in for how long. A country this size, where we stand in relation to other countries ought to be at the very heart of our political ideology. Domestic affairs we can leave to the Council of Elders. Yet nobody here knows a thing about the outside world. I'm the only one who knew enough to build a framework for future relations with the major powers. That was my job and that's what I was doing. And *that's* why I had that know-nothing Tamang snuffed out!"

"Indeed," says Lee Bo, trying to calm him down.

Matías looks upset that he's come out with the forbidden topic of assassination. Peeved and moody, he continues talking. "Of course, an airline's just a symbol. Whether on our own planes or Philippine Air or Continental Air Micronesia or JAL, we'd still get where we're going. But symbols are everything in politics. Petty officials can manage things as they stand because it's all practical matters, but a politician has to present a vision of the future, which calls for showmanship and myths. We need to go abroad of our own doing, see what there is to see and bring back what we ourselves want. And for that we need three secondhand 727s. Cut-rate rigs, Boeing's best sellers of the century, Third World specials that'll still have plenty of spare parts thirty years from now. In the beginning we'd have to hire foreigners like that cracker who flies the Islander, but eventually we've got to see our Navidadian boys grow up to be pilots. Navidadian girls for stewardesses too."

"Fine flagships you fancy, eh?"

"Yeah, especially 727s and Islanders. But there are any number of ways to go."

"Tho I daresay, you tangled your own spinnakers when you met those two, Ketch and Joel, or else when you soiled your hands with the hostelry money. But perhaps I do you wrong. Yours was no error of judgment, only a lapse of luck."

"That airfield, that five million up in smoke. Was it really Jap ghosts that did it?"

"'Twould seem so," allows Lee Bo. "Your island gods do not allude to it."

"Outside powers, then?"

"Such as may be construed."

"Then it couldn't be helped."

Matías looks relieved to know at least the island spirits haven't deserted him.

"Might we talk of something else?" asks Lee Bo hesitantly.

"Why sure," says Matías, realizing he's been monopolizing the conversation. Lee Bo is so easy to talk to, the words just flow. Now it's his turn to listen to the ghost.

"In Palau, not twenty years ago, there was an old crone who lived in a tiny village on Babelthuap Island. She raised chickens and pigs, and tended her field most ably for her age. One day, a Yankee traveler came to the village driving a hired carriage on his way to the tip of the island where a quaint old abai lodge with colourfully painted walls was to be found. Either he was all in a dither searching for the abai or he'd quaffed a peg ere leaving his lodgings, but he was in a goodly hurry when, passing the old lady's house, suddenly a chicken ran out into the road."

"Common enough story. Chickens don't know about cars. Go on."

"Aye, uncivilised fowl they are. The carriage hit the chicken and sent it to its Maker. The Yankee quickly halted his carriage, alighted and gathered up the dead bird. He was distraught, for without thinking he had killed a bird of no little value to poor country folk. Out of his own cultural waters, what could he say? A sensitive lot, it would seem, these foreigners."

"A few of them."

"I bow to your greater knowledge. In any case, this one did not simply run off. He took it upon himself to go, dead hen in hand, and apologise to its owner."

"Which caused a big fuss."

"Naturally. The old lady made such a to-do you would have thought the bird was her own beloved grandchild. As tho she were to bury it in the family grave instead of plucking it for the pot. So the Yankee pulled out his purse."

"The decent thing."

"Well, at the sight of the green bills, the old lady's eyes changed colour too. She proceeded to tell the Yankee about her bird: how clever, how beautiful, how noble it was, the pride of the village, practically a god in feathered form, but never did she name a price."

"Smart move."

"In countries rich and poor factors in a transaction pit themselves at opposite extremes o'er what they deem fair recompense. No mere percentage, but often figures apart. The old crone was determined to make him name the first price."

"Wasn't there a market value?"

"In which market? Of course, chickens have value in the village market, but not in dollars. 'Tis all barter: one chicken for a bunch of bananas and some taro, or so many reef fish or a day's work."

"Like Navidad in the old days."

"The search for the abai now all but forgotten, the Yankee finally proposed a figure. A simple sum, which she multiplied by ten, and led him on, allowing the dupe to bargain her down to four times his original offer, whereupon the old lady accepted with a show of great displeasure."

"Complete victory."

"Tho wait, there's more to tell. As the old woman made to go inside, the Yankee stopped her and held out the dead bird."

"Can't say I'm surprised."

"Being of no mind to keep it or take it to his lodgings to have it cooked, he gave the fowl back. What else could he do?"

"Must have surprised the old woman, though."

"That it did. She had no idea white folk could be so gullible. Once more she put on a woebegone air and accepted the feathery corpse as if to go bury it."

"And that evening, she and the neighbors had roast chicken, eh?"

"Laughing one and all at the fool and his money, praising the stubborn old lady. She, meanwhile, had learnt a good lesson."

"To always drive a hard bargain?"

"Nay, that when a foreigner meets a fowl, money falls from the heavens."

"Hmm," mutters Matías, detecting a note of mockery in Lee Bo's morality tale. This can only lead in an undesirable direction.

"Thereafter, in any idle moment, the old lady would wait in the shadows for a motor carriage to pass. And lo, they did, three or four times of a week. How difficult could it be to time a bird's release with the approach of the tyres? Then to slip back inside the house and wait with a long face for the Yank or Jap to come knocking? Ah, the sad stories, the tears, the better to drive up the price..."

"...and salt the roast chicken that evening."

"With each success, she would invite the whole village, and receive

bananas and taro in return. Three birds with one stone, as it were. But…"
Lee Bo pauses for effect. Matías leans forward to hear him out. "Then she
began to consider the poor defenseless victims and tried to teach the birds
to fly."

"So what are you saying?"

"Oh, nothing. Mere palaver."

"You mean I'm the old woman and the people are my chickens, is that it?"

"Not in so many words. But all things being relative, shew me the man so
singularly good, the policy so perfectly right. Where is the wholly wicked man
or bad policy? Nay, you've been a fine chicken lady," chides Lee Bo. "Crafty
and forthright in equal measure, you've done well by your life. You knew the
limits of your greed. Selfish but confident, the requisites of a politician. None
dare question that. Nay, 'twas the Brun Reef ruse rais'd the bar too high. Not
for the common people, nor e'en the Elders, there were unseen others who
remonstrated. The murder of Tamang sufficed to convince the Elders, but
'twas really Brun Reef that did it."

"That was big money. If it came off, I could've started up Air Navidad. It
would have provided the capital base for developing the country, enough for
industry to kick in. At least I thought so. A way for this country to take an
active role among the major powers."

"A big, fat pig for ev'ryone to roast and eat."

"A necessary sacrifice."

"The pig would not think so. And the ancestors are on the side of the
pig," he gently observes.

"It was them who sent Améliana?"

Lee Bo doesn't respond and Matías doesn't press the issue. In the ensuing
silence, the candle flickers and drips, consuming their attention yet never
getting any shorter.

"One thing I'd like to know," Matías finally asks.

"That being?"

"What am I supposed to do now? What's the right next move? Not that
you ever say much about anything important. You give me more minute particulars than anyone could possibly want to know about the past, present, and

future, but since when have you ever given me any real advice? Maybe I should know better than to ask. Still, there is one detail you might oblige me with."

Lee Bo gives a sly smile, as if he already knows what Matías is going to ask. He raises no objection, meaning he won't give him any practical tips.

"Several times since I became president, I received anonymous letters from someone in Japan. Know anything about that?" Matías asks straight out.

"Your 'Friend of the Islands'?"

"That's right. Every time I had dealings with Japan, those letters leaked inside information. Saved my neck more than once, though I have no idea who was writing me or why. I doubt any civilian could get access to so many classified government files, so was it an official or a politician? Who among them would know so much about Navidad—or care? Like there was a Navidad spy burrowing in the Japanese nerve center, but there's never any talk of pay-offs. Maybe just twice a year, some crucial clue-in arriving by ordinary mail."

"Witness the letter about Brun Reef and the secret plan for a Japanese cantonment there. Sage counsel, yet you did not accept."

"Right or wrong, that was my political judgment. Let's drop it, I can think that one over for the rest of my days. What I want to know about is the mole. Is he someone close to Kurokawa? Or a bureaucrat somewhere in Foreign Affairs? Why would anyone up there be so interested in this country? Or have access to so much information? It's not like some South Pacific department flunky just photocopied whatever papers passed across his desk. That data was purposefully collected. Risky business. Who'd risk his neck on such a stunt? Not once, but repeatedly?"

"A man from Ponape."

"A Ponape islander in the Japanese Ministry of Foreign Affairs?"

"Nay, nothing like that. Your pimpernel was one Daniel López, many years dead. Or rather his shadow... 'Tis a long story."

"I've got plenty of time."

"During the Great War, many a Pacific native was press'd into Imperial Army service and deployed on the front lines, López being one such conscript. Were he alive today, he would be five years your senior. His ankle was shattered by a volley in New Guinea, but he received scant attention before being pack'd home to Ponape. Lacking a doctor's care, he was crippled for life. Unable to work, he proved a burthen upon his family. The lean years right after the war must have worn heavily upon him, tho eventually he married, opened a small general store and e'en fathered a child."

"Common enough story," repeats Matías, as with the chicken lady fable.

"Aye, a most common plaint in the Imperial Japanese Domestic South Seas, tho 'twas not the end of the tale for López. Hearing that the newly form'd democratic government of Japan was duly compensating its war-wounded with welfare purses, he wonder'd: had he not been ordered to go to war by the Japanese government and maim'd in the line of duty? Were not his injuries as grave as any inflicted on a Japanese soldier? Why did he not merit like payment? The injustice of it! He was told upon conscription that he was a citizen of the realm, that his willing service made him a full imperial subject. Should not his pain be address'd as that of an imperial subject? The lack of compensation was insuff'rable to him."

"Hard knocks," mutters Matías, not that he was unaware of this side of Japan—or of all big countries, for that matter. It's precisely hardships like these that show up the arbitrary arrogance of colonial power to the small and downtrodden.

"The hard truth will out indeed. Yet López did not believe so. Consequently, he wrote a letter of enquiry contriving to suggest there must have been a serious mistake: surely his papers had been mislaid? And lo, he received a response, tho not the tidings he hoped for. Nay, the official writ declared that the new administration could not assume all responsibilities for the previous government—without a word about disbursements to Japanese veterans not applying to Domestic South Seas conscripts. 'Twas an unabashedly short set letter, a common instrument of dismissal, one of thousands posted by the Ministry of Welfare to settle like requests from the former colonies."

"Tell me about it. Plenty of our boys sent angry demands to Japan too, especially in Cornelius's time, but nothing ever came of them. Even in my day, I made a show of trying on behalf of my long-suffering countrymen, but I knew better than to push."

"López refused to credit the letter. It made no sense; this was wrong. Other lads would have cried themselves to sleep at this point, yet López believed in justice. Something of a moralist he was. He may have return'd home gimp, but what of the many who died? López did the impossible and made passage to Japan."

"To lodge an appeal?"

"Aye, in person. Given to snap decisions, it would seem. Eventually he found his way to the ministry, where he was offered much the same explanation as in the letter. Like you, López spoke good Japanese, but talking obtained no progress. Entertaining no illusions now, he promptly fix'd his aim upon another mark. Quick on the trigger, that one... still is."

"You've talked with him recently?"

"Aye, good mates we are," confides Lee Bo. "López did not hurry back to his island, but stayed on in Tokyo to launch a one-man campaign. He penned a placard in Japanese decrying his unfair treatment and paraded in front of the Ministry from dawn to dusk."

"Full of fight, I'll say that for him."

"Hardly—he limp'd, dragging his right foot. He verged on despair inside. Tho when a friendly newspaperman wrote a sympathetic article—alas, no change of heart did it buy at the Ministry—a few contributions trickled in from local readers. López was able to go on protesting for several fortnights, e'en tho the Japanese Consul in Ponape spread malicious rumours about him. In the end, his money and mind spent, López decided to go home."

Matías clears his throat. Had his own age and circumstances been only slightly different, he'd have been another López. Used by Japan instead of the other way around. Would he have had the guts to go to Japan and protest? But then again, had he allowed Japan to build a secret base at Brun Reef, could he still really claim to have the upper hand? He risked crippling the whole of Navidad himself.

"Half a year after faring back to Ponape, López died. A rheum afflicted in Japan inflamed his lungs and finally consumed him, as no remedies were to be had on his island. Soon enough, he was in a spiritual way."

"Do those who die unsatisfied become ghosts?" asks Matías. It's something he's been meaning to ask for ages.

"I know not myself. Some become ghosts and some become birds."

What Matías really wants to know is what it'll be like to die—for him personally— but can't bring himself to say the words.

"Why do certain ships take different courses?" Lee Bo continues. "Since his death, the Ponapean oft visits Japan, much as I call upon you here. In due course, López met a minor official at the Ministry of Welfare and talks with him not infrequently. This befriended clerk then goes home and writes missives about what he's learnt at work, informing people in Micronesia of things they ought to know. One of his addressees being His Excellency Matías Guili."

"But what about Japan's national interests? His bureaucratic station? His job?"

"He seems unconcerned, no contradiction does he see. An able deckhand who shall ne'er, I daresay, climb higher than midshipman, he may yet play a part in some greater charting of policy for the region. He takes secret delight in all things South Pacific, a fond pastime if you will. He enjoys his talks with López and e'en relishes the challenge of a double identity, thus keeps writing letters incognito."

Not that any of those letters will be reaching President Guili anymore, thinks Matías. That's Jim Jameson's job now.

"You've met the man," says Lee Bo, much to Matías's surprise.

"I have?"

"Aye, he directed the veterans delegation to Navidad. That last letter was posted from here. At the welcoming ceremony at the airfield, the Japanese who interpreted for Jameson, Matsumoto, who went missing with the others on the motor carriage, who reappear'd just yesterday, was it? *He's* your Friend of the Islands."

09

Matías doesn't remember a thing about his mother's death, but the entire sea voyage afterwards is as clear as day. The two of them had been living in Baltasár City. This was more than a decade into the Japanese colonial era, and Japanese settlers and businesses were on the rise. Among the many immigrants to these "Tearful Islands," as the Japanese called Navidad, was the *katsuobushi* maker Chujiro Miyakura, the man Matías arbitrarily claims as his father, who only stayed a couple of years, then left before the boy's birth. Matías's mother was helping out at a Japanese-run barber shop, though why exactly she left Melchor or what she was doing working there or who got her pregnant under what circumstances, no one ever told him.

When Matías was three and a half, his mother died of tuberculosis, which had spread unchecked through the islands. She'd been coughing horribly for months, not going to work half the time, until finally she was too weak to get out of bed. A fortnight later she was dead. Even so, Matías can't really picture her lying there in any detail. Did he actually see the body or did adults from the neighborhood merely tell him about it? Who found her? Who arranged what kind of funeral? How did he get by in the days that followed? His memory is a complete blank.

He doesn't remember his aunt coming from Melchor to fetch him either; it could have been three days or three months after her death. All he retains are random flashes, hazy images in no appreciable order. Why do some memories linger and others fade into nothingness?

The next thing he remembers after living in that tiny room near the barber shop is boarding a ship in the harbor. Matías has always liked transportation, which is partly why he put so much effort into developing the island bus system when he became president and why he was so unreasonably intent on setting up Air Navidad. His first sea trip from Gaspar to Melchor—his first ride in any vehicle—left a vivid impression. The ship looked impossibly big and grand to his infant eyes, though in fact it was just an old Japanese Inland Sea tramp steamer. But this was in the days when there was only one three-story building in the whole of Baltasár City, so that coal-burning clunker probably rated as one of the most advanced contraptions around.

His aunt from Melchor tidied up the room where he and his mother had been living, packed what little there was to take, and led her nephew by the hand to the port. This, too, was a first-time-ever adventure for the boy. At first sight, he thought the ship was some kind of building at the water's edge: oddly shaped, painted black and white, smelling of oil, entered by crossing a footbridge onto a burning hot metal deck spread with woven palm frond mats. Already a crowd of people was huddled there, and his aunt had to elbow her way in to secure a space for them and their few bags. Squeezing down among all the families and crates, Matías could feel the slight vibrations from the hull under his behind. His aunt told him he could take a look around the ship, but the boy was too timid to move.

They boarded before noon, but the ship didn't get under way until that evening. The vibrations got stronger and a whistle screeched overhead, then suddenly everyone was moving about and waving as black smoke belched from a big fat upright pipe and the ship jerked into motion. That's when he finally understood what the "building on water" was all about: it was taking them somewhere else. Wow! This was great! Suddenly the rumbling under his behind felt nice, the wind that sometimes blew smoke toward them smelled nice too. As they passed through a break in the coral reef out to the open sea, the "building" began to rock and pitch, making him so giddy his aunt had a hard time keeping him quiet.

He fell asleep under the stars that danced in the vast, dark heavens to the rhythm of the waves. As he lay there, belly full of taro and bananas from his aunt's basket, with the ship humming secret, soothing music to his spine, how much did he even really understand about his mother being dead? He was happy, his head against his aunt's warm body, not knowing he was missing his mother's warmth.

The following morning was bright and hot, but later that day they ran into a squall. With no roof over their heads, everyone on deck was drenched; luckily no one had anything with them that rain might spoil. By the third day, however, the sea was so rough they all were at the rails throwing up. How he hated the ship then for playing nasty tricks on them, but he knew they had no choice but to ride out the storm until they got where they were going. He felt miserably sick and retched his stomach dry, ate nothing more and tried to sleep.

The next morning, the sea was calm. He was woken by his aunt to see a beautiful sun burning through the haze ahead, where in the glow off to the left the smooth-shouldered silhouette of an island lay low on the horizon. Bird cries greeted the new day from across the water as they approached, calling welcome to the boy's ears.

"That's where we're going," whispered his aunt. "That's Melchor." To his eager yet sleepy eyes, it seemed to promise lots of fun. A new home, it made him feel all fuzzy inside. Maybe his mother dying wasn't so bad after all. But no, even a three-year-old couldn't think such thoughts without a tinge of doubt clouding his expectations.

All this was sixty years ago. Now, on the tatami mats of his private quarters at the Presidential Villa, Matías slowly comes to his senses. Wallowing in the past won't do shit for him in his present straits. The Melchor he'd traveled to on a boat a generation older than the one that carried Améliana there is the very same island where the Council of Elders have just condemned him. They recognized him as a native son of the island, but no longer a man to respect. He isn't worthy of the office of president; they'd proclaimed it to the whole country.

Just possibly, though, Melchor might still take him in like sixty years before. Why not go and see, he thinks, and immediately calls Jim Jameson to have him arrange a flight. Not out in front of the airport terminal, he hastens to add, have the plane wait at the end of the runway. So an hour later, for the first time in days, he's sitting in the Nissan President chauffeured by Heinrich.

⚡

The car heads straight through town to the airport. He sinks deep into the back seat so he doesn't have to see the faces of any pedestrians and they can't see him. As if it's any secret that the Nissan limousine—the only one in Navidad—has the disgraced President inside. As if he expected to be invisible or had some other vehicle at his disposal. Immediately the word spreads that the Old Man is going somewhere, and the public imagination starts to seethe. Matías still has a few privileges, he can still fly to Melchor in the Islander—the Council of Elders didn't take that away from him. He's under no legal constraints. No one throws stones at him in the Elders' name. But it's just as painful to know that the good citizens of Navidad will no longer have anything to do with him. He's not only been stripped of power, he's been made a nonentity.

The Islander is waiting on the runway as arranged. The engines are silent. The American pilot lies sprawled on the grass nearby, looking up at the sky, presumably unaware of the fate that has befallen his employer. At the sound of the approaching limousine, he sits up. Matías gets out of the car, and the pilot hurries over to his plane. He has on a white short-sleeved shirt with epaulets and gold-embroidered wings on his chest, but no cap. Instead of black uniform trousers, he's wearing jeans and rubber flip-flop sandals—he's that kind of guy. Can he really work the pedals in those things?

"Take me to Melchor," shouts Matías into the wind.

"Anywhere you like, just as long as she's got fuel," the man answers loud and clear. "Safe and sure—that's the company motto." A motto for a one-plane company that doesn't even exist. Air Navidad has a thing or two to live down before it ever gets off the ground.

"You call yourself safe?" Matías asks pointedly. "You already crashed once."

"I did at that," admits the pilot with a grin. "Totaled the plane. But me? Not a scratch. Never kill me. I'm immortal, that's what I am."

Sure, you survived, thinks Matías. *What about the fifty million yen that went up in smoke? If it weren't for you, I wouldn't have to cower in my limo in fear of my angry countrymen, ordinarily the friendliest people on the planet. If you'd died and the fifty million survived, Tamang wouldn't have won that election. He'd still be heading up the opposition party, haranguing me with empty rhetoric. Just enough to bolster his ego. Would've been better for him and better for me.* But no, those Japanese ghosts or the Yuuka or gods and ancestors prevented it. Somehow they raised the airfield, so the plane smashed its landing gear and skidded on its fuselage into a palm grove, tearing off a wing and catching fire in the process. The pilot barely managed to escape with his own life; there was no time to rescue the duralumin trunk with all the money (nor had he been informed about its precious contents) before the whole thing blew up. If the plane had rammed straight into a palm tree instead of ripping open a fuel tank under the right wing, the pilot's skull would have been crushed and the money spared. That would have changed everything. Fifty million would have been more than enough to put a damper on Tamang's popularity. It would have given Matías a sure third term.

Leaving these thoughts unsaid, Matías opens the right-hand door and climbs into the third seat back, just like when he flew to the Yuuka Yuumai festival. The pilot gets in and starts the engine, but doesn't talk either. He probably thinks the President will be changing into shorts and an aloha shirt like before.

The pilot is right: not long after takeoff, Matías unbuttons his suit and tie, leaves them on the seat along with his starched shirt, socks, and shoes, and dons more colorful plain clothes.

When they land on Melchor, Matías gets out and informs the pilot, "I may be returning today, or I may be sending you back alone. I'll be in touch by late afternoon. So, sorry, but could you stay put till then?" And with no further ado, President Matías Guili of the Republic of Navidad shuffles off across a grassy knoll in the guise of a crusty old local (his true island self, perhaps) and disappears into the bushes.

Reaching a dirt road, Matías notices something hard in his shirt pocket: it's Katsumata's sunglasses. He forgot to return them and now he'll probably never have the chance. He puts them on, adding a welcome margin of shade to the parched ground. A short stroll ahead brings him to the paved main road, which curves to the left toward the town. Beyond the gleaming lagoon, under a big blue sky, he can make out the whitecaps breaking on the coral reef. From the plane there were scattered patches of cloud, but from here on the ground he sees hardly a wisp; only a few faint streaks of white far off on the horizon, but no boats out by the reef, not a soul in sight.

The sugar cane is getting high all along the left-hand side of the road, though there's still some time to go before harvest. To the right, the scrub parts now and again to offer glimpses of the sea. Birds are singing somewhere. What a glorious day! Who wouldn't enjoy a stroll here on a day like this? The gentle breeze cools all who pass, regardless of their name or station; the sun pours down on everyone equally.

A pickup truck approaches from the direction of town. He hesitates for a moment, but then realizing he's just a nobody walking along a road, he waves hello. The man in the driver's seat waves back; there's no one riding on the flatbed. If he were wearing a suit and tie and no sunglasses, the fitting image of the head honcho who used to decide everything around here, would the man have waved?

Matías comes to a side road that branches off to the right into the trees, a shortcut to somewhere, puddles glinting in the sunlight. Why not see where it goes? Anyway, rubber sandals feel better on dirt than hot asphalt. The detour leads into the shade, where the ground is almost chilly compared to the main road. He has to watch his step to avoid the occasional cartwheel track ankle-deep in water. It's so quiet. Off in the woods he can see one lone house. Compared to here, Baltasár is a bustling metropolis. Though from here on, he can do without all the cars and people.

How about a life in exile, though? He has plenty of money to live out his days comfortably in a developed country. Even if he returns the bulk of it, he should still have enough left to live off the interest. He could move to the Philippines with Angelina. Or to Japan, for that matter. The Philippines are too close; the Japan idea is better, though not in Tokyo—some out-of-the-way town in view of Mt. Fuji. But no, Angelina would never go along with that. Okay, then, how about living alone? Buy a little house, read books and gaze at the sea, write his memoirs. He might even get Itsuko to do the housekeeping for him, the same as now. Live a simple life and reassess all the things he did for Navidad. He could write a handbook of helpful hints for his successors. Or a critique of regional relations in the Pacific. Or sign on as a consultant to a number of foreign powers. There are posts for peace-minded people like him at the UN.

What's realistically possible for him at his age? Say he left here and went north, what would he do all winter long? Would he be happy? Itsuko might well refuse to go back to Japan. Angelina probably wouldn't want to return to the Philippines either. Should he even consider living all by himself out in the cold? Could he survive abroad nowadays? Whatever it was like when he was young, can this South Seas darky face grow old in that climate of constant low-key racism? Can he take it? No, the prospect of living in exile makes him shudder. Let the Elders curse: leaving the land of Yuuka Yuumai would not be a smart move for any native son this late in life.

The path descends a gentle slope through the woods into a coconut plantation. The wind rustles the fronds high overhead, their shadows flickering over the white sand. It makes him dizzy, but happy. The smell of the sea is refreshing.

He thinks about his benefactors. So many people have helped and sheltered him over the years. Probably the first was his aunt. Of her own free will, she dropped everything and came rushing to Baltasár City to rescue her orphaned bastard nephew sight unseen and bring him back to Melchor, begged to get him into a home already crowded with distant relatives' children, checked in on him from time to time, and generally tried to see that he was raised properly. He has only sketchy recollections of his aunt, but without her where would he be? Then there was Ryuzoji—or rather, Ryuzoji and Japan. Sure, he must have had an early gift for languages among other things, but in a society like Navidad where merit alone counts for nothing, the chances are his talents would have been passed over. No, he owes his success to having brought back modern ideas from Japan, no two ways about it. And in Japan, Tsuneko helped him with favors he can only regard as acts of unreasonable kindness. She accepted him for what he was—a bush boy from some tiny backwater where they probably didn't even bathe, who'd go back to his island never to be heard from again—accepted him and loved him all the same. Then, back in Navidad, it was María Guili: at first with her husband, by hiring the young returnee, then later when widowed, by accepting him as her protector and provider. From Matías's point of view, she was goodness personified, a mother hen. Never uttered a critical word, only encouragement whenever he ran up against island attitudes. Few know how much it was her efforts that made him the top businessman in the islands, though Angelina also taught him a thing or two. True, in the case of Angelina, it was he who provided her with a life-changing opportunity, which turned out well for both of them. His nights with her, talking and touching, the consolation they brought, can't be overestimated. And let's not forget the great Cornelius, who promoted a businessman into a politician, who handpicked him as his comrade-in-arms during the struggle for independence, then essentially gave him the country gift-wrapped...

Matías emerges from the coconut grove onto the shore, an expanse of white sand flecked with buff and pink. The beach is quite broad here, describing a clean arc, a scene he seems to recall but cannot place. His head is overflowing with thoughts about the past. It's time he sorted through his memories.

He may have been a despot, but he was never overconfident, never imagined he'd come this far under his own steam. The path to power was a long one, with many people pushing him along, especially at first. None of that he'd ever lose; it's all part of his grounding, his constant landscape. A politician's job is to see what's in the offing, but for that he needs a headland from which to scan the seas and warn his people of incoming ships. Not all will bring wealth, of course, not right away. That's why he stood his high ground and agreed to the Brun Reef plan, a token exchange for all the precious Japanese cargo he could see further over the horizon.

Stop making excuses, he hears a voice saying. *You're just an old biddy brooding over her dead chickens, like Lee Bo was trying to say.* It's a strain just listening to himself. He plops down on the sand, the hot sun in his face. All this walking must have overheated his system. He wipes the sweat from his forehead. He's made too much of himself; he's not so special one way or another. If only he could defend his record before the Council of Elders, tell them that if he hadn't come along, somebody else would have. If it hadn't been close ties with Japan, then it would've been America or the Philippines or Taiwan. Someone who'd gone abroad in his youth would have played up those connections.

Or is he rationalizing again? Still, he's hardly a dictator, not by a long shot. He never killed anyone—well, aside from that one man—never detained or tortured ordinary citizens. He may have taken his share of kickbacks, but that's just standard business practice. He never drew on the national coffers for his own pocket money. Everything deposited in a Swiss bank account is legally his, and he planned to return it all anyway. He didn't cruise the streets in his limo looking for pretty girls to take back to the villa. He was first and foremost a citizen himself. If only Tamang hadn't been such a pompous ass. If only the fool had addressed himself to the real national concerns at hand instead of poking his nose into the ex-president's misdemeanors to boost his own popularity. If only that fifty million yen weren't jinxed and had been delivered safely. If only, if only, if only—a swirling spiral of self-justification.

There's no one else on the beach. It's so peaceful, so nice just to sit here and watch the waves roll in for hours on end. This far inside the coral reef, he can't even hear the roar of the surf. Look, hermit crab tracks on the sand. Clouds are lofting on the horizon, but overhead the azure blue is as clear as ever.

What to do? Should he retire here, withdraw into seclusion on this island? Not that he has much choice, now that no one will give him the time of day anymore. Would people leave him in peace, let him live in that house he owns here? Would they accept his money at the market in exchange for fish and vegetables and instant ramen? Would they let him take part in the next

Yuuka Yuumai eight years from now? Of course he'll relinquish his chairman-ship of the M. Guili Trading Company and parcel out his various duties there to the respective department heads. No matter what happens, he won't speak up. He'll publicly renounce all political aspirations. He'll lie low, for whatever the quiet life might be worth.

There *is* something familiar about this beach. Maybe he just doesn't rec-ognize it by day. Come back on a moonlit night, he might see a place where he used to play as a boy. Or no, the memory seems too near, too clear, yet somehow the vantage point is wrong. He must have been looking from over there between those two tall trees.

Suddenly it hits him: he's at Sarisaran, the very last ceremonial site where the Yuuka formed a circle afterwards and changed clothes. That's where they were, over there. The air surges with absent figures.

Out of nowhere, a butterfly flits across his vision—a lilac butterfly. He hadn't seen it against the dazzling sea, but now his eyes follow it . . . and there's another. Seemingly blown about on the breeze, but actually winging their own way, still more of them appear. Before they can engulf him, Matías turns around and—

Sure enough, Améliana is standing there, looking straight at him, arms folded in front of her white dress. Of course they would have to meet up here in Sarisaran: the symmetry of it strikes them both at the same time.

Matías rises silently to his feet. Three paces away on higher ground, she is the taller of the two. Have they ever stood face-to-face like this before? At the office, he was always sitting. At Brun Reef, she had stood beside him.

He just looks at her. Is there anything he should say? Améliana must have something to tell him, but she doesn't speak. He can't read her even, unbeau-tiful features—neither attractive nor ugly, a mysterious face. Odd snatches of emotion all blur into one strange sensation. Here he is, alone with the person who brought him down, and he feels nothing like animosity. No, her presence here seems inevitable, as all she did was inevitable. She wasn't the will behind it. Any more than he willed himself to go abroad, or build his own company, or climb the ladder to the rank of president—and eventual disgrace. Nothing in this world is shaped by individual volition; everything molds to the contours of the terrain, the ley lines that run through us. Even his leadership followed the rise and fall of these islands. He sees it all: Navidad made Matías, Navidad now gathers up the pieces.

He nods slowly, takes one brief glance at the sea, then—just as he did on the last night of the Yuuka Yuumai—signals to Améliana, who silently starts walking several steps behind him. The sun is high in the sky, but Matías doesn't even feel the heat.

⚡

The house is cool inside. He'd have thought the place would get all hot and stuffy closed up like this, but no, the interior is much cooler than outside. For a second, he almost thinks it's air-conditioned, but this isn't an artificially manufactured chill. The shades are drawn against the sun, yet he feels a draft from somewhere.

Coming into the main room, he sees a patch of sunlight through a curtain, a cheap cotton print with big green leaves and yellow flowers. The color combination reminds him of something. As he stares at the softly billowing folds of light on the floorboards, he hears Améliana's footsteps entering behind him. Green and yellow—the colors of the bus, it's that nowhere-and-back-again bus.

He runs his hand over the top of the large desk in the corner of the room; there's not a trace of dust. The old caretaker must really be doing his job. He had too many other things on his mind last time to notice, but this time he's impressed. If he remembers correctly, there was a typewriter in the big bottom drawer. As he bends down to look, he senses that Améliana is taking a seat on the sofa diagonally opposite. Her movements are fluid, without hesitation.

Matías tries not to think about that last time he was here together with her, the bed that must still be in the back room. No, mustn't dwell on what he did then, on what it might mean. Too late the realization that not all acts are born of due consideration; some things simply cannot be contained. Whatever the eventual outcome, at least she herself doesn't seem concerned.

Just like the time before, she's followed him in and now sits waiting on the sofa in this yellow-green room. Let her wait.

He opens the drawer to find the ancient Smith-Corona that he bought to write business letters in the back room at Guili's store. It brings back memories of his startup days. He carefully lifts the heavy old machine and places it on the desktop, then finds some letterhead stationery in an upper drawer and puts it in the platen.

Immediately he feels the urge to type and sits down at the desk. For the moment, he forgets all about Améliana's presence as clear, well-ordered directives claim his thoughts. Sentences come into his head fully formed and unhindered by entangling sentiment. His fingers pound at the rusted keys. The H and C keys stick, the M lands halfway above the line while the K and P dip below, the letter L invariably strikes at a slant, but somehow it still works. Can't type too fast or the lever arms jam; hunt-and-peck speed is just about the limit. The old baby is dusty as all hell. Should have told the caretaker to keep this clean too—but no, he mustn't go off on a tangent, he has to concentrate. Got to keep up his rhythm. What he's writing is important. Keep it simple and to the point. No over-blown phrases. People distrust exaggerated expressions even before they get what's being said.

An hour of typing and he's done. Améliana has sat there and said nothing throughout. He reads over what he's written. Fine, everything's in order. He pulls several envelopes out of the drawer, addresses them, then folds and stuffs the appropriate letter in each. That was simple.

Matías gets up and walks over to Améliana, admiring her relaxed, half-reclining pose. But no, she also rises. She's much taller than Matías even here. More than outside, the white dress sets off her dark skin, her emotionless face as she waits for him to speak.

"I'm leaving these with you. Please see that they get to the right people. Doesn't have to be today or tomorrow, by boat will be time enough."

Améliana nods and takes the envelopes. Their hands touch.

"Just don't you and your brothers paddle them over by canoe," he says, trying to make a joke, but she just shakes her head and doesn't smile.

"Well, then, I'll be going. You be well."

He turns to go, before he can say anything more stupid. She sees him out as far as the door. She just stands there, her hands folded over her belly. He walks a few steps, then turns to take one last look. Her hands are exactly at eye level. His gaze rests on the white cotton fabric and the waistline beneath, then he glances up to see her grin. A pleased, proud, confident grin.

He inadvertently asks the question with his eyes and she nods.

"It's a girl," is all she says, quite softly, then laughs.

It's the first time he's ever seen this young woman laugh. Never before—not at Angelina's, not at his office, not on that trip to Brun Reef, of course not during her stint as a Yuuka, or when he brought her to this house before—never did she even smile. Only now, at the very last. She smiles at a future in which Matías will play no part. As if a vague inkling had all of a sudden taken on reality. A future he'll never hear or see or hold in his arms. The thought fills him with great pangs of sadness. A feeling of utter hopelessness. It's all he can do to shut his eyes and breathe deeply to keep his head from spinning. It's okay, he can still stand, he's not going to keel over. It's all right to cry. He waits. Slowly he opens his eyes and looks up at the sun.

Then slowly, with only a nod, he turns his back on Améliana and his house, and starts walking toward the airfield. His shadow falls short at his feet.

⚡

The pilot is napping in the shade of the airplane wing. Matías would like nothing better than to stretch out beside him and take a little rest too, but now is not the time. He crouches down and shakes him awake.

"Wha—? Where the heck?" the man groans, straining to make out the other's face against the glare. "Aw, yeah, right. Sorry, I mean, excuse me, sir. I musta dozed off there."

He gets up and yawns. "Ready to head home?" he says finally, still looking half asleep.

"Uh-huh, going home."

"Be right with you. Just let me get a drink of water."

While the pilot trots off toward the supply shed a short distance away, Matías opens the right-hand passenger door and climbs into the same seat as before, locking the door behind him. Settling back, he watches the pilot come running back. What's the hurry? He could have walked at a normal pace—they've got all the time in the world.

The man gives the plane a quick once-over, checks all the major parts, undoes the Pitot tube covers and lock pins, removes the blocks under the wheels and throws them in the hold. Then he settles into his seat and carefully closes the door before beginning his pre-takeoff rundown of the control panel. He's a conscientious guy, not one to skip procedures. As he said himself on the trip over, he'll never die in any accident; he's reliable.

The pilot flicks on several overhead switches, turns the fuel cock to OPEN, adjusts the choke, and reads the gauges one by one. Once everything checks out, he presses the ignition, and the hum of the right engine gradually builds, the propeller starts to spin and pick up speed, and after brief adjustments to the throttle and fuel mixture, strong vibrations pulse through the plane from front to back. Now he repeats the same steps for the left engine. Outside the window, the tall grass whips back in the slipstream. He conducts one last check, then dons his headset, switches on the radio, selects the frequency and calls in for clearance to take off.

The pilot turns to look at his passenger a couple of rows back.

"Seat belt fastened, sir?" he shouts over the roar of the engines.

"All set," Matías shouts back, poking his head up between two seats in the middle row. He could have just nodded, but the words came out first.

"Door latch?"

"Locked."

"Well, then, shall we?"

"Hang on, I've got a request," Matías speaks up before he can face forward.

"What's that, sir?"

"Before heading back to Baltasár, could we circle a couple of times over Melchor?"

"Sure thing. She's your plane," shouts the pilot. His standard line. As loud as ever, always cheerful and eager to please. "I'll take her around as many times as you want, just tell me when you're ready to make for Baltasár. Fair enough?"

"Fine, thanks."

The pilot puts his hand on the throttle and by only the slightest maneuver pushes both engines to high velocity, then releases the parking brake, and the plane creeps forward.

No one else is leaving or landing at this hour; the long runway is all theirs. Like a clumsy stiff-winged bird on a pebbly path, the tiny aircraft rattles over the rough tarmac. Until it attains flight speed, until airborne, the Islander is an ungainly thing.

At the end of the runway, the pilot brakes one wheel and revs the opposite engine to bring the plane about in a U-turn. The flaps are down, the runway stretches wide open before them. Now comes the tricky part: taking off and climbing to cruising altitude. The roar of the engines redoubles, sending shudders down the fuselage, as the pilot coaxes out the full power of the machine, then slowly lets out the brakes. Warily at first, like a captive animal suddenly set free, the plane needs gradually to get up the nerve to make a break for open spaces. It runs and runs, picking up speed. The drooping wings buoy up on the wind and spring taut. Still the pilot reins in the eager plane, pacing the engines until they gain sufficient thrust to fly. Gently he pulls back on the stick to nose the aircraft up; the front wheel lifts off the ground, the weight eases up on the wheels behind, and the plane rises skyward. Air temperature twenty-nine degrees Celsius, combined pilot and passenger weight 160 kilograms, headwind eight knots—and 225 meters of runway in which to clear the nine-meter palm trees—flying is an exacting business.

"Circle a couple of times above Melchor" must mean his passenger wants to view the scenery below, the pilot assumes, so when they reach the three-hundred-meter mark a minute later, he levels off and trims the engines. The plane is all confidence now, ready and willing to take the two of them wherever they want to go for the next few hours.

One nice thing about the British Norman-built Islander is the raised-wing design, which allows an unobstructed field of vision below. Matías gazes down fondly at the peaceful hills of Melchor like some obliging carpet dealer unrolling rare kilims for an unlikely customer. The plane circles clockwise with its right wing dipped slightly, affording Matías an even clearer view of the topography. Seen from this height, Melchor looks so big and bountiful. Directly below is Sarisaran Beach, where he stood and faced Améliana only hours before—a point in time now speeding off into the distance.

Unlike flying over unknown territory, viewing familiar places from above is oddly poignant. So near and dear yet far out of reach, the now-deserted landmarks seem to lie there beyond real life. It's as if every coco palm, each trunk, is now untouchable, inviolate. Tin-and-thatch rooftops cluster in a pattern recognizable as Zaran, chalk-white streets stringing the houses together into a necklace knotted with childhood memories, sandy paths never to be walked again. The tropical rainforest canopy offers up a damp leafy smell, but no trace of the fragrant flowers hidden beneath. The sugar fields radiate an intense emerald gleam, but the forbidden fun of chewing stolen sugarcane, the sweet trickle of milky green juice, escapes him. There at arm's length is a Yuuka Yuumai site, a clearing by the beach the size of his hand, but nowhere he will ever visit again to share in the fervor of his fellow islanders. This must be how Lee Bo sees the world: each particular in uncanny clarity, the entirety remote and unapproachable.

The pilot completes the first circuit, bringing them back over the airfield to start another loop. Presently Sarisaran comes into view. It won't be long now.

⚡

The pilot doesn't think anything special as he starts the second go-around. He's fine just taking orders. Do as many circuits as requested, then head back to Baltasár City. There's plenty of fuel, the weather is perfect for flying. Maybe the President is trying to make his presence felt overhead. Everybody knows this government Islander is used almost exclusively by him; flown at this altitude, everybody on the ground will know it's the President up here. A good leader needs to keep his eye on the people, and what better way to get a general perspective on all the villages? Or maybe he just wants to reminisce, to revisit childhood haunts and courting places?

Just as he's thinking this, a sudden gust of wind bursts into the cabin and the plane veers sharply to the right. On the left side of the control panel, a warning light flashes on. He steps hard on the aileron pedal by his right foot to correct the yaw and glances back over his shoulder to find the right-hand passenger door ajar. Through the narrow opening he glimpses a dark mass drop away and disappear, before the wind slams the door shut. The pilot quickly banks the plane to the left, jamming his foot on the left pedal to send the plane into a tight spiral while he cranes his neck to look behind to his left. Far below, at the edge of his field of vision, his eyes barely catch the tiny black speck of a falling object. He strains to see, even as it vanishes into the green mosaic of the ground below.

He reduces altitude and circles several times, but can see nothing moving. From above, the lightly forested white sand beach looks perfectly peaceful, fulfilling the prophetic words:

The earth shall accept thee

To: Executive Secretary of the Republic of Navidad Jim Jameson

Dear Jim:

I enclose my formal letter of resignation; I leave the rest up to you. I also enclose papers assigning you provisional powers as acting president in my stead. Inasmuch as Navidad doesn't have any vice president, and given that Tamang and I were the only two candidates to stand in the last election, you would seem the person most legally entitled to the office. So for the time being, the country is yours. Up to now, I've kept you in the dark about things you didn't need to know, so you might as well continue to disregard them. Stick to the cards on the table. There's no need to get your hands dirty.

If Suzuki should show up from Japan, don't listen to him. Just send him away. Nothing will come of that scheme we talked about at Brun Reef. Letters from Kurokawa can go straight in the bin. He's no one you need to deal with.

You should probably reconvene the legislature. All their hot air never made much difference anyway. Just let them say what they're going to say, then go ahead and do what you've got to do. (Here I am telling you to keep your hands clean, then I bend your ear with unsolicited advice—read on and just ignore what you will.) Among the legislators, Arenas the plantation owner is the most trustworthy; he's got no ambitions greater than his own present standing. He's easygoing, but shrewd—he knows right from wrong. Arenas and his men are good people to have on your side.

In terms of policy, be sensible: you want to be a good caretaker. You're still young and inexperienced. Big gestures invite big failures. Err, if you must, on the side of thoroughness. You don't need an ideology to run a country; in fact, you're better off without one. It's probably more prudent for a small country like Navidad to see where the prevailing winds and currents take it rather than try to power through on its own. Don't think of it pessimistically. This way we won't need to get too close to America or Japan; we can be friends with Palau, stay on good terms with Yap and all the Micronesian Federation, and invite in just enough foreign investment to keep us afloat. Don't push economic growth at all costs. You're smart; I have every confidence in you.

Now, one immediate item of business. A Swiss accounting firm will be contacting you about transferring a large sum of money to the Navidad National Treasury. Having no heir, I made prior arrangements to have savings there disbursed in case of the account holder's decease. You can let the legislature debate what to do with it all, but it would please me greatly if a portion could be used to establish an education fund in my name (laugh at an old man's vanity if you will).

Sorry to bother you, but one more thing: there's my own personal account at the Baltasár City branch of the Bank of Hawaii. It won't come to much, but can you please make sure that Améliana gets it. Also my house in Melchor. Ask her why if you want to know. She'll explain if she feels like it, but don't press the issue.

I know it must be confusing to have an entire administration shoved into your hands, but believe me, running a country is not all that different from driving a car. Just make sure you don't crash into things. Other than that, if you feel like accelerating, do it slowly. It's your prerogative, but it's also your neck. Speeding leads to accidents. And especially, ignore backseat drivers. Remember: you're the one in the driver's seat, not them.

That's about the size of it. I'll be watching you.

Long live the Republic of Navidad!

Matías Guili

P.S. In my private quarters at the villa, beneath the box room—what Itsuko calls the nando—there's a vault. Itsuko has the keys and can show you the trapdoor. Everything you find down there I want you to load on a boat and dump in the ocean. The crates are full of submachine guns, the arsenal I laid in for keeping order after Tamang died. I issued them to Island Security for one day only to keep the legislators quiet and help smooth the political transition. I regret having used them, but by now that's just one small part of the mess I made. Was I a dictator? I really can't say. I'm not asking for a statue, just a decent grave. About the guns, though—they're all fakes: Japanese toys made of heavy-duty cast metal that wouldn't fart blanks if they tried, though they still ran twenty thousand yen a pop.

No one in Island Security even knew they weren't real. I had them issued one morning out of nowhere, with orders never to lay a finger on any trigger. Strictly shoulder strap guns, their sole function was to frighten people. Paraded around town that once, then crated away that evening and never seen again, I doubt anyone could tell the difference.

Those toys did the trick, but it was a desperate measure. Functional or not, pointing firearms at people takes serious resolve. I can't imagine you'd ever have call to use them, but just knowing they're there might prove a little too tempting. And if it later came out that it was all a bluff, you'd be even worse off than you started. The sooner you dump them in the sea the better. Sorry for all these loose ends, but this ought to be the last of them. —MG

My Dearest Angelina,

Forgive me. I didn't think it would all come to this.

It's not your fault that the I.W. Harper ran out, or that Ketch and Joel packed up and left. These things just happened, and neither of us had any power to stop them.

You're free now to close up shop and go back to the Philippines if you want, but I imagine you'd do better staying on here. You've always had a knack for business. You're sure to keep pulling in customers even without the shadow of presidential protection.

Having you by my side these last ten years has been heaven. You've made me happy body and soul, and I'm grateful for every minute. Please be well and live a good long life. May your business prosper. I hope you find another man who will be good for you.

A champagne toast—to us, my dear! All my love,

Your Matías

Late one afternoon, as the sweet smell of *sanpaguita* blossoms wafts in on a breeze beneath a high blue sky brushed with silken clouds, a woman of a certain age comes knocking at Angelina's back door and tells the young Filipina who answers that she wants to see the "Madame." Asked her name, the woman will only say, "She'll know me when she sees me."

The girl is obliged to go find her boss, who is busy balancing the books and scarcely looks up to inquire if the visitor is a foreigner. Yes, but not white and not Filipina either. Japanese? Korean maybe? Angelina's helper can't tell the difference, but says she's about the same age as her own mother and nicely dressed too.

Angelina rises from her accounts and walks slowly to the back door. She's hardly seen anyone these last few days, leaving nighttime duties to the girls themselves except when they're really short of hands to greet a crush of customers in the salon, and even then she can't quite turn on the charm like before. She knows it's not good for business, but what's she supposed to do? She functions mechanically, lacking the will to do anything of her own accord. How long is it going to be like this—the awful sense of loss.

Outside the back door, planted in rows against the afternoon sun, the swaying banana trees dapple the alleyway with shifting shadows. How beautiful, she thinks to herself, then remembers someone who will never see things like this again. Or no, the dead probably see everything, everywhere at once. But now's not the time or place for this. Leaning out the door, she sees a woman standing under the bananas—Japanese, by the look of her. No one she can recall ever meeting, but somehow familiar. How can that be?

"Hello?"

"Ah, Angelina?" asks the woman. So, neither knows the other.

"Yes, I'm Angelina."

"My name is Itsuko. Until a few days ago I worked for President Guili."

The pieces of a complex puzzle now click into place: it's Matías's housekeeper, who used to wash all his clothes, including the shorts Angelina always used to help him out of. So this is the woman who laid out his futon when he went home from here to sleep, who prepared those big sashimi breakfasts for him. The sister of his lover from his Japan days, wasn't that the story? Though according to Matías, he never had anything going with her—at least there was no reason to ever doubt him. No, to see her now, this woman clearly wasn't any hidden treasure, though the two of them will have lots to talk about for sure. It's consoling to think that she must miss him too.

"Really, you welcome at the front door! Please, come on in."

Itsuko seems hesitant but follows her inside, where she is shown a seat on a divan in one corner of the spacious salon, which is completely empty during the day. Itsuko looks around, pleasantly surprised at the decor. Even in daylight, not a thing looks cheap or make-do: the wallpaper is a pale cream flocked with olive green pinstripes, the various pieces of furniture wouldn't be out of place in a Yokohama Bluff mansion. The reproduction Tahiti- and

Marquesas-period Gauguins on the walls may be nudes, but certainly no more titillating than anything one might see at the beach.

"As you may know, I looked after the President for many years," begins Itsuko.

"Yes, he say many nice things about everything you do," says Angelina, still trying to puzzle out what she is to this woman and vice-versa. It's as if they split the main functions of a wife for Matías between themselves.

"But now after all that's happened, nobody uses President Guili's private rooms anymore. Acting President Jameson lives at home with his wife and family and commutes to the villa. I heard talk of turning it into an official guest house, but it's too Japanese for most tastes, so they've closed up the place for now."

So she's out of a job, is she? Has she come to bum return fare to Japan? No, Jim's a good guy, he'd give her plenty of severance pay to cover that. Probably still owed some salary too. And anyway, a single woman living rent-free on government wages in the islands, she can't possibly be broke. What could she spend her money on here? She wouldn't be giving her hard-earned pay to some young lover boy, would she? Doesn't look the sugar mama type, but you never know about people.

"So you see, I have nowhere to go."

So it *is* money she's after! What would Matías have done? Just hope this woman isn't too greedy. Would be nice to talk to her just once before she goes back to Japan. After all, they've seen the big man from two different sides. Not that Angelina can divulge the more intimate details to a proper-looking lady like her, though she *would* like to hear about the Matías this woman knew. Angelina rambles on in her thoughts, only to be startled by the actual favor that Itsuko has plucked up courage to ask.

"So I was wondering if I could work here?"

What a fantastic idea! The short, skinny woman sitting in front of her, never a beauty even in her twenties, must be in her late fifties. Plainly dressed, not much of a talker, and yet there's something about her. Angelina likes the idea of her signing on at the brothel, but doesn't want to get ahead of herself. They'd better talk this through first. From now on, Angelina has to make ends meet here all by herself. Who ever said anything about going back to the Philippines?

"Okay, tell me what you can do."

"I do ordinary housework, like any woman. Cleaning, washing, a little cooking. Most Japanese dishes I can handle."

Well, she might really come in handy. With Ketch and Joel gone, there's no one to do the daily chores. They were so good at what they did, kept everything in order. Pretty much how Matías used to describe this Itsuko's work habits. The girls know this is a crucial time for the house, and there's only so much their boss can do herself while trying to think of everything. So many little things to do around the place that the girls just don't see. Sure, they're young, and nights are their real work. Still, she would appreciate a little extra help, but is that reason enough to hire this woman? *Of course she can clue me in on the Matías I never knew*, thought Angelina, but no, there's got to be something more business-related.

"How about Filipino food?"

"*Adobo, carne mechada.*" Itsuko rattles off the names of some Filipino dishes, looking quite proud of herself. "If you can find me some *bagoong* shrimp paste and *ampalaya* bitter melon, I can even make *pinakbet*. And we can get almost all the ingredients for *sinigang* sour guava soup here already." Then lowering her voice to a whisper, as if letting her in on a trade secret, "There are a few tamarind trees here on Gaspar, you know." Back in her job interview tone, she adds, "I've made chicken adobo any number of times, and President Guili's Filipino guests always praised the results."

"Wow, that just incredible! Most of my girls are *Pinay*, and they get tired of the same old same old every day. Cook we got now, he make nice hors d'oeuvres and grill a mean steak—Western dishes his specialty—but can he roll a *lumpia*? Or stir-fry a *pacit guisado*?"

Itsuko looks honestly relieved. She really does want to work here.

"You don't wanna go back to Japan?" asks Angelina, just to be sure.

"An old woman like me? Even if I did, there'd be no good jobs, nowhere I'd fit in. People in Japan can be awfully cold toward anyone returning from abroad. And then, I'm not long for this world anyway."

This cuts a little too close to why Angelina herself doesn't want to return to Manila. Better not pursue this line of discussion until they get to know each other better.

"What about your salary?"

"I'd be happy to get what I was getting at the villa. Or even less…I won't complain."

Itsuko cites a figure that is roughly what Angelina had thought of paying her. A regular salary. Definitely this woman was nothing special to Matías.

"I happy to give you a job here. You're hired."

"Thank you," says Itsuko.

"No need for thanks. We make contract, just like for all the girls," says Angelina, indicating another Filipina passing through. "For sure, I gonna be thanking you."

The girl brings over two cups of coffee and the two older women hash out the terms of employment. Finally, with that out of the way, they both can relax.

"So what's new at the villa?" There must be other things to talk about, but nothing else comes to mind.

"Jameson seems to be doing a good job. All I hear is rumors, so I don't really know the political situation, but people generally have good things to say about him."

"Pretty much what I hear. They say he not overstepping his Acting President title. Acting like a stand-in, playing down the president part. After *him*, better Navidad get somebody young and able, somebody not so bossy."

There, she's gone and passed judgment on the late great President Guili. Speaking out when she's the one who's supposed to be asking. Luckily Itsuko lets the topic drop.

"Many more people are coming to ask favors," she leans closer to say. "There always was a queue out in front of the villa before, but now the whole fountain area is full up. The kids selling food are having a field day."

"People 'specting a lot of Jim."

"So it seems. There's even talk of doing away with the rule limiting it to outer island petitions only."

This woman is more in the know than she lets on, thinks Angelina. None of the media has picked up on this news yet. She's probably worth her keep just as a source of information. Probably gets gossip fresh from every fish and vegetable seller who comes to the kitchen door at the villa. In that sense, she qualifies as an honorary Navidadian—another reason to hire her.

"Just now, on the way here, I heard something very interesting," confides Itsuko in hushed tones.

"What's that?" Angelina leans in to ask.

"A tour bus has gone missing." Itsuko's face flushes red with mischief. She knows her listener will want to hear more.

"Who? Where? How?" Angelina takes the bait.

"A scuba diving tour from Japan, left the Teikoku Hotel and never reached their chartered boat at the port. One of those 'last chance' vacation packages for pensioners. The plaza's buzzing with rumors."

"And nobody go look for them?"

"Oh, they'll show up sooner or later. Younger and happier than before. It'll become a mainstay of the tourist industry here," declares Itsuko.

"You think?"

"Who knows? That's the appeal. You come here on a tour, board a bus, maybe it disappears and maybe it doesn't. The uncertainty, the anticipation—that sells. Especially to stupid Japanese."

"I see beginning of a beautiful friendship," says Angelina with a twinkle in her eye.

⚡

Ketch and Joel are sitting at a shiny wooden table, just the two of them. Drinks before them, of course: two tall glasses of ice water, two shot glasses and a bottle of I.W. Harper's finest (though in reality none-too-exclusive) distillate. They've found their quarry.

Where can this scene be? It's actually hard to say. They could be any-where—at the Sanur Hotel in Bali, the Ambarrukmo Palace Hotel in Jogjakarta or the Shangri La Hotel in Kuala Lumpur. Maybe even the old

Raffles Hotel bar in Singapore, were not the place already gone, or the Bamboo Bar at the Oriental in Bangkok (the two men being travelers, hotel bars are the likeliest destinations).

Wherever they are, just picture them reminiscing at a small burnished rosewood table, but with no half-naked girls around to interrupt the conversation.

"Nice story. It improves with age, like our favorite drink here."

Ketch raises his glass. "Like we once told Angelina, alcohol's a real boon to the imagination. Are you sure we didn't dream up those islands?"

"Hard to believe, but such places *do* exist." Joel's eyes seem bluer since leaving Navidad, his hair more platinum blond.

"Finding it was a stroke of luck."

"For us?"

"For the tale that needed telling. Good thing we happened along at the right time."

"You said it. We can be halfway around the globe, but set some glasses down in front of us and we'd still be telling it. Though it helps having each other to remember all the details."

"Words are such dialectic things. Two talkers are always better than one."

"So talk we shall, till we polish off this bottle. You start this time: tell us about Matías and his women and that naughty bus."

"Yes, and the land. The three islands. The sea and palm trees and sky. The tiny propeller plane. The Yuuka and the Elders. And Matías's unborn daughter."

"How about it, shall we start all over again from the beginning? From the first faint hints of dawn, the part about all good stories starting at daybreak?"

"Fine by me. We've got all the time in the world," says Ketch, casually refilling their whiskey glasses.